JAGGED
FATE

Also by Steve Santel

Soccer Dreamin'

JAGGED FATE

A Novel

STEVE SANTEL

iUniverse, Inc.
New York Lincoln Shanghai

Jagged Fate

iUniverse books may be ordered through booksellers or by contacting:

iUniverse
2021 Pine Lake Road, Suite 100
Lincoln, NE 68512
www.iuniverse.com
1-800-Authors (1-800-288-4677)

ISBN-13: 978-0-595-38797-7 (pbk)
ISBN-13: 978-0-595-83178-4 (ebk)
ISBN-10: 0-595-38797-7 (pbk)
ISBN-10: 0-595-83178-8 (ebk)

Printed in the United States of America

For My Family

Your love and support has allowed me to pursue my dreams. None of it would mean a thing without you.

PREFACE

As a very young boy, I can remember sneaking peeks at the TV miniseries *Helter Skelter* through a partially obstructed view. My parents had allowed my brother and me to watch the series, but we were instructed when it was time to cover our eyes. As a normal young person, I still saw much more than I was supposed to and instantly became fascinated by the story.

To me, the simple act of killing another human being is the darkest, most forbidden action on this planet. To better understand what causes people to commit these crimes, I've spent years researching the topic. The things I learned led me to write the text in the following pages.

A degree in psychology and some background work with the underprivileged gave me a glimpse into this bizarre and terrifying world. The scary thing about *Jagged Fate* is the fact that not only could a story like this happen; but also that it does.

CHAPTER 1

▼

The man had obsessed about this moment for weeks. Since their fateful encounter, he had thought of nothing else. Stalking her and planning for this precise moment had become his calling. It wasn't the first such calling he had answered, and it certainly wouldn't be the last.

Earlier in the evening, a sinister smile had spread across his face as he admired himself in the mirror. He was feeling very confident about his plan. Dressed as a police officer, he would boldly stride up to her front door and gain entrance into her house without resistance. Every detail had been perfectly thought out. Pulling it off would be no problem at all.

He laughed at the irony of his impersonating a member of the law enforcement community. He had taken on many roles in his life, but this was his first stint as a cop. He doubted that many real cops had ended a tenth as many lives as he had. In fact, he would have been shocked if the majority of them had ever even squeezed off a live round, other than at the firing range.

The woman he had targeted would be added to a long list of victims he had brutally butchered over the years. He would own her like he had owned all the rest, and he would do so without rhyme, reason, or remorse.

*   *   *   *

Nick Lacour was late when he could least afford it. He pulled out of the parking garage. It was a nasty December day in St. Louis. Sleet pelted the windshield of his black Lexus as he merged with the crawling traffic. Rush hour had become a nightmare in recent years. In bad weather, it was indescribable.

As his car plodded down Tenth Street toward the highway, he patted the pockets of his London Fog overcoat, looking for his cell. He found the phone and deftly avoided an overzealous traveler, hell-bent on making the traffic light. He cussed the driver who cut him off while he fumbled with the phone. Seconds later, the voice of his wife, Pamela, greeted him.

"Where the hell are you? You know how important this is to him. Don't even think about telling me you're canceling." Pamela was referring to their five-year-old son, Justin.

"Calm down. I'm on my way. Traffic sucks, and my deposition ran way over. I promise he won't miss the game." He tried to convey his heartfelt desire to make sure Justin saw every minute of his first National Hockey League game.

"Is he ready?" Nick asked stupidly.

"He had his Blues jersey on at three. He hasn't stopped talking about the game all day."

Nick laughed, offering a moment of levity to the situation.

"Well, I'm on Highway 40 now and will be there in under an hour. Have him at the door at seven, and we'll make the opening face-off, I assure you." He hoped his voice sounded more convincing than he felt.

"He'll be ready. Don't disappoint him, OK?" It was more of a plea than a demand.

"I won't, babe. You have my word. I'm just as excited as he is. We'll take a helicopter if necessary, but he *will* see the game."

"I'll see you in a little bit. Be careful out there. The weatherman is calling for seven inches."

"He has about as much chance of getting seven inches as I do," he said sarcastically. They both laughed.

"I love you, Nick," she said.

"I love you, too, sweetheart. I'll see you in a few."

Her words had caught him off guard. Of course, he knew she loved him. As much as he loved her, and they never failed to let each other know it. He just didn't expect to hear it right then.

He clicked the phone off and dropped it onto the black leather passenger's seat. Traffic was barely moving. He had to keep his promise to Justin. He dipped the car off the highway at Clayton Road and began to weave through back streets. He had seventy minutes until game time. He could still make it.

As he battled the heavy traffic, panic-stricken drivers, and glazed streets, he thought of his wife. Pamela was an amazing woman. He had fallen in love with her the second he had laid eyes on her. He could still vividly recall that moment.

It was right after a soccer game during his senior year in college. His team had slumped off the field after a disappointing 2-1 loss to a rival school.

He walked over to the team's giant Igloo water cooler, filled a Styrofoam cup, and looked dejectedly into the stands. Immediately, his eyes found Pamela Martin. She was leaning against the rail in the first row looking right at him. A tightly buttoned leather coat concealed her frame, but the beauty of her face was striking.

Looking at her had literally taken his breath away. He stared down at the cup of water in his hands, unable to hold her gaze. She was stunning, and he couldn't believe she was looking directly at him. When he returned his eyes to the stands, she was gone. He shook his head in disbelief, wondering if she had been an apparition or the most beautiful girl he had ever seen.

Later that evening at a campus bar, while watching the crowd with a group of friends, he saw her again. He was delighted to see that she was a living human being and not a product of his imagination. He didn't usually approach girls in bars. He couldn't recall ever impulsively approaching a girl he didn't know to ask her out. It just wasn't his style, and, quite frankly, he didn't need to be a player to get dates.

More than six feet tall, he had the body of a well-trained athlete. Long, lean muscles tapering toward a slim waist gave him the appearance of a professional athlete or an Olympic swimmer. Along with his athletic physique, he possessed the classic good looks that most women swooned over. Tightly cropped blond hair framed his chiseled face, making him look like a poster boy for Calvin Klein. He had deep-set blue eyes and a boyish charm that made him even more endearing. The fact that he didn't realize it probably enhanced the allure.

Something about this girl had been different, though. He had known that if he didn't talk to her, he'd regret it the rest of his life. His dad had once told him that only a handful of life-changing moments come along, and how he chose to deal with them would forever define his character and alter his future. This had clearly been one of those moments.

He had tried to force his way through the sweaty bodies that were jam-packed into the small room. Smoke had hung thick in the air like a nicotine-saturated rain cloud, while loud music pulsated, rattling loosely hung pictures and overhead fixtures. He spotted the object of his desire on the other side of the bar, but he couldn't quite seem to get to her. She had seemed to notice his approach and returned his gaze, smiling seductively before once again disappearing among the masses.

He had rubbed his hands through his hair in frustration and searched the room, hoping to spot her once more. Just like at the game, she had vanished before his very eyes. Who was this girl, and why had he never seen her before? He hadn't stopped thinking about her since their first quasi encounter after the game. She had dominated his thoughts so thoroughly that he had completely forgotten about his team's depressing loss.

He had summoned the bartender and ordered a Bud Light while continuing to scan the room for his mystery girl. After the beer arrived, he had bounced a wrinkled five-dollar bill on the bar and waited for his $2.50 in change. He had pocketed the tattered bills and left the coins swimming in spilled beer on the bar. The bartender had given him a look that said, "Really? I get to keep the whole fifty cents?"

Just as he had taken his first drink, he spied her again. She had been waiting in line for the restroom halfway across the drunken patron-cluttered bar. He had grabbed his beer and made another effort to wedge his body through the crowd, throwing elbows in the process.

One jab had caught a guy in the ear, prompting an angry rebuttal. But, when the guy realized it was Nick, he had cooled down and said, "Nice game, dude."

"Thanks, man," Nick had replied.

Before the fan could offer another word, Nick had resumed his battle toward the restrooms. When he finally reached his destination, the door swung open and the beauty he had been searching for disappeared behind it. Continuing his uncharacteristic behavior, he had followed her in, not wanting her to get away again. Shrieks of disapproval came from the room's other occupants, but he hadn't noticed. He tapped the girl on the shoulder.

"Hi, my name is Nick."

"Do you make a habit of stalking strange girls in the ladies' room, Nick?" she had asked as the other girls in the room laughed.

"Uh, no, not really," he had replied with some embarrassment. His face started to redden, and he began to regret his bold move.

"If you'll excuse me, Nick," she had said, disappearing into one of the stalls and closing the door behind her. The girls had giggled again as he felt each pair of eyes on him.

Mortified, he hastily retreated, muttering to himself all the way out. What had he been thinking? When he had made it back to the relative safety of the bar, he leaned up against the nearest wall and stared at a ceiling fan, feeling like a complete fool. While he had contemplated exiting the bar altogether, he felt a light tug on his jacket sleeve. He had looked down and was shocked to see that it was her.

"I'm Pamela Martin," she had said.

Before he could utter a response, she pulled him close and kissed him gently on the lips. The act had left him fighting for breath. She had knocked the wind out of him once more, leaving him totally speechless. When he finally recovered, their courtship officially began. It was a moment he would describe much later with "I just knew." Throughout the years, when asked about their first meeting, he had uttered those three simple words: it had become a credo.

Of course, he rarely admitted that the first kiss had led to infinitely more that first night. He hadn't been prone to one-night stands, but this situation had clearly been different. After barely an hour's worth of exchanging pleasantries, he had taken her back to his dorm room, where they engaged in the most passionate lovemaking of his young life. Even now, when reflecting upon that first night, he got turned on. He only wished he could still manufacture that many "rounds" in succession some ten years later.

A willingness to jump in the sack so quickly might have turned him off to most willing female participants, but not her. Instead of thinking of her as promiscuous, their first night together simply added to her attractiveness. He liked the way she had asserted herself and went after what she wanted. He would later find out that she had never done anything like that before, but he didn't need her words to provide that confirmation. As he got to know her, he learned that she truly wasn't that kind of girl.

It took some time before they would know each other on that deep level, however. They had spent the first three weeks of their relationship in bed, alternating between steamy hot sex and calls to Domino's Pizza for delivery. The interlude nearly got them both ejected from school. They missed several classes, and their grades began to suffer tremendously from giving in to their primal desires.

Nick hadn't cared. He had been so immersed in Pamela that he would have been content spending the rest of his life in that dorm room with her. God, she had been beautiful. He had never met a girl that pretty before. She had looked like a Victoria's Secret model. Jet-black hair hung over her shoulders like fine, oriental silk. She had high cheekbones and an exotic olive complexion. Her nose was small, button-like, and in utterly perfect harmony with the rest of her facial features. Her lips were full, pouty, and collagen-free. She didn't need lipstick or makeup and, in fact, wore none. Her body was as perfect as her face, but it was her eyes that most captivated him. They were like emeralds, and they bore a hole right through him. He simply couldn't get enough of her.

She had felt the same way about him. She had only participated in one sexual relationship in her life and had only seriously dated three guys, including Nick. This was the first time she had ever given into physical urges, and it had scared her. She had never been so wrapped up in another person and wondered if it was healthy to feel this way. As she would learn over time, she had a much deeper soul connection with him than she could have had with any other human being.

After three weeks of intense sexual gratification, they had finally come up for air and started to get to know one another. Their sex life hadn't diminished, but they had actually ventured outside the dorm for school and other necessary endeavors. When not mired in life's responsibilities, they had been joined at the hip, and had remained that way ever since.

They graduated on the same day, just six months after that first night. Nick received a BS in criminology and Pamela a BS in biology. He went on to law school while she aborted her dream of becoming a biologist. They had been married two weeks after graduation, and Pamela had vowed to take several jobs to help support her new husband as he learned the law. After he passed the bar exam, he had promised that she would never have to work again. He had remained true to his word during the next six-plus years. In fact, if his current income level continued, neither of them would have to work very much longer.

Nick was truly a gifted lawyer. He was generally considered one of the region's best. Six years in the firm, and he was already a full partner. The law firm was now called Evans, Masters & Lacour. He was well off financially, but that wasn't the most important thing. His family was all that really mattered to him. He still got a twinge in his chest every time he looked at his wife. He loved her so much that his heart literally ached. He wondered if that feeling alone would eventually kill him. When she almost didn't survive giving birth to Justin, he had thought he was going to die himself. Her two weeks in the intensive care unit had been the most brutal days of his life. He had thought he was going to lose his reason for living. To his great relief, she had survived and was now more physically fit than ever. She worked out four times a week and still had the body of the twenty-two-year-old he met that night in the bar. Men of all ages still checked her out. Nick especially. He couldn't believe that June would mark their ten-year anniversary.

The blast from an approaching truck's horn snapped him back to the present. Apparently, the traffic had loosened somewhat, and he was able to continue forward. Forty minutes to game time. He might just get his son into the arena before the opening face-off.

✶   ✶   ✶   ✶

Nick pulled into the driveway at 7:02 PM. He hadn't even opened the car door all the way when an excited five-year-old rocketed out of the cold and into the pleasantly warm automobile.

"Hey, Dad. Are you ready to go?"

"You bet, son. Let me say hello to your mom, and then we'll go," he said with a laugh.

"Come on, Dad. We're going to be late!"

"Have I ever gotten you anywhere late before?"

"Remember T-ball last summer?"

"OK, one time. We won't be late tonight, though. I promise," he answered, still laughing.

He got out of the car and battled the wind-borne flakes of snow. He slipped on the front walk as he made his way to the house. He made a mental note to salt the walk and driveway after the game. That is, if there wasn't two feet of snow on the ground by then.

"Hi, babe."

"Maybe you did take a helicopter. I didn't think you would make it."

"Have I ever let you down before?"

She wrinkled her nose.

"OK, don't answer that."

"Here, eat this on the way," she said, handing him a cold hamburger wrapped in paper towels with pictures of pandas decorating the border.

"You're too good to me," he replied, taking the blue-panda-covered burger.

"Remember that when you get home tonight, I might want a little *payback*."

He looked at his watch as if to inquire whether or not they had time for the payback right then. She read his mind and slapped him on the shoulder.

"After the game!" she exclaimed.

"Oh yeah. I almost forgot about the game."

"Come on, Dad," whined Justin from the front doorstep. "It's time to *gooo!*"

"Wait up for me Pam, I think I might be able to pay you back several times tonight," he said, grabbing his wife in a tight embrace and kissing her deeply.

"I'll be in bed, wearing nothing but those red pajamas you gave me." The "red pajamas were actually a skimpy negligee he had given her for her birthday in October.

"In that case, count on me paying you back at least four times."

"Oh, I like the sound of that. Is that a promise or a threat?" she purred.

"An emphatic promise."

He pulled her close again and pressed his cold, slightly chapped lips to her forehead. He could feel a stirring in his boxers. If they didn't leave right that minute, he might not be able to leave at all. She still turned him on like no other woman ever could.

Justin tugged on his olive green trench coat, imploring his dad to hurry.

"All right, champ. Let's go see a hockey game."

"Yeaaa!" cried Justin.

They were off. Nick looked in his rearview mirror. Pamela, shrouded in swirling snow and partially obstructed by his frosting rear window, remained on the front step, waving to them. He couldn't think of another time when he felt more love for her. He pictured her in that red teddy, waiting for him in their candlelit bedroom, her smooth, long legs reflecting the fire's glow. He felt another stir below the belt. It was time to refocus, he thought. There was a hockey game to attend.

$$* \qquad * \qquad * \qquad *$$

Father and son rushed into the arena four minutes before the game started. They hurriedly presented their tickets to the usher, who scanned and returned them. The ticket taker told them to enjoy the game. Nick raised this son onto his shoulders and began to weave his way through the crowd. They might actually see the opening face-off yet.

$$* \qquad * \qquad * \qquad *$$

Pamela closed the door and left the December cold outside. She locked the dead bolts and climbed the stairs to the second-floor master bedroom. She smiled as she thought about her son and husband on their first journey alone together. It was just the beginning for them. She thanked God frequently to be a part of this family. She loved Nick more and more every day, and Justin absolutely completed their world. He had her eyes and Nick's smile. She hoped he would have Nick's tenacity as well.

Pamela Lacour would not disappoint her husband tonight. She had some untested lingerie from Victoria's Secret. She had about three hours to clean the house and take a hot bath. She would then fill the bedroom with scented candles and make up with him for the spat they had that afternoon.

She hurdled the last step and veered left. She entered the master bedroom and began to pick up the clutter. Clothes from the morning's frenzied rush to work littered the floor. She assembled them into a laundry basket and made her way to the bathroom. Two slightly damp purple towels clung to the white ceramic floor tiles. Normally, they would not have left the room in such disarray, but a particularly lengthy lovemaking session had been their introduction to the day. They had left the sweat-laden, disheveled sheets on the floor and hurried into their morning routines. Both were late for work, but the interlude was well worth it.

After she finished picking up the last of the morning's wake, she stuffed the basket and made her way to the washing machine on the ground floor. Sometimes, she walked through their five-thousand-square-foot home and couldn't believe the life she had grown accustomed to. Raised in a home with modest luxuries, she was now a wealthy woman. The wealth went beyond money. She had health, love, and happiness. The bank account was merely a sweet bonus. It allowed them to reside in this small mansion and surround themselves with some of the finer things, but that wasn't what mattered most to her.

She finished loading the washing machine, fixed the settings, and turned the machine on. The laundry room was adjacent to a spacious kitchen, which had been decorated primarily in yellow. She had always wanted a yellow kitchen, and she was given free rein with the decorations. The kitchen had oak cabinets, which were stained light brown. The cabinets had somehow avoided the canary onslaught that infected most of the room. Large, pale yellow ceramic tiles covered the floor. The refrigerator was an eye-popping lemon color, but the rest of the appliances were stainless steel. The Formica countertop had a faint yellow tint. It blended well with the place mats and daisy-splashed wallpaper.

It was by far the ugliest room in the house, but she didn't care. She wanted yellow and got it. Their home was comfortable. It was not something copied out of a Martha Stewart magazine. The yellow probably would have been cited as a fashion faux pas, but it was cheery. The kitchen in her parents' house had been white and sterile. It epitomized her upbringing—cold and affectionless. She vowed that her own home would never conjure up childhood memories.

After loading the dishwasher with the evening's dishes, she drew a bottle of chardonnay from the refrigerator. She poured a glass and cursed as she spilled some on the counter. She never could pour wine without incident. She took her glass into the living room for a few moments of quiet and relaxation.

The living room was Nick's favorite spot in the house, other than the bedroom. It had a vaulted ceiling and a large stone fireplace. A tan leather couch and matching love seat occupied the center of the room. The leather was soft and supple—perfect to cuddle and watch the television, which happened to be a sixty-two-inch monster flanked by the finest stereo equipment on the market. Tower speakers, a DVD/VCR combo player, CD player, and stereo receiver filled the shelves that had been built into the wall. It was a black, menacing conglomeration of knobs, buttons, and LED displays.

The room was lightly decorated with plants and a couple of cream-colored standing lamps. For the most part, it was simple and comfortable. It was the living room of a family with means.

Pamela placed her wine on the glass coffee table and clicked on the TV set. She channel-surfed for a couple of minutes and finally landed on a '90s sitcom in syndication. She sipped her chardonnay and laughed at a bit she had seen several times before. Some shows were timeless.

It wasn't often that she got to sit down and relax in her own house. An energetic child or equally vibrant husband usually filled her time at home. Even though she felt empty with them gone, she relished the opportunity to kick back for a few minutes. She leaned into the comfortable couch and became enveloped by the warmth the leather had absorbed from the roaring fire in the nearby fireplace. She hated winter but loved building fires in the great room. Reflections of the fire danced off the blond hardwood floor. She became mesmerized by the glowing, rhythmic patterns.

She closed her eyes and let her mind wander. She had some time before her husband and son returned from the game. She could use the moment of relaxation. Her mind drifted back to her own childhood. It had been so different from the life she now had that she sometimes felt as though her childhood was an illusion. Her dad would get home late from work drunk and abuse her mother. Pamela, her brother, and her sister would seek refuge in the bedroom they shared. Their house had been a small two-bedroom bungalow. The family of five had shared one bathroom and very limited living space. She opened her eyes to remind herself that things had definitely improved. She breathed deeply and inhaled the smell of burning firewood and expensive leather. She closed her eyes again and drifted away. The aroma of bourbon and stale Old Spice replaced the smell of leather. Her dad, glassy-eyed and shit-faced, had just staggered into the bungalow on Chelsea Street.

CHAPTER 2

▼

His short-sleeve button-down shirt (gas company issue) had been partially untucked and mostly unbuttoned, revealing a sweat-stained undershirt. He had reeked of cheap bourbon and cigarette smoke. The long since departed after-shave had offered a slight odor that didn't mix well with the stink of the bar where he must have spent the past several hours.

"Where's my dinner? I'm hungry!"

"Dinner was two hours ago, Ralph," Pamela's mom had answered.

Deidre Martin had been a meek woman. Years of physical and mental abuse, courtesy of Ralph, had robbed her of the beauty she once had been known for. She had looked pale and weak. Her flowered sundress had hung from her bony shoulders like a sheet that had been loosely draped over a hanger. Her skin was pale and had taken on a grayish hue. Once-luminous brown eyes were sunken in their sockets, and it was difficult to discern their true color. Dark bags under the deep sockets punctuated her returned-from-the-grave look. She probably hadn't slept in more than six years, at least not at length. It had been starting to show.

At only thirty-eight years old, she had looked fifteen years older. This former Miss Nebraska would have never again turned heads like she had when she was in her early twenties. Twenty years prior, she could have had her pick of men. Suitors had lined up for a country mile trying to win her hand. She had chosen Ralph.

"I said, where's my goddamned dinner?" her husband had slurred.

"I already told you. It was two hours ago. There are leftovers on the counter." That had been a particularly bold move for the frail Mrs. Martin.

"Don't give me no lip, woman, if I wanted fucking leftovers, I would have eaten the shit at Jimmy's Pub."

"Well then, you better call Jimmy's and see if they are still serving shit tonight."

Pamela, now hiding in her closet, had heard this remark and stifled a laugh. She had never known her mom to talk back to her dad, much less cuss in the process. Despite finding the exchange humorous, she had been fearful for what was sure to follow. Tears of fear and disgust had seared the corners of her eyes, replacing the suppressed laugh. She soon gave those tears the latitude to flow freely down her cheeks.

"That's about enough crazy talk from you, you fucking bitch. Now, take your bony ass into the kitchen and make me some fucking dinner!"

"I made dinner, and you weren't here. If you want something, you will have to get it yourself," she had said as tears began to burn her eyes. Years of beatings and exchanges such as these had worn her out. She was no longer afraid of the man who had ruined her life. Her tears had been born from the same anger and sadness that inflicted her youngest daughter in the next room. Deidre was tired. Tired of the arguments and tired of being afraid. What was about to happen was no mystery to her. She braced for the beating.

"If I want something, you will get it for me. You got that, bitch?" ranted Ralph.

Pamela's mother had not replied. Her part in this exchange was over. She had summoned up happier memories from a different life. She had escaped to a beauty pageant. The whole world had revered her. She cried then, too, but those tears had an entirely different meaning.

"I didn't hear an answer, smart mouth. Maybe I'll just have to knock one out of you."

An ugly man, marinated in cheap bourbon, tobacco, and the remnants of Old Spice, had stumbled across the brown shag carpet in the living room and did what he did best. Ralph Martin had done the only thing he was able to do with any dexterity. He had beaten his wife to a pulp.

Three children had hugged each other and cried in the neighboring room. They were too young and too small to help their mother and too afraid to conceive of a way out of this hell. Muffled cries had faded into the distance, and the only sound had been that of fist on bone.

*   *   *   *

Pamela woke with a start. She wasn't altogether sure where she was at that moment. She was surprised to feel drying tears on her cheeks. The hollow thumping sounds that had epitomized her father's abuse of her mother were still resonating in her mind. Actually, they were echoing in her home. As she gained total consciousness, she realized that the sounds were not fists on flesh, but rather a fist on her front door. She groggily shook the fading memory of the dream from her now-awake mind and got up to answer the door.

*   *   *   *

Justin Lacour was beside himself. He was experiencing sensory overload. He was witnessing an actual hockey game just a few rows in front of him. His lap was full of various vendor delicacies—peanuts, popcorn, and ice cream. The animated crowd shouted and cheered virtually every nuance of the game. Justin figured this was about as close to heaven as a living being could get. To top it all off, he was able to share the experience with his dad. He was the person Justin admired the most in the whole world.

"Go Blues!" shouted the euphoric boy.

In a seemingly direct response to their newest fan's plea, the Blues' right-winger broke in on goal. Two Detroit Redwing defensemen remained near the goalmouth, with one breaking away from the pipes to track the flying skater. The right-winger released a bullet pass across the front of the goal crease that seemed to have eyes as it avoided the lingering defensemen and found its way onto the stick of another fast approaching Blue. The Blues' center one-timed the pass into the upper corner of the netting, behind the flailing goalie. An obnoxiously loud horn signified the home team's success. Seven minutes into the first period, and the Blues were on top, 1-0.

"Yeahhhhhhh!" shouted Justin.

Everyone in the Savvis Center was standing and wildly cheering their approval at the recent turn of events. Even Nick was smiling ear to ear, but not so much because the Blues scored. He was happy they had, but his smile was directed more toward his son. The boy was enjoying himself even more than Nick thought he would.

He reached down and ruffled his son's hair. As the boy looked up, Nick put out his hand, summoning a high five. Justin obliged with all of his young might.

Father and son enjoyed a moment of male bonding. This is only the beginning, thought Nick. He continued to watch his son, who applauded with the rest of the crowd. Thank God his job hadn't made him miss this moment, Nick thought. Pamela sitting on Justin's other side would have been the only thing that could have made it any better. He was indeed a blessed man.

*   *   *   *

The man at the front door decided to ring the doorbell. His cold fist was taking a beating on the hard wooden surface. It probably wasn't wise to make that much noise anyway.

Not that anyone could hear. The neighbors were too far away, and the cold, breezy night deadened the sound of his pounding fists like a thick blanket, leaving just a dull thud that was audible only to someone within twenty feet of the house. Beyond that, one could only hear the howling wind as it blew flakes of snow that bit into the surrounding trees and shrubs like frozen shards of glass.

Being at the front door was a mistake all by itself. The man usually didn't work that way, but he was inspired this time. That combined with the fact that the basement windows were four-inch blocks of glass mortared together. They wouldn't pass inspection, nor would they allow anyone to gain entry to or exit from the basement.

The man knew all of this from his careful surveys of the residence. He had come across the woman and her son a couple of weeks ago at McDonald's. She had actually spoken to him while they waited in line. From that moment, he knew he had to have her. She probably had teased every man she met. At McDonald's, the dry cleaner, the grocery store. It didn't matter. She waved her sexual appeal in their faces like a crisp, unattainable thousand-dollar bill. Teasing each of them. Flirting, teasing, and then going home to her clean-cut, money-making husband. The man hated her and everything she stood for. He was too lowly to have a high-society bitch like this, but she continued to flirt with him anyway. It was cruel the way she played with people. It was time someone played with her. It was time someone taught her what a cruel and heartless bitch she was.

He could still see the way her tight gray workout pants had crept up her ass. It had been obvious she had no panties on. The cotton had been still damp around her crotch from her workout. He could smell the sweetness of her perspiration mixed with the perfume she was wearing. Imagine that. Getting all dolled up to go to the gym. She probably had spent half the time coming on to instructors and other patrons, shaking her tight ass in their faces. She had been begging them to take a look before she gathered up her kid and went back to their mansion in west St. Louis County.

The man doubted her husband had ever treated her like the slut that she was. She probably teased him, too, using her sexiness to get what she wanted. The man pictured her parading around the house in provocative clothes, teasing him until she actually needed something. Then, reluctantly, she would give it up. She was going to give it up right now. She just didn't know it yet.

✳   ✳   ✳   ✳

Between periods, Nick took Justin to the concession stand to load up on more junk food. They got tortilla chips smothered in processed cheese that had the color of a Sunkist orange. It was already starting to congeal, forming a thin layer of skin on top. Mixed into the cheese-like substance were diced, brutally hot jalapeño peppers. It would require half of beer to extinguish the flames those monsters lit. At $7.75 a beer, Nick decided not to eat too many of the peppers. Even with his income, the price was absurd.

Nick also bought a soft pretzel with so much salt, he feared it had been carved directly from one of the blocks sitting in the bottom of the restroom's urinals. This was yet another ploy to get the fans to drink gallons of overpriced liquid. He added a beer for himself, a watered-down Coke for his son, and an ice cream for the two of them to share, should they have any room left.

This should hold them over through the second period, if it didn't kill them first. The total for this unhealthy purchase was $19.50. Nick handed the attendant a twenty and gathered up his items. He didn't mind spending the money but thought it was robbery to charge so much for a bunch of crap that probably cost the arena two dollars, tops. He wondered how most normal people could afford to go to sporting events. By the time you got your tickets, paid for parking and visited a couple of vendors, you were out two hundred bucks. Oh well, Justin was enjoying himself immensely. This night was well worth the money.

"Dad, can we get a hot dog, too?"

"Let's try to eat this first, OK, son? I wouldn't want to take you back home to Mom with a stomachache."

Nick knew it was past the point of averting a mere stomachache. An ulcer was more likely.

"I can handle it, Dad. I ate two hot dogs and nachos at the baseball game last summer. Remember?"

"Yeah, I do. I got a stomachache watching you. Where do you put it all?"

"Right here," Justin said, protruding his small belly while patting it proudly.

Nick laughed at the exchange. Justin was definitely taking after the old man. He could eat like a horse and use his gifted metabolism to ensure that it never showed.

They worked their way through the crowd and back to their seats just before the puck dropped for the second period. After all this food and excitement, Nick doubted Justin would make it through the entire game before fizzling out.

*   *   *   *

The man blew warm, moist air into his closed fist. It was getting colder out. However, the cold outside wasn't nearly as frigid as the ice queen on the other side of the door. The man figured he would be able to warm her up pretty quickly. He pulled leather gloves from his back pocket and slid them on. He used the gloves to sweep away any invisible prints his knuckles may have left on the door.

He stood on the front porch, dressed in a policeman's uniform. He had actually bought the guise himself earlier in the evening when he admired himself in the mirror. He had paid cash for the outfit at a costume shop. The half-stoned clerk probably couldn't remember yesterday, much less a couple of months back. He wasn't concerned about them ever tracing the purchase to him.

Parked in the long driveway was a white Ford Crown Victoria. He had boosted the car several weeks ago and painted it white. To add to the effect, he had installed a spotlight on the driver's side door and added various antennae to the roof and trunk. Stolen plates rounded out the look. No one, except an actual cop, would suspect a thing.

Because they were affluent, this couple could afford to live in near seclusion. This was one of the rare subdivisions in St. Louis that had large lots. Trees and darkness provided a cloak of privacy that was impenetrable on this moonless night. The nearest neighbor, some one hundred yards away, would have to leave his house and cover the distance through mind-numbing cold and stinging pellets of snow to see the fake cop car on the driveway. In this weather, that was unlikely.

It was still highly risky going to the front door, but the man wasn't worried. He had become invincible. The risk was part of the thrill. Any amateur could embark on this kind of thing and get away with it by taking every possible precaution. He had been careful enough. Not a soul would question his presence at this home. Not a soul would know he was there unless the husband returned early. He doubted that would happen since he had heard the mother talking to her son at McDonald's about the hockey game.

The thought of the potential dangers heightened his excitement. He was now fully ready. From beyond the door, he heard the bitch say she was coming. He could barely contain himself. In a few minutes, he would be where those tight stretch pants had been.

✳   ✳   ✳   ✳

Midway through the second period, the Blues scored another goal. This time, a slap shot from the blue line eluded the Redwing goalie, who had been screened by several players. Again, the obnoxious horn signified the home team's success. Again, Justin joined in with the raucous crowd.

Nick watched in admiration as his son whooped and yelled with the best of the fans. The atmosphere was starting to resemble an English league soccer game. Drunken fans, red-faced and hoarse, cheered virtually everything the Blues did well. In addition, they cussed virtually everything that didn't go their way.

As the period wore on, the fans got progressively worse. A fight broke out several rows up and to the right of Nick and Justin. A heavyset, bearded fan had evidently pushed his insults too far with another spectator two seats over. Wild punches were thrown, mostly into empty air, as the two rednecks tried to get at one another. After about twenty seconds of alcohol-induced attempts at an altercation, the two clowns were pulled from their seats by four security guards. Their night at the Savvis Center was over.

Nick watched with amusement. He figured that they had exhausted a good portion of their weekly wages to attend the game, and now they were being pitched out on their duffs with six and a half minutes to go in the second period. He always felt that alcohol, sporting events, and limited intellects didn't mix well. As was evidenced, it was a recipe for disaster. Or, in this case, entertainment for the rest of the paying masses.

"What's happening, Dad? I can't see!"

"Two idiots were fighting, and now they're getting thrown out."

"Hold me up. I want to see it."

"Nothing to see, son. It's over now."

"Oh man, that would have been cool to watch."

"Believe me, the scrapes during recess at your school are more interesting than that."

Nick chuckled as the heavier of the two sluggers was dragged into the aisle and out of the arena. His Blues jersey was slightly torn, and blood trickled from his nose into his crumb-covered mustache. Nick guessed that the guy would have to go out and buy a new number 16 Hull jersey this week, even though the scoring star had long since departed St. Louis. It always amazed him to see a grown man wearing a replica jersey worn by another grown man.

The heavyset slob tried to resist the guards but was clearly exhausted from his thirty-second fight. Well-worn jeans had slipped to nearly mid-ass, exposing much more than the crowd had bargained for.

"Gonna be a hell of a day at the construction site tomorrow," Nick ventured to himself.

*   *   *   *

"I'm coming, I'm coming," Pamela said as she approached the front door.

Who could be visiting at this hour on a Monday night? How long had this person been pounding on the door? She looked through the peephole in the solid oak door and saw a police officer standing a few feet away. He looked to be in his late twenties. He had dark hair, which was neatly quaffed and combed forward, probably to conceal a receding hairline. He was clean-shaven and not overly attractive, but not ugly, either. He seemed to be the quintessential cop, standing about six feet tall with a medium build. Dark, thick eyebrows accented his deep-set brown eyes, and he had a strong jaw. His badge indicated that he was a county cop named Malone.

"Just a minute," she said as she unlatched the two dead bolts and pulled on the heavy door, wondering what an officer would be doing at her home on a miserable winter night.

Suction from the blustery wind outside created some resistance, but she was able to yank the door open. Piercing cold and windswept snow stung her eyes and skin the moment the door gave way. She brushed the flakes from her face and greeted Officer Malone with a look of confused curiosity.

"Good evening, officer. What can I do for you?"

"Sorry to disturb you, ma'am, but there has been a break-in two doors down. The perpetrator bolted from the residence and headed this way."

"Oh my God!"

"I apologize for causing you alarm, but he is armed and considered dangerous. We have reason to believe he might be the same man responsible for a rape in this area last week. He fits the description."

"Was anyone hurt?"

"Just shaken up. The woman of the house noticed a window open on the ground floor. She must have startled the perp before he had a chance to finish his business."

"This is awful! We have never had something like that happen in this neighborhood."

"I know. It is highly unusual for this part of town. I guess there is no limit to where the freaks will go these days."

"How can I be of assistance?"

"Well, we just wanted to make sure all neighboring houses are secure and that all inhabitants know what is going on."

"I appreciate that. I better call my husband and get him home right away."

"That's probably a good idea. In fact, I'm late for home myself. My wife is probably really worried because I haven't called her. Do you mind if I use your phone? My cellular seems to have picked the wrong time to quit working."

She didn't give it a second thought. It didn't register to her that he could have easily called his wife through the police dispatcher. He seemed honest and concerned.

"Certainly. Please come in."

*   *   *   *

Nick was getting restless. He didn't know exactly why, but something in his world didn't seem quite right. The balance of nature had been altered somewhere, and he was starting to feel uneasy. This had happened to him a few other times in his life. Once, at the age of seven, his mom had picked him up from school. When she had gotten there, he was in tears.

"What's wrong with Grandma?"

His mom hadn't seemed to know how to respond. All she could manage in a shaky voice was, "What do you mean?" He didn't answer her question. He only buried his face in mitten-clad hands and cried the whole way home. As it turned out, his grandma had suffered a stroke that afternoon. She died a day later.

On a few other occasions, a sudden onset of anxiety had led to other visions that proved correct. When he was eleven, he had hugged his dog Ginger before he had gone to bed and sobbed into her ear that he loved her and would miss her. His dad had asked him why he was carrying on since he'd see the "stupid dog" again in the morning. He had told his father, "No I won't," and went to bed with tears streaming down his face. The dog died in her sleep that evening.

Now, similar foreboding feelings were starting to overcome him. It hadn't happened in years, and he didn't know what to make of it. As he mulled over his confusion, Detroit scored a power play goal during a wild scramble in front of the net. Neither Nick nor Justin saw the puck slip past the goal line, but they did see the red lights flash, signifying that it had indeed been a goal. This turn of events had really caused the crowd to become unruly. With the enemy team only one goal down, Nick thought this would be a perfect time to head home.

"What do you think, champ? Want to bug out and go see Mom?"

"But Dad, it's a really good game."

Justin wasn't tiring as quickly as Nick thought he would. It was past his bed-time but he had gotten a second wind.

"I know, Justin, but Daddy's getting tired. I've got to get up pretty early tomorrow."

He felt guilty feeding the boy that line. He didn't have to get up any earlier than he normally did but felt it was imperative that they leave the game as soon as possible.

"Can't we stay for just a little while longer? You will still be able to get up in the morning."

A wave of guilt crushed him as he watched the sincerity on his son's face. The kid had looked forward to this night for weeks. Now Nick was asking him to cut it short just because he had a weird premonition that something wasn't right. Even worse, he didn't have a clear vision about what might be wrong in the first place. It was probably nothing at all.

"You bet, son. This is your night," he relented.

"All right! Thanks, Dad."

Nick smiled and patted Justin on the head. After all, he had promised him this game. Only a jackass of a father would pull his son out of the arena when things were really starting to get good.

"One thing, though. Let's call Mom and tell her what a good game this is."

"OK, but then can we come back and watch some more?"

"Yeah, Justin, we can watch some more."

It was too loud in the seats to use his cell phone. He scooped up his son and made his way toward the concession stands. It was only slightly less noisy there, but he would have a better chance of actually hearing Pamela.

✳   ✳   ✳   ✳

The man heard the woman say she was coming. "Isn't that prophetic?" he thought.

He stood on the front step waiting for her. His weight shifted restlessly as the arctic wind knifed through his fake cop uniform.

"Come on bitch, I'm gonna freeze to death out here," he muttered under his breath.

He tried to look professional and poised, the way he had seen officers look on TV. He had no doubt that she would fall for the ruse. While the latches on the door clicked, the man realized that this was his twentieth mission of this sort. He liked to refer to each nighttime assault on an unsuspecting woman as a mission. Twenty, a nice round number, he thought.

That didn't mean he would end them at twenty. Thirty was a round number, too. Fifty sounded even better. In fact, there was no set goal toward fulfilling his destiny. He suspected he would continue to imbibe himself in these pleasures until it just wasn't fun anymore. He doubted it would ever come to that. Each mission brought new delights and new gratification.

No, he would continue to satisfy these needs until he either died of old age or was caught. He preferred the former and considered it to be the most likely possibility. Getting caught no longer seemed plausible. The idiot law enforcement agencies had no clue who he was. They couldn't tie the same person to any of his nineteen missions.

The man wasn't making it easy on them. That much he knew. He adhered to no predictable patterns and left no calling cards. He had no consistent modus operandi. He defied the behavior of the modern serial killer. Serial killer. He didn't like the sound of that. It didn't begin to define the sum of his parts.

Calling the man a serial killer was an insult. It insinuated that he was no more special then the likes of Ted Bundy or Charlie Manson. They had been foolish. They had been caught. He would not suffer the same fate. He would not leave consistent pieces of evidence that would help the police or FBI tie his endeavors together. Right now, his previous missions were nineteen unsolved and unrelated crimes.

His thinking broke the patterns illustrated in the psychology textbooks. He wasn't a classic serial killer. Not even a famed mind hunter from the FBI would be able to read what was in his head. Hell, the man barely knew what he himself was going to do next. That is what made him dangerous. It made him unpredictable and, in his own estimation, unstoppable.

He wasn't just a dysfunctional youth from a childhood gone awry. He didn't kill because he was an abused kid or the by-product of a messed up environment. He killed because he could. Furthermore, he killed because he enjoyed it. He was a faithful servant to the dark side of the universe, fulfilling his earthly destiny until it was time to be called to a higher plane.

The man didn't fear getting caught. Oh, he supposed it was possible. He supposed that someday, he would want proper recognition for his works of art. He even supposed he might get just careless enough to lead an unsuspecting idiot cop to his trail. He didn't fear the prospect. Sometimes, he even welcomed it.

Besides, it didn't matter what happened in this world. He would continue fulfilling his prophecy until he was chosen to move on to the next level. Life on earth didn't matter. It was what came afterward that held his interest. He was special. He knew his work in this world would not go unnoticed. He knew it would not go unrewarded.

Until that time came, he would continue to execute his missions. He always knew when it was time to start another one. He was hit with inspiration, and he acted accordingly after the summoning. This bitch had filled him full of intoxicating desire. She had virtually asked him to become number twenty. The man had seen it in her eyes. He heard it in her voice. Hell, he even smelled it in her sweat. She begged for this visit. She was out of control and it was up to the man to come and control her. He was all about that.

As the door swung open, he realized he was about to fulfill her internal wishes. Her subconscious call to him was getting answered. He shifted his train of thought to the matter at hand and addressed the woman in just the manner that a real cop would have. His sentences were professional. Even his mannerisms would have made Dirty Harry proud. His lines were perfectly believable. After all, he was just a civil servant out on a cold winter's night, trying to keep the old neighborhood safe. He almost laughed as he saw the fear register in her eyes when he spoke of the perpetrator loose in her neighborhood. The dumb broad didn't realize that the perp was standing on her porch.

He almost puked when he spoke of his "worried wife" at home. But it worked. He was invited in. The man stepped into the dimly lit foyer, and kicked snow off of his boots and onto the mat placed just inside the door. He took a couple of squeaky steps on the hardwood floor as he followed her to the phone. Mission number twenty was about to be fulfilled. He couldn't wait to get started.

CHAPTER 3

▼

"You can use the phone in the kitchen. I would offer you the cordless, but I can't find it," chuckled Pamela.

She led him through the foyer, past the winding staircase, and into the yellow-drenched kitchen.

"Sorry about all the yellow. I guess I got a little carried away."

"Are you kidding? You should see what my wife did to our kitchen. Yellow would be a welcome change."

They both laughed. It was the kind of laughter that you issue as a pleasantry in the company of a stranger. Neither found the exchange to be particularly funny.

"The phone is on the wall next to the laundry room. Help yourself."

"Thank you. I appreciate your kindness," the man said as he stepped toward the phone.

He turned abruptly to face the woman before he got there.

"I hate to continue to be a burden, but could I trouble you for a glass of water? This weather has started to take its toll on me."

"No problem. Do you want ice?"

"That won't be necessary. Thanks, though."

Pamela drew a glass from the cabinet next to the sink. It was a water glass with the smiling image of Bugs Bunny on the side. She got the whole Looney Tunes collection while filling up with gas at the nearby Mobil station. Justin had loved them. They were now a staple in the Lacours' everyday place settings.

"I hope you don't mind Bugs Bunny. We got them for our son."

She filled the glass with water from the kitchen faucet. The pipes were cold, so the water didn't need ice cubes to lower its temperature. Condensation, resembling a thin silk veil, immediately formed on the glass and obstructed Bugs's view. Officially, the only eyes on the man were now hers. She shut off the tap and walked across her pale yellow tiles toward the officer, who now held the phone receiver in his gloved hand.

"Thanks again," he said.

He began speaking into the phone while he waited for his cartoon-decorated glass of water.

$$*\qquad*\qquad*\qquad*$$

The third period had begun. Nick could not shake off the uneasy feeling that had overcome him moments ago. He had received a busy signal when trying to call home. This wasn't reason for panic, because she could have been online. Laziness had prevented him from setting up a separate line devoted to the Internet. It had become a hassle for people who tried to call them while they were using the computer.

After unsuccessfully trying to catch her on the home phone, he called her cell phone. The phone went immediately to voice mail, indicating that it was turned off. This did nothing to calm his nerves. He had become more agitated by the minute.

"Champ, I'm kinda worried about Mom. Whadda you say we blow this Popsicle stand?"

"Dad, you promised! You said we could watch the third period."

"I know I did, but Mom didn't answer the phone. I think we ought to go check on her."

"She's probably using that dumb old computer again. You know how she gets."

Smart kid. That was his first thought, too. Sometimes it was hard to believe his son was only five. Nick was sometimes convinced that there was an adult trapped in that little body.

Now torn between keeping the promise made to a little boy and giving into his paranoid delusions, he decided to sit tight for a little bit and try Pamela on the cell again in a few minutes. He was acting like a fool. Of course she was all right. How many times had he left her alone while he spent amazingly long hours at the office? She was a big girl. She could certainly take care of herself. Still, he couldn't shake the feeling that something wasn't quite right.

In answer to his conflict, divine forces intervened and allowed the Redwings to score two goals, just a minute and a half apart. Three minutes into the final period, the visiting team had the lead. With it, they had also stolen the crowd's enthusiasm. Fickle St. Louis fans had already started for the exits. It hadn't always been like this, but recently, when the Blues fell behind, they stayed behind. Nick saw this as the perfect opportunity to give in to his instincts.

"Things don't look too good now. What do you say we beat some traffic?"

He hated himself for projecting a defeatist attitude. The real Nick was quite the opposite. Adversity spurred him on and gave him an incentive to work harder, not give up.

"We can't leave now. They're only down by a goal. They can come back."

"They might be able to, son, but it doesn't look great. You see how they keep turning over the puck in the neutral zone? I think they might be in trouble tonight."

Actually, he hadn't really paid attention. He wasn't a huge hockey fan and didn't even know if his assessment was pertinent. Justin seemed to buy it, though. Justin didn't look quite as sure of himself and his argument was losing weight. The last of Justin's fight was done in by a final bolt from fate's lightning rod, which came in the form of a fourth Redwing goal. Now down by two, the Blues truly did look defeated.

"What do you think?"

"All right. We can go," Justin said dejectedly.

Nick knew Justin didn't want to give in, but the last goal had sucked the enthusiasm out of him like air from a punctured balloon. Apparently, the rest of the crowd felt the same. With fourteen minutes to go in the contest, more than half the fans pushed for the exits. The remaining, belligerent thousands booed from their seats.

Nick grabbed Justin and attempted to fight his way through the departing sea of blue and gold. He was now completely riveted with anxiety. He didn't know why, but he was convinced that he had to get home immediately.

*   *   *   *

Pamela started toward the officer with the frosted glass in hand. Suddenly, it seemed odd to her that he held the receiver in a gloved hand. He had been in the warm house for several minutes, yet he still had his gloves on. Her gaze traveled from the gloves to his eyes. He no longer looked like a civil servant, out to ensure the safety of her neighborhood. Something had changed. His eyes looked dangerous. They were filled with lust and hatred. How had she missed that before? She didn't want to tip him off, but she began to panic. It wasn't just a hunch anymore. She was now completely convinced that the man holding her telephone was not a policeman.

Almost in direct response to her fears, he dropped the receiver and rushed her. She had been standing about twelve feet away. Despite the warning signs, her reactions were too slow. He covered the distance in milliseconds, closing the space with long, lightning quick strides. He must have noticed the change in her demeanor. He pounced on her like a cat that had cornered a mouse. She dropped the glass of water onto the porcelain tiles. It shattered in a silver spray of glass fragments and water droplets.

A gloved hand reached for her mouth. She had been spun around and was now immobilized. His other arm was around her midsection. He held her so tightly that attempts to break free scarcely made a ripple of movement in her fear-ravaged body. Holding her in this awkward position, the man whispered into her ear. Hot, rancid breath filled her nostrils.

"Make a sound, and I will snap your neck," he said matter-of-factly.

He meant it.

Her wide, terrified eyes filled with tears. Her heart jackhammered, pressing violently against her chest wall. Like every other fiber of her being, it was trying to escape this nightmare.

The man dragged her into the living room. He slammed her firmly against the wall. The force of the impact broke her nose. Blood poured down her face as she screamed in pain. With one arm, he held her against the wall. His free hand ripped her shirt from behind. He yanked her sweatpants down below her waist as she cried out in terror. He popped her head against the wall again. A gash was opened over her left eye. Blood, mixed with tears, poured down her cheek and sealed her battered face to the now red-smeared wall.

This wasn't happening. It couldn't be. Her panic-stricken mind searched the vast expanses of its resources for an escape. She tried to conjure up the memories of everything she had heard or read about rape. Some viewpoints said don't fight it; give in and you are likely to survive. Some said that escaping in the first few minutes is imperative. Delay and you could perish.

Her mind raced until instinct took over. When the pressure against her back seemed to loosen, she drove an elbow backward with all the fury her 110-pound frame could muster. Bull's-eye. The elbow found a landing place on the fake cop's solar plexus. He stepped back a foot, more from shock than pain.

She used the split-second to flee from the room. Her stocking feet slipped on the hardwood floor like tires spinning uselessly on a heavy sheet of ice. She skidded onto the floor, landing hard on her left hip. Her half-downed sweatpants obstructed free range of movement. He was on her again.

She frantically pulled on the leg of a table that was against the wall in her foyer. The lamp on top crashed to the floor beside her head. She grabbed a piece of broken glass and slashed at the man on top of her. The serrated edge caught the flesh behind his left ear, creating a nasty cut.

He winced in pain and reached for the bleeding opening. She brought the jagged piece of glass down again with full force. It caught on his police jacket and tore into the stuffed lining. Resistance from the coat forced the glass to slide across her hand. She lost possession and watched as her newest wound opened. A thin smile-shaped cut covered her hand. It immediately began to drool red.

She wriggled and thrashed against her much heavier attacker. Her left hand found the base of the lamp and gripped it tightly. She brought it forward with surprising strength. The brass base slammed into the man's jaw with a resounding hollow thud. It careened wildly after impact and escaped her outstretched hand. She clawed furiously at the empty space that had once been occupied by her last remaining weapon. Her hand drew back nothing but air and part of the lamp cord that was now trailing behind the bouncing base, wriggling like a brown snake. It too escaped her grasp. Her hand closed on its ghost in futility.

"I thought I told you not to fight this!" he raged, before striking her with an open-handed shot.

The heel of his right hand drove the back of her head into the floor. He released the grip on his seeping neck cut and grabbed her hair with his left hand. He slammed his hand into her head again and she fell into unconsciousness.

*   *   *   *

When Pamela awoke, she was on her back. Her hands were cuffed together and bound to the headboard of her son's twin bed with a pair of nylons. Her legs were spread apart and tied individually to the bed's footboard corners with strips from a torn sheet. Distorted images from the Superman sheets that once covered the bed dug into ankle flesh. She had been gagged with another pair of panty hose, which were tied tightly behind her head. Blood continued to flow from her nose and from the cut over her eye. It formed a meandering rivulet down her face. It had pooled around the leg wear fabric, forming a dam.

Her head felt like it would explode at any second, showering the room with skull fragments and brain matter. The pain clouded her vision and caused her to wince with even the slightest movement. Blood from her cut hand moistened the panty hose bonding and dampened the fabric around her wrist.

The man stood at the foot of the bed and was naked from the waist down. She cried out and thrashed with all her remaining strength. The silk nylons muffled her cries and reduced the shrieks of terror to deadened moans.

He entered her with surprising force. His eyes rolled back in his head, and he embarked on an avalanche of obscenity-laced cries and ramblings. He called her every name she had ever heard and a few he may have made up. He rocked back and forth with rage-inspired strength while he drove himself into her like a flaming hot railroad spike. She blacked out again.

When she awoke, his face was inches from her own. His eyes shone like those of a serpent, and she saw the essence of pure evil glowing within them. He no longer resembled a cop or any other living, breathing human being. His face was twisted by a blinding rage and anger so deep that she immediately closed her eyes for fear that gazing into his spectral pupils would draw her into the depths of his possessed soul.

Pamela Lacour knew that she would never see her family again.

*   *   *   *

"Come on, you cocksucker! Get the hell out of the way!"

Nick hated to talk like that in front of his son, but he was now in a full-fledged panic. Traffic was barely moving. He had received a busy signal the last two times he tried to call home. Something was very wrong. With one hand glued to the horn, he yelled again. The man driving a blue Pontiac in front of him missed another traffic light. He was beside himself. Justin tried to pretend he was sleeping in the backseat. He had never seen his father this worked up before.

Nick couldn't take it anymore. He pulled into the oncoming lanes on Market Street and punched the accelerator. His car resisted at first, its tires spinning uselessly on the slick pavement. The rubber finally gained traction, and he was off. He swerved through the intersection, running the red light. Tires squealed as he narrowly avoided two oncoming motorists while he fishtailed onto Jefferson Avenue.

He was going eighty miles an hour a half mile before the entrance to Highway 40. He slowed the car too quickly and it began to skid. He gained control just before the entrance ramp and gunned the accelerator. The car straightened out and roared onto the highway. Traffic was slow but spaced. He began to weave in and out, cutting off several cars in the process. Horns blared, but he paid them no attention. He was in a zone. The only thing that mattered was getting home. He sped along the interstate, endangering the lives of both himself and his son. Caution was thrown to the wind. Nothing mattered now but getting home as fast as possible.

His pulse racing, Nick had broken into a cold sweat. Both hands gripped the steering wheel so hard that it seemed like it might snap like a twig under the pressure. He had to get home. Traffic began to loosen up after Hanley Road. His exit was less than a couple of miles away. He was now going over one hundred miles per hour on dangerously slick streets. Thankfully, the snow was barely coming down now, and the street crews had done a sufficient job of keeping the highways clean. He would be home in ten minutes.

$$* \qquad * \qquad * \qquad *$$

"You fucking bitch! You think it's OK to tease men like you do?"

Pamela was wide-eyed. The man held a knife to her throat. The cold steel creased her tender skin and threatened to pierce the surface at any moment.

"God, please let this horror show end," she pleaded to herself.

He had raged on, almost incoherently, for several minutes. His rampage blistered forth with gaining force and was now at a volcanic crescendo. She was completely helpless.

The fake cop pulled the knife from her neck. He sat up and raised the handle to his chin. A silver cobra head had been carved into the steel and perched above the knife's handle grip. The snake sneered down the length of the shining blade and seemed to be looking directly into her eyes. The cobra's ruby eyes mirrored the smoldering hatred embedded in its owner.

She shuddered and closed her eyes again. She felt the knife drive into her chest like a sharply pointed anvil. She could faintly hear the sound of bones cracking as it came to a stop halfway through her chest. He had not hit her heart.

Her eyes briefly fluttered open and she saw the knife being raised for another pass. Time had slowed. She no longer felt pain in her head or her chest. She was dying. She waited for a tunnel of light to appear before her. She closed her eyes again for the last time. The only picture in her mind was that of her husband and son, waving to her from their moving car. They were alone together on their first father-and-son excursion. A thin smile formed on her lips. She loved them both so much. She would hold onto that love for all of eternity.

The knife tore through her chest again like an exploding shotgun shell. This time, it did not miss its mark. Her body shuddered, as if it had been pulsated by ten thousand volts of electricity. She twitched several times. She was gone.

*   *   *   *

The man stared down at victim number twenty. That's all she was to him, another number. This one had exacted a toll, however. Drying blood crusted on his neck and surrounded the back of his ear, where it had finally coagulated. His head throbbed from the blow it had absorbed from the lamp. With gloves covered by his victim's blood, he pulled the knife from the woman's chest.

She had obviously taken the worst of the encounter. Her face was battered and nearly unrecognizable. Her chest was completely covered in blood so dark that the scene resembled a low-budget slasher flick. Once attractive to men, she was now a blood-soaked mangled corpse. He briefly admired his work and got off the bed. Jacket partly torn, ear bleeding, head hurting, he groped around the dimly lit room for his pants.

A single lamp partially illuminated the thick blue carpet. The wallpaper was now splattered above the headboard. The mess obstructed some of the sports figures decorating the paper. The remainder loomed in the shadows of the room like undaunted spectators to this unnatural carnage.

"Feisty little thing, this one," he thought.

It didn't matter. She met with the same fate as all the rest. He was kind of pissed that his stay here had taken so long, though. He hurriedly pulled on his costume cop pants and slipped into his boots. He had taken much too long. It was time to get the hell out of the house. The man put his blood-slathered knife back into the strap, which was affixed to his leg. One last look at the dead woman brought a smile of contentment to his face. She had been his greatest triumph yet.

The killer rushed from the room to the landing above the steps. He took the steps three at a time. He had left too much behind this time. Fire-hot intensity had made him sloppy. He couldn't let it happen again. With a quick pull, he had the front door open. He slipped from the residence just as assuredly as he had entered. Fumbling for his car keys, he bounded down the front walk and jumped into his car. It would be the last time he would use this particular vehicle.

The man jammed the car in reverse and pressed heavily on the accelerator. Snow sprayed from the tires and showered the shrubs next to the driveway. Now, facing forward, he shifted into drive and left the premises. Tire tracks, filling with gently falling snow, were left on the long asphalt driveway. From everything he had left behind, even the local cops would be able to determine the make of car he had driven. He was sure some of his blood would be found at the crime scene. From that, they could get his DNA. Footprints he had left on the walk would allow them to speculate on his height and weight.

He already pictured them hurrying around the crime scene, trying to take in every bit of evidence that had been left behind. It made no difference, however, because they had nothing to match it to. His only trouble with the law had come when he was a juvenile. His adult record was completely clean. Besides, he was about done with this town, anyway. It was time to make some new friends in a different city.

The man laughed to himself while envisioning the Keystone Cops trying to piece together a solid case designed to bring about his demise. His car angled onto McKnight Road and plodded toward the highway. In minutes, he would be miles away from the dead woman's body. A fast-moving Lexus bolted past him as he continued down McKnight toward the entrance ramp to 40 East. It was one of only a few cars he'd pass the rest of the way.

The town was dead, so to speak. At least, some of its inhabitants were. The remainder hunkered down inside their homes, anticipating a blizzard that would probably never come. Better for him, because there would be less resistance on the roadways. That meant fewer people to claim they had seen his car.

He would torch the car and his uniform. A couple of days from now, the only remaining link to this night's savagery would be a headstone and burial plot. The stone would not bear his name. Mission number twenty was almost complete.

*   *   *   *

Nick slid onto McKnight Road and barreled forward. He was almost home. He turned right on Litzinger and continued to throttle ahead. The snow had almost stopped falling. An icy stillness filled the winter air. Seconds later, his home came into view. As he pulled into the driveway, he immediately noticed another set of tire tracks. His worst fears were starting to be confirmed. He scrambled for his cell phone and rapidly punched in the number of his next-door neighbor, Tom Chilcote.

"Tom, it's Nick Lacour. Sorry to bother you at this hour," his voice cracked with fear.

"What's wrong, Nick? You sound awful."

"I'm not sure. Can you do me a very big favor?"

"No problem. What can I do for you?"

"Can you come over and take Justin home with you for a little while?"

"Yeah, sure. What's going on?"

Tom now sounded as choked with fear as Nick.

"I can't really explain right now, but you would really be helping me out."

"OK, I'm on my way."

Tom had become a good friend of Nick's. They golfed together during the summer and Tom's son, Brett, often stayed with Justin. The two boys were only a year apart and enjoyed playing together.

Justin had stirred in the backseat during the phone call. He awakened just as Nick asked his neighbor to pick him up. Now the boy was concerned, too. Though very young, he was able to sense that something was definitely wrong. Crying softly in the backseat, he couldn't understand what was going on. He wasn't upset about visiting the neighbors but was visibly shaken by his father's demeanor.

"Why do I have to go to the Chilcotes'?"

"It'll be all right, Justin. Go with Tom, and I will pick you up shortly."

"But I want to go with you," the boy whimpered.

He was now nearing hysterics of his own.

"Don't fight me on this, OK? I need you to go with Mr. Chilcote, and I will pick you up real soon. Can you do that for me?"

Justin nodded his head. Face glistening; he was absolutely certain something was happening. Something that was not at all good.

At that moment, Tom pulled into the driveway. His house was only a hundred yards away, but he had elected to drive his silver Toyota 4Runner to pick up Justin. More tracks now confused the tire depressions on the Lacour driveway. He pulled up alongside Nick's car, which was still running. He leaped out, wearing a look of deep concern.

"Is everything all right, Nick? You really have me worried right now."

"I think everything will be fine. I just have to take care of a few things."

Nick knew he wasn't making sense, but he absolutely had to get into his home, and he was sure it was not currently a place for his young son.

His explanation didn't seem to put Tom at ease, but he still obliged his friend's request.

"Come on, slugger. Let's go to my house and see what Brett is doing."

Justin reluctantly climbed into the backseat of the utility vehicle as Tom flashed Nick one last look of concern.

"If there is anything I can do, anything at all, I'll be glad to help," he assured Nick.

He meant it. Tom could be depended on.

"Thanks, Tom. I know you will. I'll see you in a little while."

Tom jumped into his Toyota and backed down the length of the driveway. Nick was rushing for the front door of his house before Tom's headlights swung onto the street.

*   *   *   *

The killer slogged along Highway 40 toward downtown St. Louis. The roads had cleared considerably, but he still didn't want to risk a mishap. It would be exceedingly difficult to explain his blood-covered clothing. The knife might draw some inquiries as well. It was exhilarating to think that he was risking his freedom by driving in poor conditions with a ton of evidence covering both himself and the worn leather interior of his makeshift cop car.

He passed the downtown area and continued across the Poplar Street Bridge into Illinois. Lights from the city cast a faint silver glow through the mist-laden December air. It was unusually bright in the city because of the pale gray clouds and flurrying snow. Downtown St. Louis was mostly deserted. The man passed only two cars on his way toward the other side of the river. No additional movement cracked the frigid pall that had dropped like a lead sheet over the city. Not a single sign of life offered disruption to the deathly still night.

The Ford rolled into Illinois and exited in the area that boasts the country's worst crime rate per capita—East St. Louis. On any other evening, a white man's trip into this *Escape from New York* setting would have been suicide. Tonight, not even the gangs had ventured out. Things couldn't be moving along any more smoothly. The man could disintegrate the mission's props and be home in time to watch *Jerry Springer*. He loved that show.

He took a side street that angled toward the river. Not a living soul was in sight. Anyone seeking refuge in the woods flanking the river would pose no threat to the killer while he ditched his ride and blood-dipped costume. From the side street, a dirt road now under the siege of the recent snowfall jutted into the woods, leading toward the river's edge. A fire might attract some attention from the Missouri side of the Mississippi River, but fires in East St. Louis were not uncommon. Efforts to investigate would be minimal at best on this night.

The man turned the car off the road into a small clearing surrounded by leaf-less trees and winter-deadened shrubs. He cut the engine and popped the trunk open. He extracted a heavy pair of boots, a pair of jeans, a dark green flannel shirt, and a heavy fleece pullover. He then completely undressed and changed into the new gear. The clothes from mission twenty were dumped into the trunk.

He finished the process by pulling on a pair of heavy wool gloves and removing a five-gallon can of gasoline from the trunk. Slamming the lid closed, he circled the car, dousing it with gas. With the vehicle now glistening in petrol, he reached through the open rear window and withdrew an empty glass bottle and a rag from the backseat. After stuffing half the rag into the bottle, he lit the exposed end and hurled it through the open window. He started his jog into the woods. Behind him, the interior of the car began to ignite. The flames slowly began licking the dash and front seats.

Soon the gas-covered exterior would catch, and the entire car would be engulfed in orange and gold destruction. Jogging at a steady pace, the man was rapidly putting distance between himself and the burning Crown Victoria. He continued toward the river and would have to run another five miles before he got to his own vehicle.

He had left his truck in an abandoned warehouse in the stockyards. The area wasn't as rough as some of the more infamous portions of East St. Louis. It was littered mostly with drunks and prostitutes. Finding a hitch back to the city hadn't been a problem a day ago, when he left the truck. He hoped it was still there.

An old pimp named Tommy had promised him the truck would be well-guarded. The price for security and maintenance was one hundred dollars. The man obliged in cash. He now hung his hopes on the promised word of a pimp. He had punctuated the meeting with a slight bit of roughhousing that seemed to keep the old guy honest. When he left his truck, the old pimp was leaning against it, wide-eyed. He wouldn't dare risk pissing the man off. His fearful look said as much.

CHAPTER 4

▼

Nick noticed immediately that the front door was ajar. He no longer clung to hopes that everything was all right. Almost afraid to enter, but terrified not to, he pushed open the heavy door. His eyes immediately focused on the destroyed lamp, its pieces scattered and littering the foyer floor.

"Pamela! Pamela! Pamela, where are you?"

His desperate cries were the only sounds breaking the uncomfortable silence in the house. She wasn't here, he thought. He raced past the lamp and into the kitchen. Puddles of water and more broken shards of glass covered the floor. The phone receiver hung limply by its cord, looking like a dead man hanging from a gallows pole. Like everything else in the house, it had long since stopped moving.

"Pamela, honey, where are you? Please answer me!"

His voice was starting to crack. He was terrified of what he might find next. He left the kitchen and moved into the great room. The worst sight yet—blood on the floor and wall. Nothing else was out of place. What the hell happened here? Now immobilized with fear, Nick's eyes rapidly searched every space of the room. He was looking for a sign, any sign that told him his wife was OK. He shifted his efforts back to the foyer. Avoiding broken glass, he assaulted the stairs. Taking the winding staircase several steps at a time, he reached the threshold in seconds. He immediately bolted into the master bedroom. Nothing. Not a sign of Pamela ebbed through the tide of stillness washing over the room.

"Pamela! Paaaamelaa!"

He was getting hoarse. His throat cracked, and his voice trailed off into a rusty croak. His wife was gone. Now frantic, he turned circles in the middle of the master bedroom. He looked under the bed, in the closet, and all around the bathroom for his missing wife. Still no signs of life.

Heart hammering, eyes beginning to water, he bolted out of the room into the hall. He quickly checked the hall bathroom. His wife was not there. He moved back into the hall and looked into the spare bedroom. No sign of Pamela there, either. He continued toward the last room on the upper floor, the one belonging to his son. Before he even entered the room, he noticed a smudge on the carpet. Heart beating wildly, he entered Justin's room.

Nothing his mind could have dredged up prepared him for the scene he was now witnessing. He approached the mess on the bed. What had once been his beautiful wife was now a brutalized corpse. Nick fell to his knees next to the bed and draped himself across Pamela's bound, blood-drenched body. He began to convulse spasmodically as huge sobs shook his frame. The love of his life, the mother of his child, lay dead before him.

*   *   *   *

Tom Chilcote couldn't take it anymore. He knew that Nick told him to wait for his return, but something was wrong.

"Honey, watch the kids. I'm going over to check on Nick."

"Is everything OK? You don't look so good."

His wife, Angie, wore a fearful expression.

"I'm fine. Nick just seemed a little weird. I'll just see if there is anything I can do."

"Maybe he wants to be alone. You shouldn't just pop in on him like that."

"I know, but this is different. Something isn't right."

"What do you mean? Do you think he and Pamela are having some problems?"

"No, nothing like that. He just seemed really nervous. I can't explain it, but something tells me I need to go check on him."

Angie looked skeptical but relented.

"Fine. I'll be here with the little monsters."

Tom kissed her on the cheek.

"Thanks. I will be right back."

He dug into his pocket for the 4Runner keys and forged into the December wind. He could have easily walked, but avoiding extended time in this cold held a lot of appeal.

Within seconds, he was parked in front of the Lacour home. He noticed immediately that the front door was open and that Nick's car was still running. He now knew something wasn't right.

Shifting into park, he cut the engine and jumped out of the truck. He jogged to the front door and entered the residence.

"Nick? Pam? You guys OK?"

From the second floor, he could hear muffled sounds. He did not hear voices but knew something was going on upstairs.

"Nick, it's Tom. Are you up there?"

He held the banister, one foot on the bottom step, poised but reluctant to ascend. There was still no reply. He started up the steps. The sounds coming from the second floor got louder. What he heard was crying—not the whimpering of a child, but the hysterical sobs of a grown man.

At the top of the steps, he could tell the cries were coming from the end of the hall. He proceeded to Justin's room. Faint light cast a shadow-distorted glow on the hall carpeting. He stepped into the doorframe. Stunned eyes fell on the sight before him. Like his neighbor moments earlier, his first impulse was to drop to his knees. He did so and retched on the floor just inside the room.

When he regained his composure, he struggled to his feet and approached his friend. Nick held his wife fiercely as he fought with the many emotions that had overcome him. Tom rested a hand on Nick's shoulder. No words seemed adequate.

Stunned by the events that had transpired and queasy from the carnage engulfing the small bedroom, Tom didn't know exactly what to do. In a low, broken voice, he told Nick that he was going to get help. Taking slow, unsteady steps, like an infant exploring the world for the first time, he staggered out of the room into the hall.

He sucked in deep breaths, gulping fresh air as if he had been trapped underwater for several minutes. He pulled a cell phone from his pocket and dialed 911. The ambulance that would be the first emergency vehicle on the scene was much too late to do any good.

*　　　*　　　*　　　*

The man was slightly surprised but delighted to see that his truck was not only where he left it, but also exactly how he left it. You know what they say: crooks are the most trustworthy people out there. He stifled a laugh at that thought.

Emotionally and physically drained from his struggle at the woman's home, the man slipped into his truck and decided to rest for a bit. Risking the poor driving conditions at this hour no longer seemed fun. He wanted to reflect on the night's events. He was relishing every delectable memory, each still fresh in his mind.

Besides, the burning car by the river would have attracted attention by now. No point in subjecting himself to scrutinizing eyes. He could sleep for a couple of hours in the truck and then get back to his apartment after daybreak. He wasn't working in the morning, so he really had no sense of urgency. Not that he ever did. His actions were his own. No one would ever be able to hold him accountable for anything.

Still recollecting the encounter from earlier in the evening, he drifted into a dreamless sleep. He would be home and free of suspicion in the morning. Another successful mission accomplished.

*   *   *   *

It had taken seven minutes for the ambulance to arrive on the scene. The first police cruiser appeared forty-five seconds later. It was followed by two more five minutes later. Now, twenty minutes after Tom's 911 call, the Lacour residence was crawling with people.

News crews from all four major networks had camped out on the front lawn. More than a dozen neighbors stood shivering in the street, trying to peer beyond the yellow police tape. Lights from the TV camera crews had illuminated the yard, making it look like a miniature version of Busch Stadium.

Nick sat at his kitchen table. An untouched cup of coffee in front of him, he stared blankly at the floor. He was in a deep state of shock. Angie Chilcote had made the coffee and was now trying to run interference so that he was not overwhelmed by crime scene technicians and detectives. Her husband was attempting the same, but with far less patience.

"Leave him alone. Can't you understand what he is going through?"

Tom's requests died on the vine. The detectives still had a job to do.

"Mr. Lacour, I'm Detective Ramsey and this is my partner, Detective Valentine."

Nick didn't raise his head to meet their gaze, nor did he acknowledge that he was addressed.

Ramsey stood over him dressed in the traditional *Columbo* overcoat. He was in his early fifties, but years in the trenches had creased his face with a look that spelled mid-sixties at the youngest. He had thinning gray hair, tightly cropped to his smallish head. Attached to his pea-sized head were larger than normal ears, which stuck out at an odd angle. Their tips were flanged with a tint of red that matched his bulbous nose. The beak was no stranger to a bourbon or three and had grown in proportion to the oversized ears. His disheveled look certainly didn't inspire a vote of confidence regarding the apprehension of a homicidal maniac. Still, somewhere underneath the comic book features resided a professional and diligent cop. His intensity was well displayed through bright blue eyes that had not been dulled by more than twenty hard years on the force. They still held a razor-sharp stare that had buckled many a felon during his hard-edged interrogations.

"Mr. Lacour, I know this is a very difficult time for you, but we really do need to ask you some questions."

Detective Jack Ramsey again tried to penetrate Nick's veneer.

"I told you, leave him the fuck alone. His wife was murdered for God's sake," Tom snapped. He couldn't take watching this. He was beginning to unravel.

The detectives ignored Tom and redirected their attention to Nick. After a long silence, Nick looked up at them. Eyes glazed and distant, he looked toward the detectives but appeared to be staring right through them.

"Mr. Lacour, we hate to have to speak with you right now, but time is critical. If we don't determine the nature of this crime right away, we lose precious opportunities at arresting the perpetrator."

Detective Raymond Valentine had done the speaking this time.

"Murder," replied Nick.

"I'm sorry. What did you say?" asked Valentine.

"You asked the nature of the crime. I said murder."

He again fell silent and stared into the abyss of black coffee before him.

"Yes, sir. That is correct. However, we need to start building a case right away. Do you mind if we ask you a few questions?"

Nick said nothing.

"Very well. We would like to start by asking you to recap everything you can remember about tonight. It is very important that you leave out no details. Time frames are critical right now," said Ramsey.

In a dull, flat voice, Nick began to summarize the events of the evening, as he knew them. With a lawyer's detail but a voice lacking emotion or inflection, he recounted every minute aspect of the day's events. He began with his car ride home from work and ended with the grisly scene in his son's bedroom. His recounting of the day was so thorough that he even included some of his conversations, verbatim.

Remaining in control throughout the lengthy dissertation, he finally began to break when recalling his anxiety about entering his home. His recollection of time was pinpoint accurate. When he began to speak about his tour through the home, his voice rose and started to crack. By the time he came to the part where he saw Pamela on the twin bed, he broke down with emotion.

Words were choked off by sobs. He buried his head in his hands and bawled without restraint. Angie put her arms around him and started to reassure him that things would be all right. She wasn't convincing.

"That's enough, officers. I think Nick has had quite enough tonight," said Tom, rudely intervening the detectives' interrogation.

It was clear that they both had plenty more to ask, but they nodded in begrudging agreement. It had been apparent that Nick was not a suspect. This would be proved when the coroner determined the time of death. He had been at a hockey game when his wife was brutally murdered. Detective Ramsey knew that this evening's questioning was over.

"Thank you, Mr. Lacour, for your cooperation at a very difficult time like this. We are extremely sorry about your wife. Please call me if there is anything I can do," finished Ramsey.

He placed a business card on the table next to the cold cup of coffee.

Nick pulled his head from his hands and looked at Ramsey through bloodshot eyes.

"There is something you can do, detective."

"Anything. You name it."

"You can catch the motherfucker who did this to my wife."

"Believe me, Nick, nothing would make me happier. You have my word that I will use every resource, every man hour, and every ounce of twenty years of experience trying to do just that."

Nick nodded briefly and dropped his head into his hands again. He had never felt more numb or helpless in his entire life. His world had been ransacked. None of this felt real. He could not believe he would never see his wife again. It didn't completely dawn on him until that moment. With this sobering revelation driven into his mind like an ice pick, he broke down again.

CHAPTER 5

▼

The man awoke spread across the front seat of his pickup. It was still dark in the abandoned warehouse, so he had no concept of time. He didn't wear a watch but guessed that it was after daybreak. Rubbing his eyes, he winced at the pain in his neck. That bitch had done a number on him. A thin, ugly smile parted his lips as he recalled the confrontation.

He got the better of her. That much was obvious. How could she think that she had a chance against him? No one had ever bested Gerald Rucker. That was his name, but few people knew it. If he had friends, he supposed they would call him Jerry. However, he had none. When he drifted to new towns, it was always under an alias. Right now, he was Carlton Lewis. That was the name of a bum he whacked in Indianapolis last winter.

Old Carlton had the nerve to break into his car and spend the night, trying to escape the January cold. He could still remember the man's eyes, big as quartz crystals, when he awoke with a knife to his throat. Amazingly, Mr. Lewis had a wallet. No money, but a driver's license and Social Security card. Maybe he had been a contributing citizen at one point in his life.

After Rucker slit his throat, he dumped the body in a nearby alley. No one would miss this guy. He would be toe-tagged as John Doe and incinerated at the morgue. Rucker would borrow his identity for a while. He had been Carlton Lewis for nearly a year. The new name had landed him a job in St. Louis. He even obtained a credit card.

Gerald Rucker lived in an apartment in downtown St. Louis. He used a post office box for his mailing address. It had been registered under the name of Carlton Lewis. No one ever questioned the fact that he didn't look anywhere near forty years old. That was the age Carlton made it to before taking the knife.

Recovering from a few poor hours of sleep in the front seat of a truck, he sat up and decided it was safe to vacate East St. Louis. Taking slow steps, still sore from his battle with the woman and his run along the river, he slid open one of the large double doors of the warehouse. The sun was out, and it stung his eyes. It looked like a whole new world compared to the night before. Melting snow was already running down the street and gurgling in the drainage pipes that ran along the corners of the building. It was time to go home and regroup.

He got back into his truck and turned the key. The engine sputtered at first but finally caught. He pulled out of the warehouse, giving a silent salute to the old man who had promised to watch the vehicle for him. He was on his way back to the city. He felt alive and cleansed from the completion of yet another successful night of murder.

*   *   *   *

Nick woke up in unfamiliar surroundings. Still groggy from the tranquilizers he had reluctantly accepted from his neighbor, he wasn't exactly sure where he was. A quick glance around the room made him aware that he now occupied a spare bedroom in the Chilcote residence. He glanced at his watch. It was 6:17 AM. He had only been asleep for about two hours. Complete mental fatigue had forced him into a brief slumber. With the suddenness of an earthquake, he was again pierced by the realization that his wife was gone. He had hoped to awake and discover that it was all a nightmare. It was not.

Now, he had to face the unpleasant task of starting the rest of his life without her. He would love nothing more than to take another handful of tranquilizers and drift away into complete unconsciousness. He could not. He still had his son. He was completely responsible for helping him through this brutal time and ensuring that he somehow recovered and learned to live a normal life, free from the scars that the loss of his mother would leave on his soul.

He still felt numb. How could this have happened? Who could have possibly wanted Pamela dead? He had been unable to contemplate these questions the night before. Now, with the finality of her death constantly imposing itself on his mind, he had to face grim reality. But first, he had to summon the strength and courage to tell his son that he would never see his mom again. When he had arrived at the Chilcotes' home, Justin was asleep. He had been too dazed from the sequence of events to remember much about leaving his own dismembered residence. He vaguely recalled being helped into Tom's SUV. From there, the events of the night were fragmented blips in time. He recollected resisting the tranquilizer tabs at first but finally succumbing to the appeal of escapism that they would provide. After that, nothing else seemed to matter.

He couldn't escape any longer. He didn't know where to start, but he did know that Justin would be up in about an hour. After somehow explaining this to his son, he had to start making funeral arrangements and deal with various other unpleasantness. The next several weeks in his life would be hellish. Not even time would serve as an adequate remedy for his pain.

After sitting on the bed for several minutes deliberating, he shifted into lawyer mode. He would somehow have to be able to tune everything out and rely on his uncanny ability to focus and perform like a machine on autopilot. He left the bedroom and headed down the stairs to the kitchen. He could smell fresh coffee and frying bacon. Normally, both smells would have been a delight to his senses. Right now, they just brought on a wave of nausea.

Angie stood by the stove, turning the bacon and tending to eggs that were cooking in sizzling butter and bacon grease. He swallowed hard and resisted the urge to vomit.

"Thought you could use some breakfast."

Angie was trying to be helpful.

"I'm really not hungry, but thanks anyway."

He couldn't tell her that the mere sight of food was about to make him sick.

"Really, Nick, you are going to need your strength. Try to eat something."

"I can't. Maybe later."

"Didn't you hear the man, Angie? Nick doesn't want to eat right now," Tom interjected.

He had rescued Nick from a nearby room and now appeared in the doorway to the kitchen. He was dressed in business attire, ready to face another day's grind at the office.

"Nick, I would stay here with you, but I have a meeting that can't be rescheduled. I'll be back as soon as it is over."

"I understand. You have already done enough. Thank you both so much for being there last night. I don't know that I could have handled it alone."

Tom simply smiled and nodded his head. Again, no words would adequately sum up the feeling.

"Nick, you and Justin are welcome to stay here as long as you like," Angie added, trying to be helpful. In her way, not addressing reality was the best formula for coping.

"Thanks, Ang, but I have a lot to do. I am going to have to face this, no matter how badly I don't want to."

"Well, just know that you are welcome here anytime."

He attempted to force a smile and mouthed his thanks. Smiling just didn't fit his face right now.

"You mind if I use your phone? I am going to have to start letting people know what happened before they hear it from the media."

"The cordless is on the kitchen table. Help yourself."

Angie avoided eye contact, feeling that avoidance would return life to normal. "Thanks."

He picked up the phone and began to embark on a series of calls that would deplete the last reserves of his mental strength. The first would be to his brother in Boston. Then he would call his parents, followed by Pamela's mom. He asked that they help him by calling other relatives and close friends.

His brother, Jim, was stunned silent when he heard the news. Choking back tears, he only managed to say that he would be on the next flight to St. Louis. The entire conversation lasted less than a minute.

The next two calls didn't go quite as well. His parents had always adored Pamela. They repeatedly told her that she was the daughter they never had. They took the news very badly. Jane Lacour, his mother, passed out. His father handled things only slightly better.

After surviving that call, he stared at the phone for several long minutes. It was possible that Pamela's mother already knew. After all, no one was aware that he was at the Chilcotes'. The murder had undoubtedly appeared on the morning news. Calling her father would not be necessary. He had died from a heart attack five years prior.

He began to dial the number to Deidre Martin's home. He got stuck on the last digit, but after a lengthy pause, he pressed the lit "8" on the keypad and put the phone to his ear. Deidre had lived a hard life. She managed to survive mental and physical spousal abuse for more than twenty years. When her husband died, she was born again.

She was now a mainstay at the Lacour home. She was Justin's chief babysitter in times of need. She visited her daughter and grandson nearly every day. So much so that Nick had jokingly referred to her as his other child.

"Deidre, it's Nick."

He was fiercely fighting with his emotions, a battle he would soon lose.

"Hi, honey. How's my beautiful little grandson doing?"

"Uh, Justin's fine."

"Something's wrong. You don't sound like yourself."

He resisted the urge to put this off any longer.

"Deidre, uh, something awful has happened. Pamela is dead."

He knew the words weren't chosen carefully enough, but he couldn't prolong this any more. The lawyer in him got straight to the facts.

"What do you mean? I just spoke with her yesterday."

Deidre's voice had risen to a hysterical pitch.

"Last night, while Justin and I were at the hockey game, an intruder broke into our home——"

He couldn't finish the sentence. For what seemed like the hundredth time in the past ten hours, he came apart, completely ravaged by the devastation of loss.

"This can't be. I just talked to her yesterday."

Deidre did not want to accept this news, but the broken tone of her voice suggested that she already had.

Struggling against the tears, he tried to continue but could not. Angie relieved him of the phone and attempted to resume the conversation.

Emotions also besieged her. She only managed to tell Deidre that Nick and Justin were at their house before she dissolved into tears as well. Deidre said she would come over as soon as possible.

During all the commotion, Justin had awakened and was now standing in the kitchen. A puzzled, fearful look creased his angelic face. He had never seen his father cry before. He couldn't begin to understand the complexity of the situation.

Nick saw his son standing in the doorway, a small blanket gripped in his hand. Flannel Superman pajamas clung to his small body. Seeing Justin fractured his heart like a chisel that had been forcefully driven into stone. How could someone take away this innocent little boy's mother?

He rushed to his son and gathered him into his trembling arms. He would now have to embark on the daunting task of explaining to Justin that his mother was gone and that he would be raised in a single parent home.

*   *   *   *

Gerald Rucker entered his dimly lit apartment. Small factions of light had illuminated the edges of the drawn window shades. The apartment was small, so he needed no light to navigate his way. He deftly avoided a coffee table and walked down a small hallway to the bedroom. Without bothering to remove his clothes or shoes, he fell into the bed. His mind had envisioned last night's interlude for quite a while. The culmination of events had exhausted him. Mentally and physically fatigued, he immediately fell asleep.

While he rested peacefully in his one-bedroom flat, the lives that he had torn to shreds were struggling to repair themselves enough to face another day. His only dreams involved the woman on the bed. Fear in her eyes, but longing in her heart. He just knew that she had begged for him to come into her life. He had fulfilled her wishes. A dream-induced smile covered his face. The man felt he had saved another person from life's misery.

By releasing them from this life, he was also ensuring his own personal freedom when the time came for him to receive a call to a higher plane. He was certain that with each successful mission, he was rapidly gaining the acceptance of the forces that ruled the dark world that he longed to be a part of.

He rolled onto his side and let his subconscious seek out the next woman worthy of his touch. He could almost see her. It wouldn't be long. The opportunity would again come to satisfy his needs while moving closer to an eternity in hell.

*   *   *   *

The sun didn't deserve to shine on this day. Nick cursed its life-giving light. In his heart, there was no light, just putrid darkness. Telling his son about Pamela's death was the hardest thing he had ever done. Dealing with it himself was running a close second. An emotional wreck and unable to cry anymore, he had to enter the house. He didn't know if he had enough resolve left to do it, but he had to. Somewhere in the former semblance of his home lay answers to his questions. He had to deal with the pain. But to cope with it, he would have to gain an understanding.

He was only able to pull halfway up his driveway. The remaining half had been roped off with crime scene tape. Sidestepping the yellow tape, he saw streaks of red on part of the driveway. At first he thought it might be blood but then realized it was print wax used to make casts of the tire tracks.

He took a deep breath and entered the house. There were still people on the scene. Crime technicians dusting for prints and gathering bits of microscopic evidence scurried about. He didn't recognize any of them, but they seemed to know who he was. With sullen nods, they continued about their business. People were starting to treat him as if he were a leper. At a time like this, few people know exactly what to say or do. For many, avoiding the wake created by life's miseries is the best technique. None of the technicians bothered to tell him not to disturb the scene of the crime. They seemed more comfortable staying at arm's length and steering clear of any conversation.

He stood motionless in the foyer. As he glanced up the stairs, he immediately had a flashback to the evening before. It was an eerie déjà vu that made him tremble. He knew he had stood in the same spot just twelve hours prior; however; he hadn't known the extent of the situation at that point. Now, as he stood there once again, he had complete awareness of what had happened.

The house looked different in the light but still held the foreboding darkness from the night before. When his wife was removed from this place, it lost all of its appeal and charm. A once comfortable residence that he called home had metamorphosed into a crime scene. This had been his dream house, the place where he thought he would grow old with his spouse while they watched their children grow and eventually bring families of their own to visit.

The residence no longer captured that essence. It would forever be recognized as the place where his life took a devastating turn. It was now the building his wife died in. The walls witnessed the spectacle and retained its visuals, but nothing about the place even resembled his home anymore. As he ascended the staircase, he realized that nothing in the building was familiar to him. It was almost as if his subconscious mind had blocked all pleasant memories of the life he was in the midst of carving out when hell came through the door and shattered his dreams.

At the top of the steps, he felt his pulse begin to rise. He knew that down the hall, the room he once viewed as his child's bedroom had since been transformed into a room occupied by death's shadow. He forced himself to take a step in that direction.

With pulse racing and a thin line of sweat forming on his forehead, he forged down the hallway. He didn't know why, but he knew that he had to go into the bedroom again. He had to see the room while it still harbored an air from the events that had transpired just a short time ago. His legs like lead and heart racing, he covered the distance and stopped just a few feet shy of the doorway. Poised outside the room, he saw the yellow police tape forming a thin shield between him and the room where both his wife and a part of himself had died the night before.

He still didn't know why he needed to enter the room. It was almost as if an unseen force was guiding him, pulling him in that direction. He took two more steps and stood in the doorframe. At first, his eyes would only focus on the police tape blocking the entrance. He stood, almost confused, feeling as if he were in a dream.

As his eyes broke their stare with the tape, his gaze shifted deeper into the shadowy room. At first glance, everything looked virtually undisturbed. The shelf unit he had built for Justin still contained the same books and stuffed animals. The St. Louis Cardinals batting helmet he had gotten for his son at a baseball game last summer still sat on top of the white dresser. It was resting next to a small Tiffany lamp that Pamela had loved. The lamp was on and its glow reflected off the shiny red helmet and polished dresser top.

Most of the room's artifacts were in the exact place they had been when Nick and Justin left for the hockey game. Justin's toy chest remained in the corner of the room. Partially opened, he could see some of the toys threatening to spill out of the overstuffed box. A small desk, which matched the dresser, occupied the opposite corner. Above the desk was a corkboard. Justin had tacked pictures of his favorite athletes on the board. Sports figures adorned the wallpaper as well. A large poster of Albert Pujols hung over the bed. The quintessential baseball slugger was Justin's favorite sports star. Pujols' image stared into the distance, following some ball that he had launched into hyperspace off the head of his ominous looking black baseball bat.

It was at this point that Nick's conscious mind registered the change in the room's appearance. He looked from the poster to the bed and was immediately catapulted back to the night before. Pamela no longer lay on the small twin bed. She had been replaced by a white outline illustrating the position he had left her in when he initially mourned her.

Blood had stained the rumpled sheets and bedspread crimson. Splatter marks covered the wall behind the brass headboard and the floor surrounding the bed. He stared at the chalk outline, still in shock. His mind didn't want to accept what had taken place here, but his heart had already been penetrated by reality's jagged edge.

He didn't know what he was looking for, or why he was looking into the room at all, but it seemed like something he had to do. He remained outside the doorway, peering past the crime scene tape like it was the steel bars of an animal cage. He just stood there, unable to move, barely able to comprehend what had taken place in the same room where he had read a bedtime story to his son just a day and a half ago.

Turmoil was raging inside his mind. He fought the aching of his loss and the anger toward its precipitator. His heart was filled with anguish. He fully understood that Pamela was gone, but he had not been able to deal with the consequences. The wound was too fresh to inherit the aftermath. He was now a widower and a single parent. The emptiness formed a gaping cavity in his chest.

Fighting back the tears again, he began to feel something new press in on him. It was a mixture of blind rage and woeful devastation.

"Why!" he cried out, unable to contain the mounting force.

He struck the wall next to the door with full force. His hand crashed through the drywall, drenching the air with a spray of white dust and paper fragments. He drew his fist out of the hole and struck the wall again with equal force, enlarging the first hole to about ten inches across.

Murmuring on the ground floor grew louder as several of the individuals in the house began to climb the steps to investigate the outburst. He crumpled to the floor. Fists still clenched, he began to slam his head against the wall, crying, "Why? why?" over and over again.

Detective Ramsey was the first to arrive on the second floor. He had come back to the house to meet with the crime scene technicians. He saw Nick sitting on the floor and sat down next to him on the thick Berber carpeting.

"Cracking your head open isn't going to bring her back."

Nick stopped banging his head into the wall and looked at the detective. Pain and anger seared his eyes. He was completely helpless. He said nothing.

"In some ways, I understand what you are going through."

"Why did this happen?" Nick posed, ignoring Ramsey's statement, feeling that no one could understand what he was feeling.

"A million reasons probably. Some sick fuck randomly chose your wife as his target. No one really knows what causes someone to commit a crime like this. I can tell you what the psychology books say, or you can hear what twenty years of criminal investigation has to say."

"Spare me the psychology bullshit. Let me hear from twenty years of experience."

"Then the answer is there is no answer. A mentally disturbed individual snapped and committed a heinous crime. Unfortunately, it happens every day."

"Why here? Why Pamela?"

"I wish I could answer that. More than likely, he saw her somewhere, and she fit a profile he keeps tucked away in his disturbed mind. She tripped some alarm wires in his brain, and he became obsessed. He probably staked her out for some time before making his move."

"How do you go about catching this maniac?"

"We will gather as much evidence here as we can. We will put it into our computer and look for matches. I will interview everyone who knew your wife, as well as all your neighbors. We will look for witnesses and start to compile a case."

"Do you have anything so far?"

"It's pretty early yet," replied Ramsey. "We know that he drove a large sedan. You could tell that from the tire marks in the snow last night. Your vehicle and your neighbor's SUV disrupted most of them, but we got some decent readings. We also think he came through the front door."

"How do you know that?" Nick looked alarmed at the thought.

"He couldn't have gained entrance into your basement through the windows you had installed. None of the windows on the ground floor had been opened. There were no prints in the snow surrounding the outside of the house."

"Pamela wouldn't have let a stranger into our house. She was much too careful for that."

"That leads us to think that she either knew him or he was posing as a professional of some kind."

"What do you mean *professional?*"

"He was probably dressed as a cop or gas company employee. It doesn't happen that often, but it is not out of the question."

Nick was trying to digest this information. He was searching his mental Rolodex trying to think of anyone who might be capable of this kind of a crime. He couldn't think of a single person. Everyone who knew Pamela liked her. She had no enemies. She was active in the community, the school, and their church. Anyone who had met her would agree that she was a great person.

"Nick, I know this is going to be hard for you for a long time, but we will be relying on your help."

"Anything I can do, Detective Ramsey. I want this guy caught."

"Call me Jack."

"OK, Jack. I want this beast caught."

"So do I, son. So do I. But to do that I need your total cooperation."

He looked at Ramsey and nodded. He was recovering from his fit of rage. His mind was currently focused on finding the person who had walked through his front door and murdered his wife.

"We can start by getting off this floor and going somewhere to talk."

Ramsey got up and helped pull Nick to his feet. They went down the stairs to the ground floor.

"How about some coffee?" he asked as he motioned toward the front door.

"OK."

The two men got into Ramsey's undercover police vehicle and left. Birds chirped from the barren trees lining the driveway. Terror had exited the neighborhood and was waiting to wreak havoc somewhere else.

CHAPTER 6

▼

Rucker opened his eyes. Very little light illuminated his small apartment. It must be near nightfall. He rolled over toward his nightstand and looked at his alarm clock through sleep-blurred eyes. Squinting slightly, he was able to discern that it was 4:15 PM.

Stretching, he crawled out of bed and sauntered into his kitchen. He was hungry and hadn't eaten in more than twenty-four hours. He had been too focused on the task at hand. Now he was famished.

He opened the refrigerator door and saw a half-empty mayonnaise jar, lid askew. Behind the mayonnaise were a bottle of Budweiser and a jar of pickles. Only one spear floated in the murky green liquid. On the inside of the fridge door stood two plastic bottles of mustard, both with crusted brownish remnants on their caps.

The door's bottom shelf held a jar of Welch's grape jelly and a block of cheddar cheese, once orange but now crusted over with green and white mold. Rucker looked at the paltry display with disgust. He hated to do it, but it was time to go grocery shopping. He grabbed his jacket from the back of a kitchen chair, picked up his keys and wallet from the countertop, and left the apartment. He would go down the street to the local grocery and replenish his food supply. He felt good. The yearning inside had been satisfied last night.

Anxiousness was replaced by a peaceful feeling of resolve. He took the second floor steps outside his unit to the parking lot. His white Ford truck was parked, straddling two of the lot spaces. He must have been tired this morning.

He got into the truck and sped off to the grocery store. Punching through radio stations, he finally landed on 97.5 FM. It was a local rock station specializing in hard rock from the '70s and '80s. Sammy Hagar was singing about unsatisfactory speed limits. Rucker turned up the dial and sang along.

It was only two miles to the grocery store. The night had brought cold temperatures back to the city. Water from the previous day's snowmelt was beginning to form a thin layer of ice on the streets and sidewalks. He pulled into an open spot near the building but misjudged his speed and tried to stop too quickly. The pickup skidded on the freezing water and grazed the metal stand holding the shopping carts. The stand swayed from the blow. He laughed.

He got out and headed into the market. He hadn't felt this good in a long time. Mission number twenty had been exactly what he needed. Since his work was seasonal, the bad weather had brought about a lull. He had been going crazy staring at the walls of his apartment. Killing the woman in the county eased his restlessness. His only hunger right now was from lack of food.

The automated doors swung open as he entered the store. He grabbed the first cart he spied along the wall just inside the doors. The cart's wet wheels left dirty tire marks on the white speckled tile floor.

He hadn't purchased food in a long time, so he decided to go all out and buy a full supply. He started in produce and grabbed some healthier items. While mulling over the purchase of bananas, he saw her. She was just a few feet away, filling a plastic bag with apples. He could feel a churning in his stomach. The woman before him was almost as attractive as the one he butchered last night. She had on a black rain suit that swished when she walked. It was the kind you wore home from the gym. The jacket was unzipped, revealing a black sports bra that barely contained her large chest.

Her hair was up in a ponytail, which had been pulled through the back of a ball cap. The cap was yanked down tight over her forehead. He couldn't get a good look at her face but was able to see the smooth lines of her cheekbones and the tip of her nose. Suddenly, his appetite had changed.

*   *   *   *

Joe's Sports Café was a dusty hole in the wall a few miles from Nick's house. The front door creaked its disapproval as the two men entered the dimly lit establishment. It was early Tuesday afternoon, and the only other people in the bar were Joe, who was the bartender and owner, and a couple of locals. The place smelled of spilled beer and must. A few brown tables with Formica tops stood in the center of the small room. Beyond the tables was a bar that covered the entire back wall. A shuffleboard table was pressed up against the wall to the left of the front door. The opposite wall had two electronic dartboards and some Miller Lite posters. Each poster had a different bikini-clad woman holding a bottle of beer.

The only light in the room came from the neon signs that hung behind the bar and on both sidewalls. The signs promoted various kinds of beer. The bar itself was lit by recessed lighting built into the structure and positioned under a glass surface. Bottles of liquor stood on top of the smoked glass. The light gave their contents a mystical glow.

Two locals occupied each end of the bar, looking like sentries. They were both middle-aged men seeking refuge from life in general. Regulars at Joe's, they always sat at the bar ten feet apart and rarely spoke.

"Gentlemen, what can I get you?" Joe asked.

He swept a cloth over the bar top, drying an imaginary spill.

"Two Buds and two shots of whiskey," Detective Ramsey said as he took the liberty of ordering for the both of them.

Jack and Nick pulled two wooden stools away from the bar, which slid with some resistance over the dirty floor.

"Pretty strong coffee for a Tuesday, huh, Jack?" Nick said with a smile that appeared for the first time in a day.

"Yeah, pure Colombian gold," Ramsey replied, returning the grin.

"More like downtown St. Louis gold," Nick answered as he accepted the draft and the shot that Joe had placed before him.

"Here's to catching bad guys and making the world a better place," Ramsey toasted, raising his shot glass.

Both men downed the amber ounce and a half of liquid fire and grimaced.

"Maybe I should have stuck with coffee," grunted Nick through partially clenched teeth.

They sat at the bar staring at their drinks for several minutes. Neither spoke. They were both lost in different versions of the same daydream. The only sound in the rundown place came from a nineteen-inch television mounted in the corner near the ceiling. It was spewing out questions from a game show that only the book nerd contestants could answer.

"Nick, is there someone you know who might have been capable of this crime?" Ramsey asked, breaking the long silence.

"I have been thinking about that all morning," he said while shaking his head. "No one disliked Pamela. She was almost too good a person. No one that she knew would have been able to do what was done..."

His voice trailed off as he recollected the grisly scene in his son's bedroom.

"I don't want to insinuate that someone close to your family murdered your wife, but I am relatively certain it was someone who knew her in some way. Even if he was only an acquaintance or someone who had come into contact with her recently."

"I know that most murders are committed by a person who knew the victim, but that doesn't seem possible in this case."

"I just can't buy the fact that some nut job randomly chose your home on a shitty December night, knocked on the door, went in, and killed your wife."

Nick didn't respond. He agreed that it didn't seem plausible, but he was still having trouble accepting the fact that someone who knew Pamela would want to kill her.

"What kinds of hobbies did Pamela have? I know she didn't work full time, but what did she do to occupy her daytime hours other than help raise your son?"

"She was incredibly active. She went to the gym a couple of times a week; she helped out at Justin's school, and at St. Pius, our church. She was probably involved in ten or more charitable organizations. She also worked a couple days a week at Borders."

"I was hoping you would say that she only went to one or two places on a regular basis. It would narrow the list of suspects."

"Not Pamela. She couldn't stand idle time. I never met someone with more energy."

Nick gazed at the television without focusing on the program. He raised his glass and took a long drink from his beer, draining more than half the contents.

Ramsey had been taking notes. He fell silent again and began to ponder some of the information Nick had given to him.

"I want you to make me a list. I know you are going to be busy, but this is very important. I want a list of every organization, gym, school, and charity that Pamela visited on a regular basis. I am absolutely convinced that the person who did this knew her in some way."

Nick nodded. He would compile the list. He would also make funeral arrangements, tie up loose ends at his firm, raise his son, spend time with relatives and adhere to all the other responsibilities that makes up a life. He didn't know how he was going to get any of it done. Right now, all he wanted to do was sit on the barstool and drink beer. Drink beer and forget.

"Tell me about Pamela. I mean, it seems obvious that she was a good person, but give me some details. I want to get to know everything about her that I can."

Nick took another drink and emptied his glass. He summoned Joe over for a refill and began to speak about his wife. He spoke for more than an hour. At times, he seemed on the verge of losing control. Just when he appeared to be ready to crack, he would pause, drink from his glass, and resume where he left off. He gave Ramsey as much detail as he could. He told the detective how he had met Pamela and how they had fallen in love that very first night. He gave sporadic details about their nine-year marriage. Most of all, he told him how big a part of his life she was and how devastating life would be without her.

When he was done, he set his glass back on top of the damp coaster. He was mentally exhausted. His recounting of the details had made Pamela come back to life in his mind. Once again, he was struggling with his composure and her departure.

Ramsey had been watching Nick intently. After he had finished, Ramsey let out a sigh.

"I'm envious of you. I don't know that I have ever met someone as deeply in love as you are. It sounds like Pamela was an amazing woman."

"What's next?" Nick asked, while wiping away the moisture that had formed in the corners of his eyes.

"Well, we sort through the crime scene information and start our interviews."

"Was this an interview?"

"No, not really. We know that you are not a suspect. I just wanted to get to know more about Pamela's life. The kind of person she was. The kind of person she might have met who would want her dead."

"Did you learn anything?"

"I learned that only a sick bastard would have wanted to kill her. Then again, only a sick bastard would willingly kill another person period."

"Have you?"

"Have I what?"

"Have you killed another person?"

"Not like that. But, yes. I have killed a human being."

Nick looked at Ramsey. He was starting to respect this man. He felt that if there were a detective capable of finding the killer, Jack Ramsey was that person.

"Ten years ago, I was staking out a building in North St. Louis. I was with narcotics at the time, and we had been tipped off about an incoming shipment of cocaine. The tip came from a druggie we had busted three times. The third time, he earned himself a trip to the state prison. He decided to roll over on some 'friends' to lighten his sentencing."

Ramsey continued on and told Nick about the bust.

"From the very beginning, something didn't seem right. I can't explain it, but it felt more like a setup." Ramsey rubbed his cheek and drew the beer glass to his mouth, taking a drink and motioning to Joe for a refill. "To make a long story short, I was forced to pull my piece. I shot a sixteen-year-old kid in self-defense. It was him or me. Knowing that doesn't make it any easier."

Nick stared at his beer. The story did nothing to shake his confidence in Ramsey. If anything, he felt a deeper respect for the man because of his compassion.

"What happened next?"

"I got buried in about three months' worth of paperwork. The department had a hearing. It was decided that I fired with no alternative. I was cleared of all sanctions and allowed to return to work."

"So it wasn't like *NYPD Blue*? You couldn't just kill a bad guy and hit the street that same day looking for more?"

"Unfortunately, our job has little resemblance to television or movies. Only in the movies can a cop kill a bunch of civilians and be treated like a hero. Christ, a simple bust leads to a day's worth of reports."

"Doesn't sound too glamorous."

"It's not."

"Well, don't feel bad. Neither is being a lawyer. My courtroom battles come after several months of research, reports, and interviews...It's nothing like the movies."

"I think we have a lot in common."

"As long as we both want the same thing. As long as we both want to nail the son of a bitch who killed Pamela."

"You got that," replied Ramsey.

He took a pull from his fresh beer and threw a twenty on the bar.

"Come on. Let's get out of here."

They pushed through the battered door and exited the dingy bar. Both men squinted against the bright, late afternoon sunlight. They got back into Ramsey's car and headed toward Nick's home. There was a lot of work to do.

*   *   *   *

Rucker hovered in the produce section, pretending to check the ripeness of a cantaloupe. He watched the girl as she filled her basket with fresh produce. She must be a health food freak, or worse, a vegetarian. From a safe distance, he followed her through the store. Occasionally, he would pluck an item off one of the shelves, giving the appearance that he, too, was shopping. At one point, in the frozen food aisle, she abruptly turned and started to head toward him. He tried not to show surprise. Had she known he was following her? She whisked past him and opened a freezer door a few feet behind his cart. Apparently, she had for-gotten a half-gallon of Edy's ice cream. OK, so she wasn't a complete health nut.

When she walked by, he could smell the fresh scent of her shampoo. It had a strawberry essence. He could also smell her clean skin, probably covered in body lotion. It, too, smelled of berry, a raspberry scent, possibly from one of those swank underwear stores. She didn't appear to be wearing much makeup. Her features looked very natural and clean. She had too dark a skin tone for this time of year, so he suspected she paid homage to the tanning gods via an electric bed. Her mouth was small but sensual. She had large brown eyes and a pointed nose. It wasn't too big for her face, but it upturned slightly. It did little to detract from her raw appeal.

In the forty minutes that he had been following her, he felt the rage building deep within. After committing a murder, like he had done the night before, he was usually quenched for a long period of time. This woman inspired him. Normally, he wouldn't feel anything the day after a successful mission. This time, he did. She was driving him wild. He could already feel the smooth texture of her skin and the suppleness of her breasts.

He was doing everything in his power to contain his building fire. If he hadn't been more disciplined, he might have jumped her in the parking lot. He chose discretion as the better part of valor. He would check out at the same time she did. He had fewer items in his cart, so he could beat her to the parking lot and follow her home.

After taking a carton of cottage cheese from the dairy section, the dark-skinned beauty was done with her shopping. She pushed her cart down the remainder of the aisle and began to angle toward a checkout register at the front of the store. Luckily for him, the lines weren't too long. He would be able to time this perfectly.

Rucker had eight items in his cart. He qualified for the express lane. With only two registers open—regular or express—he assumed a position, fourth in line, at the express checkout.

The first two patrons went quickly. Their limited items were scanned and bagged. Both customers paid with cash. This was going better than expected. The woman was two registers away. He peered over the top of a candy shelf and saw that she was only about halfway through the process.

Only one customer remained in front of him. She was a little old lady. In her basket was a gallon of milk, a loaf of bread, two cans of soup, and a Bit-O-Honey bar.

"How would she be able to chew that?" he thought. She looked like she was about ninety years old.

"That bar will pull her dentures right out of her head." Again, he kept his observation to himself.

"Ma'am, that will be seven dollars and twenty-two cents," said the pimply faced kid at the register.

"I'm sorry, son. What did you say?" asked the elderly lady.

"Turn up your hearing aid, you old bag," Rucker mumbled to himself.

He was surprised to see the kid behind the counter grin. It looked like he may have overheard. Whoops.

"I said the total is seven dollars and twenty-two cents."

"You are going to have to speak a little louder. My hearing's not what it used to be."

Rucker was getting anxious. He made a quick check over the candy shelf. Good. She wasn't done yet. She still had a few more items to go.

"He said the total is seven twenty-two," Rucker half-shouted to the elderly woman.

"Oh. OK. Let me just write you a check," she said to the checker, who was now smiling again. He seemed to be enjoying this exchange.

She fumbled in her purse for her checkbook. Rucker was starting to seethe. He couldn't believe how long this was taking. He glanced over the candy rack again. The woman was still there but all of her food had been rung up. She was in the process of swiping a credit card through the machine.

"Come on. Come on. Let's get this moving," he mumbled.

The old woman finally found her checkbook.

"Now let me just find a pen."

She went back to her purse for another lengthy search.

"Ma'am, I have one here," the checkout kid said as he handed her a pen, which was attached to a thin chain.

The old woman accepted the pen into her bony hand. She dropped it twice. It fell off the register, stretching to the end of its chain, but coming up well short of hitting the floor. Rucker was starting to perspire. His blood was boiling. This was taking forever. He took surveillance over the candy rack only to see the woman waiting as plastic bags of groceries were loaded into her cart.

Finally, the old woman had control of the pen and her checkbook.

"What did you say that total was again?" she asked, blinking.

Her owl-like eyes were magnified to ten times their actual size through the Coke-bottle bifocals she wore.

"The total is seven twenty-two. Now write the goddamn check so the rest of us can get the fuck out of here!" Rucker snapped.

He couldn't take it anymore. The brown-skinned woman was wheeling her cart out the front door just as he launched into his mini tirade. He wanted to give pursuit, but it would be too suspicious. It wasn't worth the risk.

"Why, I've never…" she grunted, looking up at him in astonishment.

With that said, she commenced on the longest check-writing display in the history of that particular Jacobson's market.

Rucker tried to look out the front window to see what kind of car the woman was driving, but it was too fogged up from the combination of cold temperatures outside and warm air inside. He was fuming. She was going to get away. He glared at the old woman as she completed writing her check like she was signing the Declaration of Independence. She had a spiteful look on her face suggesting she knew that she had won.

The cashier finally received the check. He placed it in the cash drawer and handed the old bag her receipt.

She fumbled in her purse for her keys, unwilling to move an inch until everything was situated.

"Are you done? Because if you are, why don't you get the fuck out of the way, so those of us who can still breathe can pay for our groceries," Rucker said, still glaring at her.

The kid behind the register nearly burst into laughter. He couldn't contain his grin.

Rucker knew he had made too much of a scene to come back to this grocery store in the near future.

The old woman didn't acknowledge the outburst. She continued to take her sweet time until she finally had her things in order. She slowly began to shuffle out of the store, pushing the cart unhurriedly as if it were loaded down with six hundred pounds of stone. Little did she know she had just saved a young girl's life.

Rucker stared after her. He had half a mind to follow her to her giant Buick and cut her head off in the parking lot. Instead, he paid for his eight items and went home, completely unfulfilled.

CHAPTER 7

▼

It was Thursday, three days after the murder. Nick was preparing to honor one of the most morbid customs in the American culture, the wake. Nothing more than a full day of looking at a dead body while grieving. He felt like he had already cried for more than a year. Another day of it didn't seem possible. Now he would have to suffer through the patronization from well-wishers. In addition, he would share space in a room occupied by the casket containing his soul mate.

This promised to be an extremely long day. Pamela and Nick had rarely discussed death. However, both had been adamant about one thing: no matter what the cause of death, the casket was to be closed to the public. He took it a step farther. He made sure it was closed for the family viewing as well.

Nick had arrived at the funeral home at 11:30 AM. The family viewing was from noon to two. The public could arrive anytime thereafter, up until ten that evening. For him, it would be ten and a half hours of emotional torture.

Thirty minutes early, he entered the mortuary and looked for the mortician. He was a meek man, around forty years old. With eyes sporting heavy bags, and silver hair, his profession had aged him beyond his four decades. He had perfected a compassionate expression. It was a look he wore throughout his business day. Nick wondered if he kept it on at home around the wife and kids, or if an alter ego came out. So tired of caring all day, maybe he became Mr. Hyde in the comfort of his own home. For now, he appreciated the compassionate side. It even appeared genuine.

"Hello, Mr. Bailey," he offered to the mortician, whom he found arranging flowers in Parlor A.

Parlor A, as it were, contained the body of his departed wife.

"Hi, Nick."

Peter Bailey offered a hand with a solemn look of compassion stamped on his face.

"Quite an arrangement," Nick said, accepting the handshake.

"Yes, your wife was dearly loved," Mr. Bailey replied, while making a sweeping gesture toward the twenty or so flower arrangements that had already arrived at Bailey & Sons Funeral Home.

"Yes, she was," Nick responded as his eyes surveyed the room.

It already looked like a floral shop, and he was starting to wonder where the mourners would stand or sit.

"I hope you find this suite acceptable," Mr. Bailey said, again sweeping his hand like Vanna White introducing a new puzzle to solve.

"It will do just fine," Nick replied. He neglected to add that every funeral parlor looked the same to him: cream-colored wallpaper with gold accents, plush burgundy carpeting, and Victorian decorations. The dim, amber lighting cast by the brass lamps was supposed to make you forget about death and pretend you were visiting a luxurious English parlor. He found it curious that Mr. Bailey referred to the room as a suite. This wasn't the honeymoon suite at the freaking Hyatt. It was the place his wife was being laid to rest.

"Are you still sure you want the casket closed? Your wife was a beautiful woman, and we did a fine job capturing that beauty."

"Yes. I'm sure. It was her wish."

Nick loved how people attending wakes would reference the corpse as "looking great." How great can you look when you're dead? To him, all dead people looked dead. The one thing making them alive, the soul, was always noticeably absent. All that remained in the silk-lined box was a remnant of who they once were. A shell, if you will. He never thought the shell looked great.

"Very well. It is important to honor last wishes."

Nick didn't respond. He was still looking about the room trying to figure out where everyone would be hovering.

"I know you will hear this more than enough in the days to come, but I am sincerely sorry for your loss," Mr. Bailey said with compassion.

Nick accepted the first words of patronization. He believed the man but knew he would tire of hearing that sentence. He just wanted to be alone right now. Hearing this crap all night would not bring Pamela back. Reliving the nightmare would further wear down his frayed emotional state.

"Mr. Lacour, if you will excuse me, I have to attend to Mrs. Wilson's suite," Mr. Bailey said and patted Nick on the shoulder, as if that gesture would brush away the weight of the world.

Nick relished the solitude. Oddly enough, despite the cheap ambient attempts to calm the bereaved, he did find the funeral home somewhat relaxing. He almost wished he could take a seat on the couch nearest his wife and spend the next ten hours alone with her, saying his private good-byes without interference. He would have no such luck.

The first to arrive was Nick's brother, Jim. The two men embraced tightly. They had been close their entire lives. Nick was only two years older than Jim. Despite living more than a thousand miles apart, they talked nearly every day. Their closeness transcended the miles and time.

Jim still didn't know quite what to say. He still seemed to be noticeably shaken by the passing of his sister in law. After the two men separated, wiping their eyes, Jim excused himself and went to the kneeler next to the casket. He knelt and paid his final respects to his sister-in-law. Nick watched him with admiration. Before Pamela arrived, Jim had been the person he was always closest to. They still shared an unshakable bond. Nick was glad to have his younger brother nearby at the most difficult time of his life.

Next to arrive at the funeral home were Nick's parents with Justin in tow. His parents looked like they had aged ten years in the past three days. He greeted them with the same embrace he had given his brother. He paid especially close attention to his son, who looked so lost and alone. The scene looked like a Lacour family huddle, with Jim joining in. They all wept openly. This was going to be an emotionally tumultuous day for each of them.

*   *   *   *

Rucker sat at his kitchen table looking at the *St. Louis Post-Dispatch* he had purchased on a whim at a nearby gas station. The effects from his grocery store debacle a couple of days ago had finally worn off. He was starting to feel good again. He opened up to the obituary section. He loved death. He enjoyed reading about the demise of other human beings while imagining the discomfort their deaths had caused the people around them. He viewed the obits much like a normal person would the comics. Reading about mortality always brought a smile to his face.

There it was—Pamela Lacour's obituary. He had become familiar with the woman's name by watching the local news. He always cut out newspaper articles pertaining to his victims. He was starting to build an extensive library of clippings.

"Pamela Lacour, wife of Nick, mother of Justin..."

Blah, blah, blah. He read the paragraph and got to the end where it spoke of the funeral arrangements. He was tempted to attend the service, but it probably wasn't a good idea. The stereotypical killer always returns to the scene of the crime in some capacity, so they say. He wondered who "they" were.

He had little fear of the local police but suspected that even these small-city cops would have the inclination to stake out the wake and the funeral. Why take an unnecessary risk? He had achieved a large body of successful work by performing carefully and taking risks only when it was absolutely necessary. This wasn't the time or the place.

He was curious, however. He wanted to see the mourning loved ones as they said good-bye to their precious little slut. Imagining the scene gave him a shiver of enjoyment. He read the paragraph several more times, reveling in his contentment. The grocery store failure was now completely forgotten.

Rucker finished his repetitive reading and adjourned to the brown, well-worn couch in his living room. It was just after noon. Work had been called off yet again. Times were slow in Rucker's line of business. He was a concrete worker and could count on virtually unlimited time off in the winter. It was beginning to get tiresome. He was forced to spend endless days lying on the couch, watching TV, and daydreaming about his next mission. Twenty-one.

Stretched out on the couch, he mentally returned to the first murder he had ever committed. He was fifteen. It was long before he started performing his coveted "missions." She had been an eighty-two-year-old woman. She had lived four doors down from the home he shared with his fifth set of foster parents. Young Jerry had not been a well-mannered child. True to the textbooks, he had exhibited the kind of behavior that typically predicts the development of a dysfunctional member of society.

At that time, he was just like most of the heroes of his field when they were young. He had tortured animals, set fires, and took part in any activity that would shock and disgust adults. His list of foster parents was growing longer by the year. The fourth set had lasted only two months. They didn't appreciate Jerry hanging their cat from a showerhead in the master bathroom.

That little stunt had earned him six months in a juvenile psychiatric institution. It didn't matter to him. He had feigned rehabilitation and had been released to another set of foster parents. Couple number five had been like all the rest.

Do-gooders who had thought they could save Jerry by heaping large quantities of love and attention on the misguided youth.

Mike and Sarah Sanders had disgusted him. They were a middle-aged couple that had failed in their biological attempts to have children of their own. Jerry had learned that Mike's *boys* didn't swim. Attempts at in vitro fertilization had failed as well. They had elected to provide a home for the poor, unloved drifter Jerry Rucker.

At first, his stay in the Sanders' home hadn't been so bad. They hadn't known quite how to adjust to the new addition. For the most part, they seemed to have feared little Jerry. He loved the respect he had already commanded from these saps. For six months, he had repaid their fear by generally behaving well. He had used the time to familiarize himself with his surroundings. In so doing, he had gotten to know about the neighbors and the general lay of the land.

It was at this time that a strange stirring had begun deep within his subconscious mind. He no longer had achieved great enjoyment from torturing household pets or killing small animals in the nearby woods. Fires hadn't held much luster anymore, either. He was changing. He couldn't pinpoint it at the time, but he had known he was destined to do much more.

That July, six and a half months after the Sanders had taken him in, Jerry Rucker came of age. The day had started much like the previous two hundred. He had gotten up, eaten breakfast, and gone outside and smoked cigarettes while his foster parents made the mistake of leaving him home alone. They had dashed off to their respective jobs and trusted him. Imagine that.

While sitting in the backyard smoking a Marlboro and listening to the annoying chirping of birds, he had seen an old woman tending garden a few houses away. She had looked as frail as one of the chirping birds, hunched over and laboring in the sweltering summer heat. He had laid odds that she wouldn't last the day. He had been right; however, the end wouldn't come at the hands of the heat or the yard work. He had fortuitously made his own prediction come true.

After watching her for nearly an hour, he had become restless. He kept waiting for her to drop over from heatstroke or a heart attack. He had been sure that she wouldn't live through the day. Frustrated and tired of watching her struggle in her meager garden, he had decided to pay her a visit.

"Ma'am, you look like you could use some help."

Startled, the old woman had looked up from her gardening. She smiled when she saw a smallish, clean-cut young man standing before her offering assistance.

"Why, that would be lovely," she had cackled, looking and sounding like a witch.

Jerry began to assist, all the while becoming increasingly more agitated and restless. Finally, she had offered him some lemonade. It was time for a break. This would be his opportunity. He had followed her into the small house, which contained decorations from another era. He had felt as if he'd been transported backward in time some sixty-plus years. Accompanying the outdated appearance was the smell of mothballs and decay. He would soon provide a contribution to the decay smell.

"Would you like a fresh lemon in your glass?" she had offered.

"Yes, please," Jerry had replied.

He had watched her shuffle around the room as if the simple process of making a glass of lemonade was something used to whittle away an entire day. His disdain for her existence had been deepening by the second.

"You seem like a nice boy. Why aren't you out playing with the other kids on the block?"

"Playing? I'm almost sixteen years old. I don't play anymore," he had said to himself.

She had stood with her back to him, carefully slicing wedges from a lemon she had taken from the icebox. He had watched with disgust. She was too old to still be living. Without warning, he had leaped from his chair and jumped on her. She had squealed in terror, completely stunned by this turn of events. Immobilizing her in a hold, he had wrenched the knife from her arthritic hand and drove it into her stomach. He pulled away, almost as shocked as she was. She had slumped to the floor, holding her abdomen and muttering something about God.

"He won't help you now," Jerry had muttered.

She had been too weak and too old to create much of a disturbance. Her moans had seemed distant and virtually soundless. Jerry had resumed his seat at the kitchen table and watched her die. He had been fascinated by the changing expressions on her face and her labored, erratic breathing. After several minutes, she finally lay motionless in a pool of her own blood.

He had continued to watch her for many more minutes, somewhat shocked by what he had done, but oddly fulfilled. On that July day, young Jerry Rucker had become a man in his own mind. A natural killer was born. Unfortunately for him, that killer had not been careful. Two neighbors had seen him enter the home. The dead woman wasn't found for more than a week, but his prints had covered the knife and her kitchen table. He was confined in juvenile detention for one year and transferred to another psychiatric home for two more.

It had taken his best acting to convince the doctors that he was finally healed and ready to return to society. He had belabored the point about his brutal upbringing. He had reiterated time and again that he had never known a family of his own. They had seemed saddened by the fact that he had bounced from house to house, city to city. He had never truly been loved. No one wanted him. It had been a theme he kept going back to; he had been smart enough to realize it was making an impact on his caregivers. They were starting to buy his "feel sorry for me" line of bullshit. Even young Jerry had become so wrapped up in the act that he fleetingly felt there might be some merit to the stories.

For two years, he stuck to his guns. He had remained firmly entrenched in his role as the neglected, abused child, struggling to exist in a harsh world. He even broken down in tears when he felt his words were having no effect on a particular psychiatrist. The entire act worked to perfection. It worked so well, in fact, that one psychiatrist took quite a liking to him. Her name was Nancy Spicolo. She was in her mid-thirties, never married, and without children. In some ways, Nancy and Jerry had been alike. She didn't have a lust for killing, but she was misplaced. Her upbringing had been more normal, but her lot in life had been almost equally as depressing.

Nancy had been a crucial contributing factor to his eventual release from the institution. They had fed on each other. While he couldn't quench his thirst for death, she had kept him satisfied in other ways. Nancy had taken his virginity and helped stoke his physical fire toward the opposite sex. For eight months, they had participated in a well-hidden affair. Other patients had suspected, but they were either too far gone or too paranoid to ever say a word. For the most part, the sex had been well concealed. It ended the day he was released. Nancy had given him a good-bye blowjob and a thousand dollars cash. He had promised to call her after he got settled.

On his eighteenth birthday, just three years and seven days after he committed his first murder, he was released back into the civilized world. This time, he wouldn't be so careless. This time, he wouldn't get caught, but it took all he could do to fight off three years of urges that very first day. He had half a mind to off the guard who escorted him past the pearly gates of the institution. He had been able to keep his desire in check.

He had used some of the money to buy a used Cutlass that barely ran. The remainder was put into a deposit on an efficiency apartment in downtown Memphis. Nancy had also helped him obtain his first job. He was hired as a gas station attendant just two miles from where he took up residence. The transition into civilian life had been smooth. He paid Nancy back a year later. She had the honor of becoming his first successful mission.

While institutionalized, he had spent three years honing his craft. Even if it was only mentally, he still felt he had perfected his skill set. Now, he needed to learn discipline. He needed to fight off his urges and wait for the appropriate time.

Two weeks after his release, he resumed where he had left off that summer of his sixteenth year. Equipped with a driver's license and a beat-up car, he began to embark on the kind of activity that would keep him satisfied for the next ten years. He killed three people in the year preceding his reunion with Nancy Spicolo.

The three killings had been like training exercises. Each one was designed to iron out imperfections in his approach. They helped him gain confidence and learn from his minor mistakes. It all led to his calling. His true birth came with Nancy. In the ten years following her "disappearance," nineteen others helped him begin to carve out his legacy.

*　　　*　　　*　　　*

Emotionally wrung out, Nick sat down on the gold-colored couch that had served as his first perch of the day. It was 10:33 PM on Thursday. The last of the well-wishers had left the funeral home. He sat alone in Parlor A with the embalmed corpse of his departed wife.

"What happened?" he muttered to himself.

Just a week ago, he and Pamela had gone to their favorite Italian restaurant. They went out dancing afterward. Justin was at home with Nick's mom while they stayed out until 1:00 AM. They had a great time. It had only been six days ago. Six days. Who could have predicted what the next week would have in store? He rubbed his eyes and yawned. It had been a long day. He was still numb from everything that had happened. He knew things weren't going to improve for quite a while.

Tomorrow would be the funeral. He would say his final good-bye and be expected to pick up the broken pieces of his life. Furthermore, he would have to be strong for his son. The way Justin dealt with this tragedy could affect the next several years, maybe even the rest, of his life. Nick contemplated that sad fact deeply as he sat on the crushed velvet couch, staring at Pamela's casket.

"I miss you already. How can I continue this journey without you?"

He could almost hear her reply. She would be saying, "You have to, because you are Nick Lacour. You are the strongest person I have ever met. Now, you are going to have to be strong for both of us. More specifically, you are going to have to be strong for our son. You will have to go on because I love you, and it's what I want you to do."

The words weren't spoken, but he could hear them in his mind almost as if they had come directly from her mouth. And he was right. That is exactly what she would say if she were able to appear to him.

He sighed. It was time to go home. Rather, it was time to go somewhere. He didn't feel like he had an actual home anymore. He had agreed to stay with his parents for the next few days because Justin was comfortable there. His parents thought that having people around would help. He wasn't so sure but agreed anyway.

His parents weren't kidding. There would be people around. Jim and his two kids would also be there. It would be like a giant slumber party in a medium-size, three-bedroom house. Maybe it would be for the best, at least for the time being. He couldn't bear the thought of settling back into the house that he and Pamela had called home. He would not be able to escape the constant reminders. Not only reminders of the happy life he had before this unthinkable tragedy, but also the persistent memory of what had occurred just three nights ago.

Reluctantly, he got up from the couch and decided to head for his parents' house. He grabbed his overcoat from a coatrack in a neighboring room and ducked back into Parlor A to take one last look at the casket before he left. Just three days ago, he had held his wife in his arms after they made love. He distinctly recalled thinking that he had never been happier. How ironic, because at this exact moment, he had never been more miserable. What a cruel game life can be.

He draped the coat over his shoulder and headed out to the parking lot. A chill was in the air after an unseasonably warm December day. The night was foggy and looked like the perfect setting for a horror film. Streetlights, shrouded in mist, lit up the parking lot with an eerie glow.

He got into his car and drove for ten minutes before realizing that he wasn't even going in the right direction. His mind had been elsewhere. A million memories had come back to him in the past seventy-two hours. The last few days were spent in a continuous daydream. He couldn't shake the memory of Pamela cuffed to his son's bed. The image was emblazoned in his brain forever. The person who did this had to be caught, and he had to pay for it.

He hummed along Highway 270 at speeds that far exceeded the sixty-mile-per-hour limit. Nick barely knew that he was driving. All he could think about was the faceless, nameless man who had burst into his home and shattered his perfect life. His thoughts were now torn between mourning and a rapidly developing anger.

At first, all he could think about was losing Pamela. Punishing her killer wouldn't bring her back, but it would serve to provide closure to this nightmare. The anger had slowly been welling inside. Now, it was starting to dominate his thought patterns. He was becoming obsessed with this man. The psycho killer had to be punished. He had to pay a heavy price for his actions.

He continued clipping along the highway, drifting deeper and deeper into his reverie. Complete sorrow was starting to share equal time with rage. He would see to it that the killer got his due. If the cops couldn't do it, then he would do it himself. He didn't know where to start, but he couldn't continue to sit around idly and wait for someone else to avenge Pamela's death.

The thought of finding the killer was giving Nick new life. It would be his driving force, his obsession. Tomorrow, after Pamela was buried, finding this maniac would be one of the only things that mattered. He would dedicate part of his life to seeing this through. He knew Pamela wouldn't approve, but he also knew that he would lose his sanity if he didn't accomplish this goal.

Nick would find him. He would punish him for this senseless crime even if it were the last thing he ever did. Thinking about it made things better already. He downshifted into fourth gear and exited the highway. He now had a goal, a dark purpose that would fuel his thirst for revenge.

CHAPTER 8

▼

Friday. Nearly four days had passed since the murder. Nick was getting dressed and preparing to bury his wife. Thunder shook the St. Louis landscape. An oddly placed thunderstorm was rattling the dreary December morning. He realized that it had rained at every funeral he had ever attended. Never did it seem more appropriate than right now. The charcoal clouds accentuated his mood.

After methodically putting on his black suit, he took a deep breath and cut a path toward his parents' kitchen. Jane Lacour stood in her customary spot before the stove. He must have seen her there a million times in his life. The pose never changed. Neither did the quality of the cooking. Imbibing in her own culinary skills had expanded her once-petite body to a frumpy buck and a half, which didn't compliment her 5'2" height. She had a kind, caring face that was now doused with concern for her son's well-being. Soft brown eyes matched her Clairol-colored hair, giving the misguided impression from afar that she might be under fifty. Upon closer inspection, frown lines at the corners of her mouth and eyes would dispel that myth. Years of chronic worrying had reshaped her face, and she commonly wore an intense look of fear and apprehension. No worldwide tragedies escaped her notice, and she seemed to take many of them to heart.

On any other day, he would have eaten ravenously at this particular kitchen table. Today would be different. He hadn't had an appetite in days. In fact, he couldn't remember the last time he ate. It might have been at the hockey game.

"Sit down, Nicky. Let me fix you some pancakes."

"No thanks, Mom. I'm really not hungry."

He hated when she called him Nicky.

"You simply have to eat. You're going to wither away to nothing."

"I don't think you have to worry about that. I could stand to lose a few pounds," he said with a chuckle while mockingly tugging on his flat stomach.

"Don't be silly. There isn't an ounce of fat on you."

He couldn't say much to that. It was true. He was in nearly perfect physical condition, at least for a thirty-year-old beer-drinking man. In actuality, he was probably in better shape than he had been in college.

"Seriously, Nick. I'm worried about you."

"I know you are, Mom, and I love you for it, but I have to handle this in my own way. Right now, my way is to not eat. I promise, you will be the first person I visit when I am hungry again."

His mom gave him the kind of worried look that most mothers acquire almost immediately upon giving birth. She had it mastered, and it never failed to make him feel ashamed. He hated to see her worry, but right now he had other things on his mind.

After choking down a glass of juice and a couple of vitamins, he went looking for his son. Pamela's death had struck Justin harder than anyone else. His initial response to the news had been a show of strength and maturity that caught Nick completely off guard. Shock had probably cushioned the blow initially. Since that time, he had become distant and quiet. His eyes seemed to be perpetually filled with tears and his despondence had Nick extremely worried.

"Mom, have you seen Justin?"

"Yeah, he's in the basement with your father."

"They're not playing that video game again, are they?"

"What do you think?"

Since Nick and Justin had taken up temporary residence in the senior Lacour home, Justin and Nick's father, Mike, had played a computer golf game incessantly. Mike was a youthful sixty and still fit from years of physical activity. His solid features could have easily passed him off as a much younger man. His hair had escaped the onset of age and still hung as a thick shock of brown across his dome. Intense blue eyes reflected the fire of his youth. They had been passed down to two additional generations of Lacours.

And, all three were now crowding the small computer table in the basement as the young boy handled the game's controls. He couldn't get enough of the golf game. He was starting to play pretty well and boldly predicted he would be "whipping Grandpa's butt in a few days."

"What are you playing?" Nick asked, knowing the answer well before he issued the question.

"Golf," Justin said simply, unable to offer much more of a response than that. He was trying to extricate his animated golfer from a precarious sidehill lie.

"What do you say you ride with me? OK, buddy?"

"Can I finish this hole?" he asked, gripping the controller with fierce intensity.

"Two more shots, and then we have to go."

"Good. That's all it will take."

Nick and his father shared a grin. The boy was already getting cocky. He was following a long line of Lacour men, confident with the ability to back it up. He swelled with pride as Justin remained true to his word, landing his shot from the rough onto the putting surface and then sinking a twenty-footer for birdie, while letting out a little yell to further impress his two interested fans.

"Get your coat. It's time to go."

Justin got up and fished his miniature suit coat off the back of the chair he had been occupying. Nick scooped him up and climbed the basement steps. More than anything else he was feeling right now, he was extremely worried about his son. Justin had cried himself to sleep each night. During the day, he seemed almost catatonic. The only time he had shown vibrancy was when he was playing computer golf. For that reason, Nick never denied his request to play, even though he didn't think all that computer time was good for him.

Justin wrapped his arms tightly around Nick's neck. His hold suggested that he fully understood that his father was his one true beacon in a sometimes savage world. Nick hugged him back, fighting off the urge to cry. It was incredibly cruel that this young boy would have to go through life without his mother's strength, love, and guidance.

Nick loaded Justin into the vehicle. After buckling the boy into the backseat, he assumed his position behind the wheel. They were about to attend an event that neither of them was prepared to handle.

*   *   *   *

They arrived at the funeral home twenty minutes early. Nick was surprised to see that Jim and his family were already there. Jim, six foot two and a spitting image of Nick, was one of the pallbearers. The six men chosen for this thankless task would carry the casket to the hearse parked in the circle drive in front of the building. After loading it in, they would drive separately to the church, where they would unload the casket and carry it to the back of the church.

Nick and Jim shook hands. Their closeness alleviated the need to speak much at this awkward time. After ten minutes of small talk, other people began to arrive. First upon arrival were Nick's parents, followed by Pamela's mother. Deidre Martin may have taken this whole thing the worst, at least physically. Always a thin woman, she now looked like a skeleton. Nick guessed she weighed less than one hundred pounds. Her cheeks were more sunken than ever. This once-attractive woman of fifty-two looked nearly seventy. He wondered if she would survive the ordeal.

Hugs ensued, complete with tears. If Nick thought the wake was long, then the funeral process was going to be a marathon. After the service, close family and friends would adjourn to Mike and Jane Lacour's home. A bounty of food would decorate every flat surface. Alcohol would flow, and each bystander would go through the motions of pretending to acclimate to life after the loss. Nick's acting skills weren't up to the task. He would need every ounce of reserve strength he had left to get through the day.

They entered the church at a little past ten. Stale incense lingered in the air. The organist was busy warming up with chords from church hymns, some of which would be performed this morning. As Nick walked down the aisle toward the first pew, he tried to tune everything out. He had attended a lot of funerals in his life, more of them recently, now that some of the family and their long-time friends had gotten along in age. He never thought he would have to attend his own wife's funeral, though.

The walk to the front of the church seemed like it was a thousand yards long. He could feel every pair of eyes in the building upon him. They pricked his skin like pins inserted by an acupuncturist. He walked along, holding his son's small hand in his own. The sacristy was dimly lit. The remainder of the church was slightly brighter. Cloudy skies prevented natural light from illuminating the beautifully designed stained glass windows, which adorned all sides of the building. The brilliant blue, red, purple, and gold in the glass faded into the walls like distant paintings that had been pressed directly into the church's maroon brick.

The Lacour men finally arrived at their appointed seats, front and center. Nick's parents fell in beside him and Justin. Pamela's brother and sister, along with Deidre, rounded out the remainder of the first pew. Silence had fallen in the church. An occasional cough or whisper periodically broke the quiet.

A priest entered from the left side of the altar. He emerged from the sacristy while the organist announced his presence on cue. Two altar boys flanked him. They held brass bowls of burning incense, which were emitting odors that replaced the scents from their departed ancestors.

After allowing the organist to complete the hymn, the priest raised his hands to once again evoke silence. Sniffles were starting to accompany the coughs. All whispers were gone.

"We are gathered here today to celebrate the acceptance of one of our beloved sisters into the kingdom of heaven," started the priest.

Nick glanced at the priest as he began but spent most of his time watching the coffin, just a few feet from the entrance to his pew. He stared at the draped metal box with intensity, trying to wish his wife back to life. He half expected her to thrust the lid open and jump out, putting an end to this cruel joke.

The Mass continued in the tradition of most funerals. Readings were taken from the Old and New testaments. The priest addressed his flock with an air of sympathy and compassion. He flowed through the proceedings using the same symbolic program and mannerisms he had employed many times before.

During his homily, the priest spoke of Pamela and the family and friends she left behind. His words were kind, but they lacked true understanding. He barely knew the Lacours. As he finished and began to signal the altar boys that it was time for communion, there was an interruption. Nick had risen to his feet. Clearing his throat, he asked if he could approach the altar and offer some final words on behalf of his wife. The priest, unaccustomed to this kind of thing, was slow to react at first. But, he then extended a robed arm and pointed the way to the pulpit.

When Father McCulley had met with Nick and his family at the wake, they had decided that the priest would offer the eulogy. Nick had felt that it would be too difficult for any member of his family, particularly himself, to speak the final words. He appeared to have changed his mind as he approached the altar with unsteady strides. Expectant eyes followed his every step as he took his place behind the podium. Adjusting the microphone to his height, he spoke.

"I apologize for the interruption, and I thank Father McCulley for giving me the opportunity to speak. I hadn't planned on coming up here today. I didn't feel I would have the strength to give Pamela a proper eulogy."

He paused and tried to compose himself. After taking a deep breath, he continued.

"Pamela was the love of my life." His voice wavered but held its tone. "We met nearly ten years ago. I knew the minute I laid eyes on her that she was the person I wanted to spend the rest of my life with." He paused slightly, then resumed. "I know that sounds cliché, but it's true. Pamela literally took my breath away. Every time she walked into the room, my heart skipped a beat. She was the strongest, kindest, most beautiful person I have ever known, and I love her more than any one person has the right to love another…" His voice trailed off, leaking with emotion.

Struggling to resume, he took several deep breaths. His voice continued to falter as he spoke again.

"I'm not mad at God right now, but I certainly don't understand why this happened. I can't comprehend why someone like Pamela could be taken from us so prematurely." As if to offset his touch of anger and confusion, he added, "Despite that, I am thankful for having had time with her. I am also forever grateful to her for bringing our son into this world."

Eyes glazed, he drew in another breath and pushed onward, fighting to stay in control.

"Pamela, if you can see me right now, I just want you to know that I will take care of our son. I also want you to know that I will love you every day for the rest of my life. You were my inspiration for living, and I will never be the same without you. Good-bye, sweetheart. Save a place for me in eternity."

With the last words of his speech still echoing in everyone's mind, Nick returned to the pew with some assistance from his father and brother. Justin climbed into his lap, and the two embraced. The priest didn't know how to follow this unlikely episode. He, too, was crying. After a pregnant pause, he completed the Mass.

As the choir sang "Amazing Grace," the procession filed out into the winter rain. A steady drizzle thumped the tops of umbrellas as the gathering of people circled the hearse and watched the pallbearers load the casket into the vehicle. With headlights on, each car followed behind the hearse and limousines to the cemetery.

Nick and his son rode in the lead limousine. Nick stared out the slightly tinted window and watched the rain drown the area with gloom. Eyes losing focus on the outside world, he could now only see gathering raindrops beading on the window and eventually streaming down the glass in zigzag patterns.

With a heavy heart, he tried to think of better times now passed. All that remained of his marriage was a lifetime of memories. He turned to his son and saw the legacy Pamela left behind. He couldn't fail Justin or his departed wife by giving up now. He draped an arm around his little boy and elected to press on into the strong headwind life had unleashed upon them. He would have to summon up another surge of courage as the limousine pulled into the cemetery. It was time to offer a final farewell.

*   *   *   *

Rucker woke up in a fog. He had slept until past 4:00 PM on Friday. Not working was starting to take its toll. A half-drained bottle of Stoli lay on the floor next to the couch. Twelve ground-out cigarette butts filled the ashtray on the coffee table. Specks of black, white, and gray ash decorated much of the tabletop. He could still taste the stale combination of vodka and tobacco.

He rubbed his throbbing head while pushing himself into an upright position. He had gotten up too quickly, and the room was spinning. He fell back into a half-crouch. There was entirely too much light in the room. He hated the light. In another life, he might have been a vampire, he guessed. It seemed to fit. He loved blood and hated light.

"Let's try this again," he thought.

This time, he made it all the way to his feet. Standing unsteadily, he staggered into the kitchen. Boredom had led to a hard night. Shuffling toward the refrigerator, he looked for something to blunt the aftereffects of too many cigarettes and far too much vodka.

He opened the door and saw the same thing he had seen a day earlier—nothing. He reached for the only edible item in the fridge, a Budweiser. Cracking open the can, he drained the entire contents in less than ten seconds. He wiped his mouth on his shirtsleeve and released a tremendous belch. The empty can was fired in the direction of his trashcan. It missed badly, clanking off the wall and skidding along the kitchen floor, leaving foamy droplets of beer along the way.

Feeling slightly better, he ambled into the bathroom. He didn't like what he saw in the mirror, bloodshot eyes with complementary dark circles underneath. Unshaven and generally unclean, he grunted his disgust. He turned on the shower and got in without removing his clothes, figuring they were as dirty as he was. The scalding water began to burn his hangover away.

After about twenty minutes of swaying beneath the showerhead, he shut off the water and stepped onto the cold bathroom tiles. Dripping wet, he left puddles all over the floor. This time, a look at the mirror wasn't as depressing. It was too steamed to produce a reflection.

Still dripping, he managed to work his way into the dark bedroom. Stripping off soaked clothes, he picked up a towel from the floor and began to dry off. When he was mostly dry, he reached for a pair of sweats that lay on the bed. He had spent most of the previous three days in those pants. In his estimation, they were good for three more. He pulled them on, electing to go commando. He found a sweatshirt on the floor a few feet from the towel, which had been tossed back to its original position. He pulled the gray sweatshirt over his wet hair. He was ready to face another night.

Vision clearing and head reaching a dull throb, he determined it was time to seek out number twenty-one. The inspiration hit him just after midnight while he was watching music videos. The yearning had not subsided during his sleep. He was now quite certain that it was time to answer his calling again. Not even a week had passed since mission twenty. He had never killed more than one woman in the same month. In fact, the shortest time between killings had been four months. This could definitely become a personal record.

Still moving gingerly, he stepped into a pair of high-top tennis shoes and grabbed his keys and wallet from the nightstand. He may not actually murder a woman today, he thought, but the search was going to begin. His yearning was still in the early stages. He would be able to hold it off for a few weeks if necessary, but it was time for the hunt to start. He loved the anticipation almost as much as the killing.

CHAPTER 9

▼

The day after a funeral is supposed to provide reckoning. Nick still felt numb. Things had happened too quickly and without his permission. He woke up in his parents' house for the fourth straight morning. At last, the smell of cooking food didn't elicit instant nausea. He was surprised that his appetite was starting to return. He guessed that the body's needs would eventually win the ongoing battle with mental anguish.

Slipping into a white cotton robe and a pair of well-worn brown slippers, he padded down the hall and into the kitchen.

"Morning, Mom. What are you cooking?"

"I'm going to get you to eat yet," she said. "You can't possibly resist your favorite breakfast."

On the table was a basket of fresh-baked biscuits covered by a red-and-white-checkered towel. Several complementary jellies and three-quarters of a stick of real butter bordered the basket. Next to the biscuits was a large bowl of grits, steaming under the rapidly melting, remaining quarter stick of butter. Jane was busy at the stove making sure the rest of the food was cooked before the biscuits and grits got cold. She flipped four eggs, over easy, and slid them onto a plate. She garnished the plate with four strips of bacon, extra crispy, and handed the plate to her son.

"Now, fill the rest of this empty plate and start eating, for God's sake."

To Jane's surprise, Nick did as he was told. He heaped a generous portion of grits on the plate and shoved aside the bacon and eggs, freeing room for two biscuits. The final tally looked like something he would have eaten on a regular basis in high school. She smiled her approval.

For the first time in several days, Nick blocked out his feelings and attended to the needs of his stomach. After polishing off the last bite, he dropped the plate in the sink, drained a glass of juice, and thanked his mom for yet another wonderful meal.

"I'm just happy to see you eating again. I was beginning to think you were going to look like one of those Ethiopian kids we see on the television."

"Does this make you happy?" he asked, protruding his full belly in exaggerated fashion.

"Go clean up. You're coming to church with me this morning," she said with a smile as she swatted him with her dish towel.

He started to protest like he might have when he was an actual resident there, but his words stopped short when she held up a hand indicating that she wouldn't hear any excuses. He figured that some divine exposure couldn't make things worse. He would appease his mother and join her at Mass. Before he could leave the kitchen, however, the phone rang. He glanced at the "Birds of the Wild" clock on the kitchen wall. The big hand was touching a cardinal, and the little hand had just pushed past a robin. It was only seven fifteen.

"I'll get it, Mom," he said, grabbing the receiver off the wall phone with concern etched on his face. "What now?" he thought.

"Lacour residence."

"May I speak with Nick Lacour?"

"Speaking. Who's this?"

"Nick, this is Jack Ramsey. Have I caught you at a bad time?"

"No, not at all. In fact, you may have saved me from going to Mass," Nick said as he flashed his mom a devious grin, which she volleyed with a look of disapproval.

"Nick, a few things have come up in your wife's case. Are you free to meet me this morning?"

"Absolutely. Let me clean up, and I'll be there in twenty minutes. Can you tell me anything before I get there?"

"Yeah. We think we may have found the car used by the killer."

"OK. I'll be right there."

He hung up the phone and hurried toward his bedroom. Before he had completely vanished from sight, Jane interrupted his progress.

"What is it, Nick?"

"I'm not sure. Evidently some new evidence has turned up."

"What is it? What's going on?" Her worried look deepened.

"I don't know exactly, but I'll fill you in when I get back."

"Where are you going?"

"I'm going to take a shower, and then I'm off to the county police station."

He didn't stick around long enough to catch another one of his mother's expressions. She was only doing her maternal job, showing concern for her son. He raced to the shower. He couldn't wait to find out what leads had turned up. Maybe this sick jack-off would be caught after all.

*   *   *   *

Rucker had gotten home at five o'clock in the morning from the previous night's carousing. When his jaunt to a few popular bars in town failed to pique his interest, he elected to visit some of the seedier spots across the river. It was on the Illinois side where people could satisfy their darker desires. Establishments featuring naked women could be found on virtually every street corner in certain towns. Some of them were whorehouses that were merely fronted by strip clubs. He had found his way into a few of those joints.

In the last one he visited, The Pie Factory, he came across a very interesting prospect. Her name was Lola. At least that's how she introduced herself. She was taking customers' orders for drinks and other "off the menu" items. Lola told him she was twenty-one. He guessed she was really closer to eighteen.

She definitely walked like a woman. The place had taught her well. She was The Pie Factory's number one attraction. Part of her appeal was her role. She never stripped. She merely walked around the room carrying a tray and enticing the male customers. She even turned the heads of the few female customers that visited the Factory out of curiosity.

He watched her move gracefully throughout the room. She wore a French maid outfit, complete with fishnet stockings and four-inch pumps. Her white cotton blouse was frilled with lace at the collar and around the cuffs. The blouse was unbuttoned halfway down, revealing the most perfect cleavage he had ever seen.

Peeking out from behind the open buttons was a red silk bra that barely contained her supple breasts. When she came to take his order, she lifted a pump and rested it on his thigh. He traced his way down her leg and revealed garter straps attached to red silk panties. He had to have this one. Her eyes glowed as she looked him up and down, acknowledging that in this setting, she was not the prey. She was the hunter.

He took his eyes off of her silky smooth legs. He met her appraising look. Her face was angelic. She had dark, mysterious eyes and thick lashes. Her skin was creamy and without an imperfection. He felt sure she was under twenty years old. Her pouty red lips curved into a devious smile.

"What can I get you, baby?" she asked.

After ordering a Jack and Coke and trying to conceal his growing interest, he scanned the rest of the room. There were four girls dancing, two each on different stages. A handful of stragglers, mostly older perverted men, surrounded both stages. Rucker sat at a small table off to the side, away from the center of activity. There were eight similar tables scattered throughout the room.

The red carpeted room was dark and smoky. It smelled mostly of cigarette smoke and unclean individuals. The corners of the square building were exceedingly dark. Each corner had a booth, which was equipped with a curtain that could be pulled shut to ensure relative privacy. Lap dances and other activities were going on in each corner. The curtains had been closed at each booth.

As he was watching one of the curtains, it slid open. A man probably in his late sixties, stumbled away from the booth. A young girl with red hair and alabaster skin followed him out. She was wiping her mouth and clipping her skimpy, see-through bra back on. He guessed that the old-timer had received a little more than a lap dance. It was amazing what the pharmaceutical industry had done for the senior set, Rucker thought. He turned away from the old man and was startled to see Lola standing next to his table.

Instead of pulling up one of the three open chairs, she seductively slid onto his lap. She wrapped her free arm around his neck.

"Are you still nursing that drink, or do you want another one? Or, maybe something else?" she inquired seductively, winking after the last question.

He read it as an implication that he, too, could take up temporary residence in the booth now vacated by the old man.

"Another Jack will work. For now," he said, leaving his options open.

"Coming right up, sugar."

She got up slowly, protruding her tight buttocks directly in front of his face. She bent over, acting like she was fixing the straps on one of her pumps. While bent over, her skirt came up in the back, allowing him to gain another glimpse of her red underwear. He continued watching as she walked to the bar. She looked back at him and smiled. It was the kind of look a cat might give a mouse, before playfully slapping the hell out of its new quarry. He felt his interest growing by the second. It was now quite clear that she had been placed before him as a sacrifice. It was his obligation to once again answer his calling.

She returned in minutes with another drink. He had finished the last third of his first one while she was away. He pushed the empty glass aside. Lola placed the fresh Jack Daniels on the same coaster and plopped onto his lap again.

"Are you sure I can't get anything else for you? You look like you could use more than just a Jack and Coke," she said, laying a little more emphasis on the word *more*.

"What else did you have in mind?" he asked without breaking his stare, which was fixated down her blouse. All the while he pictured her tied to a bed, firm tits sticking straight up in the air like highway cones.

"We have just about anything you could want."

"Sounds interesting."

Lola giggled and threw her head back, displaying a smooth tanned neck. Rucker wanted to grip that smooth, coffee-colored skin in both hands and choke off the last oxygen molecule bound for her brain.

"Why don't you think about what you want, and I'll come back to take your order," she said, stressing *order* this time. "You see that table in the corner?" she asked while pointing toward the vacated booth.

"Yes, I see it."

"My friend Kara is waiting on anyone who wants to sit at that table," she indicated, while enunciating *waiting* and *sit* the loudest. "She can get you anything you want."

"How about *you*? Can you give me *anything* I want?" he asked. He had decided to play her little game.

She laughed again, throwing her head back and brushing long dark hair away from her silky neck. He started to salivate. In his mind, he could hear the bones cracking in her neck as his hands closed together around her windpipe.

"Baby, I can't cover that table, too. I have all of these," she said with an all-encompassing gesture toward the empty tables surrounding the stages.

She winked again, implying that working the booths wasn't part of her job.

"Well, if you decide to work that booth, I might have an order for you," he responded, while pointing at the booth just as Lola had done.

He further mocked by stressing the word *work*. He certainly was enjoying the game.

Lola smiled and lightly brushed her long, ruby red fingernails across his face. She gave him another wink, got up, waved her ass in his face again, and was gone. She had never responded to his last remark, leaving him even more intrigued. He was now absolutely certain that mission number twenty-one had just begun. This one might just be more fun than all the rest.

*   *   *   *

Nick had wasted no time getting to the police station. En route, he had considered what Ramsey had said about the evidence found. For the first time in days, all of his attention was drawn to something other than Pamela. He felt guilty for leaving Justin with his parents yet again, but he silently vowed to make it up to him soon. He had been feeling helpless around the boy, and it was driving him crazy. He hoped that things would return to relative normalcy sooner rather than later.

He barely slowed when he reached the entrance to the police station parking lot. He could hear his tires squeal on the blacktop as he pulled in. It would be truly ironic to be ticketed for reckless driving while entering the station, he thought. He was opening his car door before he had even shut off the engine. He set the parking brake, slid the car keys into a pants pocket, and made a dash for the front door.

Pushing open one of the glass double doors, he entered the St. Louis County Police Station. He had rarely been to this venue and was forced to glance around, lost at first. A receptionist seemed to sense his confusion.

"Can I help you?" she asked with a bored and condescending tone.

It was apparent that she didn't relish having to work on a Saturday.

"I'm looking for Detective Ramsey," he panted, winded from his sprint.

"May I ask who is looking for Detective Ramsey?" she inquired, with more boredom mixed with slight touch of snootiness.

"My name is Nick Lacour," he responded, barely able to hide his contempt for her attitude.

After hearing his name and pondering it for a second, the receptionist looked like she might have had a moment of recognition. Her demeanor seemed to change from loathing to pity. He thought he might have liked loathing better. He watched as she picked up a phone and signaled that it would be just a second.

"Detective Ramsey, uh, there is a Nick Lacour here to see you," she whispered into the receiver with a voice that was saturated with sadness.

At least she was capable of some compassion, Nick thought.

"He will be with you in a moment. Can I get you anything? A Coke or cup of…?" she asked, trailing off before finishing the question.

"No thanks. I'm fine," he answered, aware that she wanted to offer condolences but wasn't familiar with how to go about it.

"OK," she somehow managed, searching for additional words that never came.

At the conclusion of this brilliant repartee, Ramsey appeared in the lobby.

"Hello, Nick. Thanks for coming down here this morning," Ramsey said, greeting Nick with an extended hand.

"No problem. I'm glad you're starting to mount a case," Nick said, returning the shake.

"Why don't you follow me? I want to show you what we have so far."

Ramsey waved a key card across a security box adjacent to the department's entrance. The card was attached to a chain around his neck, and it registered a beep from the box upon recognition. On cue, the door buzzed. He opened it, ushering Nick into the homicide department and toward his office. They passed a row of cubicles, all unoccupied except for one. In it sat a young officer. He looked to be filling out a report and was inflicted by the same "I don't want to work on Saturday" disease as the receptionist.

They entered an office situated in the far left corner of the room. The engraved nameplate read "Detective Jack Ramsey." Ramsey entered the office first and went around to the other side of his desk. He pulled out a high-backed swivel chair and sat down.

"Have a seat, Nick," he said, motioning to an uncomfortable looking blue chair placed directly in front of his desk.

Nick sat down and looked around the small office. The walls were mostly bare except for a map of St. Louis County and a picture of Ramsey with a woman that Nick presumed was his wife. The office had no additional decorations. Stacks of paper cluttered the top of Ramsey's desk and the credenza behind him. A bookshelf occupied the open wall to Nick's left. It was filled with volumes, mostly textbooks and manuals. He didn't recognize any of the titles.

Ramsey folded his hands on the desktop and sighed.

"There have been some developments in Pamela's case," he said, as Nick watched him, waiting for more. "We believe we may have found the car used by the killer. At least, what's left of it."

Nick was unable to ask questions or offer any comments. He was a prisoner to the information that Ramsey had to share and was unable to say a word.

"We found a mostly charred 1992 Ford Crown Victoria in East St. Louis. It had been white at one time. It was decorated with various antennae and a spotlight. To the untrained eye, it may have resembled an unmarked police cruiser." Ramsey paused before adding, "We know it's the right car because the killer made the mistake of turning around in one of your neighboring driveways. The driveway belongs to a Mrs. Olsen."

"Sweet old lady. She lives a couple of doors down."

"Yes, well 'sweet' Mrs. Olsen happens to be somewhat paranoid. She has closed circuit cameras mounted all around the perimeter of her house. One of the cameras captured our boy's car. The plate matches that of the car we found on the other side of the river."

"Did the camera get his face?" Nick asked, starting to get excited by the rapid developments.

"No, but a kid at Jimmy's Costumes might have," Ramsey answered.

He watched the detective intently. He was hanging on every word as Ramsey forged ahead.

"In the trunk, we found the remnants of a police uniform and a badge. The badge was a replica but bore a strong resemblance to the real thing."

"What about this costume shop?" Nick asked, finally absorbing the information while recovering from his brief inability to speak.

"We found a button on the floor in your son's bedroom. It was blue and went along with the remnants of the uniform we found in the trunk."

"How does that tie into the costume shop?"

"We went to every uniform and costume shop in town. The only police officer uniform rented or sold in the past couple of months was at Jimmy's. The kid there gave our sketch artist a solid description of the renter, who had elected to pay for the uniform as opposed to renting."

"Do you have the sketch?" Nick asked, looking sick but still wanting to see it.

Ramsey unfolded a copy of the sketch that lay on his desk. Nick stared at the hateful eyes and sharply contrasted features for what seemed like an eternity. His blood boiled. He was now more sure than ever that he must be the one to bring this guy down.

"There's more."

"What else?" he asked weakly, while looking up from the sketch. He was not sure if his mind could digest anymore.

"There were blood smears on the foyer floor along with tissue samples taken from underneath your wife's nails. The forensic biologists are testing them right now. It'll take several days before we have the DNA results back and are able to run them through CODIS."

Nick was familiar with the Combined DNA Index System. The picture was getting clearer. He could imagine a man dressed in a police outfit knocking on his front door. Worse, he could almost see him entering his house and…He closed his eyes trying not to complete the thought.

"We'll know more soon enough. However, this would explain quite a bit. It explains why the perpetrator pulled into your driveway and gained admittance to your residence through the front door."

"Where do we go from here? Does this help narrow the list of suspects?"

Nick was reaching. He knew it didn't explain much, but it was a start.

"It's hard to say right now. If this is the car used by the killer, at least it places him in a certain area around midnight. We can use the information to question people in that area."

"Yeah, but how many would have been out after twelve on a night like that?"

"You'd be surprised. The area we found the car in doesn't have deluxe accommodations. There are a lot of homeless. Maybe we'll get lucky."

"What else does the information tell you?"

"It starts to rule out the fact that this was a random killing. There was definitely planning involved. To be premeditated, the killer had to know your wife."

Nick shuddered at the thought. He was having a difficult time accepting that possibility. He was thankful the sketch didn't resemble anyone he knew.

"There is more," Ramsey said, not waiting for a response from Nick as he continued right away. "We think we may have matched a footprint. Our crime scene technicians were able to use an electrostatic dust lifter to pull a footprint from your foyer. The killer had obviously entered with wet shoes and had left a print on your hardwood floor. We wouldn't have thought much about it, but there was a noticeable gash in the left heel. We ran it through the computer and matched it to a plaster cast taken outside the home of a murder victim in Tennessee two years ago. With some luck, the DNA will match another crime, too," Ramsey finished, letting Nick soak it all in.

"So, in your professional opinion, what does all of this mean?" Nick asked, but he was pretty sure he already knew the answer.

"It means that we may be dealing with a serial killer."

"What now?" he asked, mildly disappointed that Ramsey had confirmed his fears.

"First thing's first. I'm telling you all of this because I like you. I respect what you have done as a lawyer in this town, and I feel for you as a fellow human being. I lost my first wife. I know what you are going through."

"I'm sorry. I didn't know that."

"I know. It's not something I talk about all that often," he said. He paused to finish his stale coffee before adding, "Anyway, I understand your pain, and I want you to be kept up to speed. I also want you to understand that this information is not public knowledge. Sharing what I have told you with anyone else could severely jeopardize this investigation. We certainly don't want the media involved any more than they already are. If rumors start circulating that there is a serial killer on the loose in town, then panic will spread like wildfire."

"I appreciate that and will not say a word to anyone. Thank you for sharing this with me. It gives me hope that this guy might actually get caught."

"We will do everything we can, that much I can promise. We are going to face certain limitations now, however."

"What kinds of limitations?" Nick asked skeptically, concerned by Ramsey's remark.

"Now that there is a possible link between murders in different states, the FBI is going to get involved."

Nick's involvement with the FBI had been limited. He had spoken to special agents on occasion during the course of some of his trials. He knew their reputation but didn't know how it would affect this case. None of the agents he had met had taken a great liking to him. After all, he represented the "other side."

"This can be good or bad," offered Ramsey. "They certainly have more resources than we do, and their success rate is fairly impressive when it comes to multistate killers," he concluded, noticeably avoiding the term *serial killer*.

"But?" Nick asked.

"They have also been known to disrupt local investigations. Their approach is global, and I appreciate that. However, when it comes to a murder in a smaller city, they don't have the community ties that we do."

"I guess I don't understand," Nick said, now unclear as to how this was good or bad.

"They don't have the local contacts. They go around questioning everyone but don't have a relationship with the criminal element in this town."

"Will you stay on the case?" Nick asked.

"Yes. We will just have to work around them."

"And risk interfering with their investigation?" Nick asked with sarcasm, prompting Ramsey to laugh at the obvious irony.

"Yes, we may interfere with 'their' investigation, but we will do it in a tactful way."

"What can I do? I want to be involved."

"Right now, the best way you can help is by remembering every detail you can from the past several months. Somewhere, somehow, this joker came into contact with your wife. You may not know it because it seemed insignificant at the time, but she may have told you about a meeting, or something in passing."

Nick had been thinking about recent conversations with Pamela but couldn't recall discussing anyone who had been previously unknown to them. He agreed to keep trying.

"Do you want me to show you out?" Ramsey asked, rising and signifying that the meeting was now over.

"No thanks. I think I can manage," Nick replied as he started toward the door.

"Nick?"

"Yeah?"

"We'll catch this guy. I wouldn't normally promise something like that, but I can feel it in my gut. It has become my personal mission."

Nick responded with a half-smile and nodded. He hoped it was true, but he wasn't convinced yet. He felt it was time to put his amateur detective skills to the test and start conducting his own investigation. However, he certainly wasn't about to share that intent with Ramsey.

Over the years, he had become extensively involved with the St. Louis criminal world. He was the most popular defense attorney in town because of his impeccable record. In fact, he had never officially lost a jury trial. He knew that there were several questionable characters around town who owed him their life. It was time to cash in a few favors.

CHAPTER 10

▼

Lola. Rucker couldn't get her out of his mind. It was noon on Saturday. He was still half-dazed from the alcohol, cigarette smoke, and long night. There had been a lot of long nights lately. He tried to rub the haze out of his eyes, then searched the room for his phone book. He found the book and thumbed to the section in the Yellow Pages for night clubs. After turning two pages, he found an ad for The Pie Factory. It was decorated with the image of a curvaceous young lady busting out of the middle of a pie. The drawing looked like Lola.

He scribbled the number on a pad and got dressed. He would go to QuikTrip and get a cup of coffee. From there, he could use the calling card he purchased at Wal-Mart and call The Pie Factory to find out when Lola would be working again. Lola. He could still see her cleavage. He had a clear picture of her long legs and delicate features.

When he arrived at QuikTrip, he purchased a pack of Kool Filter Kings and a sixteen-ounce black coffee. He set his purchases on the roof of his truck and walked to the pay phone, which was just a few feet away. He punched in the number for The Pie Factory. It advertised as a twenty-four-hour establishment, so he knew someone would answer.

"Yes. I was wondering if you have any specials this week?" he asked, while trying not to raise any suspicion.

"What kind of specials do you have in mind, sweetie?"

The girl who answered was not Lola. Her voice was husky from years of hard smoking, drinking, and who knows what else.

"I don't know. I just thought you may have some special entertainers this week," he replied with growing agitation.

All he wanted to know was if Lola was working.

"We always have special entertainers. Why don't you come by, and we'll introduce you to some of them?"

"Is Lola dancing this week?"

"Everyone wants Lola," the girl chuckled. "No, she doesn't dance, but she will be here."

"When will she be there?"

"Lola works just about every night. Come on by, and you'll see."

"OK."

He hung up. It didn't specifically answer all of his questions, but he didn't want the people in the place to think Lola had a stalker. They might develop good memories after Lola's body was found hacked to pieces. He didn't want them thinking ahead.

After the unsuccessful call, he grabbed the coffee and cigarettes off the roof of his truck. He pulled the lid off the coffee and threw it on the floorboard. He drank the piping hot liquid in a single gulp. For him, it was always mind over matter. Pain was a state of mind. He never allowed the synapses to carry pain sensations to his brain.

He was still thinking about Lola. He had to come up with a tactful plan to find out her work schedule. From there, he could follow her home. It might take weeks to set up the perfect situation to complete his mission, but she would be worth it.

Pulling into his apartment complex, he decided he would return to The Pie Factory this week. He didn't want to become too frequent a visitor. Within a week, he suspected he would know where she lived, what she drove, and who might stand in the way of his prize. The planning had just begun.

*   *   *   *

Just over a week had passed since Pamela Lacour was brutally murdered in the home she shared with her husband and son. Nick couldn't believe it had only been nine days ago. The rest of the world had moved on. He was trying to learn to live all over again.

On Monday, he had gone to his law offices and met with Ronald Evans, senior partner at Evans, Masters & Lacour. Evans was a bitter man. Years of too much work and too little recreation had hardened him into the stereotypical cynical, sour old man. He had been a member of the firm for forty years. He breathed, ate, and sweated his job. It had cost him three wives and five children, none of whom maintained contact with him anymore.

Nick was slightly nervous about meeting with him. Evans was famous for unprovoked tirades. Nick wasn't in the mood for one of his outbursts. Nick thought his reaction to just such an episode might land him out of a job.

Despite his apprehension, the mood of the meeting was not at all what he had expected. Evans was kind, almost docile. Nick had been surprised to find the founder of the firm in his office sitting on a leather couch reading the comics section of the daily paper. Even more astonishing, he had a smile on his well-worn face. Nick couldn't remember a single time that the man had smiled in all the years he had known him. His normal sullen expression was accentuated by too many wrinkles for his sixty-two years and too much red. The maroon coloring was presumably from a tumultuous relationship with single malt scotch.

"Lacour, come in, son. Have a seat."

Evans gestured to a shiny brown leather chair positioned adjacent to the couch he was occupying.

"I hope you got the arrangement the firm sent to the funeral."

"I did, sir. Thank you."

Truthfully, Nick wasn't quite sure if the flowers had arrived. Many of the firm's members had shown up at the wake, however. That had been good enough.

"Terrible tragedy, what happened to your wife and all. I'm sorry I couldn't attend the funeral. Firm business. Surely you understand."

He slid his glasses to the tip of his nose, further enhancing his appearance as a tyrannical old man.

"I do understand, Ron."

Nick thought to himself that he couldn't give a shit if the old guy had shown up or not. He watched as Evans adjusted his frames again and thought to himself that the man either needed a different pair of glasses or a bigger nose.

"What can I do for you today?"

"Well…" Nick paused.

He had been dreading this meeting for days.

"I would like to take a leave of absence."

He blurted it out all at once. He was too overwrought to offer additional explanation.

"I see. I see."

Evans was scratching his chin, as if to contemplate this outlandish request.

"Well Nick, you have done exemplary work for this firm. We are proud to call you one of our own. I think that under the circumstances, a leave of absence would be appropriate."

Nick, who had been building an argumentative case to combat whatever Evans said, sat in stunned silence. His jaw literally dropped. He would never have expected the old man to grant his request.

"How long were you thinking?" Evans expression changed from understanding back to cynical.

"About a month, if that's acceptable." Nick almost winced as he said it, fully expecting Evans to blow up. He held his breath, waiting for the volcano to erupt.

Evans again scratched his chin and adjusted his bifocals.

"I think a month would be adequate time to repair your life after this senseless tragedy. Consider your request granted."

Nick was still shocked. He could barely mumble his words of thankfulness. He began to rise from his chair, anxious to vacate the office before the imposter Evans was replaced by the much uglier version.

"Of course, Nick, we won't be able to pay you during this time, unless you have vacation accrued. I'm sure you understand. We rely on a lawyer's billable hours. On leave, you aren't much use to us financially."

"I understand, Ron. The money is not my chief concern right now. I need to attend to family matters," Nick said, relieved to find that the old Evans was back and that alien forces hadn't overcome his body.

"Very well then, Nick. Tend to your business, and come back in a month, refreshed and ready to do what you have done so well in the past," Evans said.

He looked disappointed that Nick hadn't disputed the point. Nick knew the old man was always up for a light argument no matter what the circumstances were.

"Make lots and lots of money for us, of course," Evans added, in answer to the confused look on Nick's face.

They shook hands and Nick hightailed it out of the office, convinced that Evans had either completely flipped out or had gotten laid recently. He voted for the former option.

"Transition your open casework to Bronson before you leave, and give my regards to your family," Evans called out just as Nick exited the office.

Nick didn't even respond, fearful that any comment would jolt the old-timer back into his harsh, unforgiving character.

On his way out, Nick met with Rich Bronson and went over his caseload. Most of it had been in the early stages. Nick was glad that someone else was going to compile research data. He hated that part of the job and was very thankful to Bronson for his assistance.

He left the office still shaking his head when he got to his car. Like most of the events of the previous week, this one seemed equally unfathomable. He still wasn't sure the meeting with Evans had gone as well as it had. No matter. He felt he deserved some kind of a break. A weight had been lifted from his shoulders. Now, with his job secure and waiting for his return, he was free to embark on some amateur detective duties. He had one month to catch the man who had ripped his life apart. It wasn't much time, but it was a start. For the next thirty days, this would become a major focus in his life. He would waste no time feeding his obsession.

✳   ✳   ✳   ✳

Wednesday. Rucker had thought the day would never arrive. He was impressed with his self-control and ability to wait until the self-appointed day to revisit his future quarry. The daylight hours had passed exceedingly slowly. He had actually been called to work. The weather had broken, and his boss had called to offer him a job pouring a driveway.

At first, he considered turning down the offer, but he needed the money. He had barely worked in the past month, and funds were running low. He begrudgingly accepted and showed up at the job site at 7:30 AM.

Throughout the day, he went about his business, barely speaking. He had a difficult time concentrating on the job. Twice, he was scolded by one of the cement finishers for screwing up. Normally, this would have pissed him off. Today, it really didn't matter. Lola was the only thing on his mind.

The job took what seemed like an eternity. It was cold out, and everyone was moving slowly. After digging out the area and setting forms, the crew was finally ready to pour concrete by 1:00 PM. The first mixer truck arrived carrying nine yards of concrete. His company was using a full crew, because there really wasn't any other work available.

They finished the job in the dark, just after five thirty. He was tired, but still had the energy to visit The Pie Factory. He hurried home, and after a ten-minute shower, he dressed, forced down a couple of slices of partially molded bread, and left his apartment. It was only six thirty. Places like The Pie Factory didn't really get going until much later on.

He had intended to arrive early. He wanted to familiarize himself with the area. This part of his mission was like a stakeout. He would get accustomed to the various cars on the lot. His careful surveillance would tell him when and how Lola arrived at work. He figured she had a fairly consistent work schedule. If customers had been asking for her by name, the establishment would want her there on certain days. He stayed in the parking lot for nearly thirty minutes. He pretended to be reading something while he observed the lot and the bordering area.

The Pie Factory was one of four strip clubs within a quarter-mile stretch. It was the last club before the road jutted out into nothingness. He had driven past the Factory to get a sense of what lay beyond. As soon as he passed the club, all signs of civilization faded. He drove for three miles, past open fields and sparsely wooded terrain. There wasn't a building of any kind for four miles.

At the four-mile mark, he passed a farm. The land contained a ranch-style house and a barn that stood several yards to its left. No lights were on in the house or the barn. A Ford F-150 truck occupied the gravel driveway leading up to the house. The home was about fifty yards from the main road. Beyond it, there were no additional buildings for another three miles.

Finally, he came to a small town, one that was straight out of *The Andy Griffith Show*. A few small shops, a gas station, a convenience store, and a restaurant made up the bulk of the structures. There wasn't much going on there, either. Satisfied with what he had seen, Rucker headed back to The Pie Factory. He was already determining his escape in the event that he abducted Lola outside the bar. That would not be his first choice, however. He would prefer to find out where she lived and get her there.

He pulled into the gravel parking lot outside the bar. His headlights bore a hole through the dust that had been dredged up when he swerved into the lot. Stones crunched under his tires as he came to an abrupt stop. More dust filled the cold night air. He shut off his headlights, killed the engine, and did one more survey of the lot.

Five cars were parked close to the building. He guessed they all belonged to workers. He made a mental note of each car and decided to go in. Upon entering, he thought the bar was closed. No music emanated from the overhead speakers. He didn't see a soul in the bar area. A glance to his right revealed two strippers leaning against one of the stages. They looked to be sharing dancing tips.

His eyes swept the remainder of the small room. A bartender came out from one of the back rooms carrying a case of beer. It looked like the bartender and two dancers were the only people in the bar. Rucker's heart dropped. He was overcome by disappointment. He didn't want to look suspicious, so he decided to order a drink. As he stood at the bar rail, he felt a hand rub across his shoulder. He slowly turned and saw Lola standing behind him.

"I can get your order, sugar," she said.

She wasn't dressed in the French maid costume tonight. Her outfit was simple. She wore a pair of low-cut jeans, skin tight and unbuttoned at the top, and a white cotton shirt that was unbuttoned past her cleavage line. He noticed that she had on a skimpy white lace bra, and her nipples protruded from underneath the fabric. They were as erect as the member in his pants, and he couldn't respond at first, again overtaken by her appearance. It took him a moment to catch his breath.

"OK. I'll take a Jack Daniel's on the rocks with a splash of Coke."

Lola smiled and rubbed her hand down his shoulder and across his forearm. She went over to the bartender, who was unloading the case of beer he had retrieved from the stock room.

"Jack and Coke, Lenny."

"Uh, huh," Lenny grunted while he continued to empty the box of beer into the cooler.

Lola looked back at Rucker and smiled again. She then disappeared into the same stockroom the bartender had emerged from a few minutes earlier. He watched her walk away. It was all he could do not to follow her and end this mission right there and then. She had overtaken him.

From his peripheral vision, he noticed movement. He turned toward the far right corner of the room in time to see a man, probably in his fifties, exit one of the curtained booths. An African-American dancer followed him. She was buttoning up her top and sliding into a small, leather miniskirt. It didn't take a genius to figure out what had just happened.

Rucker was relieved to see another customer in the room. It drew some of the attention away from him. He looked around again and saw that the two strippers were still comparing dance moves. They were oblivious to his presence. Lenny was still laboriously putting beer bottles, one by one, into the cooler. Rucker thought he could have unloaded eight cases in the time it was taking Lenny to put away twenty-four bottles.

The older gentleman who had been in the booth was slightly disoriented and breathing heavily. He took a seat next to one of the stages. Music began emitting from the speakers. Rucker didn't know the song. It was one of those new techno dance cuts. He hated that shit.

Behind him, he heard the front door open and felt a blast of December air hit him in the back. Four men had entered the bar. They looked to be in the same field as he was. Each man was wearing worn jeans and a dirty flannel shirt. One of the men nodded at Rucker as they all filed past him on the way to a spot next to the older man.

One of the talking strippers left her post and jumped onto the stage surrounded by the construction workers and the man from the booth. She launched into the routine she had been trying to share with her coworker. He watched her dance but felt nothing stir inside. It was Lola who now occupied his unmentionable thoughts. By the way, where was she? She had gone to the stockroom several minutes prior and had not returned. He hoped she hadn't left already. His fears were quickly relieved when she exited the stockroom and again took up a spot next to the bar.

"Got my Jack yet, Lenny?" she shouted, trying to be heard above the annoying music.

Lenny again grunted. He had finally finished unloading the case of beer. He pulled a glass from underneath the bar and filled it with ice. He poured Jack Daniel's over the cubes, doused the contents with Coke and slid the glass across the bar to where Lola was standing. Lola took the glass and headed toward Rucker.

He loved to watch her walk. The way she swung her hips and cocked her head to the side drove him wild. He had never been this riled up by a woman.

"That'll be four dollars."

Lola handed the glass of whiskey to him and brushed hair from her face with her free hand. She winked at him as he took the drink and fished in his shirt pocket for some money.

"Here you go," he said as he handed her a five, while waving off the dollar's worth of change.

"Thanks, sugar," Lola said with another wink.

She delicately lifted a portion of her bra and slid the wrinkled dollar under the lace as he watched with keen interest. Her expression let on that she recognized the fact that he had enjoyed this act.

"Maybe you can help me next time," she said.

He tried to feign disinterest and made an expression like he didn't know what she was talking about. Inside, he was getting fired up. At one point, he had imagined that he saw a nipple.

Lola winked again and strutted back to the bar. She probably hadn't bought his disinterested act. He watched her walk away again, all the while fantasizing about putting something else under her bra, something that was shiny, cold and dream-shattering.

*   *   *   *

Nick hadn't been to North St. Louis in quite some time. He had actually grown up not too far from the 'hood that he was now driving through. His parents had not been well off. While his dad was a hard worker, he never made enough money to be able to afford a house in a better part of town. His old neighborhood hadn't been that bad when his parents had first moved there, but cheap housing and an influx of city dwellers had diminished the property value and the safety of the area.

This forced him to learn how to fight for survival at an early age. He was only of average size while growing up in that rough part of town. His dad had taught him how to defend himself at an early age. When he was ten years old, he came home from school with a black eye. It had been the third time in less than a month that an older, bigger kid had kicked his butt on the playground. Pouting in his room that night and vowing not to go back to school, his father had thought it best to teach his son some of the finer points of self-defense. A former Golden Gloves boxer, Mike Lacour had shared some of his knowledge with his distraught son. He had proved to be a quick learner.

A week later, the same bully had confronted him at recess. The bully, John Neighbors, was two years older than he. He was big and generally the most feared student at North County Middle School. This time, John had been in for a surprise. The whole school, including Nick, had shared the same surprise when some of Mike Lacour's new moves had been put to the test. The end result had been a badly beaten bully and a new North County legend in the making.

Nick found that not only had he been able to use some of the skills his father taught him, but also that he had been very good at it. Furthermore, he had enjoyed the rush it gave him. This had become a deadly combination for most of his teenage years. It hadn't taken long for his reputation to spread throughout the school district. As the new king of the hill, Nick had found that other kids were eager to try to knock him off his pedestal. Nick would never lose another fight. That feat, however, landed him in jail three times in high school and earned him five school suspensions and one expulsion. Street smart and tough, Nick had made it out of North St. Louis with only one nasty scar; it ran across his abdomen.

He had never quite lost his fondness for kicking ass. His wife actually had helped to settle him down. Nick couldn't remember the last time he had been involved in a physical altercation. It had to have been early in his college career.

Pamela had made sure that his penchant for honing his fighting ability was put on hold. She had helped him grow up and stop seeking trouble. Because of her, he had made it through college and law school while staying out of jail.

He still had street savvy but was more leery of fighting, especially in the modern era. Fists had been replaced by guns and knives. He had never feared driving through this part of the city in the old days, but he was cautious today. It was just after 4:00 PM. It was getting dark, and the neighborhood he was cruising was not a place to be at night. That was his intention. He still had some contacts on the street and would have a better chance of finding them at night.

His goal was to locate Tyrell Jones. He had helped Tyrell beat a murder rap two years prior. Flaws in the crime scene investigation had rendered several bits of key evidence inadmissible. The case drew national attention and some comparisons to a couple of very famous trials. Tyrell wasn't a famous person, so the comparisons were based mainly upon similarities between the ways the investigations were conducted.

Nick's victory in that case had made him a hero on the street and a thug in the courtrooms. The inadmissible evidence was so compelling that scarcely anyone doubted whether Tyrell had actually committed the crime. Twelve people did doubt it, however; hence, Tyrell was a free man.

Tyrell Jones had been charged with murdering his mother's boyfriend and two women the man happened to be accompanying that night. Tyrell had taken few precautions to conceal his crime. He was accused of shooting both women at point-blank range and stabbing his mother's boyfriend to death, beginning with several well-placed cuts to the groin area.

Arriving officers had destroyed the crime scene and apparently tried to cover up their mishaps by planting evidence at Tyrell's apartment. Nick was able to obtain expert testimony proving that blood and other key evidence had actually been placed long after the night of the murder. Tyrell walked. He now owed Nick his life. It was time to cash in a favor.

Nick exited Interstate 70 at Grand Avenue. He drove three miles into the heart of one of the most dangerous neighborhoods in St. Louis. He parked his car in front of Leroy's Bar. Leroy's was one of Tyrell's former hangouts, as of two years ago, anyway. He was hoping someone might know his whereabouts.

White men in North St. Louis after dark draw attention. White men driving fifty-thousand-dollar cars in North St. Louis after dark stop traffic. He could feel many pairs of eyes upon him as he got out of the car and clicked the remote lock. He was starting to question his own judgment as he entered the bar.

As soon as the front door creaked shut behind him, all conversations at Leroy's came to a halt. He stared into a wood-paneled, smoke-filled room while ten young black men looked back. He was a little uneasy, but he didn't dare show it. That would be an instant kiss of death. He glanced around the room, looking for Leroy or any other recognizable face. He found none, so he cut through the dense smoke toward the bar. Nick had many close friends in the black community. He felt he could really use one right about now.

"Leroy around tonight?" Nick asked the bartender.

"He off today," came the reply.

The rest of the room was still silent. All twenty eyes watched Nick walk to the bar, and they continued to watch him as he addressed the bartender.

"Can I get a Bud?"

At first, there was no answer, making him think he wasn't going to get served. He did his best to hide the mounting nerves that had triggered beads of sweat on his forehead and a trickle down his back. After a long pause, the bartender pulled a Budweiser from the cooler and slid it across the bar toward him. He didn't bother to remove the cap.

"Say, have you seen Tyrell Jones lately?"

Nick found that this question met with the same resistance as his request for a beer.

"What you want with Tyrell, white boy?" came a voice from the back of the room, finally penetrating the silence.

Nick followed the sound of the voice to the left rear corner of the room. A well-built man, probably in his early twenties, was leaning against the back wall. He held a beer in one hand and a pool cue in the other. Nick noticed his grip on both had tightened, showing off the muscles and veins in his forearms.

"Tyrell and I are old buddies," Nick responded with an air of false bravado.

He now hoped the lighting was too dim to reveal the mounting sweat on his brow.

There were some murmurs in the crowd. Another voice cracked the silence from the opposite side of the room.

"Tyrell gots no white-boy homies," a voice piped in, while a couple of the onlookers laughed. "You got that right," chimed in another.

Plotting his next move and still fighting to conceal his discomfort, he caught a break. One of the young men standing closer to Nick approached. Nick held his ground, fighting the impulse to escape. He stopped breathing, expecting the younger man to lead a charge toward him. Instead, he stopped a couple of feet from Nick's barstool.

"You the dude that got Tyrell off, ain't ya?"

Nick nodded, relieved that he might hold some esteem in this part of the world.

"Hey everybody, this is the cracker that saved Tyrell's sorry ass."

It was all Nick needed. Suddenly, he felt like he had just come home to a family reunion. All ten tough-looking kids in the bar surrounded him, but their intentions had changed completely. He exchanged more high fives and low fives and felt more back slaps than a quarterback who had just won the Super Bowl with a touchdown pass.

"Here, this one's on Leroy," the bartender said as he slid another Bud toward Nick to occupy the half-full bottle in his hand.

A broad smile revealed more gold-capped teeth than enamel.

"Tyrell will be here later on. You can hang with us until he gets here," the bartender offered, still smiling with gold gleaming in the dim lighting.

Nick spent the next hour giving a detailed recap of Tyrell's trial. All ten of the customers at Leroy's and the bartender listened to every word without taking their eyes from him. The stares were considerably less threatening now. They all looked like little kids, sitting around a campfire, listening to a well-articulated ghost story. They were each captivated, only interrupting periodically to ask a question or two.

Nick had just finished describing Tyrell's reaction to the verdict when the front door opened. In walked another black man, well-dressed in a burgundy suit and black overcoat. He stood well over six feet tall and had the build of an NFL running back. He had a clean-shaven head and a large flattened nose, which had been shattered in numerous street fights. Nick had not seen Tyrell Jones since twelve strangers had salvaged the fate of his future. The large man immediately broke into an ear-to-ear grin.

"What the fuck you doing here, honky?" Tyrell said, breaking into laughter. He crossed the bar and held out an enormous paw that would have made a basketball look like a grapefruit. They went through a series of neighborhood handshakes.

"How you doin', Nick?"

"I'm OK, Tyrell. How have you been?"

"Can't complain. Got my hoes, my freedom, and a regular income."

"Good to see you. I hope your regular income isn't going to require another trip to my office."

The comment elicited a sly smile from Tyrell, who didn't respond.

"Now, what the fuck are you doing in the 'hood after dark? You could get shot, or *worse*, up in here."

"I was looking for you. The prosecutor has some new evidence and wants to reopen the case."

"What the fuck are you talking about?" Tyrell asked, looking like he had been shot, or worse.

Before Nick could answer, the snickers in the room let Tyrell off the hook. By now, Nick was laughing, too.

"No, no. I actually came here because I need *your* help."

"My help?" Tyrell asked, looking at Nick quizzically, but then interjected, "Anything, man. Anything. You know that."

"If you got a minute, take a ride with me."

"You gonna let some nigga off the street ride in that sweet-looking chariot out front?"

"Come on. I'll buy you dinner."

"After you, white boy," Tyrell smiled.

*   *   *   *

Nick took Tyrell to a local barbecue joint a couple of blocks away.

"You must be doing OK, judging by this phat machine you got wrapped around you," Tyrell said while admiring the interior of Nick's car.

"No thanks to you. I can't take many more freebies from you street punks."

Tyrell laughed, but it faded quickly.

"Hey man, I was sorry to hear about your wife."

"Thanks," Nick said with a nod.

They drove together in silence before Nick broke the conversational drought.

"That's kind of why I'm here."

Tyrell answered with the same confused expression he had worn when Nick asked for his help at Leroy's.

"I was kind of hoping you might know something," Nick said.

"What the fuck would I know 'bout dat?" Tyrell asked, looking slightly ticked off.

"Settle down. I don't mean to say you had anything to do with it. Relax," Nick said. "I was just hoping you might have heard something on the street."

When convinced that Tyrell had calmed down, Nick handed him a copy of the police sketch. "Here, this might be the guy."

"No man, none of the brothers would have been involved in something like that. We not into that shit, man," Tyrell said, taking in the sketch.

He still appeared slightly skeptical about Nick's motives, but he was no longer offended.

"I don't think it was one of the brothers. I do think it was someone who might have a pretty extensive history of this kind of thing, though," Nick said. "Look, the reason I'm here is because the car the killer drove was ditched in East St. Louis. I was hoping you could do some checking around and find out if anyone knows anything," Nick added as he parked in front of Jimmy's Bar-B-Q on Grand.

He killed the engine and looked at Tyrell, who now appeared to be completely relaxed. He no longer seemed skeptical of Nick's intentions.

"Sure, bro. I'll do some axin'," Tyrell replied. "Now you gonna buys me some B-B-Q or what?"

"Sure, man. And I'll come back and buy you all the food you want if you can help me with this."

"I'll do what I can, Nick. You know that," Tyrell said, more serious this time. "Look, dude. I owe you my life. A brother doesn't forget something like that."

"Between you and me, Tyrell, I would have offed the cocksucker that was cracking your mom around, too."

The comment inspired an even broader smile from Tyrell.

"I knew you was a bad motherfucker, Nick. I could see it in your eyes. Now, can we *please* get some food?"

"Let's do it," Nick responded.

The two men from different social tiers, but oddly linked, got out of the car and headed into Jimmy's. Nick's personal—and private investigation—of Pamela's murder had just begun.

CHAPTER 11

▼

"St. Louis County Police Department," came the dry, uninterested response on the other end of the phone.

"Hi, my name is Nick Lacour. I need to speak with Detective Jack Ramsey."

"One moment, please, while I connect your call."

One moment became five minutes before a live voice broke through the monotonous drone of canned music on the line.

"Ramsey here."

"Jack, it's Nick Lacour."

"Nick, I was just thinking about you."

"Yeah?"

"I have you on my list of people to call today."

"Really? Has there been a breakthrough in the case?"

"Nothing major. Just wanted to see how you're doing."

Nick let out an audible sigh. For a brief moment, he thought that the police might be on the verge of apprehending this prick.

"I'm holding it together."

"That's good," came Ramsey's fatherly reply.

"Well, since I saved you a call, why don't you fill me in regarding the case?" Nick said.

"Nick, you know I'm not at liberty to share the details."

"That's a crock of shit, Jack. This is my wife we're talking about. Besides, I probably have more contacts in the field than you do."

"OK, settle down. You're right, that was insensitive of me to lay the upstand-ing cop b-s on you."

"So, what have you got so far?" Nick inquired, not yet detaching himself from an edgy tone.

"Unfortunately, I don't have a ton to tell you right now," came Ramsey's somewhat dispirited reply.

Nick breathed in deeply and let out another frustrated sigh. "Surely you've found something." he quipped while beginning to lose his patience.

"The guy was truly a professional."

"You make it sound like this creep was in my home installing a stereo system. What do you mean a *professional*?"

"What I mean is he didn't fuck up."

"I once read that a person who commits a murder makes about a thousand mistakes. Are you telling me he made none?"

"Well if he did, we haven't found many yet."

"Then you're not trying hard enough," stammered Nick, on the verge of losing his cool.

"Listen, Nick, I know you've been through the wringer and back. I want this guy caught nearly as bad as you do."

"Then go catch him, and stop telling me about how professional he is!"

"I wish it were that simple. The bottom line is he just didn't leave much behind."

"Much? That means there was something."

"All right, here it is," Ramsey said, mirroring Nick's sigh. "I really shouldn't be sharing the details of the investigation with *anyone*, but I'm going to go off the record and tell you what we've got if you promise to keep this to yourself and let us do our jobs."

"I promise. Now what have you got?" Nick asked, becoming further annoyed by the conversation.

"As I said, we ain't got much. The guy was almost *too* good. After tearing apart the crime scene a million different ways, we have come up with very little."

It all seemed so detached to Nick. The "crime scene" Ramsey callously referred to was his home—a home that was built by love, sweat, and hope. The hope had been destroyed. The love was still there, but one of the people who inspired it had been destroyed as well.

"OK, I heard all that the first time. What did he leave behind that you can use?" Nick asked, now in a near-frantic state of anger, frustration, and exasperation.

"Well, I already told you about basically all we have," Ramsey started. "Except..." he trailed off.

"Except what?" Nick asked, losing patience for this game.

"It's not much, but we also found traces of concrete."

"*What?*"

"Concrete. You know, the kind you use to make driveways and such."

"I don't understand," came Nick's reply.

"He wore boots. As he tracked through the snow on your driveway, the boots became wet and left prints on your hardwood floors. The prints had dried, but we were able to lift tracings of concrete."

"No shit? Wow, what a breakthrough! Seems so improbable that he could have picked up concrete while walking on a concrete fucking driveway!" Nick added with heavy sarcasm.

Ramsey continued, undaunted by Nick's outburst.

"The concrete wasn't picked up on your driveway, although we thought of that. The concrete was Mississippi pea gravel, and it had come from his boots. Your driveway is composed of a completely different kind."

"OK, so he had concrete on his boots. What does that mean?"

"He also had it on his skin. Your wife managed to take a decent-size chunk out of his body during their altercation. The skin under her nails also had traces of concrete and lime."

Nick was getting tired of this conversation. To him, the little evidence they had didn't amount to squat. *Traces of concrete...are you kidding me?* Nick thought. *How could that possibly help?*

"Look, I know it's not much, but it might tell us he's a construction worker of some kind," Ramsey said. "Like I told you before, she may have known or met him. Can you think of any blue-collar workers she may have been in contact with recently?"

"No, not off the top of my head," he said. "She had been on me to get a new patio put in the backyard, but I wasn't aware of any bids going out yet."

"Good, that's a start. If you come across anything along those lines, call me immediately. This may be a bigger break than you think, Nick," consoled Ramsey.

"OK," Nick replied disconsolately. "Anything else?"

"Maybe," Ramsey offered hesitatingly.

"I'm listening."

"It seems as though the pieces of skin may have shown us something else, too."

"OK?"

"The DNA was run through the FBI's crime system computer. There's a high probability that it matches the DNA found in traces of blood left at an Indianapolis murder site three years ago."

"So your hunch that he's done this before was right on?" Nick mused in an almost inaudible tone.

"I told you, he's good at it. Yes, I'd say there's much better than an excellent chance that he's done this before."

"So that makes this a random killing?"

"Killings are rarely random. If he has done this before, your wife was *chosen*. You don't take the methodical measures that he employed in a random, isolated incident."

"So let's cut the bullshit, Jack. What exactly does all of this tell us?"

"It confirms our fears and tells us we're definitely up against a serial killer."

"How does that change things?" Nick asked, already knowing the answer before finishing the question.

"It's a federal case," Ramsey stated flatly.

Nick emitted his third audible sigh of the conversation. *Great*, he thought, *now the fucking FBI would be involved*. He had rarely had a good experience with the "fibbies," as they were known in the law enforcement world. He had witnessed them screw up a couple of cases. In fact, as a defense attorney, he didn't mind terribly when they were called in because it sometimes aided his cause. Unless, of course, they took over the case and it became a federal trial. He loved it best when they were called upon as "consultants." They had been known to muck things up badly enough on occasion to provide the defense team with a better chance of proving reasonable doubt to a jury.

"That's what I was afraid you'd say," said Nick.

"It's still early. We haven't finished our investigation of the crime scene or our interviews with your neighbors," Ramsey interjected, trying to add some hope to the situation.

"Hey, I apologize for being such a prick with you just now."

"Don't apologize. I'd be a much bigger prick if I was going through what you are," said Ramsey.

"I just feel so damn helpless."

"That's why we're here. It's our job to help, and that's what we're going to do."

"I know. I just hope you get the chance."

Both men knew what that last sentence meant. If the fibbies took over the case, the local police would more or less be removed entirely. The FBI saw local intervention as a nuisance. The Bureau's arrogance prohibited it from acting in unison with the locals. Once it took over a case, it was truly "their" case.

They spoke for a few more minutes about the weather, Anheuser-Busch's entry into the low-carb market, and the upcoming baseball season. When they hung up, Nick felt more out of sorts than he had before placing the call. It was now apparent to him that he must proceed with his own investigation without alerting the FBI. In some ways, maybe that was the best thing, anyway. After all, he was the only one who had a truly vested interest in the apprehension of the man who had taken Pamela away from him.

*   *   *   *

Nick's cell phone had been ringing for an undetermined amount of time when he finally corralled it and pushed the flashing blue button.

"Hello?" he groggily answered.

"I think I got something fer ya," replied the voice on the other end.

"Who is this?" asked Nick as he clumsily tried to rub the sleep from his eyes.

"Who you think it is? It's Tyrell, man. Who else gonna call you at this hour?"

"Tyrell, how's it hanging, my man?" Nick asked, trying to sound more hip than he felt after being yanked from the first sleep he had in days.

"It's hanging, it's hanging," Tyrell responded. "Anyway, you wants to know why I called or what?" he asked.

Nick pushed himself upright and fumbled around for his glasses. A lifetime contact lens wearer, he couldn't see an elephant from ten paces without the aid of corrective lenses.

"Yeah, lay it on me. What you got for me?" Nick inquired, still trying to sound hip and not quite as out of it as he had been a few seconds earlier.

"Well, there's this dude. Rough-looking cracker been hanging out at a joint called The Pie Factory. You know the place?" Tyrell asked.

"I might have spent a bachelor party or two there," Nick answered.

"Anyways, this rough-looking prick asked old Tommy Hunt to watch his truck a few weeks back. Old Tommy said he was real nervous-looking when he picked it up."

"OK. So, what has that got to do with me?" Nick asked, now more confused than ever.

"Well, you see, this freak mumbled something about, 'The bitch is gonna get what she deserves,' when he was paying Tommy his money," Tyrell said.

"I'm still a little confused, Tyrell. I can't figure how that applies to me," Nick responded, still not fusing any useful connections in his mind.

"Maybe it don't. It's just that Tommy found it kinda odd. Especially since the dude picks up his car the same night that they found a burning car near the river."

"Cars burn all the time in East St. Louis, Tyrell. That still doesn't tell me a great deal."

"Might be a coincidence, but the whole thing happened the night your old lady got did in," added Tyrell. "And there's one more thing."

"Yeah, I'm listening," Nick said.

"Tommy said the dude looked like that picture you gave me."

"You've got my attention. Tell me more," Nick said.

He was now sitting bolt upright and trying to digest what he had just heard. Tyrell's words were still hanging in the air like a cartoon balloon that was ready to burst.

"Seems that this ugly sumbitch asked Tommy to watch his truck at a warehouse for a couple o' days. Tommy didn't think much of it at the time but said the dude was kind of weird-looking."

"What do you mean *weird-looking*?" asked Nick.

"The kind of weird that says you done something you wasn't 'posed to, but can't wait to tell somebody about it," explained Tyrell.

It was starting to add up a little for Nick. The assailant steals a car, commits a murder, burns the car, and then escapes from a different part of town in his own vehicle. The pickings were slim, but oddly, they made sense.

"When the dude said that part about the bitch getting hers, Old Tommy wasn't too surprised. Like he said, the man looked like he was up to no good anyways," Tyrell said.

"So how do I get a hold of this Tommy?" Nick quickly asked.

He still felt the story was somewhat sparse but better than anything else he had. Besides, recognizing the man from the police sketch and tying him to the car Ramsey's crew connected with the killer went well beyond coincidence.

"I was thinking you might be axin' me dat," Tyrell answered. "Now be the best time. Get yo' shit together and meet me in the stockyards in half an hour."

The phone clicked dead on the other end. Nick sat staring at his cell phone trying to compute what he had just been told. It still seemed like a long shot, but he had to follow up on it just the same.

He pulled on a sweatshirt, wrestled himself into a pair of jeans, and left his parents' house in the still of the night. He was no longer half-asleep, and his heart hammered with the anticipation that he'd just had a major breakthrough in his quest to find the guy who killed Pamela.

✳　　　✳　　　✳　　　✳

Tyrell sat on the hood of his car smoking a Benson & Hedges as Nick pulled up along side the pimped-out red Cadillac that Tyrell proudly drove.

"A little cold to be sitting on the hood, isn't it?" Nick asked through his lowered window.

"Nah. I like the fresh air. Keeps me sharp, if you knows what I mean," Tyrell chuckled.

"Hop in," Nick said, not really knowing what Tyrell meant at all. "Let's go meet this Tommy."

"We don't need to drive anywhere. Old Tommy just inside that crib right there," Tyrell said.

He was pointing toward a dilapidated structure that didn't look strong enough to bear the weight of a few starving field mice.

"OK," said Nick, "Let's go talk to him."

He climbed out of his car and joined Tyrell next to the Cadillac. Tyrell pitched his cigarette onto the pothole-riddled street and stepped away from his car. The two men walked toward the shack together in silence. This was a place, and a neighborhood for that matter, which Nick would never dare go alone at night. He was only marginally more comfortable with Tyrell as they plodded through the icy stillness of another brutal winter night.

"Yo Tommy, gets your old ass out here. Gotta man who wants to talk to you," yelled Tyrell.

"Whachoo doin' up in here, Tyrell?" came the reply from the rotting structure sagging some fifty feet from the street.

Nick tried to peer into the coal blackness of the building but couldn't see anything that resembled a living being. A few seconds later, a smiling black man, probably in his sixties, appeared in the crumbling doorframe. He wore an untucked flannel shirt that had probably not been washed in a lifetime. He was fumbling with a pair of well-worn jeans as he moved forward. Nick was just able to make out the slackness of his skin and yellow of his eyes as he drew nearer.

"Nice pad," Nick remarked as the man hopped off the decaying front porch of the house and onto the rock-strewn yard.

"This ain't my house, you fool," came the reply. "I's just taking care o' some bidness," he added, while hitching up his pants and cinching his belt.

A young girl, probably no more than seventeen, followed him out of the house. She was rubbing her jaw with an embarrassed look on her face. She wore a skirt so short that Nick was sure he'd be able to see her privates were it not for the darkness filling the yard.

Before parting company, she held out her hand and waited for the meager reward that would somehow make this degrading experience worthwhile in her mind. Tommy handed her a wrinkled, slightly torn ten spot and slapped her on the ass. He broke into an ear-to-ear grin and looked like an old man who had just hit all six lottery numbers as he watched her clip-clop down the street in her busted pumps.

"So what's you doin' up in here, Tyrell? I thought you was done with these parts?" he asked with a grin, still grabbing his crotch.

"I told you, old-timer, I broughts this man to see you," Tyrell replied.

"Well shit, boy, I ain't blind yet. I can see that much," he cackled, maintaining a stronghold on his groin and wearing a look of deep contentment.

"Tommy, my name's Nick. I'm a, er, a friend of Tyrell's," he explained, not too convincingly.

"Some friend you must be, driving your white ass out here in a Lexus," the old man said, holding out his hand.

Nick took the hand but hoped to God it hadn't been active in the after-hours party that had just concluded in the beat-up shack behind them.

"Watcha need, Nick?" asked the old man, now all business.

"Well, Tyrell tells me you came across some strange character recently. Said he paid you to watch his truck," Nick answered. "He even said the man may have resembled a sketch I gave to him," he added.

"Are *you* asking?" Tommy inquired, while scratching his head and balls simultaneously. He looked to be searching for the magic response that would trigger his memory, which Nick anticipated by handing the old guy a better-pressed version of the ten he had parted with moments earlier.

"Tyrell speaks the truth. What is it you want to know?" the old man asked, now wearing a modified look of renewed contentment as he accepted the gratuity.

"It's an extreme long shot, but someone broke into my house that same night. It's probably ten million to one that it's the same guy, but Tyrell said you indicated this man was odd. The way he said it intrigued me," said Nick.

"The cracker was a whole lot mo' than odd," responded Tommy. "He had eyes that could look right through your head, just like the ones in that picture Tyrell showed me. Kept muttering something about some bitch who was gonna get hers. I didn't rightly know what he was babbling about, but it sounded like some serious shit."

"What makes you think there is a connection to the guy who came to my house?" asked Nick, omitting the part about what he did while at the house.

"I didn't really thinks much of it myself," answered Tommy, "but the picture talked me into it."

"Why don't you tell me about the guy?" asked Nick.

"Well for one, I can't be all dat sho' he's the same cracker as the one who burnt that car. 'Sides, I don't need him coming back here no mo'," Tommy said with the hint of a tremble edging his voice.

Nick didn't ask Tommy to qualify the last part. He could tell by the look on his face that the man had shaken Tommy up pretty badly.

"Anyway, I see this cracker at The Pie Factory all the time," Tommy added. "Well, maybe not all the time, but definitely mo' than once."

"What makes you think he's the same guy who ditched the car by the river?" Nick asked.

"'Cause he comes here all smellin' like smoke, out of breath and sweatin' on a night when you needed two coats to keep warm," Tommy answered with conviction. "I figure he must have run a long way just to pick up his truck. I could hear the fire trucks in the distance when he got here, but di'nt know a car had been burnt 'til the next mornin.' Dat's when I think something was kind of funny 'bout that cat."

Nick looked like he had just seen a ghost. It wasn't odd for cars to burn in this part of town. It wasn't strange for seedy people to be into covert things in this area, either. It *was* somewhat abnormal, though, that a white man would show up in the middle of the night and pick up his truck right on the heels of another vehicle burning a mile or so away. For that matter, it was even more unsettling that the man's face bore strong resemblance to the police artist's sketch of a possible suspect in his wife's crime.

It was still a one in a million, but Nick was starting to get a vibe that there was more to this than just coincidence. It was possible that a drug dealer or a john was doing business in the area that evening. But like Tommy said, it was a little too cold to be sprinting around the woods—especially a white man in a completely black neighborhood.

"Thank you, Tommy," Nick said, filling the old man's withered hand with another ten. "You've been real helpful, but I might need you to do me one more thing," Nick said.

"What's dat?" he inquired with a hint of paranoia, which had reduced his grin somewhat.

"I need you to let Tyrell know the next time you see this guy at The Pie Factory, OK?" asked Nick.

"What I get out of this?" Tommy responded, still wearing a worried visage.

"Enough of those," said Nick, pointing to the bills in Tommy's hand, "to take care of your next bit of *bidness* in a hotel instead of this piece of shit shack." Nick motioned to the remnants of a building that surely wouldn't survive another winter, or even a strong gust of wind.

"You on!" Tommy cried, clapping Nick sharply on the back, leaving Nick slightly stunned that the little man possessed such might.

CHAPTER 12

▼

"So whatta ya having, sugar, Jack 'n' Coke?" asked the girl wearing a name tag that read "Lola."

Rucker nodded affirmatively and intently watched her walk away after he had confirmed his usual order. He was a little surprised that she remembered his drink preference and couldn't decide if that was a good or bad thing. After giving it very little thought, he decided it was good. He wasn't sure, but he even imagined that she had smiled at him a little more warmly that time.

He'd been to this dump on a few occasions now and each time had ordered his drinks from Lola. He knew it was a little risky frequenting the same place, but he simply couldn't resist the pull she had on him. It was almost as if she had cast a spell that he was now powerless to break. Each time he went to The Pie Factory, he felt her magnetic draw getting stronger. He'd never been in this position before and liked the role reversal. He imagined that once he finally wasted her, he'd really appreciate the game they had played together.

"There you go, honey. That will be four dollars."

He handed her a ten and waived off the change. She smiled sweetly and touched him on the arm.

"Thanks, baby. That's really nice of you," she said.

His eyes followed her as she left the table. He loved watching her ass shake when she walked through the bar. He could tell she was wearing a thong and wondered what color it was. He broke into a sweat just thinking about it.

It had taken him a couple of weeks to hammer down her schedule. She worked on Monday, Wednesday, and Friday nights. He wasn't sure what she did with the rest of her time, but he planned to follow her home soon. There was no big rush, though. He was enjoying the chase and could tell she was starting to warm up to him. She had made a couple of comments during his last visit acknowledging the fact that she remembered him.

Oddly enough, the chase was strangely rewarding this time around. None of his previous girls had survived that long. After watching them a few times, he couldn't stand it anymore and had to own them. With Lola, he felt like making his move too early would spoil the experience. She was more exotic than the rest. Every time he scanned her voluptuous frame and angelic face, his breath halted and his pulse quickened. Yeah, she was definitely a good one, and he had to plan the final act very carefully—and before the impulse to have her became something he could no longer control.

For now, he was content making small talk and watching her slink around the joint in her tight little costumes. He paid close attention to other customers who appeared a little too handsy with Lola for his liking. One night, he was forced to smack some poor nerd around after watching him clamp his hand on her ass several times. He followed the guy outside to his car and slammed his head on the roof several times before the clown even had a chance to open the door.

Rucker left him bleeding in the parking lot and beat a hasty retreat before someone noticed. Poor sap never saw it coming and still probably doesn't know what he did to earn it. Rucker chuckled to himself every time he thought about the incident. Whatever the risk, it was worth it because the guy hadn't been back since.

"How's that Jack? Need a little top-off?"

Rucker nodded.

Lola came back a minute later with a fresh glass.

"Here you go. This one's on the house," she said as she handed him the new drink.

Rucker took the glass and gently grabbed her arm. He looked into her eyes and could tell she was not alarmed. He was impressed by her fearless attitude.

"Thanks for the drink. This is for you," he said as he slid a rolled up ten under her bra.

His fingers lightly grazed her soft skin, and for a minute, he thought he might pass out from the excitement. He quickly composed himself and attempted an awkward smile.

"Thanks, sweetie," she said, while returning his smile and touching his hand invitingly.

He sensed strength in this girl that he had never encountered before. She'd be a formidable conquest in the end, and he looked forward to their final meeting. It was still a little too soon, though. He wanted to enjoy the dance for a while first.

*   *   *   *

Angela's shift at The Pie Factory ended at 3:00 AM. She was so tired she could barely stand erect as she staggered out to her car. A blast of cold air stung her eyes and made her more alert as she inserted a key into the faded red door of her 1985 Ford Escort. The car wasn't a whole lot younger than she was. On nights like these, they both seemed equally worn out.

The old "scort" turned over roughly and sputtered through a few tense moments before the engine finally caught. *Thank God*, she thought as she sat shaking uncontrollably waiting for the heater to make each visible exhale a little less prominent.

It's a good thing the car started this time, because she couldn't bear the thought of getting a ride home from one of the bouncers or the bartender. No matter how emphatically she stated it, she never seemed to be able to convince any of those thugs that she wasn't interested. Her verbal emphasis had been replaced by a physical exclamation point one night as she had been forced to slam her knee into her least favorite bouncer's groin region. This had come after several minutes of fighting off his drunken advances with quick hands and expletives. The knee had been much more effective than the two previous methods.

With the car finally warm enough to pull out of the lot, she shifted into drive and started home. Oh, how she hated this time of year. She lived ten miles from The Pie Factory and on most nights covered the distance before the interior temperature of the vehicle rose above freezing. Tonight would be no exception. She drove with teeth chattering and gloved hands clutching the frigid steering wheel. Her mind passed the time by dreaming of a better life.

Though only twenty-five, she already felt fifty. What brought her to this place? It was a question she had asked herself a thousand times without once being able to utter a single acceptable answer. She was a victim of circumstance, she supposed. Playing the role of the chronically abused in every home she had ever occupied, she had finally been able to escape. She now made enough money to afford a paltry apartment in this one-horse town. At least she was finally alone. She was thankful every day for that blessing.

Her former roommates all had shared the same characteristics. They each had used her body to take out their fury, whether the discontentment was sexual frustration or a hatred for life in general and the cruel lot they had drawn from it.

The first abuser had been her own father. Fortunately for Angela, he died of a drug overdose when she was twelve. That hadn't prohibited him from robbing her of her virginity when she was eleven, however. It hadn't stopped him from driving his fist into her jaw, either. She still wore a slight scar along the corner of her mouth, where his high school class ring had laid her flesh open. She sometimes mused at the irony of being hit by a ring that she doubted had been acquired by intelligence or hard work, things she long since knew her father had not possessed.

After Daddy's exit, her mother had taken up with a series of losers who had made dear old Dad look like an altar boy. One right after another paraded through the house, taking whatever appealed to him. Angela had managed to avoid their sexual perversions but not their violent outbursts. Both she and her mother had suffered numerous beatings at the hands of these societal misfits. Only one had been even decent to the two of them. Sadly, her mother hadn't been bright enough to recognize it because she dumped him after they had been together for just two short months.

Once the train of derelicts had passed, so did her mom. Never one to be outdone by her husband, Mom followed his lead onto the heroine horse and rode herself right out of this world. She had died with a needle in her arm when Angela was sixteen. She had absorbed the loss of each parent without having shed a single tear. She cursed them for bringing her into the world and despised the life they had subjected her to.

And, as if it could have gotten worse, she got knocked up and married when she was seventeen. She lost the baby before birth, and her husband died a year later. It wasn't drugs this time, though. He had succumbed to a lead foot that didn't combine well with a fifth of vodka. His car had careened into a bridge abutment one night after a twelve-hour drinking binge. He left her a checking account balance of thirty-nine dollars and a new scar across her abdomen to overshadow the one on her face. That one had been a constant reminder of the night he tried to end her life.

That had been seven years ago. The physical wounds had long since healed, but the emotional cuts still ran deep. Rarely a day went by when she didn't wonder what it would have been like to grow up in a normal environment. Now, just half a decade into her twenties, she felt used up and spent. She wondered what any decent guy would ever be able to see in her. She lacked the confidence to realize that she had true beauty. Not just the physical kind, but also a spiritual beauty that gave her an almost paranormal glow.

She had a way about her that couldn't quite be explained. People wanted to be near her and were instantly drawn to her. Whenever she entered a room, all eyes turned to her. She always assumed it was her body they wanted, but it was actually much more than that. She had a magnetism that everyone who had ever encountered her wanted to feed off.

All she ever saw when she looked into the mirror was a tired woman who felt twice her age. She wondered what she had done to deserve this life and whether it would ever improve. She often fell asleep dreaming of a handsome, charming man who would be able to see past the pain that masked her soul. She didn't know if he really existed. She certainly found it hard to imagine every time she pulled on her work outfit and made her way between the countless tables of perverted losers who were only able to see her as an object and not as a human being.

With teeth still grinding, but not quite as violently, she finally pulled into her apartment complex. Apartment 2A of the Knollwood Villas was nothing special, but it was hers. She relied on no one but herself these days, and she wouldn't have it any other way.

After prodding her keys into three different locks, she mustered a last bit of strength to force the front door open and took an exhausted step across the threshold. Finally inside her home, she felt the warmth and comfort of being able to seal everything else outside her closed door. She finally had a refuge to escape to and shelter herself from the hostile and uninviting world she had come to know and hate.

Throwing her scarf and wool coat over the back of a faded green couch, she stumbled down a short hallway to the unit's sole bedroom. Too tired to even flip a light switch or brush her teeth, she flopped onto the bed and immediately drifted away into a dreamless sleep.

*   *   *   *

Rucker sat outside the apartment complex, impervious to the cold and darkness infiltrating his parked vehicle. He had been staring at the second apartment building's entrance for more than an hour. Freshly ground-out cigarette butts littered his ashtray, and the truck reeked of stale smoke and booze. Taking a final pull from the last inch of his Kool, he ground it out and started the engine. His reconnaissance paid dividends on this night, because he finally found out where Lola lived. He had hoped to follow her on one other occasion, but her car wouldn't start and she had to bum a ride from a coworker. He had been tempted to offer her a ride himself, but thought the better of it. A premature move like that would cheapen the dance. Now he had a bead on her homestead and could show up anytime he liked.

A minor tug from within beckoned him to her apartment, but it was late and he wasn't ready. The burning inside had been building, but it hadn't reached a final crescendo. He was still content playing the game with her. She intoxicated him, and he didn't want to ruin it by making a clumsy, unplanned move toward her apartment. No, now wasn't the time. Not yet.

He drove out of the small parking lot with his lights off. Following her had not been easy. They seemed to be the only two vehicles on the road, and he had to be very careful not to tip her off. Lucky for him, he was able to let her get a couple of turns ahead and he still could figure out where she was going. It was almost as if he sensed her presence and followed its gravitational pull.

The last few miles were covered without headlights. It was a little risky, but he enjoyed the challenge. He hadn't met a cop yet who he couldn't persuade to release him. The message was usually verbal, but he wasn't opposed to combining words with a more physical approach. In his thirty-one years of life, he had been pulled over only four times. The first three times, he had been caught speeding and was dismissed with a verbal warning. The fourth time had been for running a stoplight. The officer on the scene was now walking with a severe limp. Giving Rucker a ticket had led to a severe beating, followed by two months in the hospital. His shattered kneecap would never fully heal, and the cane in his right hand would be a permanent reward for that ill-fated decision. The altercation had forced Rucker to seek a new alias and a new car, which was probably the most irritating thing about the event to him.

Nevertheless, he was happy not to be traveling that "road" again on this evening. He was getting close to the girl and couldn't risk being forced to avoid this part of town. He silently cursed himself for taking the chance but then laughed for giving it a second thought.

Lola. The name had been etched on his brain for quite some time now. He went to sleep at night muttering it to himself and woke with its two-syllable echo still ringing in his ears. Her image had left an indelible impression on his psyche, and he wondered if he would ever be able to shake it free. Sometimes, he would stare off into space and picture her standing right before his eyes.

Who was this girl? Why did he feel so strongly this time around? Each mission had been about doing a job. This one was more about prolonging the mission to avoid doing the job. Still, he could hear that other voice in his head. The one that cried out and told him to stop screwing around.

"Get to work," it said. "You still have a job to do."

He had always obeyed that voice in the past but had tried to ignore it this time. He didn't want to end the chase. Even so, he knew the voice couldn't be put off forever. It always won. Always. The question now was when would it emerge victorious over Lola. He pushed the last thought aside and concentrated on the road. It was nearly rush hour, and he didn't want to attract attention on his way home. Lola. The name kept popping into his head. Nothing seemed to be able to stop it.

He turned on the radio, half-expecting The Kinks to be paying similar homage. Instead, he listened to the mindless drivel of some early morning talk radio program. The only words he seemed to hear sounded like "Lola." He drove into the early morning hours seeing her face and hearing her name whispered into his ear.

*   *   *   *

Angela awoke with a headache. She squinted at her alarm clock, which displayed large yellow numbers illustrating that it was 11:37 AM. It was still dark in her room, due to the tightly drawn shades that conformed to the theme of keeping the outside world out.

Struggling to pull herself from bed, she sat up and rubbed her eyes until she was sure they'd be forced from their sockets. She didn't have a single drink the night before, but she still felt hungover. She wished she could lie under the warmth of her down blanket all day, but she had things to do. Her body had somewhat adjusted to her odd work hours, but her mind would never reconcile the schedule. She longed for an eight-to-five job that didn't involve slobbering drunks, drug addicts, pervs, or other freaks.

Her bare feet hit the cold tile floors of the bathroom, and she winced. She turned the shower nozzle marked *H* to full blast and waited while the pipes groaned their disapproval. A pipe bursting in this old building wouldn't shock her. In fact, she couldn't believe it hadn't happened yet. Oops, scratch that thought. Bad karma.

The hot water cascading over her skin felt good. She closed her eyes and let the piping hot stream rush over her body for what seemed like hours. After enduring this process until her skin was tinged red, she shut off the valve and grabbed a large thick purple towel from the rack. She could barely see anything because of the steam, but she welcomed its warming effects.

Dressing in a pair of faded jeans that fit her slim figure like paint and a bulky gray sweatshirt that read "Duke" in large blue letters, she was ready to face the day. Her last boyfriend had left the sweatshirt behind. She could scarcely believe that it had been nearly two years since she had been on a date. All she ever seemed to do was work and sleep. When she wasn't moonlighting at The Pie Factory, she was scanning groceries at the local Jacobson's market. All told, she logged more than sixty hours a week with very little coin to show for it.

Today was a Tuesday, however, and she was off from both jobs. It was her only free day of the week, and she planned to make good use of it. First, she would go check out Belleville Area College, which was a little less than twenty minutes from her apartment. Angela had obtained her GED a couple of months prior. She then filled out an application to attend BAC. To her delight, she had been accepted. Now all she had to do was find the time and money to attend classes.

No one in her family had ever attended college. In fact, the GED would have made her one of the family's brightest academic stars. Few in the Graves family had advanced beyond the ninth grade. Angela had only logged two years of high school before a premature pregnancy and ensuing marriage had forced her out. Taking college classes would be a major breakthrough in her life, and she was excited by the prospect.

Eager to begin her future, she sped off to BAC armed with lofty aspirations. Perhaps she'd escape the mind-numbing depression caused by long work hours and scant moments of near comatose sleep. If she were going to make something of herself, she'd have to do it alone. She learned early in life that she couldn't rely on another soul to aid her success, much less survival, in this world.

She now had a plan and felt better about herself already. It was another overcast day in this smog-filled annex to St. Louis, but she felt the psychological clouds lifting. Maybe the sun would pop through soon, too.

*   *   *   *

Nick tried to reconcile what he had learned the night before. Many of the puzzle pieces were still jumbled, but he felt that he might be onto something. Rising from bed after just two hours of sleep, he was unable to subdue the adrenaline rush he had experienced while obtaining a possible lead in the case. It was still a long shot, but he believed there was a connection between the man described by

Tommy and Pamela's murderer. Either way, he was set to investigate the remnants of the burned car in East St. Louis this morning.

After shoving down a cold cherry Pop-Tart and some pulpy orange juice, he escaped his parents' home before anyone else was out of bed. He felt guilty about leaving Justin so much these days, but he couldn't bear the interrogation he was sure to receive from his mother regarding his late-night departure. She always had hearing keen enough to detect the slightest sound, even while sleeping. It almost seemed like she could hear a dust particle settling on a piece of furniture. Her hypersensitive hearing had made it nearly impossible for him or his brother to leave the house after-hours as teenagers or return past their curfew. They both still joked about the multiple times they thought they were out of the house undetected, only to see Mom standing in the front doorway looking like she might very well dismember each of them for the attempted violation of a house rule.

He was more than a little surprised that she wasn't up yet, since it was nearly seven. Recent events and advancing age had definitely softened her demeanor. Nick guessed that watching Justin all day and bearing the emotional wreckage left behind by the passing of her daughter-in-law had sufficiently exhausted her.

He placed the juice glass, now containing nothing but the slimy orange fragments he detested, in the sink. Why did she still insist on buying juice with pulp? She knew he hated it. He shook his head and silently crept out of the house. True to the pattern of his youth, he could see his mom peering at him through the front window as he pulled out of the driveway. He tried to avert her gaze but was unable to escape her disapproving look. Now in his thirties, he still couldn't get anything past her.

After battling the heavy line of traffic heading eastbound on Highway 40, Nick finally crossed the Poplar Street Bridge signifying passage from Missouri into Illinois. The murky depths of the Mississippi River passed silently under the bridge, some two hundred or so feet below. His mind ricocheted between visions of Justin, whom he hadn't been spending much needed time with lately, and a faceless killer. The latter he abhorred and wanted to shred with his bare hands.

Once in Illinois, he took the first exit, marked East St. Louis, and headed south toward the riverfront. It was now light out, so he felt relatively safe in this poverty-stricken, crime ravaged neighborhood. A Caucasian driving a Lexus would normally be an open invitation to disaster in this town, but it was too early in the morning for the real threats to be out of bed. All-night drug and alcohol binging complete with various forms of felonious behavior usually rendered most of the seedier individuals in the community lifeless come early morning. A trip to East St. Louis after dark would have been another story entirely.

He pulled his car off the main road and onto a gravel path blocked by a No Trespassing sign. He guessed the car Tommy described was less than a mile away. Getting out of his car and shivering in the early morning winter cold, he unhooked the chain connecting the sign to a couple of rotting posts and dropped the disconnected end onto the ground. He clambered back into the car and continued down the road for a little over a mile before coming upon the burned car's wreckage, half buried among a grove of barren trees.

He pulled his car alongside the skeletal remains of the vehicle and got out. From the looks of the car, it had burned for quite some time. The interior upholstery was reduced to blackened seat springs and a melted plastic dashboard from which a distorted steering wheel protruded.

He poked around in the interior for a few minutes before turning his attention to the trunk. He pried the lid open, revealing the equally demolished contents of the car's rear compartment. The smell of burned rubber and melted vinyl filled his nostrils. Trying to breathe through his mouth, he used a tree branch to root around the trunk space. The ashen remains of what appeared to be clothing littered the trunk bed. A grossly misshapen spare tire that bore the brunt of the fire was centered toward the rear of the cavity.

A little frustrated by being unable to reveal significant clues, Nick decided to go home. But just before he left, his eye caught something wedged between the spare tire remnants and the black encrusted interior sidewall. He protracted the item, which looked a little bit like a short, triangle-shaped spatula. The handle was gone. The shiny chrome-like appearance of the head had since been replaced by obsidian markings resulting from exposure to 1,600 degrees Fahrenheit.

Turning the item over and over in his hand, he decided it was some kind of tool. He vaguely remembered his dad having one in the basement and was able to place it as an edger used for concrete finishing. He shoved the tire off to the side and found another tool. This one was a flat piece of metal with two prongs jutting out of its center. The prongs had once been connected to a handle. He immediately recognized it as a trowel. Not exactly sure what to make of his finds, he wrapped them in an old towel from the floor of his backseat and deposited the tools into his trunk.

He drove home wondering what significance, if any, the tools had. He recalled Ramsey describing the concrete tracings the killer had left behind. It was possible that the evidence found by the police drew a line to the burnt tools in his trunk.

They might even draw a connection to the strange character Tommy described and the perpetrator he was seeking.

Not completely satisfied with his early morning field trip, he begrudgingly headed back to his parents' house, where his mother would certainly be waiting to interrogate him in a manner that would make Andy Sipowicz from *NYPD Blue* swell with pride. He grimaced at the thought and immediately began thinking of a story that might throw her off the trail and abruptly end the line of questioning. It would take him the entire forty-minute ride to concoct something believable, and even then, it only stood a fifty-fifty chance of fooling her. Dear old Mom. He smiled to himself, admiring her intuitive skills when it came to her children.

Wide awake from his early morning visit to Illinois, he decided he didn't feel like returning to his parents' just yet. He briefly considered going to the office but nixed the idea quickly, feeling that he couldn't deal with the awkward attention and sympathy he'd receive. He still wasn't comfortable around consoling individuals who meant well but only made matters worse.

Instead, he drove to his own house. He hadn't been inside since the day after the crime. His neighbor had helped him pack a couple of bags that first evening, and he had managed to stay away ever since. It still hurt way too badly to enter the house. Pamela's presence was engraved into every square foot, and being there reopened the gaping wound in his heart that was still a long way from healing.

For some reason, his investigative trip to the river that morning had inspired him to check his own house for clues. Maybe the police had missed something. After the way the LAPD cops had allegedly botched O.J. Simpson's arrest, he wouldn't put it past the locals to have missed something, either.

Standing on his front porch, he braced himself for what he'd see inside. He had been in a state of shock the last time he was there and probably didn't notice the many signs of battle that had scarred the residence the night Pamela died. Fighting back the onset of an anxiety attack, he unlocked the front door and dodged the lines of police tape barring entrance to his residence. At first glance, things didn't look much different from they had the night he left for the hockey game with his son.

It almost seemed like yesterday; he could still feel Pamela's lips on his as they embraced for a last time in this same doorway. He had no way of knowing that would be the last time he'd ever touch her or see her living face. A wave of grief-stricken nostalgia overcame him, and he felt his legs go out from under him.

Tumbling to the foyer floor, he sat up against the closed front door and sobbed with his head buried in his hands. He wasn't going to get very far if this was the way it was going to be, so he made an attempt to compose himself. After taking deep breaths and spending several minutes trying to detach from the cloud of grief hanging over the house, he finally rose to his feet. He would have to be a lawyer, not a husband, if anything useful was to come of this visit.

Making his way through the foyer and into the den, he visually scanned the great room of his house as if he were seeing it for the first time. Blood streaks stained the blond hardwood floors and one of the walls. He fought extremely hard not to connect the aftermath with his wife's demise. He tried to fool himself into thinking he was checking out the crime scene of an unknown victim. His intentions were good but not very effective. Every step bore reminders of the life that had once existed within these walls. At every turn, he could see Pamela's smiling face and feel the love they had shared for nearly a decade. When he wasn't imagining her face, he was actually seeing it in the many photographs that still lined the deserted hallways and rested atop dust-covered tables.

Now convinced that he had made a mistake in coming back so soon, Nick decided he couldn't do any good there. In fact, the desire to conduct his own investigation was starting to fade. What was the use, anyway? Even if he did catch the guy, it wouldn't bring her back. Despite that indisputable fact, a lingering desire for revenge still motivated him. It was a primordial instinct that he just couldn't shut off. It mixed with the pain of loss and formed a toxic potion that he didn't have the power to escape. No, he couldn't bring her back. But he could still serve justice and avenge her death.

He spent the next hour wandering around the ground floor, halfheartedly hoping something out of the ordinary would appear. The crime scene investigators had done a thorough job examining the premises. Not a trinket or piece of furniture had escaped their probing hands and eyes. Fingerprint dust was still everywhere, and hundreds of orange evidence cards marked virtually every square inch of the house, making it more like a museum for the dead than the Lacour family home.

It was becoming obvious that Ramsey's team had conducted a complete search. Nick was all too familiar with crime scenes and the telltale signs of the misguided act that created them, but he began to seriously doubt he'd find anything that the professionals had missed.

He went to the kitchen and decided to look for something to supplement the Pop-Tart he had eaten hours earlier. It had taken him several days to feel any hunger pangs after the tragedy. His body's will to live had assumed its own role, and he now ate out of necessity. In just a short time, his belt had begun to explore holes that he hadn't used since his teens. He guessed he had dropped fifteen pounds already but wasn't overly concerned about it. His mother's insistence that he feed himself was finally getting through. He now robotically forced himself to eat a few times a day, even if he didn't think he had the stomach for it.

He pulled open the refrigerator door and stared at its aged contents for several minutes. Nothing looked good. In fact, nothing looked good *literally*. He began to pitch expired items into the trash while trying to ignore the stench of rancid, spoiled food.

When the contents of the fridge had been mostly emptied, he settled on a carton of yogurt that wasn't yet past its prime and a package of processed turkey that probably wouldn't kill him. Closing the door, he jumped up on the island in the center of the kitchen and methodically began to chew his way through rolled up pieces of meat. The once pleasurable act of eating had become a chore. He slowly forced down the food while desperately trying not to conjure up the many memories that threatened to burst through his mental dam and flood him with pain.

He gazed at the yellow refrigerator while spooning out the last couple of bites of strawberry-flavored yogurt. He couldn't draw the distinction between flavors of any kind and merely ate because he had to. Strawberry might just as well have been liver for all he knew. His taste buds hadn't been conveying such information to his brain because the latter was too occupied with other thoughts.

As the last bite went down his throat, he hopped from the island and carried the empty carton to the trash can next to the fridge. With his gaze still fixed on its hulking yellow mass, his eyes caught a displaced Post-it Note. Trapped behind the many magnetic pictures and handwritten lists his wife had cluttered across the refrigerator's surface was the orange note.

He removed a three-by-five-inch plastic magnet housing a picture of his son sitting on a swing at school and peeled the item from the refrigerator door. "Fritz Brothers Concrete" had been written across the top in Pamela's penmanship.

Nick turned the Post-it over and over in his hand, remembering what Ramsey had told him about the traces of Mississippi pea gravel found on his floor. His mind also flipped to the blackened tools that now rested in the trunk of his car. Too many references to concrete had occurred in a short period of time. His mind raced as the sum of each component was added together. Concrete-bleached skin from the killer's body, traces of pea gravel on the floor, burned concrete finishing tools found in the abandoned car. It was all too coincidental to be just that. He fixed his gaze on the orange paper in his right hand.

"Fritz Brothers Concrete," he said to himself.

He didn't know anyone at that company, but Pamela must have, or their refrigerator wouldn't be holding reference to it. His mind now went into overdrive trying to calculate the implications. Had she been having an affair? Nah, he immediately dismissed that thought. Pamela was far from an adulteress. But still, could she have been? He slapped the indiscretion out of his mind and reprimanded himself for considering the possibility.

He pondered the mystery for a long time, trying to come up with an explanation. Finally, he remembered a conversation several weeks prior to her death. He had come home from work late one night and was exhausted. Pamela had greeted him at the door like she usually did and had asked him about his day. He had been so mentally fatigued that he wasn't in the mood to speak or deal with her chipper attitude. He could recall having snapped at her and feeling guilty about it later.

"I'm sorry, honey, you didn't deserve that," he had apologized that night when they finally went to bed.

"Deserve what?" she had asked, playing dumb.

"My insolent asshole attitude, that's what."

"Don't you mean, dickhead asshole attitude?" she had clarified.

"Yes, I'd say that's an accurate assessment," he had responded, while pulling her toward him in a playful headlock.

"Good. Now that we have that straight, I'd say you owe me a twenty-minute massage as penance."

"How about ten minutes? I'm really tired."

"Want to try for thirty, counselor?" she frowned while doing her best to look disgusted.

"No ma'am, twenty it is," he answered and began to massage her shoulders and back.

"That feels so good; I could go to sleep right now."

"Hey, I'm the one who worked all day. Shouldn't I be getting the massage?"

"Correction, you went to an office all day. I *worked*."

"Oh yeah?"

"Yeah. Want to trade? Tomorrow, I'll lounge around your office, and you can clean house, grocery shop, do laundry, and look after an attention starved five-year-old."

"No thanks!" he shot back quickly while continuing with the massage.

"So how was the office, anyway? Must have been shitty to put you in such a rotten mood."

"Oh you know, same old crap," he had said. "Some days it gets to me more than others, I guess. Anyway, enough about that garbage. Tell me more about *your* work."

"Well, let's see, after spending the morning picking up toys and drowning in laundry, I took your son to lunch and did some grocery shopping."

"What was on today's menu?"

"The usual—chicken nuggets."

"Geez, does the kid eat anything else?" Nick had chortled, picturing his son as a future KFC mascot.

"Not much. I think he would eat them every day if given the chance."

"Great, I'm going to be father to a pimple-faced fat kid when he gets older."

"Fat? Are you kidding? With his energy, he could eat cheesecakes all day and never gain a pound."

"Good thing he has your metabolism."

"Yeah, right," she smirked. "Oh hey, I almost forgot. I found someone who will pour us a new patio like you promised."

"Really, who?"

"Oh, just some guy I met in line at McDonald's."

"Picking up guys at McDonald's, huh? Must be desperate."

"You know how I love sweaty, blue-collar types," she had giggled.

"I guess tomorrow I better get down to the union and apply for a construction job," he had responded in mock redneck twang.

"You don't know how badly that turns me on," she had laughed, while rolling over to face him.

The minor squabble had been forgotten. They had made up like they always did. They had promised early in their marriage that they would never go to bed mad at each other, and it was a promise they had faithfully kept all the way to the end.

Nick hadn't thought about the discussion since. It was wintertime, and he hadn't been too keen on starting any yard projects until the spring. Pamela didn't bring up the patio again, either. This had been several weeks before her murder, and it seemed so insignificant at the time. Could the guy at McDonald's have been the one?

Still looking at the orange Post-it, he felt nauseated. A chance encounter with some maniac at a McDonald's might have led to his wife's death. He sprinted to the lower level bathroom and discharged the processed turkey and yogurt. He might not have been able to distinguish between food flavors, but the taste of bile was still poignant to his senses.

CHAPTER 13

▼

Rucker drove home in the early morning light, fighting off the sleep that threatened to overcome him. He'd been awake for nearly forty-eight hours and had imbibed several drinks during that time. He was finally hitting the wall and couldn't wait to get to his apartment, where he could pass out for the next half day.

With the weather still questionable, he doubted he'd be called on to work today. The foreman of his crew had told him the previous day that he didn't think they would need him anymore this week. He could use the money but wanted the sleep even more. Besides, it wasn't beneath him to rob a convenience store or an innocent bystander when he was really strapped for cash.

The seemingly endless drive home was almost over. He turned into his apartment complex, fighting desperately to keep his eyes open for another few minutes. He was so tired that his eyelids felt like lead, and keeping them open had become somewhat painful.

Swerving to avoid a pothole, he drilled a confused squirrel as it attempted in vain to get back to the safety of the trees bordering the road. Dumb fucking animal, he thought. They don't even try to cross until a car is nearly upon them. He enjoyed watching the animal bounce off his truck and into the grass lining the curb. He looked in the rearview mirror to see it flop a final time before succumbing to the fatal blow.

He had always hated animals. He had tortured a cat at his fourth foster home, earning him a trip to a juvenile psychiatric ward. The cat had irritated the shit out of him with its incessant purring and cold, uncomfortable stare. One day when the family was out, he cornered the frightened feline and jabbed at it with a fireplace poker while it hissed and slapped at the intrusive weapon.

Becoming bored with the game, he swung the poker violently at the cat, catching it squarely on the skull. He had watched in fascination as it staggered out of the corner and weaved a drunken line toward the center of the room. When it had gotten within a few paces, he charged it and punted the stunned animal back into the corner. Raising his hands victoriously in imitation of a referee, he signified that the field goal attempt had been good.

"Time for kickoff," he snapped.

He had dragged the mortally wounded pet out of the corner by its neck and considered another boot, but ended up fastening it to the showerhead via one of his foster dad's neckties instead. He watched with amusement as it twitched a few times before ceasing to move.

Upon closer inspection, he saw that it had still been breathing faintly. He jammed it into a shopping bag and took it into the woods with him where the real fun would begin. Over the next several hours, he carved out its remaining life with his pocketknife and watched the stages of dying unfold before his amazed eyes. He was particularly enamored by the blood flow, which was heavy during the animal's final moments but almost altogether coagulated once it finally perished.

The experience had been rewarding to young Gerald, and it began an animal onslaught that continued until he reached puberty. Sometimes he had tortured them, and sometimes the kills had been quick. Cats had been his favorite primarily because of their seemingly ill temper toward humans. Squirrels had been fun, too, but much harder to catch. He had devised a number of different traps and apparatuses useful for that purpose. One time he had dug a hole and managed to entice two raccoons to fall prey to his ruse.

Whatever the quarry, he always enjoyed the end result. He was merciless when it came to death's door and never let one of his captives free once he had the victim under his control. Burning ants and small bugs with lighters and magnifying glasses had been fun when he was a small boy, but it in no way had compared to dismantling a small animal.

By the time he reached his teen years, he had tired of the practice. The patterns exhibited by his trapped quarry had become too predictable, and he no longer derived pleasure from watching them die. It was on to bigger and better things, which promptly had led to his first human killing. He had never looked back from that point on, now more than a decade ago.

*   *   *   *

A day after finding the note posted on his refrigerator, Nick pulled onto the gravel road that led to the main hub for Fritz Brothers Concrete. The unpaved path joined a street in the St. Louis suburb of Maplewood and provided access to the office and equipment that Fritz Brothers used. Feeling a little nervous about drawing attention to himself, he was relieved to see there was a large gravel parking lot adjacent to the main yard. Beyond the lot stood a fenced-in piece of property, which housed dump trucks, jackhammers, Bobcats, and a multitude of other tools.

Pulling in beside an empty pickup truck, he surveyed the location from a seemingly inconspicuous perch. There were eight vehicles, mostly trucks, parked in the lot. Inside a chain-link fence there were more vehicles, each bearing the bright blue Fritz Brothers logo on the doors. He counted two flatbeds and two heavier dump trucks along with a trailer and two Bobcat machines. The rest of the load was probably out on jobs.

It was 2:00 PM on a reasonably nice day, so he imagined that the crew was busy in the field catching up on lost wages. The past few weeks had been lousy, which couldn't possibly be good for concrete work unless you were pouring inside a building somewhere.

Careful not to appear suspicious, he had borrowed his mother's Chevrolet and dressed down in a flannel shirt and pair of jeans. If questioned, he planned to say he was inquiring about work. Since many construction companies were union-fed, he thought the better of driving his foreign car to this place of business. He had heard all sorts of stories about the treatment of foreign vehicles on union lots. One of his friends had had his Volvo keyed three times at the local Chrysler plant before wising up and taking his wife's Ford to work.

A large barrel-chested man, braving the elements in nothing but a dirty white T-shirt and overalls, seemed to notice him. After eyeing him a few times while unloading one of the flatbeds, the man made his way over to Nick's vehicle. Nick got out to greet him, immediately wondering if this was the man who had infiltrated his life.

"Hi, my name's John. John Mathis," Nick said.

"Mathis? You mean like the queer singer?" the concrete worker retorted.

"Nope, not a singer and not queer, either."

"Something I could help you with, Mr. Mathis?"

Nick extended his hand and found it engulfed by the oversized meat hook of a giant. The man before him was probably six foot five and weighed every bit of 350 pounds. It wasn't sloppy weight, either, so Nick knew that if he was the perp, Pamela had never stood a chance. He watched helplessly during the handshake, hoping the guy wouldn't exert undue pressure and pulverize his hand.

"I'm Carl Fritz," the giant said; releasing Nick's hand unscathed, save for some minor discomfort.

"Hi, Carl. Good to meet you," Nick said, while trying not to show signs of pain from the man's viselike grip.

"Now, what can I help you with today?"

"I've seen your trucks in the area and was wondering if you had any job openings."

Carl looked Nick over carefully. His mouth formed the slight hint of a sarcastic grin.

"Mr. Mathis, you don't really look like the manual laboring type, if you know what I mean."

"Really? I worked on a highway crew in Tennessee for five years before moving here."

"You don't say?"

"Yeah. We repaved mostly interstates, but I had quite a bit of experience with concrete labor."

"Mr. Mathis, this is a slow time for us. Most of my crews are stuck at home because the weather hasn't been too cooperative lately," Carl replied, still not convinced.

"I know what you mean. It's not the best time of the year to be in this field."

"Uh, huh," Carl grunted. "Look, tell you what I'll do," he said, while scratching the unruly shock of hair on his chin that made him look like a ZZ Top wannabe. "Things is going to pick up for us real soon, and I'll be needing some more laborers. If you're still interested, come back here beginning of April, and I'll see what I can do."

"Thanks Carl, I appreciate it."

"Now, seeing as you're here and dressed for action, want to make a few bucks today?"

"Sure. What did you have in mind?"

"See that truck there?" Carl asked, pointing to a fully loaded dump truck at the rear of the lot.

"Yeah."

"That truck needs to be unloaded in the next twenty minutes so I can take her to another job site. If you give me a hand, I'll lay twenty bucks on ya."

"Seems fair," Nick responded, not wanting to show his growing regret for having shown up in the first place.

"OK then, let's get started," Carl said, slapping Nick on the back and nearly crushing several vertebrae in the process.

Nick suspected that this was a test. Problem was he really didn't want a job here. He just wanted to check out the crew and see if someone looked out of sorts or suspicious. Truth told he was now uncertain why he had come here at all. He guessed that he hoped one of the men would be wearing a sign that said, "I snuffed your wife," but decided that probably wasn't going to be the case. Now, as a result of giving into his curiosity, he would be forced to perform manual labor for the next half hour or so. He certainly wasn't opposed to physical work, but he could think of other ways to whittle away the afternoon.

The two men unloaded the truck in less than thirty minutes. It had been chock full of wheelbarrows, sledgehammers, lumber scraps, rolls of wire mesh, setting forms, and several other materials Nick wasn't sure about. After completing the job, Carl turned to him smiling.

"Didn't take you for much at first, but you's a pretty good worker. Yessir, I just might be able to put you to work sometime after all."

"Sounds great," Nick said feigning excitement at the prospect of getting a job with Fritz Brothers.

"OK, Mr. Mathis, you done good."

"Call me John."

"All right then, John, why don't you leave me your number and I'll be in touch?"

They walked to a small office attached to the yard. It was really little more than a twelve-by-twelve-foot square of cinder blocks with a tin roof and concrete pad for a floor. The tiny room housed a smallish metal desk, one three-drawer file cabinet, and a card table. On the card table was a coffeemaker, a thirteen-inch black-and-white television, and a fan that had so much grime on the blades that Nick highly doubted they still revolved.

"Here," said Carl, handing Nick a scrap of paper and a blue Paper Mate. "Give us your number, and I'll try to fit you in this spring."

Nick scribbled down his fictitious name and a fake phone number. He handed the paper scrap back to Carl and turned to leave.

"Oh, hey, almost forgot," Carl said as he pulled a folded twenty out of the dirty front pocket of his overalls.

With a hand so blackened from oil and soot that Nick wondered if Lava soap would ever render it clean again, Carl handed Nick the twenty.

"You know what, Carl? You keep the money. I really didn't do all that much."

"You sure?"

"Yeah, man. Just don't forget about me when you go to hire someone."

"All right, buddy, you got it," Carl responded, while immediately stuffing the bill back into his pocket.

Nick exited the yard through a slightly askew gate and moved hastily toward his car. He didn't figure Carl would try the number he just gave him but didn't want to be around if he did. He retreated to his mom's Chevy, already feeling the muscles in his arms and back screaming their displeasure at his brief employment with Fritz Brothers.

"I've got to start working out again," he told himself, knowing that the minor labor he had just performed would most likely lead to heavy soreness the next day.

As he started the car and began to back out of the lot, two additional pickups pulled in behind him. Gruff-looking workers exited each truck, giving him a passing glance on their way toward Carl's yard. He looked them both over carefully, trying to decide if either one could be the killer. He drove away from Fritz Brothers convinced that either of them could have been the guy; or maybe even big Carl for that matter. His visit to the yard had been a waste of time.

He missed Pamela, who he'd never see again, and his son, who he had virtually abandoned when he started this insane quest. Conflicted by mourning for Pamela, intense love for Justin, who needed him desperately right now, and a desire to maim the source of his discomfort; he was a jumbled mess of emotions. He had pushed this chase too far to turn back now, but it was starting to deplete his sanity.

*   *   *   *

Rucker's truck bounced along the gravel drive leading into Fritz Brothers' lot. He passed a gray Chevrolet with its reverse lights illuminated just prior to entering through the open gate. He looked at the Chevy's driver and for a split second felt some recognition, but he immediately lost interest and proceeded into the construction yard.

He could see Carl Fritz heading toward one of the empty trucks, and he hoped he wouldn't be asked to go somewhere with him. He had worked for the first time in a few days and it felt good to be back, but he still didn't want to do a ride-along with the boss. Carl was a good guy, but he asked a lot of questions and seemed to pry a little too heavily into his business. He certainly didn't have a need for that type of person in his life right now.

He was happy to be working again, though. The day had passed quickly and had helped divert his attention to something other than Lola. Now that his shift was most likely ending, she began to creep back into his thoughts again.

"Hey Carl, who's the stiff in the Chevy?" Rucker asked through a three-quarters lowered window.

"Oh, I don't know. Just some guy looking for work."

"He can jump to the back of the line then."

"Don't worry. I told him we aren't hiring right now."

"Good."

"Speaking of work, care to give me a hand cleaning up the Rothman job site?"

"Guess so," replied Rucker.

That's just *great*, he thought. Exactly what he didn't want to do is endure twenty questions from Carl Fritz today. On the flip side, it might be better than obsessing over Lola. It was becoming more and more difficult to stop thinking about her. Several times recently, he had awakened from a deep sleep wanting to drive to her apartment. He wasn't sure how much longer he could stifle that impulse. He knew that it wouldn't be long before mission twenty-one took place. He hoped to be able to toy with her a few more times at The Pie Factory before his desires overcame him.

He parked his truck next to the company issue vehicle and climbed into the passenger's side. A couple more hours of work might do him some good, as long as the fat hippy didn't overdo it with the questions.

*   *   *   *

It was five thirty and dark out when Rucker and his boss returned to the Fritz Brothers lot. Suddenly energized by a solid day's work and not wanting to let go of the adrenaline, he decided he was due for another visit to The Pie Factory. It had been nearly a week, and no matter how hard he tried to push Lola out of his mind, she had an odd knack for revisiting his thoughts on a more or less continual basis.

He had to see her again. Lola. Sweet Lola. Admiring her from afar was starting to become more than he could bear. He felt his resistance weakening and knew that during one of his next couple of visits, he would no longer be able to control himself. He began the mental preparations for their final meeting. His heart beat wildly as he played out the final act in his head. He cautioned himself to remain calm; otherwise, he might mess the whole thing up. He tried to force the fantasy out of his mind, but it was too strong. The diverted thoughts of food and sports were quickly replaced by Lola's smiling face. He had to have her, and the time was fast approaching.

He decided he'd go to the Factory one last time to finalize his plan. He needed to see her again to refuel the fire that was now stoked to a roaring inferno. One last "dance" with her at the Factory and then he'd have to give in to the mission. He still hated to end the game, but it was beyond his control. The voice that dictated much of his behavior had taken over. "Take her now," it urged. "She's ready for you." He could no longer ignore the impulse, no matter how desperately he wanted to. Yes, this would be their final meeting before he owned her. He would have one last opportunity to let her wait on him before she was no longer able to wait on anyone else ever again.

"Good day today, Carlton," Carl Fritz said as he got out of the loaded truck.

Carlton, as Rucker was known at Fritz Brothers, got out, too, and hoped that Carl wouldn't have it in him to unload the truck tonight.

"Now go on home and get some rest. I'll need you early tomorrow, and you can start your day by unloading this truck."

"OK Carl, I'll see you," Rucker said, happy that Carl was letting him call it a day.

With that, he got into his own truck and headed home. It was still early. He could shower, get something to eat, and make his way to the Factory in plenty of time to spend the evening watching Lola. Her shift wouldn't even start for a few hours, so he had plenty of time. He might even squeeze a little nap in to make sure he was sharp when he saw her.

Lola. Thoughts of her danced in his head all the way home. In a short period of time, she would be Lola no mo', he reasoned.

"Hey, that almost rhymes," he said aloud to himself while pulling into his apartment complex.

He then launched into a hideous version of the song "Lola," inserting his own key buzzwords, which followed a completely different theme.

"L-o-l-a, Lola, I can't wait to own ya," he blared while laughing at his own warped creativity.

*   *   *   *

Riding a multiday high from her recent enrollment trip to the area college, Angela was oddly ready to go to work. Knowing that her future would not be permanently dependent upon gigs like The Pie Factory, she seemed to have a stronger stomach for the usual antics that accompanied a night in that horrid, smoky dump.

Upon finishing a six-hour shift at Jacobson's, she went home to clean up. She shifted mental gears and tried to systematically make the change from the conservative look of khakis and a long-sleeve denim shirt into the "uniform" required by The Pie Factory.

Arriving just five minutes before her shift, she donned her apron and embarked on another long night of slinging drinks, kissing up to ugly misfits, and attempting to thwart their advances while still enticing them enough to earn a decent gratuity. The entire act was a delicate game that she had learned to balance perfectly. Still, there had been many times when the customer thought his tip bought much more than a pat on the butt or grazing of the breast. When that had happened, she relied on one of the Factory's beefy bouncers to rescue her. She could probably handle most of these losers herself, but it might be damaging to future funds if she rendered a regular customer unconscious. Years of physically defending herself had taught her numerous effective moves. When in doubt, attack the family jewels. That had become her motto.

Of course, enlisting a bouncer's assistance often led him to believe that the *save* had qualified him for much more than a verbal thank you. That was another aspect of being able to balance the numerous skills necessary to survive in this business. Most of the time, she was able to get off easy by purchasing the overgrown meathead a drink. If that wasn't enough, she relied on her verbal artillery to do the job. None of these stiffs could match her intellect, so the mental sparring was generally enough to save her butt. The fragileness of the male ego never ceased to amaze her. A couple of small penis remarks usually sent the muscle-bound retard away admonished.

This evening, she was prepared for nearly anything. A few years at the Factory had taught her to expect the unexpected and never let her guard down. Renewed energy involving her scholastic future had enabled her to view this situation as nothing but a temporary job. Before she knew it, she'd be on to bigger and better things. Or so she thought.

She grabbed her serving tray, pasted on a smile that was Academy Award-worthy, and jiggled her way to the first table of the night. "Great," she muttered to herself through closed teeth, "It's the creepy guy." He had been frequenting the joint lately. He first arrived on the scene a few weeks ago. Initially, he kind of blended in with all the rest of the sex-starved, maladjusted losers who showed up on a weekly or sometimes nightly basis.

After a few visits, she began to notice a pattern. He always sat in her section and never watched any of the dancers. He kept his attention primarily on her. She had mentioned it to her boss, who also doubled as the head bartender.

"What do you want me to do about it, ask him to leave? Fuck, Ang, he's a paying customer, and he's done nothing wrong," he replied.

Yet.

She accepted the minor lashing and decided to suck it up and serve him just like everyone else. Even so, there was still something not quite right about this guy. The way he stared at her kind of freaked her out. She'd been stared at plenty throughout her life, but this was different. He had an intensity about him that was completely unsettling. She couldn't explain it, even to herself, but her intuition told her that this guy was bad news. She'd have to keep a close watch on him and make sure help was always nearby when she went to his table.

"Jack and Coke again tonight, sweetie?"

Gag, she thought to herself. She wasn't sure that kissing up to this weirdo was worth the extra money. But then again, she desperately needed the money and he was an exceptional tipper.

The guy at the table nodded and smiled, making the look on his face even more uncomfortable to bear. She retreated from the table, took a deep breath, and kept telling herself that this wouldn't be going on much longer. A couple of solid years at the junior college—maybe even a promotion at the grocery store—and she'd be able to give up this nightmare job.

"Jack and Coke, Lenny."

"Ah, your buddy's back," the bartender laughed.

"Yeah, whatever. Just give me the damn drink."

"Hey, watch the fucking attitude, missy. Cheap-ass cocktail waitresses are a dime a dozen."

"Sorry, it's just that you know he weirds me out."

"Don't sweat him, honey, all of these guys should weird you out," he laughed, revealing several brown and yellow teeth that had been victimized by too much Skoal over the years.

"You're right, he's just another customer."

"Here you go, babe, one Jack and Coke for your *boyfriend*," he said. He spread the grin wider this time, revealing such a deep brown that Angela suspected he ate shit sandwiches to accompany his incessant tobacco chewing.

"OK, back to the table, smile, drop off the drink, and run away," she whispered to herself.

"Here you go, baby. That'll be four dollars," she said while wrapping the short glass in a bar napkin and setting it on the table.

"Keep the change," Rucker said, while handing her a ten. "You look happy tonight," he added.

"Do I?"

"Yeah, at least happier than usual."

"I guess I'm always happy," she winked.

"Well, the smile looks good on you," he leered.

"Thanks, baby. And thanks for the tip," she punctuated it by touching his shoulder.

The last gesture made her want to vomit, but experience had taught her that light touches to nonthreatening body parts generally inspired the customers to keep the good tips coming. She left the table trying not to look hurried but could feel his eyes on her all the way back to the bar. Not much longer, she kept telling herself. Not much longer.

CHAPTER 14

▼

"Nick, it's Tyrell."

"What's up, Tyrell?"

"Nothing man. Just wanted to let you know that the cracker me and Tommy was telling you about is back at his favorite place."

"Really?"

"Yeah. I just got off the phone with Tommy. I guess he just got there or something."

"Thanks, Tyrell," Nick said as he glanced at his watch.

It was 10:00 PM. Going out to The Pie Factory wasn't Nick's idea of a great evening, but it sounded better than tossing and turning in bed all night waiting for the sandman, who rarely seemed to visit these days. Besides, he had to know if this was the guy. It was the only real lead he had, and it felt right.

"So what's you gonna do, man?" Tyrell asked.

"I don't know. I haven't gotten that far yet."

"Needs some help?"

"Thanks, but I should probably do this alone. I don't want to get you messed up in this whole thing."

"Been messed up in a lot worse than this, Nick," Tyrell chuckled.

"You got that right, buddy, but I can handle this one on my own."

"All right, my brother, but if you change your mind, you knows where to find me."

"Thanks again. I appreciate the offer."

With that, they clicked off. Nick's mind began to whirl in circles trying to decide what exactly he was going to do when he saw this guy. Was it even the guy he was looking for? If so, how would he know? A million questions surfaced, none of which came with any clear answers. He decided to trust his instincts and see where fate took him. All the while, he tried not to let his mind wander to a place that he didn't want to go. That was the place where he encountered a dangerous and psychotic killer all because of his desire to exact revenge. He couldn't let himself consider the consequences he might face during a failed meeting with this guy, not to mention what it would do to his son, who was already one parent down. He quickly stifled the last thought and let the burning quest for revenge born of anger and despair dictate his actions. He grabbed his keys and headed to The Pie Factory in search of his unwelcome destiny.

*   *   *   *

Tommy Hunt sipped on his beer while leaning against the bar. He shifted his attention between the exotic dancers on two stages in the center of the room and the front door. He was now sorry he had told Tyrell that the strange dude was back at The Pie Factory again. His gaze bounced nervously between his two objectives. He would have loved nothing more than to take a few bills over to the stage and let a pair of big tits flop around on his face for a while. Unfortunately, he had to wait for the white lawyer to show up. He was starting to feel uneasy about the whole thing. What if this weird cracker found out he was fingering him for something? He still vividly remembered their brief encounter at the garage and had rather hoped he'd never see the guy again.

Now, he was pointing him out for some guy he didn't know, and he had no idea why. The lawyer better make good on his promise to make it worth his while financially, that's all he knew. He was too old to be messing around with shit like this anymore. All he wanted to do was belly up to the stage and buy him a little tail.

With his beer half-empty, he took another look at the front door. The lawyer had five more minutes and then Tommy was going to put his time and his money to better use. He looked at his worn silver Timex and mentally started the clock.

*   *   *   *

Nick pulled into the parking lot, which was prominently marked by a large glowing sign that read "The Pie Factory" in neon red. He couldn't believe he was there. Worse yet, he couldn't believe how his life had changed. Fate had played an ugly card, and now everything was out of control. It wasn't that long ago that a night like tonight would have been spent in front of the fireplace at home in the blissful company of his wife and child.

The heavy metal group Cinderella had been unwitting prophets. "Don't know what you got 'til it's gone," they had sung. Got that right, he thought. He parked toward the side of the lot in a space that wasn't lit by streetlights or the bar's sign. He figured he'd let Tommy point out the subject and then he'd go back to his car and wait for the man to leave. Beyond that, he wasn't sure what he'd do next. Maybe get a plate number and have it traced? He might even follow him, but he feared it would give up his element of surprise and cost him a slight advantage.

He drew in a deep breath, cut the engine, and walked toward the dumpy joint that was home to bachelor parties, lonely losers, and perverted fantasies. Somewhere inside those four seedy walls might be the maniac who had suddenly and unacceptably changed his life. Empowered by his anger, he strode across the parking lot and entered the dimly lit strip club.

$*$ $*$ $*$ $*$

Tommy thumped his watch a final time, grabbed his now warm Budweiser bottle and tipped it to the sky. Eyes watering slightly from the big swig, he set the bottle back on the bar and tried to decide which stage he'd go sit by.

Just as he made his selection, he noticed the front door swing open out of the corner of his eye. He looked over and immediately recognized the lawyer Tyrell had brought to see him in the stockyards. Not wanting to be noticed by the other customers, he waited for eye contact and motioned quickly toward the restroom. He turned and headed toward the men's room without looking back. He was confident no one else had noticed and hoped the lawyer wouldn't be obvious about it, either.

He shouldered the bathroom door open and waited apprehensively for the lawyer to follow him in. Now he just wanted to get this over with so he could turn his attention to the girls and stop worrying about the rest of this nonsense. He ducked down and checked each stall to make sure no one else was in the bathroom. Assured that he was alone, he took up a post at one of the piss-stained urinals and prepared to go about his business.

*   *   *   *

Nick's eyes, already adjusted from the darkness of the parking lot, fell on Tommy Hunt immediately. The frail black man was leaning up against the bar just twenty feet inside the room. Tommy must have recognized him, too, because he pointed into the distance and took off. Nick assumed that was his queue to follow.

He had picked up on Tommy's nervousness the last time they met. Something about the guy he was looking for had really disturbed the old man. Respectful of his fear, he was careful not to blow Tommy's cover. He looked around the room as if he was checking out the joint. He then went to the bar and ordered a Bud Light. He gave the bartender eight dollars for the outrageously priced lager and followed Tommy to the restrooms.

Once inside the men's room, he saw Tommy taking a leak at one of the room's two pissers. The smell of bad hygiene and urine filled the air. He advanced to the lone remaining urinal and continued to follow along with the absurd cloak-and-dagger act. Never saying a word, he stared straight ahead willing to let the old man dictate the next move.

"He's wearing all black and sitting at a table by himself just a little ways away from the right stage," Tommy whispered in a hush voice.

That was it. Tommy zipped up and paused for a moment at the sink, waiting for the fruits of his effort. Nick joined him at the remaining sink and washed his hands. He folded a fifty-dollar bill into a paper hand towel and left it on the sink before exiting the restroom.

Tommy appreciated Nick's discretion and waited for him to leave before snatching up the towel. He could now buy a couple more beers and probably a table dance or two. Smiling, he could no longer remember why he had been nervous about this meeting in the first place.

Exiting the men's room, Nick scanned the bar, searching for the right stage. He wasn't sure where he had to be standing to demonstrate the right versus left stage but was relieved to see that not many of the tables surrounding the two stages had been occupied.

Immediately in front of him was one of the two main stages with another just beyond it. Two dancers were on the closest stage grooving to "Shook Me All Night Long" while doing their best to live up to the title. The second stage was currently empty, but there was a guy in black sitting fairly near it. A few other customers occupied intermittent tables in between, but Nick was sure he was now locked onto the guy he was there to see.

It took everything in his power not to sprint straight to the table and tackle the guy. He let discretion get the better of him and decided to play it cool. Besides, he didn't even know for sure that this was the same guy he was hunting. Instinct, however, told him it was. Trying not to draw the man's attention, he circled the first stage, pretending to admire the show. Along the way, he stole a glance toward the man in black who didn't seem to be paying attention to much of anything. In this lighting, it was hard to draw parallels with the police artist's sketch.

He found an unoccupied table to the left of the first stage. It bore a straight-on shot of the man dressed in black. Perfect. He could observe the man and make it look like he was watching the girls. He took up a chair and began his surveillance. After doing this bit for nearly twenty minutes, he decided it was odd that the man never seemed to look at the strippers. Wasn't that the reason people came to places like this? Unless of course, you were stalking your wife's killer, he mused.

The man never seemed to be looking at anything, and it had become unnerving. He had an unsettling presence about him. Nick could tell from a distance that he was probably in his late twenties or early thirties. He had thinning black hair and an unseasonably dark tan. He wore a black turtleneck that tightly covered what Nick suspected to be a decent-size build. His features were somewhat nondescript and muted by the semidarkness of the room, except for his eyes. Even from this distance, they seemed like black diamonds, glowing in the dim bar lighting. He could see why Tommy had said that he had eyes that could look right through your head.

He staked out the man's table for more than an hour, trying to decide what to do next. He just couldn't seem to pull his eyes away from the guy, while trying to figure out if he was the one without having the benefit of any solid evidence to support his belief. After awhile, it became apparent why the man was there. He would sit motionless staring off into space, except when a certain young waitress walked by. Every time that happened, he seemed to morph into an entirely different being. Nick watched him closely and could tell that the young beauty enraptured him. He could see why; she was quite striking.

He now wondered if the man was actually staking out the waitress. He began to feel anxious, thinking that she could be his next victim. He was now more desperate than ever to find out if this really was the guy he was trying to find. He finished off his beer, dropped a couple of dollars on the table, and left the bar.

He got into his car and decided to wait for the man to leave. From his vantage point, he'd be able to see everyone who came and went. With only about a dozen cars on the lot, it would be easy to see which one belonged to the man in black. Once he left, he would attempt to follow him as discreetly as possible. His mind raced with the possibilities. What if this really was the guy? If so, what would he do once they met? The answer was always clear whenever the latter question came to mind. Now he just had to prove that he was on the right trail. Once he did, nature would take its course, and justice would be served once and for all.

*   *   *   *

It was just after 3:00 AM, and Rucker knew Lola would be finishing her shift shortly. He decided to make his way back to her apartment and wait for her. He didn't know what he would do once she got there, but he was fairly confident the voice or instinct would appropriately take over. He liked watching her enter the apartment building. He imagined what she was doing once she was home alone. She probably undressed right away and took a shower. He imagined her tight little body glistening under the running water and soon felt a fire burning in his loins.

Quieting the voice had become more and more difficult with each passing day. In the past, he had always given in to its beckoning calls. Once the message was clear, he followed its instructions without delay. This time, he was trying desperately to ignore its pleas, but they were becoming more and more insistent.

"The time is now," it said. "Don't put this off any longer, or you'll be sorry!"

He knew he wouldn't be able to continue to turn a deaf ear toward the voice. Its origin came from his master, and it wasn't wise to ignore the master. He would follow its instructions as he had always done in the past. This might even be the last time he'd be able to watch Lola go about her normal routine. He had a big surprise for her and hoped she'd be as excited about it as he was. Somehow he knew that she would.

*   *   *   *

Finally, the man in black was leaving the club. Nick shook the sleepiness from his body and looked at his watch, which read 3:11 AM. He'd been sitting in the parking lot for more than two hours. He might have dozed off a couple of times but quickly snapped himself awake each time he felt the enticing call of a peaceful slumber. Stretching to get the blood flowing through his limbs again, he turned on the car just after the man in black climbed into his own vehicle.

What now? He had been tentative about following the man but knew this might be his last chance. If the guy really were stalking the waitress, he probably wouldn't return to The Pie Factory after he had finished her off. He certainly hoped he was wrong about his theory, but suspected that he couldn't be more right. Taking care not to alert the man, Nick pulled out of the parking lot a full thirty seconds after he had departed. He could see his taillights just ahead and began to follow him. Not once in his life had he ever performed surveillance on another human being. It felt weird in a way but kind of exciting, too.

Now fully alert from the surge of the chase, he did his best not to look conspicuous as his car performed like a stealth bomber, keeping the white pickup within striking distance as it slipped into the night. Every time the man turned, Nick sped up a little to make sure he didn't miss the next turn. He was able to maintain a safe distance behind and felt confident he hadn't revealed himself yet.

A couple of times, another car pulled onto the road between them. These streets were a hotbed for after-hours activity, so it really wasn't unusual for people to be milling about at three in the morning. He was happy for the frequent interference from other motorists and used each opportunity to draw closer to the man's truck without appearing out of the ordinary.

After driving for fifteen minutes, the man pulled into an apartment complex. This was going to be tricky, Nick thought. It would be difficult to continue the chase without alerting the man to his presence. He slowly pulled into the complex and scanned each passing street, squinting anxiously into the dark for any sign of the pickup. Thankful that the vehicle was bright, Nick located it in the third parking lot to his right. He passed the lot and went to the next street, where he made a left and parked his car in an empty space. He killed the lights but kept the motor running. Somewhere just one street over was most likely the person responsible for taking Pamela away from him. He shook with anticipation and rage. It was all he could do to keep himself from immediately returning the favor. He took several deep breaths and tried to calm down. This might not even be him, he kept telling himself. His subconscious sang a different tune.

*   *   *   *

Rucker sat in his truck and felt the temperature within the cab begin to fall immediately. He lit a cigarette and blew smoke through the slightly cracked window. The nicotine seemed to warm him as he drew in another deep inhalation.

Any moment now, Lola would return. He trembled slightly at the thought but wrote it off to the cold.

He could break into the apartment ahead of her and be waiting when she got home. The idea was tempting, but that wasn't quite how he had pictured their final act. As the fire within had grown ever hotter, he realized it had started to overcome him. It was precisely at this point when he made final arrangements to answer the voice within and fulfill his appointed assignment.

After tonight, he would make preparations for the long-awaited finality he had dreamed of. He would need to boost a car this week and purchase new clothes. His knife sat in the closet, calling to him nearly as loudly as the voice. The knife had a voice of its own and, in concert with the voice in his head, could not be ignored.

It might take a couple of days to make the final arrangements. If he did it tonight, he knew he risked making several incriminating mistakes. He'd never been hasty in the past, and he wasn't going to start now. Despite the insatiable hunger within, he still needed to take all necessary precautions. He had stayed in this town a little longer than most and suspected it was probably just about time to move on. Soon he'd be searching out another location complete with a multitude of exciting new prospects. First there was Lola. Little Lola would make this his favorite resting place to date.

Thinking of her excited him in a way that he'd never been excited before. He rapidly went through the mental checklist of things to do before he could make her his own. When he was ready to make the final move, he'd pack his belongings into the truck. He had a tarp to cover the bed, so he could have it completely packed the night before he decided to conclude the mission.

It was now Friday, so he had until Monday before Lola worked again. There was much to do and not a lot of time to do it. He was so excited he could hardly contain himself. He had dreamed of this moment so often that it was incredible to think that it was nearly upon him. He shivered with delight, picturing what Lola would look like with a knife sticking out of her chest.

*   *   *   *

Shivering in his car, Nick couldn't take the suspense any longer. He had to go check out the white truck and hoped to find something that proved whether this was the man he was seeking. Maybe he'd get a better look at his face and be able to match it to the sketch. He stepped out into the cold and crept around the apartment building toward the parking lot where he had last seen the man. He thought about someone seeing him lurking around the buildings and calling the cops. That would certainly be fitting, he thought.

Following a sidewalk that circled one set of units, he spied the truck less than a hundred yards away. He began to creep closer when he saw a glowing in the front seat. The man was still in the truck.

"What had it been, ten minutes since they arrived here?" he questioned. "What the hell is he still doing in the truck?"

Then it all rang clear. The man didn't live here. With one well-crafted guess, he suspected he'd be seeing the cute little waitress from The Pie Factory any time now.

Crouching in some bushes, watching the intermittent glow from the man's cigarette, he waited. His knees began to stiffen from sitting in the catcher's position for more than five minutes. He was trying uncomfortably to shift his weight when the lights from an approaching car sparkled across the snow patches surrounding his cover.

A red Escort swung into the parking lot, grinding snowmelt salt as it snatched up the last parking space in front of the apartment building. From his spot in the bushes, he was only about fifteen yards from the car. He wasn't surprised to see the waitress from the strip club get out of the car and hustle up the wooden walkway leading to the nearby apartment building.

His instincts had proven correct. The man in black had been following the waitress, just as he had been following the man. What an unlikely triangle they made. Turning slightly to face the apartments, he saw a second-floor light come on. The silhouette of a young girl flashed across the shade momentarily, and then the window darkened.

He knelt, holding his breath, and contemplating what to do next. Would the guy break into her apartment? Expecting the truck door to open at any instant, he watched with bated breath. Nothing happened. The glowing cigarette was gone. It was almost as if the man had escaped the cab without Nick even knowing it. Had he? It was dark, but he was sure from this distance he would have noticed or at least heard the door open.

In answer to his question, the truck fired up as cold exhaust spewed from its tail pipes. He wasn't going into the apartment. He was leaving. Nick forced himself quickly from a cramped position and hurried around to the rear of the building. Breaking into a rapid jog, he pressed his keyless entry and unlocked his car door. He jammed the key into the ignition and started the engine. He now had to pull out of the apartment complex and resume his chase without tipping off the man in black.

"Let the games begin," he said.

*   *   *   *

Rucker finally arrived home. He had been awake for twenty-four hours but still felt strangely energetic. He owed that to seeing Lola again. Her face and body had cycled through his mind the entire way back to his apartment. The clock on his dash now read 4:12 AM. He'd have to get up for work in less than two hours, but he didn't care. Carl had asked him to work on Saturday to catch up on some jobs that had been put on hold by the weather. He thought it was a good excuse to keep his mind off of Lola since she wouldn't be working that evening, anyway. Of course, he *could* pay her a visit at her apartment.

No, he thought. Not yet. Despite every nerve ending imploring him to speed up the plan, he had to stick to it. Sloppiness had never been part of his missions, and he wasn't about to deviate from a successful formula this late in the game. He'd quell the voices and desires until Monday, when Lola would be forced to serve him a final time. Little did she know that drinks wouldn't be involved this time. He was certainly ready. Was she?

He had been so entranced by thoughts of Lola that he never noticed the black Lexus running in and out of his rearview mirror throughout the ride home. It was starting to appear that the hunter had become the hunted. Rucker was completely unaware as he entered his apartment, flipped on the bathroom light, and looked at the haggard reflection staring back at him from the vanity mirror.

"Who would want that?" he thought as he rubbed the premature age lines sprouting from the corners of his eyes.

"Lola, that's who, can't you tell? Didn't you see the way she looked at you?" asked the voice. "Lola wants you, and it's time you stop fucking around and take her!"

He looked away from the mirror and snapped off the light, willing the voice to disappear when he could no longer see his reflection. He cupped both hands over his ears and tried to block it out while conjuring up the sweeter tones emitted by Lola herself. Yes, she did want him, he decided. He went to bed feeling she was thinking of him, too.

*   *   *   *

By the time the man in black reached his inner-city apartment building, Nick's mental and physical tanks were both empty. It was after four, and he was riding the heels of another week without much sleep. Staying behind the white pickup had been an arduous task. Very little traffic on the roadways forced him to stay well behind the truck, but not so far that he lost it entirely.

Once they reached the city, he was relieved to find that most of the traffic lights had switched to blinking yellow. Even then, he had to let his prey get so far ahead that it was sometimes guesswork picking the right street to resume the chase. A light dusting of new snow had been falling, making the search more manageable. Following the fresh tracks helped him maintain a reasonable distance without having to reflect his headlights in the truck's rearview mirror very often.

Somehow it all worked out, because he was now parked one street away from the man's truck. His car was positioned behind the backside of the apartment building that the man had entered. He watched intently, hoping to see lights come on in one of the units of the building. Finally, a small window shrouded in frosted glass lit up with bright white lighting. Nick made a mental note that the window was on of the second floor and attached to the unit farthest to his left. He drove around to the front of the building and scratched the address onto a piece of paper: 132 Minnesota Avenue, apartment number 2C. Next to the address he added the Missouri plate number 745HK.

There, he had it. Rejuvenated from his successful detective portrayal, he drove back to his parents' house while plotting the next move. Knowing what the man drove and where he lived should make it easier to check out the apartment and search for something linking this guy to Pamela's murder.

He couldn't reconcile whether he wanted to confirm his beliefs. On the one hand, it would be a relief to know who had perpetrated the crime, thus enabling him to enact sweet revenge. On the other hand, he was almost afraid of the confirmation. That would make everything a reality, and he'd be forced to take the necessary actions. He wondered if Ramsey or the Feds had made similar progress. Would they arrive before him and deprive him of his moment? It shouldn't matter as long as the murderer was caught, but Nick still wanted a crack at this freak himself. The cliché that "it wouldn't bring her back" ran through his mind again with little meaning. Maybe it wouldn't bring her back, but it would solve the mystery and rid the world of this menace. He didn't want another human being to suffer a loss as a result of the actions of this killer. Whatever the methodology, he just wanted the ordeal to end. He knew he'd never rest again without knowing who had heinously disrupted his life and that of his son. He wanted to know the why behind it as well but figured he could settle for the who.

It was blind luck that he had stumbled upon a good suspect, which made him believe it to be an act of fate. He was by no means an investigator but had spent enough time around criminals to be able to end up on the right track. The moment of truth was fast approaching, and he'd have to prepare himself for the final reckoning.

He finished the twenty-five minute drive home in a trance, thinking about Pamela, picturing her sitting peacefully under an electric blue sky on a sugar white beach in Destin, Florida. The family had vacationed there the previous summer, and he had decided that she never looked more beautiful than the day they first arrived. She had been dressed in a somewhat conservative white bikini. He hadn't been able to peel his eyes from her voluptuous tanning body or her luminous face.

The three of them had been blissfully happy that day, playing in the surf while letting it wash away all of life's worries. He hadn't wanted the moment to end, but like everything else, it had. Now he clung to the memory with all the strength his mind's eye could muster as he prepared to unleash all of his rage and passion on the monster who had made the creation of any future memories impossible. His teeth ground together as the cold, dark eyes of the man he had been pursuing all evening replaced Pamela's visage.

"I will make you pay," he muttered through clenched teeth as he pulled into his parents' driveway.

CHAPTER 15

▼

Nick awoke to the smell of frying bacon and fresh coffee. His appetite had finally returned to normal. He looked at his watch, which read 7:35 AM. He'd only been asleep for a few hours, but he felt strangely refreshed. The gut feeling that he was onto something regarding the case had refueled his energy tank. He slipped into a pair of sweatpants and a T-shirt and headed for the kitchen. His mom would probably ask him a million questions about where he went and what time he got home, but the desire to eat a home-cooked breakfast outweighed the unavoidable interrogation.

"Morning, Mom," he grumbled, bracing for a prying avalanche of questions and innuendos.

"Good morning, honey. Sleep well?"

"Yeah I did," he responded, sensing one of her famous interrogations.

"I thought you could use a decent breakfast before you started your day."

"Sounds good, thanks," he replied warily, wondering when the inquisition would begin.

"Eggs, bacon, toast, and grits, coming right up."

Damn, was she cheerful, he thought. There has to be more to it than just this. She's softening me up before hammering me with an onslaught of leading questions, he concluded.

"Here you go, honey, a big breakfast made for a growing young man."

"Thanks, Mom," he answered, all the while thinking she was addressing him like he was a small child. "Has she gone nuts?" he wondered.

He scarfed down the meal, ignoring his mother's continual stare. He knew she was appraising him, waiting for an opportune moment to meddle without setting him off. He'd read this script with her a thousand times and knew how to throw her off the game plan—*most* of the time.

"Can I get you anything else?" she asked.

"No, Mom, that was great," he replied, wiping the last remnants of egg yoke and extra-crisp bacon crumbs from the corners of his mouth.

"Oh, OK."

"Here it comes," he thought. He knew there was no way to avoid it.

"There's just one more thing, and then I'll let you get to your day," she said.

"Yeah?" Nick asked with raised eyebrows that said, "Tread lightly."

"Look, honey, I know it's none of my business, but I was just wondering when you were going to start spending time with your son."

"Mom, don't go there," he reprimanded. "And you're right; it's none of your business."

"I know you've got a lot on your mind, and I really don't mind watching him. I honestly don't mind at all, it's just…" she trailed off.

"OK, let's get it out. It's just what?" Nick asked, beginning to lose tolerance for the topic.

"Fine, I'm just going to say it, and you can be mad at me if you want."

"Good, say it so we can stop playing this ridiculous game and I can go about my business."

"I might be wrong, Nick, but I think I know what your *business* is these days."

His eyes questioned, but he did not speak.

"You're looking for him, aren't you?"

He broke eye contact, realizing he was talking to the one person he could never fool.

"Look, you don't have to answer. I just wanted to tell you that your son needs you right now."

"You think I don't know that?" he asked, with irritation flooding his voice.

"You may know it, but you sure don't act like it," she shot right back.

"Is that right?" he added sarcastically.

"Don't get smart with me, young man. You may be grown up, but I'm still your mother."

Nick scowled at her but didn't talk back this time.

"I don't want your apologies. What I want you to do is to start living your life again. It's been weeks," she pleaded. "Whatever it is you're doing out there is not going to change the fact that she's gone."

"I know that, Mom, I just can't seem to let it go."

"Nick, it's time that you do let it go. It's time that you let her go, too. Did you ever stop to consider what might happen if you did find him? Do you even know what you'd do?"

"I have some ideas," Nick replied, maintaining an edge to his tone.

"Well, suppose it doesn't work out? Have you ever stopped to consider what your son would do if he lost his remaining parent right now? And what if you do take care of this business without getting hurt or worse? What then? Have you stopped to consider what it would be like to have your son visit you in prison?"

He hadn't really thought about that, but the image wasn't pretty. Justin had been through enough, and visiting his father behind bars would certainly add obstacles to an already difficult road ahead.

"Honey, I know how much you loved her. Believe me, we all did. But no matter what you do right now, it's not going to change the fact that she's gone."

She paused for effect, letting her words sink in.

"I don't think this is what Pamela would want, either."

The last sentence was the final dagger. Nick sat at the kitchen table, crestfallen. For the past two months, finding his wife's killer had given him a sense of purpose. It was a driving force that enabled him to not only cope, but also to avoid reality. He realized that everything his mom had just said was emphatically true. The worst part was he knew with absolute certainty that Pamela would not approve. That was the thing that ate at him the most.

"I just want you to think about these things, Nick. You're not a killer. You're a sweet person who had something horrible happen to him. What you're feeling is completely natural, but it's time to move on. Your son needs you. Your father and I adore you and want you to be happy again. Go back to work and start rebuilding your life. No one ever said it would be easy, but you have a lot of people in your corner. We'll help you get through this."

"I know that you're right. It's just so hard."

"You're a born survivor, Nicholas Lacour. I promise that you'll get through this and life will get better," she finished.

She hadn't called him Nicholas since he was about eight. Right now, he felt about as helpless as an eight-year-old. He grabbed his mother and hugged her tight.

"Thank you, Mom. I think you've helped me to see the light."

After a long embrace, he let go. It really was time to start rebuilding his life. The prospect scared him, but he knew it was the only thing to do. He got up from the table and went to his room to change clothes. He needed to visit Ramsey and clue him in on all that he knew. Despite his desire to avenge Pamela's death, he knew it was time to leave this to the authorities.

*   *   *   *

Rucker woke with another headache. The long drinking nights followed by short hours of sleep and full days of work were brutalizing his body. He'd been doing it as long as he could remember, but only recently had it started to bother him. It was after eight thirty, and he was on his way to the job site. He overslept and was forced to call Carl Fritz to let him know he'd have to go straight to the job. He made up some bullshit about having a dental appointment to fix a toothache.

With his mind still fuzzy, he drove nearly all the way to the Fritz Brothers lot before he remembered he was supposed to be going directly to the location of the job. The crew was pouring a driveway somewhere in St. Louis County and he now realized that he had also forgotten to bring along the directions he wrote down just an hour ago.

Maybe the liquor and late nights were starting to add up. He was becoming more and more forgetful and feared he'd make a crucial error when it counted most, while performing one of his coveted missions. He didn't care so much how it affected his job. He'd be leaving that shortly, anyway. Messing up while on a mission, however, was not acceptable.

He swung into the Fritz Brothers lot to see if anyone was around. The gate was locked, and all of the commercial vehicles were gone. He'd be forced to return home to retrieve the directions. He cursed himself and quickly spun the car around in the lot, spitting up gravel as his spinning tires swatted away all loose obstructions. They finally grabbed solid ground, and, irritated, he peeled out of the lot. He vaguely remembered part of what he had written, but he was barely paying attention when Carl dictated the route over the phone. Most of it was too hazy to resurrect from memory. He drove back to his apartment while exceeding the speed limit and silently cursing his stupidity the entire way home.

*   *   *   *

Before stopping at the police station, Nick felt the need to confirm his suspicions. He figured he could do so by stopping off at the apartment he had been led to the evening before. He suspected in some hidden recess of his mind that this was his last clinging desire to rectify the situation on his own. His conscious mind was able to convince him that providing Ramsey with proof would be better than leading him on a potential wild-goose chase.

He arrived at the apartment complex just before nine. It was an unseasonably warm day, so he knew that if this guy were indeed a concrete worker, he'd most likely be working. He circled the front parking lot and looked for the white pickup. It wasn't there. He drove around the back of the building and parked, trying to get up the nerve to do what he felt he had to do. He had never broken into someone else's residence. He wasn't sure he'd even know how to do it without damaging property or alerting one of the neighbors.

He decided to climb up the fire escape and try a couple of windows before checking the front entrance. He hoped that the credit card trick he'd seen in so many movies would work on the ancient window latches. The building was probably more than fifty years old, and the windows appeared to be originals.

He climbed up the rusted metal steps of the fire escape, hoping no one was watching. Each step made a resounding hollow echo as if it were intent upon announcing his arrival. When he got to the second floor landing, he paused near the rear door just next to the small window he had seen illuminated the night before.

He grabbed the weathered door handle and turned. Nothing. The door was locked and looked like it hadn't been opened in a very long time. It was most likely warped shut, too. Next up was the window that was lit up the night before. Drawing a MasterCard from his wallet, he prepared to do his best "MacGyver" imitation. Before fumbling with the latch, he pressed gently on the bottom of the window. To his utter shock, it moved ever so slightly.

With a quickening pulse, he pressed upward with a little more force. The window momentarily stuck, but then began to slide open. Nearly out of breath from excitement, he cupped the bottom of the frame and thrust it all the way open. No window shade blocked his path, so he found himself looking into the mildewed stall of a bathtub with its curtain drawn to the rest of the room.

He looked around to make sure no one was watching his felonious act. Convinced that the coast was clear, he put both hands on the inner windowsill and pulled himself through the small opening headfirst. His body lurched forward as he braced his advance against the opposite ledge of the bathtub, which was hidden by a plastic shower curtain. The curtain protested his arrival and crashed to the floor along with the molded rod. Without any further impediments, he held onto the front of the tub and pulled the rest of his body through the open window. He was in.

*   *   *   *

Rucker made it home in record time, still muttering obscenities to himself. The whole Lola affair was beginning to frustrate him. He had let his desires build too long this time, and it was starting to affect every aspect of his life. For a while, the cat-and-mouse game had held his interest, but he no longer enjoyed the chase. He would be glad to rid himself of Lola on Monday so he could move on to bigger and better things. She was becoming somewhat of a burden, and he realized he now hated her for staying alive as long as she had while within an arm's length of his dark presence.

He opened the front door of his apartment and made a beeline to the night-stand in the bedroom where he had left the job site directions. He never locked the door, figuring there was nothing in his apartment worth taking, anyway. He knew if the cops were ever onto him, they'd enter with or without the presence of a lock, so leaving it latched really didn't matter.

As he entered the bedroom, he had the strange sensation that something was slightly askew. There was the feeling that another presence shared his limited space, and he felt hairs begin to rise on the back of his neck as he plucked the scribbled directions from the bedside stand. He quickly turned, but saw no one behind him. Maybe he really was losing his mind. He gave in to a childhood impulse and quickly looked under the bed but only saw the presence of multiple dust bunnies and a two-year-old *Playboy* magazine.

He turned his attention to the bedroom closet, which was ajar. Had he left it that way this morning? He couldn't remember for sure but decided to open it up, anyway. He strode across the room toward the closet, half-expecting to find a surprise waiting within.

*   *   *   *

Nick fumbled with the fallen curtain rod for a few tense seconds before finally getting it to stick to both walls. He pushed the curtain back to the position it had been in prior to his crash landing. He then prepared to search the apartment.

Before he advanced five feet beyond the bathroom, he heard heavy footfalls outside. It sounded like someone was coming and doing so in quite a hurry. Frozen in place, he didn't know where to hide within the small one-bedroom flat. When he made the last-second decision to check out the apartment, he had done so without much preparation. He had no weapons other than himself. On most occasions, that would be more than enough, but if this guy was some crazed maniac, he might be armed.

He virtually dove into the bedroom and dropped to the ground while attempting to wedge himself under the bed. It was no use. There wasn't enough space between the frame and the floor to accommodate his body. From his belly, he saw the closet a few feet away. His ears braced for the sound of a key hitting the front door lock. Instead, he was jolted by the unexpected sound of the door crashing open without the few seconds' warning a key might have provided.

The change in atmosphere thrust him into frenzied action, and he immediately bounced from the floor while spinning toward the closet. He hastily ripped the sliding door open while trying to do so somewhat silently. With the door just a couple of feet open, he was devastated to see that the interior of the closet was cluttered with clothing, shoes, boxes, and other kinds of misplaced junk.

Now in a full-blown panic, he did his best to jam into the limited space. Somehow, he managed to fully occupy the only open air in the small closet and immediately pulled the door shut in front of him. The entire act had taken just a couple of seconds but felt like minutes as he seemingly thrashed about in slow motion in a wild attempt to avoid being caught. Breathless, he did his best to keep from gulping in the large quantities of oxygen required to feed his starving heart. He could feel his vision darken as he tried desperately to hold his breath and remain motionless. Each second floated by like a small eternity, and he was uncertain how much longer he could hold out before inadvertently revealing his position.

✳   ✳   ✳   ✳

Rucker reached for the closet door handle with tense anticipation. His breathing accelerated a notch as he prepared to unearth the monsters hiding within. Just before yanking the door open and unleashing hell's fury into the room, he stopped.

"This is ridiculous," he told himself. "You're a grown man for crying out loud, and you're behaving like a frightened child."

He must've been completely exhausted and mildly hungover, he concluded. His mind had been failing him all morning, and it was now tricking him into believing that someone or something was lurking within the dark recesses of his bedroom closet.

He withdrew his outstretched arm and turned to exit the room. Shaking his head, he left the apartment. With the elusive job directions in one hand and the front door knob in the other, he pulled the door shut behind him. If he hurried, he could still make it to the site without suffering too much of a verbal berating from his coworkers.

*   *   *   *

Nick's ears were starting to ring and stars began to sporadically flash across his blackened vision. He concentrated his hearing intently for any sound to follow that of the closing door. Nothing. The apartment had been left in silence, save for the heartbeat pulsating in his ears. His ticker threatened to knock its way past his sweater and out of his chest. He inhaled deeply and shuffled his feet, clearing the tension from his mind and body. He clung to that position for several more seconds before being convinced that he was once again alone in the apartment.

"What was he doing here?" he asked himself.

This was among the craziest things he had ever done. Breaking and entering was bad enough, but doing it at the residence of a possible homicidal maniac was insane. He slowly slid the closet door open and began to savor the mothball-free air that existed beyond the dark, tight crawl space. After escaping the temporary prison, he decided he needed to get out of the apartment as soon as possible before the owner made another hurried return.

He started back toward the bathroom, figuring a retreat from whence he came was probably his best bet. Curiosity played its unyielding hand before he could leave, however. He decided to poke his head into the other rooms first. His eyes flitted quickly across the walls, furniture, and floors. Aside from being unkempt, it was mostly bare. Sparse furnishings and little else littered the tiny apartment. Just before leaving the kitchen and heading back toward the bathroom window, his eyes caught a slip of paper on the kitchen table. It was a paycheck that had not been cashed.

He searched the check for information and immediately locked onto the familiar logo for Fritz Brothers Concrete in the upper left hand corner. That was pretty much all he needed to see. His eyes drank in the logo for long seconds as the stunning revelation ate into his brain. He was standing in the middle of an apartment leased by the man who almost certainly had killed Pamela.

Thirsting for additional confirmation, he made a hasty, yet thorough, search of the premises. In addition to coming across a couple of disturbing Polaroid pictures that captured the distant fuzzy image of a girl who might resemble the waitress at The Pie Factory, he found one more decidedly chilling collection of evidence. In the same sock drawer as the Polaroids, he came across a manila envelope littered with press clippings. The article on top of the stack carried the head-line ST. LOUIS WOMAN VIOLENTLY MURDERED. It shared space with maybe fifteen or twenty similar articles.

His heart stopped, and he began to shake uncontrollably. He sat on the edge of the bed and tried to compose himself, fearful that he might pass out and awake to the sharp edge of the same blade Pamela had succumbed to on that horrific night just two months ago.

Wanting desperately to wait in the apartment for the man to return, he kept hearing his mother's voice echoing the last words she had said to him that morn-ing. Her references to Justin and making a true orphan of the boy stung with bit-ing severity. As badly as he wanted to end this incredible nightmare with his own two hands, he knew he now had to turn it over to the authorities and hope they had good fortune apprehending the murderer.

He slid the envelope and the pictures back where he found them and searched for the resolve to extricate himself from the apartment. On the way out, he didn't bother to exit through the window. Instead, he boldly strode through the front door, not caring who saw him. Part of him clung to the hope that the man would be returning at the same time he was leaving. Then he'd have his opportunity to right this wrong and leave the outcome in the hands of fate.

Unfortunately, those hands had not served Pamela well, so there was no guar-antee he'd receive better care from their sometimes-cold grip. With his mind numb, he got into his car and prepared to drive to the St. Louis County Police station. He didn't know what he'd tell Ramsey once he got there. He didn't really know much of anything anymore.

*   *   *   *

Rucker got home from work at six thirty and was too tired to do much of any-thing. He wanted to be sharp next time he saw Lola, so he decided to stay home and get some much needed rest. The last couple of weeks had been a whirlwind for him. The realization that he had to complete his mission with Lola in a cou-ple of days had overwhelmed him. He was now starting to feel the familiar excited anticipation that came with every final encounter.

Wrecked from a brutal day of shoveling and wheeling concrete, all he could think about was a hot shower followed by a few hours of sleep. He stripped off his soiled work clothes and pitched them on the floor next to his bed. When he entered the bathroom, he started to get that strange sensation again. Earlier he had felt "watched" in his apartment. Now, he once again felt like his space was being violated.

He swept back the plastic shower curtain to turn on the shower knobs and froze. As he had watched the curtain move across the base of the tub, the sight looked unfamiliar. He realized that the plastic was riding much closer to the bottom of the tub than usual. He stared at the shower curtain for several minutes, trying to force his mind to piece together what was going on.

The feeling he had experienced that morning involving someone lingering in his apartment may not have been imagined after all. Were the cops finally on to him? A panicky sensation spread through his body, and he felt his extremities go slightly numb. What was he going to do? He couldn't leave until he had met with Lola a final time. Maybe they were watching his place right now. Another surge of adrenaline coursed through his veins at the thought.

"OK, don't blow it out of proportion," he thought to himself.

Think. He couldn't jump to any unnecessary conclusions until he had reason enough to believe that he was truly in trouble. Maybe he had readjusted the curtain himself and forgot. Probably not, but he definitely hadn't been thinking clearly the past couple of days. He decided to proceed with the shower and get some rest. Fleeing his apartment right then made no sense. Even if the cops did suspect him of something, he sincerely doubted they had enough proof to put him away. Still, in all, why was the curtain lower than usual?

As he was rinsing soap from his body, Rucker noticed something strange on the windowsill. He looked closer and saw debris scattered across the sill. Right in the middle of the refuse was a streak that looked like a shoe print. He rubbed the streak and it flaked off. He wasn't being paranoid after all. Someone had been in his apartment, but who? And why through the window?

With fear turning to anger and a feeling once again of having been violated, Rucker finished his shower and continued to mull over the possibilities. He went over and over his last mission and tried to think of something he might have done to tip them off. He also considered what evidence existed in his apartment that could conceivably tie him to the crime.

He immediately thought of the manila envelope in his nightstand drawer. He hated to part with the mementos, but those seemed to be the only shreds of evidence that could tie him to any of the victims. That along with incriminating DNA that he figured might have been left behind at one murder location or another. Even if that were the case, they'd have to get his DNA to make a match. To do that, they'd have to catch him, and he had no intention of letting that happen.

He hesitantly withdrew the press clippings from his drawer and studied them for more than an hour. He really didn't need them, he decided. The memories and visions were locked firmly in his brain forever. The articles didn't tell the true stories, anyway. They certainly didn't show any of the women's faces at that final moment.

After rereading the last article a second time, he put them back in the envelope and took them to the kitchen sink. He lit his collection on fire and watched it burn.

"Fucking cops," he thought.

They had a tendency to ruin everything. When the last of the envelope had been charred, Rucker scooped up the ashes and deposited them in the toilet. The only remaining connection he had to his masterpiece missions existed solely within his mind.

He felt the cloud of urgency settle over him once more and realized he could wait no longer. Putting it off for two more days while he prepared was no longer a luxury he could afford. He'd clear out his limited personal effects from the apartment the next day and then go to Lola's that evening. As soon as he was done with her, he'd skip town. The thought of finishing his business and, best of all, finishing Lola made him happy again. That's more like it, he thought. Enough of this delusional paranoia. It was time to get ready for mission number twenty-one. This one certainly promised to be his finest hour.

CHAPTER 16

▼

Nick entered the St. Louis County Police Department with a heavy heart. He was relieved to be handing over a bona fide suspect to the proper authorities but annoyed with himself for not having the balls to handle the perp himself.

"I need to see Detective Ramsey," he told the mousy woman at the receptionist desk.

"What business do you have with Detective Ramsey?" she whined through pursed lips.

She had wrinkled her nose and contorted her miniscule facial features, making them appear so close together that he might have been able to cover the lot with a silver dollar. Her horn-rimmed glasses had slipped to the edge of her pointed beak and appeared ready to drop off her shrunken head at any moment.

"Just tell him that Nick Lacour is here and that I have evidence for him pertaining to a murder case," he replied agitatedly.

"One moment," she crowed, while dismissing Nick to a waiting chair via the pointing of a bony finger.

He took his seat and listened as the old broad boomed into her phone receiver. Lacour became "Lafleur," but he was fairly certain Ramsey would be able to figure it out.

A couple of moments later, a door to his left opened, and Ramsey appeared, looking weathered. His dress shirt was partially untucked, and his tie was disjointed and hanging loosely around his neck. Nick felt that the man had aged ten years since their last meeting.

"Nick, good to see you," Ramsey said.

He appeared to be trying to mask his exhaustion through a feigned smile, but the rings around his eyes gave him up.

"You too, Jack," Nick responded.

"C'mon, step inside."

Nick followed Ramsey through the vaguely familiar world of cubicles until they reached his corner office. He watched as Ramsey pulled a half-empty pot of coffee off his desk.

"Can I pour you a cup?"

"No thanks."

"So to what do I owe the pleasure of this visit?"

"I think I have a suspect for you," Nick responded dryly, getting straight to the point.

"Oh?" Ramsey questioned with raised eyebrows.

He set the coffeepot back in its cradle and took his seat behind the desk.

"Yeah. In fact, I'd be really surprised if this guy *wasn't* the one."

"I'm listening," Ramsey said, seemingly taken aback by the revelation.

Ramsey listened as Nick launched into the story about his contacts in East St. Louis and the trip he took to The Pie Factory. He sat in silence, giving all of his stunned attention to the details. He fidgeted at the part when Nick broke into the man in black's apartment, but he didn't respond. When Nick finished, Ramsey folded his hands across his forehead and stared into nothingness.

After a couple of uncomfortable moments, Nick broke the silence.

"So what do you think?"

"I think you committed a minor felony," answered Ramsey, now looking even more worn-out than he had when Nick arrived.

Before Nick could protest, Ramsey broke into a grin.

"Of course, that last part of your story will be left out if this thing ever gets to court," he said, still smiling.

"What's next?" Nick asked after nodding affirmatively.

"I need to get a search warrant together first. Once we have that, we'll pay this guy a visit. If what you saw is still there, we should have enough to make an arrest."

"Then what, a long, drawn-out trial? Maybe worse, he makes bond and walks?"

"As a lawyer, you know that a first-degree murder charge will carry no bond or something well beyond his financial means. Secondly, if he is the guy, a blood test ought to tie him to your wife's murder as well as an Indianapolis homicide."

"So aren't you going to lecture me about getting involved in a major investigation?"

"Nah. Even if I felt that strongly about it, I wouldn't have the energy," he said, massaging his temples. "Besides, you just made my life a whole lot easier."

"What about the Feds?"

"It's still not their ball game. I guess they have enough on their plate right now, because they haven't involved themselves like I thought they would."

"That's a good thing, right?"

"As good as a pair of forty-two D's flopping around in your face."

They both smiled at the reference. Nick got up to leave the office, but Ramsey motioned him back to his seat.

"There's one more thing we ought to discuss, Nick."

"Yeah? What's that?"

"If anyone finds out how we got this lead, the entire case will be thrown out."

"I know. That's why I came to you."

"I just want to make sure we're on the same page. I can't have your buddies in East St. Louis surfacing in the press. What's more, I need you to stay out of it, too," Ramsey said with conviction.

The lighthearted air had sifted from the meeting, and it was now all business.

"Don't worry about it. I'll take care of my *buddies*. I can also assure you that my role in this mess is now complete."

"I just want to be sure we're absolutely clear on that point. With that being said, I'm sure I can come up with evidence that might have led us to the suspect. In fact, we weren't that far off."

"Really?" Nick questioned, sounding more disbelieving than he had implied.

"Don't look so surprised. Did you think every cop sat around eating doughnuts all day?"

"Not *all* cops."

Ramsey ignored the playful jab and rediscovered his business side.

"The truth is we've tied the killer to the car you mentioned in East St. Louis. We have a sketch of the suspect, compiled from a costume shop employee who sold him the cop suit. Along with the tissue sample, footprints, and a button from the uniform he purchased, I think we probably have enough to seal this guy away for a couple hundred years."

Nick looked disappointed. Prison didn't seem to be a harsh enough fit for the crime. Ramsey sensed the letdown in his demeanor and continued.

"Of course, I'm sure the death penalty will supersede the two centuries worth of incarceration."

"How's that? I didn't think Indiana carried the death penalty."

"Actually, both Indiana and Missouri impose the death penalty."

The disappointment on Nick's visage evaporated at once. Now mostly content that he had indeed done the right thing, he again rose to leave the office. Ramsey stood with him this time and shook his hand once more.

"We'll be in touch."

"OK. Now go get this prick."

"Don't think for a second that you made a mistake," Ramsey said, addressing Nick's lingering question. "I'm sure it would have been awfully tempting to take matters into your own hands."

Nick maintained his silence but knew they were on the same wavelength.

"Believe me, it will be a lot less messy for you and for us doing it this way. You did the right thing."

Somehow, Nick knew that was a question he'd always wonder about but nodded in agreement just the same. They then parted company.

Ramsey had a million things to do to make sure the eventual arrest and case he compiled was airtight.

Nick had his own demons to confront.

∗   ∗   ∗   ∗

Rucker was beginning to feel antsy. Despite his physical exhaustion, he couldn't seem to settle down. It certainly had a lot to do with the fact that he knew someone had been in his apartment. He wasn't necessarily afraid of whoever had entered his dwelling. He was more frightened by what that person might represent. He couldn't help feeling like a storm was building on the horizon.

Having the cops in his apartment would definitely be cause for alarm. He didn't think that had been the case, however. He knew the cops were a bunch of bumbling idiots, but he didn't peg them for breaking and entering. If they honestly had something on him, they would have most likely gone through the proper channels. There'd be search warrants and more fanfare than associated with a presidential motorcade.

Only on television did rogue detectives slyly piece together evidence and trap criminals. In the real world, law enforcement was much more predictable than something you'd expect out of a *CSI* episode. No, if they really had something, there would be a dozen squad cars outside his place right now. Lights flashing, sirens blaring—it would look like a comical circus hosted by inept members of the law enforcement community rather than Barnum & Bailey.

Believing that fact made the stillness surrounding his apartment that much more intolerable. In some ways, he would have almost preferred the brash entrance of a fleet of cops. The fact that they hadn't arrived made this morning's visitor that much more perplexing. Who was he? What had he been doing in the apartment?

The feeling that thunderheads were building overhead had become inescapable. The utter calm before the proverbial storm was more than he could bear. He grabbed his coat, threw on a pair of shoes, and prepared to launch himself directly into the eye of that very storm.

*   *   *   *

Nick left the police station feeling relieved in some ways but dissatisfied in others. For all practical purposes, he had done the right thing. By handling it in this manner, he had entrusted his future with Ramsey. It was a risk but one he was willing to accept. In all likelihood, the whole thing would be over in a matter of hours. The finality of it would provide him with the opportunity to move forward instead of living in the past.

Maybe that final thought is what bothered him the most. Throughout his amateur investigation, he had felt a purpose. More than that, he had maintained a tie to Pamela. With the mystery on the verge of being solved, he'd be forced to let go of that temporary purpose. The realization was all too sobering a reminder that his future life would be without his wife.

In addition to those pangs of emptiness, he felt something else. He hadn't been able to place the source of his discomfort earlier, but it had just seized him in a rush. What about the girl at The Pie Factory? Ramsey hadn't taken a particularly keen interest in that portion of the story, and he had glossed over the details to get to the part about the suspect's apartment.

The truth was Nick's instincts told him that she was the next intended victim. He now felt a wave of panic surge over him. What if it was too late? He had been so busy trying to prove he was onto the right guy that he had ignored the fact that this guy had most likely chosen his next playmate. He flipped open his cell phone and dialed the number for information.

"What city and state?" the generic voice questioned.

"Sauget, Illinois," Nick replied.

"Go ahead."

"Yes, I need the number for The Pie Factory."

"One moment."

A recorded voice now interceded with the number. He chose the option to be automatically connected for an additional charge and waited for someone to pick up on the other end.

"Pie Factory," grumbled the person on the line.

"Hi, I'm calling to speak with one of your waitresses."

"Which one?"

"Young girl works the tables surrounding the stages."

"Need to be more specific, buddy."

"French maid outfit. Dark hair. Very striking."

"You must mean Lola."

"Yes, that's her."

"She's not here."

"When will she be working again?"

"Are you some sort of perverted stalker, bud?"

"No, I just thought she was nice, and I wanted to see her again."

"Yeah, right," the guy answered unconvinced. "Anyway, she's off today."

"OK, thanks."

He clicked off and stuffed the phone into his jacket pocket. He knew deep down that he had to get to Lola right away. He hoped beyond hope that he wasn't already too late. He began to reconstruct from memory the directions to the apartment from when he had followed the man in black a couple of days before. He exited the highway and traversed across the overpass. Selecting the lane marked East 40/61, he re-entered the expressway and started toward Illinois. Anxiousness weighed on his foot. The needle on the dash pressed past ninety as he clenched the wheel with both hands and dreaded what he might be about to find. He had to get to her immediately, but would he make it in time?

He followed the highway across the Poplar Street Bridge into Illinois while blowing by seemingly unmoving traffic the entire way. He prayed that his obsession with confirming his suspicions hadn't caused him to put off this meeting too long. He realized now that he should have warned her the day he knew this guy might be dangerous to her. The guilt made him press the accelerator even harder. He didn't think he could stand the sight of another mutilated young woman. His imagination got the best of him as unpleasant images flashed through his thoughts. Now going more than a hundred miles per hour, he approached his exit.

"Please God, let me be in time," he begged.

*   *   *   *

Her afternoon off had nearly evaporated, and she hadn't left the couch. She couldn't summon the energy to leave her apartment to do anything more worthwhile than watch Oprah. The wear and tear of a long winter in addition to working two jobs had taken a toll on her mind and body. She shut off the television and sat in the silent, darkening room, pondering her future. She was certainly glad she'd be taking some classes in the summer, but it still seemed so far off. Working days and nights had completely burned her out. She desperately wished she had the money to take a trip somewhere exotic.

Hanging on the edge of her hand-me-down coffee table was a travel magazine she had bought weeks ago. Up until now, she hadn't had the time to leaf through it. She plucked the magazine from the table and began to flip through pages decorated with scenes from faraway lands. She could almost smell the ocean breeze as her eyes delved deeply into a spread about the Cayman Islands. Oh, what she wouldn't give to be there now.

Folding the magazine across her chest, she let her mind take her to that beautiful and tranquil place. She imagined the coolness of the white sand under her bare feet. She drank in the coconut smell of tanning lotion, which covered her bronzed body. The sound of turquoise water lapping up against the shore deepened her fantasy.

When she awoke, she was startled to see that the room was now dark. She had fallen asleep on the couch, dreaming of a trip she'd probably never take. The magazine she was reading had slipped from her grasp and tumbled to the floor. It was poised to be swept under the rug along with all the rest of her hopes and dreams.

Her peaceful escape had been interrupted by an incessant banging sound. She was attempting to impart reality back into her groggy mind when the sound made its intrusion once again. This time, fully awake, she recognized the noise as someone knocking on her door. Who would be visiting her unannounced? She had very few friends, and most of them had no idea where she lived. Family wasn't an option, either. They were all gone, either dead or never known.

She tiptoed to the door, not wanting the visitor to know anyone was home. Peering through the peephole, she saw the muted outlines of what appeared to be a UPS delivery person. She couldn't make out his facial features in the dim lighting, but he seemed young and harmless enough. He held a package in one hand

and a clipboard in the other. She began to get excited, figuring that the package contained enrollment materials for the upcoming semester of college.

She unlatched the bolts and cracked the door, leaving the chain drawn.

*   *   *   *

For the first time in Rucker's life, he was experiencing a new sensation. A normal person would label the feeling as nervousness. To him, it was merely a transition stage between anger and rage. He didn't know why he was so jumpy about this particular mission. Maybe it was the prolonged anticipation.

His mind had played out the upcoming scene over and over during the past several weeks. Lola had become his complete obsession. In some ways, she might even have been considered his reason for being. All the hype was rapidly leading to one final cataclysmic encounter. Part of him didn't want the feeling to end, but he knew that it had to. The odd appearance of an intruder in his apartment had thoroughly convinced him that the time had come to conclude his business and move on.

Fortunately for him, he'd been preparing mentally and physically for some time now. He'd swiped a UPS uniform about a week ago and had purchased an empty box and some packing tape the day before yesterday. In addition to the company issue brown garb and hat, he was wearing a large pair of glasses with non-prescription lenses. He pulled the hat snugly over his forehead so that it almost obstructed his vision. He had shaved his perpetually shaggy face and donned the glasses before he left his apartment. In the bathroom mirror, he barely recognized himself, so he was confident that Lola wouldn't be able to place him while he was cloaked in the shades of evening.

With his disguise complete, he was now ready to assume complete ownership of his coveted prize. He parked his truck behind the apartment complex and made sure it was poised for a hasty escape once he had finished what he came to do. Absence of street- or porch lights behind the building made for a much more inconspicuous locale.

Satisfied that everything was ready, he grabbed the package and left the truck. He had been sitting there for half an hour, breathing deeply and taking in his surroundings. Very few lights were on in the nearby building, and all of the shades were drawn. His truck was the only vehicle parked behind the complex. That was both good and bad. It meant on one hand that no one was nearby, but on the other hand, it drew some suspicion to his vehicle. It made little difference, however, because he'd be driving new machinery in a few hours and would be hundreds of miles away from this place.

He slipped quietly through the bushes decorating the side of the building and came out on the corner of the front parking lot. Scanning the spaces for the red Escort, his eyes lit up when he saw it parked in its usual spot near the front walkway. Thrilled that Lola was home, he tried to calm himself and prepare for their last dance together. He struggled to push the burgeoning excitement from his mind so that he would be able to accomplish the mission in a proficient manner. With his mind and body honed to the task at hand, he reached her apartment and rapped on the door. After weeks of waiting, she would finally be his.

✻   ✻   ✻   ✻

"Evening, ma'am. Got a package here for you," Rucker said in his best, most innocent sounding drawl.

"Who's it from?" came the meek sounding voice through a slight crack in the door.

"Geez, it's kinda hard to read in this light, ma'am. Want me to take it back?"

"No, that's OK," she replied after a brief pause.

The door in front of him closed. The ensuing seconds between that instant and the sliding of the chain seemed like an eternity. Convinced that he'd have to break the door down, his patience was rewarded as the door swung open sans its last line of defense.

"Sign here, please," he said, handing her the clipboard while carefully trying to conceal his facial features as soft light streamed through the open doorway from the inside of the apartment.

She grabbed the clipboard and penned her name. After handing it back to him, she reached out her arms for the package.

"This is pretty heavy, ma'am. Maybe I should just set it down inside your door."

"No, that's OK, I can handle it."

He felt the moment slipping away. He had to act quickly or his opportunity would be dashed. As he started to extend the package toward his prize, he dropped it on the floor just inside the apartment. Before she bent to pick it up, he thought he saw a glimmer of recognition in her eyes. In that split second, he realized she might have connected him to his frequent trips to The Pie Factory.

Wasting not a moment more, he thrust himself through the partially open door and pounced on her. The move was so sudden that she didn't have time to react. He was able to muzzle her with one arm and pull the apartment door closed behind him with the other.

"Now you're mine, bitch," he grunted through clenched teeth.

*   *   *   *

Angela's eyes widened in terror as she began to grasp the consequences of having opened her door to a stranger. The only additional thought that pierced her stunned mind was the sad irony that this was probably a fitting end to her rather unsatisfying existence.

*   *   *   *

Nick barreled into the apartment parking lot at an unsafe speed. He was just able to get his car to stop before it collided with a parked vehicle on the lot. He backed away from the near miss and holstered his car in a spot near the apartment building. When he got out, he immediately recognized the red Escort parked next to the walkway.

"Good, she's here," he thought.

Or maybe not good, depending upon whether or not he was too late. Glancing up at the building, he tried to determine which unit belonged to the waitress. He didn't really want to knock on every door, but decided he'd do so if necessary. Just then, a light flickered out in the window of one of the ground units. It wasn't terribly unusual, but something about the occurrence struck his curiosity. As he neared the door to that unit, he thought he heard some muffled sounds from within. Not wanting to make an embarrassing mistake, he pressed his head against the door and tried to make out what he was hearing. After several long moments passed, he distinctly heard a young girl's voice cry, "No, please!"

It was all he needed. He withdrew a few paces from the door and exploded into it with startling force. The door jam splintered under the force and the door itself flew open, slamming into the inside wall and bouncing back toward him. He deftly avoided the damaged door and bolted into the dark room. Scuffling sounds and heavy breathing were coming from the rear of the small unit. He wasted no time as he sprinted through the main room directly toward the source of the conflict.

*   *   *   *

Angela tried to close her mind to the event that was about to happen, but the man hovering over her had made it impossible to do so. He was exerting phenomenal force upon her body, and she just couldn't find a mental haven to escape the onslaught. Early in the encounter, she had tried to fight him. Though small in stature, she was incredibly wiry and fit. It was to no avail, however, against the much larger, psychotic man. He had dragged her squirming, contorting body into the bedroom as if he knew exactly where it would be.

The hand he had used to grip her torso was now holding a large knife. He pressed his other hand hard across her mouth, shoving her head deep into the mattress she was now lying on. She tried desperately to kick him off, but her attempts didn't budge his muscular frame. When she shut her eyes, he withdrew his hand and slapped her savagely across the face.

"You will pay attention to me," he barked violently, while straddling her tiring body.

To accentuate his point, he gripped the knife under her chin and used the hand that once covered her mouth to tear her T-shirt from her chest.

"Make the smallest sound, and I'll cut your fucking head off," he leered. "If you cooperate, you just might live to tell someone about this tomorrow."

Somehow, she doubted that last line. The look in his eyes burned with such supreme evil and hatred that she knew in her heart that enduring a traumatizing rape would not be the end of it. This monster had come to end her life.

Frantically, she clawed through her subconscious mind in search of a solution. Freeing herself from his hold was proving to be impossible. The effort it was taking had begun to exhaust her remaining physical resources. She probably had no more than five minutes to extradite herself from the danger at hand. Within that time, she may only have a split second of opportunity. She had to save herself for that last gasp.

Deciding that her demise was inevitable, she tempted fate and let out a last-ditch cry for help. She knew that by doing so, she'd most likely have her throat cut. Somehow, that result seemed almost endearing compared to gratifying his sexual fantasies.

"No, please!" she let out in bloodcurdling fashion, hoping that for the first time in her life an angel would heed her cry for help and rescue her from the depths of utter despair.

*   *   *   *

The scene inside the bedroom paid eerie homage to the one Nick had visited in his dreams countless times since Pamela's death. It was exactly the way he had imagined her last moments at the mercy of an insatiable killer.

His body worked instinctively as his conscious mind became unable to balance rage and fear for the girl's life. He grabbed the knife-wielding man by the neck and forcefully pitched him into a closet door. The sliding door gave way underneath his weight and bowed off its track. It collapsed into the closet with the dazed assailant draped across the leaning door. The knife flew from his hand and tumbled harmlessly across the bare floor.

*   *   *   *

Unable to comprehend what had just happened to him, Rucker heaved himself away from the fallen closet door and staggered toward the third party who had just hurtled into the room. Who was this guy, and why had he shown up? As he approached the unexpected man, he noticed a fire in his eyes that rivaled the one that stared back from his own mirror. It was the first time in his life that he had come across an adversary worthy of his respect.

*   *   *   *

With the slightly disoriented man still reeling and lurching toward him hunched over, Nick teed up a kick to his exposed jaw and watched him pitch over helplessly across a small desk near the entrance to the bedroom. He turned his attention for a split second to the girl on the bed to make sure she was still alive. When he reverted his focus back to the doorway containing his fallen captor, he was alarmed to see that the man had not only recovered, but had been able to drag himself out of the room.

He started after him but couldn't complete the pursuit until he knew the girl was not wounded and in need of medical attention. He looked her over trying to quickly appraise her physical status.

"I'm OK," she sobbed. "Go get him."

Convinced that she'd be all right, he blew from the room. He darted out of the apartment and slid across the icy walkway leading toward the parking lot.

Breathless, he rapidly scoured the lot for any signs of the escaped killer. To his utter astonishment, the man had completely vanished into thin air.

Not sure where to begin his search, he heard the scrapings of nearby bushes as they raked across the jacket of the fleeing man. Quick to take up the pursuit, Nick ran toward the direction of the sounds and saw the man trying to free himself from the shrubbery at the rear of the building. Less than thirty yards away from his conquest, he continued the chase into the landscaping. Despite tripping slightly on a low hanging branch, he was still able to close much of the distance between himself and the man he had pursued literally and figuratively for what seemed like an eternity.

After a few more strides, Nick cleared the side of the building and broke into the open again. There, just ten paces in front of him was the person who had murdered Pamela. Fueled by a thirst for revenge and hatred for the soulless animal running in front of him, he nearly flew the remaining feet, closing in on his intended victim. But instead of putting a savage end to an almost unbelievable nightmare, he could only watch helplessly as his intended captive jumped into the cab of a pickup truck.

He slammed heavily into the side door of the white truck and snatched frantically at its handle, attempting to wrench the door open. His grasp on the chrome handle slid free as the truck burst into motion and squealed from the lot. He collapsed onto the frozen ground in its wake, watching the taillights and the man within disappear before his eyes. Crestfallen from his near miss, he brushed himself off and went back to the apartment to tend to the frightened girl. He found her sitting upright on the bed, clinging to the remnants of her torn shirt while crying inconsolably into clenched fists.

When Nick sat down next to her to make sure she was indeed unharmed, she grabbed onto him and held him with all of the remaining strength she could muster. He held her trembling body in his arms and tried to usher away her fears. He was completely relieved that he had arrived in time but couldn't shake his disgust that the killer had sprung free. Somewhere in the cold night surrounding the apartment building, a beast was tending to wounds that amounted to little more than fractured pride.

CHAPTER 17

▼

Rucker was seething mad. He sat in his truck at a stoplight, pounding his fists on the steering wheel. He couldn't believe she had been saved. He had carefully planned their final meeting and had been so close to making the dream come true. Nothing could have possibly gone wrong. That is, until *he* showed up.

The man totally caught him off guard. He came out of nowhere and with incredible force. Rucker was peeved with himself for fleeing, but he had had no choice. Under the circumstances, he was unprepared for the surprise attack. He'd love to get a second chance at the guy, on equal footing. He dared him to try it again. What a sissy he was to hit him with a sucker punch. A real man would never do such a thing.

Who was he anyway? Somehow he knew he had seen him before. It had been dark, but he had caught enough of a glimpse of his face to recognize him. He had to find out who had come to Lola's rescue. The man's eyes were burned into Rucker's brain. He saw his face as clearly as if he were staring at a photograph.

Lola. Sweet Lola. He had been seconds away from making her his very own prize. Months of restraining his urges while plotting the last act. Lola was going to be part of his finest hour and now she was gone. Surely she would have to come back to her apartment. Or would she? Whoever had helped her must have known she was in danger. She may never return to the apartment or The Pie Factory unaccompanied. It certainly wouldn't be worth risking her life over.

His master plan had been foiled by some clown who looked vaguely familiar to him. Who was this joker, and why would he be protecting Lola? These were all questions that needed to be answered. He had waited long enough for her. Now she had become a liability. Both Lola and her new hero would have to pay for this night. No one escaped Gerald Rucker. No one.

After beating the steering wheel until his hands and the wheel were about to break, he composed himself. A tantrum would do him no good. He had to regroup and figure out what had just happened. He had to get another crack at Lola. The man's image continued to flash brightly in his mind. He would dream of that face until he confronted him once again. Next time, his new adversary wouldn't be so lucky. Next time, neither the hero nor anyone else would be able to save Lola from her appointed destiny.

*   *   *   *

"Hi Jack. It's Nick."

"Yeah Nick, how's it going?"

"I've got a very scared young woman with me. Our suspect just attempted to kill her."

Nick told Ramsey the entire story about his hunch followed by the visit to Granite City to try to warn the girl. He explained that he couldn't reach her at work so he opted to visit her apartment instead. When he got there, he found the killer trying to add her to his list of growing totals. When he had finished recounting the details, he paused and heard Ramsey let out a long sigh. He prepared himself to receive another fatherly lecture from the detective. Instead, he was taken aback by the outburst Ramsey unleashed.

"Nick, I told you to stay the fuck out of this investigation, didn't I?"

"Well yeah, but…"

"Look, you have no freaking idea how much damage you're doing right now," Ramsey said as he cut him off. "Every time you interfere, you lessen our chances of catching this guy!"

"I know, but I…"

"Not to mention the fact that you're endangering yourself and those around you in the process," said Ramsey, who had pounced on him again like a mountain lion attacking a foal.

Nick didn't bother to respond. He knew Ramsey was right, but couldn't help feeling satisfied that he had saved a life by meddling where he didn't belong. He let Ramsey's tirade continue for another few minutes but had long since stopped listening. He was alternating his attention between the road ahead and the girl sitting in his passenger's seat. She was curled into a tightly wound ball and almost appeared to be sucking her thumb. In the dark front seat of the car, she could have easily been mistaken for a ten-year-old.

"Is any of this getting through to you, Lacour?" Ramsey inquired after a lengthy pause.

"Of course, Jack, you're right about everything you said," Nick responded in a patronizing voice.

"Look man, I'm just trying to look after your best interests."

"Gee, thanks, Dad."

"Spare me the sarcastic crap. You know what I mean. You're a good kid and you've just suffered an awful tragedy. It's normal to want to take matters into your own hands, but it never does anyone any good when a victim responds like that," Ramsey said.

Nick paused again to let his message sink in.

"Seriously, Nick, I'm not trying to chastise you. What you've done for the girl is beyond impressive. It was goddamned heroic, and I'm proud of you. I just want you to get out of this mess once and for all."

"Thanks, Jack. That means something to me," Nick said, losing his arrogant tone.

"Now, what I want you to do is get your ass home and stay as far away from this freak as possible. Let us do our job, OK?"

"Absolutely. By the way, what are you doing to 'do your job' right now?"

"Not that it's any of your business, but we've staked out the guy's apartment. His name is Carlton Lewis. He's a virtual unknown from Indianapolis with no priors. That is if Carlton is truly his real name. Lewis is a forty-year-old man, and our guy has been described as much younger-looking than that."

"That's good, Jack. I'm happy you're on top of things."

"You being sarcastic again?"

"No sir, I mean it. I feel better knowing you're taking care of this mess."

"OK. Now get home, and I'll let you know when he's apprehended."

"Aye aye, detective," Nick said before hanging up.

When he had finished the call, he looked over at the young girl. She was either sleeping or in total shock—he couldn't tell which. They drove the rest of the way to the hospital in silence. Once the girl was released from the hospital, he'd have no alternative but to take her to his parents' house while he decided what to do next. He hadn't yet figured out how he was going to explain the new guest to his mom and dad. It certainly wouldn't make much sense, but then again, very little made sense right now.

He continued down the highway trying to figure out his next move. He had to make sure the girl and his family stayed safe while Jack and his boys attempted to arrest the killer. Seemed like a simple concept on paper, but nothing was easy in his life anymore.

*   *   *   *

Rucker made it back to his apartment complex after stopping along the way to buy a six-pack of Budweiser and a package of Advil. His head hurt from the Karate Kid's kick, but not nearly as much as his self-respect hurt from the near miss at Lola's apartment. He still couldn't believe she had gotten away. He'd never failed on a mission attempt before and wasn't dealing with the disappointment very well. His dashboard became proof positive after he unleashed a beating on both it and the steering wheel.

After popping a few Advils and washing them down with the beer, he started to feel a little better. Maybe he'd loll around his apartment and drown his sorrows in liquor and painkillers while he tried to figure out what to do about Lola. He gave the steering wheel one last thumping, as he dropped the *f*-bomb a couple more dozen times. The past couple of months had been all about Lola, and now she was onto him. Even worse, she had an unknown protector who may have whisked her off to God knows where for God knows how long.

He was still convinced that he had recognized the guy. The memory was fuzzy, but he was almost certain he had seen him or met him before. He'd spend the rest of the evening mulling it over as he attempted to devise a plan that would win Lola back and put the hero away all in one fell swoop.

Just as he got into the turn lane to enter his apartment complex, he noticed a police cruiser slipping by his street. He aborted his turn and went down to the next block. He parked his truck a half-mile from his apartment building and hoofed it in to check things out. If a stranger had been able to stop his progress at Lola's and get into his apartment, it was possible that the police were indeed onto him, too.

He slinked silently along buildings and under the cover of hedges and trees as he neared the apartment building. From a distance, he could already see what looked like an unmarked police car. All that was missing in that car was a dozen Krispy Kremes to accompany the two buffoons who may as well have had *cop* stenciled across their foreheads.

He cut over to the next block away from the apartment complex and noticed another law enforcement vehicle. This one was a lot less obvious, but he immediately recognized the older cop as someone he had seen on television many times in conjunction with the task force searching for the murderer of a West County woman. It struck him as ironic that the murderer was now observing some of those very same task force members from the bushes surrounding the net they had constructed to apprehend him.

So it was true; they really had found him. He didn't know whether to feel surprise, anger, fear, or shame. He'd managed to log many years of killings without once being in danger of getting caught. Now, he was on the verge of being apprehended for something he hadn't even done yet. That damn Lola sure was becoming a pain in the ass. His desire to finish things with her was strong, but his thirst for freedom even stronger. He decided to get back into his truck and get the hell out of Dodge quickly. He could find another identity in another city fairly quickly. He had enough money to keep him going for a while. Fortunately for him, nothing of value remained in the apartment. Aside from some useless clothing and a few odds and ends, they wouldn't find much. He kept all of his money in a strong box under the backseat just in case something like this happened. He also had a spare knife and a forty-five-caliber revolver, which he had never used. He really wasn't into guns but would use it if it meant saving his bacon.

Feeling angry and cheated, he got back to his truck and began to embark upon his escape from a place that hadn't been entirely good to him. He had never been forced from a town before. For that matter, he'd never had to run away from anything in his life. Now, he had to flee twice in the same night. He was furious but more focused on leaving this potential disaster before some punk cop found him and made an undeserved name for himself.

$$*\qquad*\qquad*\qquad*$$

Explaining to his parents why a twenty-five-year-old cocktail waitress from a strip club was coming to stay with them temporarily wasn't going to be the easiest thing in the world. He couldn't quite tell them the entire truth, because he didn't want them to know he was mixed up in a murder investigation. Much worse than that, he didn't want them to know he had most likely found the person responsible for their daughter-in-law's death.

He decided to pawn it off as a favor for a friend, stating the girl was a fellow attorney's niece, and she was having a difficult time. The story was probably going to be incredibly flimsy, but neither of his parents wanted to press him on much of anything right now other than making sure he stayed fed. They would most likely accept the fiction and never utter a word of disapproval.

Nick had taken the girl to Barnes-Jewish Hospital in St. Louis, where she endured a brief overnight stay and some fairly detailed questioning from the cops. She was still badly shaken but seemed to be getting over the shock of her near-death experience. After a comprehensive examination, she was released early the next morning. She had suffered minor shock and some bruising. Other than that, she was cleared to re-enter society without a hitch, although she was instructed by the police to stay close so they could call her as a witness once her assailant was apprehended.

Since she didn't seem to have family or any close friends, Nick was the one who greeted her upon discharge. She looked nearly as relieved to see him in the morning as she had been the night before. Matted hair and dark circles under her eyes did little to detract from her ethereal beauty. Next to Pamela, this girl was probably the most beautiful woman he had ever laid eyes on.

That meant little to him at the moment, however. She was like a frightened child, and he provided the only relief in sight. He couldn't bear to let her go back home with a killer stalking her. His last check with Ramsey had indicated that the maniac was still on the loose. Apparently, he hadn't returned to his apartment, and the authorities were starting to worry that something had tipped him off regarding their presence surrounding his domicile.

"So how did you know, anyway?" she started.

He interpreted the question and took the liberty of explaining the entire sordid tale to her, from the murder in his home to his discovery that the perpetrator had most likely selected her as his next victim. She appeared scared by the prospect, but not as utterly shocked as he expected her to be. Something told him that previous experience had made this kind of thing almost commonplace to her. Maybe not the serial killer part, but she certainly seemed to be no stranger to life's difficulties.

After hearing the story, she indicated that she was convinced he was telling the truth. It made no difference really, because to her, he was already a savior. No matter what his motives had been, she probably would have been forever indebted to him for coming to her rescue. She told him that her first thought had been that maybe he was a sexual stalker, but something in his eyes completely defied that logic. She said she was now writing the whole thing off to fate. She continued to refer to Nick as her guardian angel.

"I guess we're a match made in heaven, right?" she joked.

"What do you mean?"

"Well, both of our lives were nearly ruined by the same guy. I'd say that's fate."

"I guess you could say that, although I believe he intended to do more than 'ruin' your life last night."

"True. Still, he didn't, because you saved me," she said, smiling.

She was looking at him like a young girl might look at her teen idol.

"So, what's your name?" Nick asked, trying to change the subject.

He was now blushing a little, fully aware that the girl's complete attention had been cast in his humble direction.

"My name is Angela Graves."

"Good to meet you, Angela. I'm Nick Lacour."

"I know."

"You do. How?"

"They told me at the hospital that you paid my bill. I asked who and they said, 'Why, your Uncle Nick, of course.'"

"Yeah, I might have told them something like that," Nick said with a laugh, now slightly embarrassed.

"Well then, *Uncle Nick,* now that you've got me, where are you taking me?"

"I thought I'd take you back to your apartment and drop you off."

She looked at him wide-eyed, appearing to be on the verge of a tearful panic attack. Before it went too far, Nick bailed her out.

"I'm just kidding. I'm going to take you back to my parents' house, if it's OK with you."

"That was kind of cruel, Uncle Nick," she retorted, slapping his arm.

"I know, but I couldn't resist."

"So why your parents' house? Don't you have enough money to move out on your own?" she mocked.

"My house is kind of messed up right now."

"Oh," she replied. Now it was her turn to feel embarrassed. She had forgotten that he said the murder took place in his home.

"I'm really sorry, Nick, I was just joking around," she said, trying to overcome her guilt for making such an insensitive comment.

"Don't think anything of it. I know you were just kidding."

"Tell me about yourself, Nick. When you're not saving damsels in distress, what do you do with your time?" she asked, feeling somewhat better about the situation and wanting to change the subject as well.

"I'm a lawyer, although I haven't been practicing much lately."

"Really? Sounds pretty cool."

"It's pretty dull actually, but it pays the bills."

"Somehow you don't strike me as a dull guy."

"Beyond chasing serial killers for excitement, I actually lead a fairly uneventful life."

Nick smiled at the dark humor. The uncomfortable tension in the air had long since lifted. They had dropped into a conversational routine that mimicked the banter of a long-standing couple. Somehow, he already felt completely at ease around her.

He prepped Angela for her first meeting with his parents like she was a star witness in a major trial. She seemed to be having fun with the act and had decided to play it out to the hilt. The chance to pretend she was someone else while entering another person's world held a lot of appeal. She had promised him she would be a convincing actress and not blow the cover.

✳   ✳   ✳   ✳

Rucker had been driving through the night. He stopped once for gas and a few snacks. It was about time to find another car and ditch the truck. His head still hurt from the surprise attack. He couldn't get the attacker's face out of his mind. He had become so obsessive about it that thoughts of Lola had actually been replaced by the hero's mug.

He still couldn't shake the feeling that he had seen him in another time or place. Suddenly, like a bolt of lightning from the sky, it hit him. The guy who showed up last night was the husband of his last victim. He remembered the face from the news telecasts after the murder and from pictures in the *St. Louis Post Dispatch*.

Now he was really pissed. Somehow, the widower had tracked him and ruined his plans for number twenty-one. To make matters even worse, he had kind of kicked Rucker's ass. He wasn't keen to admit the last part, still trying to convince himself that he had been sucker punched.

Shaking with anger, he pulled his truck off of I-65 at the next exit. He was almost to Birmingham, Alabama, with no destination in mind. Knowing who had foiled his meeting with Lola had inflamed him. He couldn't let Lacour off that easily. He had inserted pain into the lawyer's life once before and was fully capable of doing it again. He wasn't about to let some chicken shit lawyer drive him away.

Sure, there was the matter of the cops to contend with as well, but he didn't care. He had managed to avoid them for more than a decade and would be able to do so for another few days. The message was now clear. He had to return to St.

Louis and find both Lacour and Lola. Once he did, he'd make a spectacle of them both for the whole world to see.

"No one makes a fool out of Gerald Rucker," he ranted. "No one!"

With that, he drove down a country road just twenty miles outside of Birmingham and began to seek out his next mode of transportation. A few cosmetic changes to his features would also ensue, followed by a triumphant return to Missouri. Once there, he'd make the hero and his girl regret the day they interfered with one of Gerald Rucker's prized missions.

*   *   *   *

Once Nick got Angela to his parents' house, he discovered he couldn't go through with their well-concocted story. He'd always been brutally honest with his folks, and this would be no exception. He told them the truth, not just for their own benefit, but for Angela's and Justin's as well. His instincts told them that the killer would come after them. He'd definitely come for Angela, and he didn't want his family to be subjected to that risk as well.

After explaining the entire story to his stunned parents, he announced that he'd be taking Angela to the lake house to harbor her out of harm's way until the killer was caught. In addition, he wanted Justin to go stay with Deidre Martin and suggested that his parents take a timely vacation. They were very reluctant at first, resisting Nick's suggestion that they flee their own home. His argument was persuasive in the end, however. His well-formulated plan began to make sense, and they agreed to go along with it. His father had made it clear that he wasn't happy with this mess but would indeed honor his wishes.

With that out of the way, Nick now had to account for his son and get him out of town before the killer made another untimely appearance. He phoned Deidre and asked if she could keep Justin for a few days. He spared her the details he had bestowed upon his parents by simply saying that his folks needed a break. Deidre gladly agreed and offered to pick him up right away.

Now the only thing left to do was escape to his lakefront vacation home in the Ozarks and wait for justice to take its course. He hoped Ramsey and his crew were making progress. His thirst for revenge had abated, and he now just wanted the entire fiasco to be over. Once the killer was caught, he could resume raising his son and trying to force his life back to normal. He knew that it would never be truly normal again but hoped that it could get better than its current state.

Somewhere in the dark recesses of his mind where his thoughts didn't want to go, there was a small hope that having Angela with him might bait the killer. He didn't want to consciously go there, but the wish was present. While burying the thought, he reminded himself that sometimes, it's best to be careful what he wished for because it might just come true.

*　　　*　　　*　　　*

Now driving a green 1992 Honda Accord, Rucker embarked on the long haul back to St. Louis. The entire way there, he realized that he didn't know for sure where he was going. He doubted very seriously that Lacour was currently maintaining the same residence. In fact, he figured it was probably for sale by now.

"Where to, then?" he asked himself.

He could probably start with Lacour's law firm and take it from there. He remembered reading that Lacour had been some hot shit lawyer, so finding out more about that wouldn't prove too difficult.

What if he wasn't working? Then he might have a bigger challenge on his hands, but he'd cross that bridge when he came to it. Right now, he had to get back to the city limits and find a place to pitch camp. With a little luck, the whole thing would be over in a day or two and he'd have the liberty to hit the road again, for good this time.

*　　　*　　　*　　　*

During the first half of the ride to the vacation home, neither of them spoke. Nick was lost in his own world, thoughts drifting among the winter trees that lined both sides of the highway. The only words spoken had been during his phone call to Ramsey. He felt obligated to let the detective know that he was harboring a witness. Ramsey responded with another mini tirade for investigation interference but finally relented. Nick had convinced him that the getaway was actually the safest thing for all those involved. The following hour of virtual silence was finally broken as his voice rose above the din of the radio.

"How are you doing over there? Need anything?"

"I'm fine, thanks," Angela responded.

She looked like her mind hadn't floated completely back to the car yet.

"So how did you end up working at a place like The Pie Factory?" Nick asked.

He was attempting to break the silence with a friendly question. It had merely been an attempt to elicit conversation, but it came off more judgmental than anything else.

"What's that supposed to mean?" Angela asked, breaking away from her hypnotic trance with the rapidly passing countryside.

Nick regretted the question the moment it left his lips, but he couldn't take it back. Actually, it had been on his mind for a while, but he never had the guts to utter the syllables. Now that it was out there, he was forced to continue.

"Look, I'm not judging you. I'm just trying to understand."

"What's there to understand? I was alone on the streets at seventeen. There weren't many options," Angela responded sullenly while she tried to shift her attention back to the moving scenery.

"I'm sorry. I was only making conversation and trying to get to know you better," Nick answered.

He had determined it was probably better to defer this line of questioning to another day. Still, he wanted to know how this seemingly innocent girl had been so brutalized by life. He wanted to protect her in anyway possible and hated picturing her in a place like The Pie Factory.

After a few more moments of driving, Angela again looked up at him. Their eyes met, and he noticed that she had been crying.

"I think it's really sweet that you're concerned about me. No one has ever really cared before," she said as her voice grew distant.

Her hand touched his free hand, which had been resting on the gearshift. She seemed so fragile, Nick thought. Despite upsetting her, he still wanted to understand.

"You know, there is so much you could do," he continued, leaving the statement open-ended and not willing to leave well enough alone.

"Yeah? Like what? I have no education, no job experience, no money…" she smirked. She was obviously growing frustrated, and anger began to leak into her voice. "What do you propose I do?"

"Anything you want, Angela. I know it sounds cliché, but you seem to have so much to offer. Why work in a dump like The Pie Factory?"

"Like I said before, there weren't any other options. Where else can a girl like me earn enough money to stay alive without an education or past job experience?"

"Well, you could go back to school for starters."

"Sure, easy for you to say, Mr. High-and-Mighty Lawyer. I don't think colleges are knocking themselves out to enroll strippers who never finished high school."

"You said you weren't a stripper."

"I might as well be a stripper. I work in a fucking titty bar."

"That's bullshit, Angela. It's a cop-out, and you know it," Nick replied with an annoyance of his own that had begun to infuse his voice.

"All you people that were born with a silver spoon in your mouth think life is so fucking easy. Try living in my world for a little while, and then talk to me about college and doing more with my life," she shot back while withdrawing her hand from his. She was getting sarcastic, and her voice had formed a cold edge.

"What I mean is you are young and bright. You could do so much with your life. I hate to see you waste it in that place."

"Can we drop this, please? I don't need advice from someone who has lived on easy street his whole life. Besides, what do you really know about me, anyway?"

"Give me your hand," Nick demanded, as he lifted his shirt revealing a jagged scar that ran from his navel to his sternum.

"What are you, some kind of pervert? Let me out!" she yelled, groping for the door handle.

"Give me your goddamn hand!" he exclaimed as she surrendered her hand, shaking and looking uncertain.

"Here, feel this," he demanded.

Her hand ran up and down the scar. It protruded above the skin and was as noticeable to touch as it was to sight.

"This is an example of the easy street I grew up on," Nick said with disgust.

He pushed her hand away and re-covered the scar with his shirt.

"What happened?" she asked hesitantly, horrified by what she had just seen and felt.

"It's a knife wound. I was in a few altercations while I lived on *easy* street."

"That looks like a hell of a lot more than just an altercation."

"There are others. Want to see?" Nick asked, softening a little.

"No thanks. I think I've had my fill for the day."

"Things aren't always what they appear, Angela. My life wasn't as easy as you think," Nick said without looking at her.

His grin had disappeared, and his attention was focused on the road ahead.

She didn't know what to say. Her upbringing had been brutal, too, but she hadn't pegged Nick as a child of the streets. From the looks of his wound, he had narrowly skirted death at least once in his life. She was embarrassed that she had assumed so much and had obviously been mistaken.

"All you see is the job, the car, and my clothes. But you don't know what I had to go through to get here," Nick said, keeping his eyes on the road and both hands on the wheel.

"I apologize, Nick. And you're right," she added, "I probably did judge you a little based on those things."

"We may be at different points in our lives right now, Angela, but we really aren't that different," he volunteered.

"I think maybe I realized that the first time I looked into your eyes. Maybe I did let the car and the job cloud my judgment," she replied.

"You're forgiven. I just wanted you to know that you aren't the only one who has been through a lot."

She grabbed his free hand again. The unveiling of the scar had made her feel closer to him. She indeed did think they shared more than just the desire to escape a madman. They were linked in deeper ways than she had realized before.

They drove on in silence. Angela's thoughts had changed. They were brought together by fate in the strangest of ways, but at that moment, their hands felt like one. It was almost as if they had known each other all of their lives. She basked in the comfort of the moment. At this, the most terrifying time in her life, she felt safe. It was the first time she had ever felt that way.

CHAPTER 18

▼

When he finally made it back to the city, Rucker immediately began an investigation of his own. He started by plucking a White Pages from an outdoor phone booth at a Mobil gas station. The book had been attached to the booth by a wire, which snapped rather easily under the strain of his knife.

He went inside to buy some chips, a pack of smokes, and a Coke. When he got back to the car, he peeled the phone book open and began to search through the Ls. Lacoste, Lacostelo, Lacour...

"Bingo," he said.

He ran his index finger down the line of Lacours in the book. An entry for the lawyer didn't exist, but there were six others to choose from. He folded the page and threw the book onto the passenger's seat. He cracked open the Coke, took a huge swig, and prepared to find a cheap hotel to call home for a few days.

Once there, he'd dial all the Lacours in the book and try to find out where the hero had gone. If that didn't work, it would be on to the law firm. Beyond that was uncertainty, but he had no doubt that he'd find him. Once he did, he suspected he'd find Lola as well. The thought of the two of them together further intensified his rage. He'd do things to them that were inconceivable. No one escaped from Gerald Rucker.

*   *   *   *

"So where *are* you taking me, anyway?" Angela asked, stretching and reaching her hand behind Nick's head.

"We're going to a little place that my wife and I bought a few years ago. It's not much, but I'm quite certain that lunatic won't be able to find us there."

"Oh, OK."

Her reply was followed by a long silence. She didn't seem to know what to say next. The entire situation had become surreal.

"When you say it's not much, do you mean 'not much' as defined by someone who drives a Lexus or 'not much' like the kind of places I grew up in?" she asked with a smile.

Nick returned her smile but didn't respond.

"So that means 'not much' is quite different than the way I would look at it, right?"

"Let's just say it will serve the purpose."

"And what exactly is the purpose?" Angela asked.

"The purpose is to keep you alive and make sure the sick fuck who's following you gets caught before he catches us," Nick responded as he turned toward her, more serious this time.

"Don't even think that you are going to leave me in the middle of nowhere while you go to look for this guy," she said, gripping his neck. "Where you go, I go, Mr. Lacour. You got that?"

"I got it, I got it. Now, can you release the death grip you have on my neck?" he winced.

Angela relaxed her grip and started to give him a gentle massage.

"That's much better," Nick said softly. "Now you're going to put me to sleep instead."

"We can't have that, can we? I'm not done with you yet," Angela said.

A sly grin spread across her face. She was obviously becoming more and more comfortable around this man, whom she barely knew.

"Oh yeah? I don't know if I like the sound of that," he said with raised eyebrows. He continued with feigned terror, adding, "If it's anything like the neck rub, I think I might be in some trouble."

Angela pulled his head sideways. She leaned toward him and gently kissed him on the cheek. Suddenly, Nick knew the rescue from a killer meant much more to Angela than just the fact that he had saved her life. What was he doing? He was alone with a beautiful woman just a short time after his wife's death, and it didn't feel right.

He had risked everything in his quest to catch the killer. He had jeopardized the life of this young girl sitting next to him. He had probably lost his job and most of his sanity. Even worse, his absence was doing untold damage to Justin.

His son needed him more than ever right now, and he was away again. He had become unable to focus on anything else but catching the psycho who had forever changed his life.

The path of his obsession was like a tornado, damaging everyone and everything in its way. Despite knowing all of this, he couldn't go back now. He had risked it all, and if he gave up right now, it would have been for nothing. Besides, he sensed the killer would be looking for Angela and him soon. He didn't know how he knew that, but his instincts told him it was a reality. He was dealing with much more than a dangerous man. He was dealing with pure evil.

"We're almost there," Nick said, while attempting to divert his thoughts.

"Good, I'm getting hungry. I hope this little place of yours comes with food."

"I think we can probably find something edible. That is if you don't mind eating sardines and crackers?"

"You better be kidding. I'd rather starve!"

"Well, for my special guests, I might be able to find something else."

"Oh, now I'm a *special* guest? You must really be hurting for guests these days, Nick."

Nick grinned. He was starting to like this girl. He forced the thought aside, though. The two of them had been drawn together by a set of circumstances beyond their control. They were both linked to a psychotic killer. It was the duress that had bonded them, wasn't it? He couldn't possibly be developing feelings for another woman right on the heels of Pamela's death.

No, it was undoubtedly the situation that had pulled them together. Despite trying to convince himself of that, he still felt close to this girl, whom he barely knew. He couldn't let those feelings come into play. He had to ensure her safety and make sure the killer was caught at the same time. Those challenges alone should be enough to occupy all of his waking thoughts. Despite those facts, there was still something about this girl that intrigued him.

Nick blinked hard and shook his head, as if that simple act would purge his mind of the recurring fantasies he had about Angela. She must have been reading his mind, because she wore a similar expression to his own. They both capitulated to looks of confusion while being strangely happy at the same time. She may have been falling for him already. Despite his efforts to the contrary, nothing could change that. The last thing he wanted to do was hurt her. In fact, it had become his self-appointed obligation to ensure her safety.

He stifled his confused thoughts and turned up the radio. A newer song by a popular group blared through the car's eight speakers. The song must have bridged the gap in their ages, because they both began to sing along. They laughed at each other's imitation of the lead singer's vocals. The laughter temporarily dismissed the gravity of their situation. For the time being, there was nothing more than the music and the impromptu karaoke of two very scared individuals.

✳   ✳   ✳   ✳

Rucker had finished calling the last Lacour on his list. To his dismay, not one of the six knew who Nick Lacour was. He couldn't fathom the fact that every Lacour wasn't in some way related, given the uncommon name they shared.

He had reached five of the six on his first try. The first three simply said wrong number and hung up. The fourth was not home, and the final two scoured their family trees but couldn't find a connection. In fact, the last call went on for more than ten minutes while Rucker listened to a thirteen-year-old ramble on about her family history. He would have terminated the call, but he held a glimmer of hope that the person on the other end could aid his search. It turned out not to be the case.

Disgusted and frustrated, he flopped onto the springy hotel mattress and stared up at the smoke-stained ceiling. He was now occupying a room at a Motel 6 for less than thirty dollars a night. His choice of neighborhoods explained the low cost and the poor accommodations. He reckoned the motel probably rented some of the rooms by the hour, judging from the noise coming from his neighbor's room.

The seventh call he placed held the most promise. After thumbing through the hotel issue Yellow Pages, he had been delighted to find a law firm containing the sought-after name.

"Well what do you know? The little prick is a full partner!" he exclaimed.

He punched in the number for Evans, Masters & Lacour and got their receptionist. Amy, as she had announced herself, was extremely chatty. Unfortunately, she was only mildly helpful. She conceded that Nick Lacour worked for the firm, though she didn't know "for how much longer," as she had put it. Evidently, Mr. Lacour had taken many liberties for a couple of months. In fact, he hadn't been to work since his wife's death, and the senior partners were growing tired of waiting for the grieving process to end. She even told him in a hushed voice that word on the street was he'd be getting canned soon.

"You didn't hear it from me," she said.

She indicated that was privileged and unofficial information, but he figured she had probably blabbed it to the entire office by now.

Having grown tired of the conversation, he tried to pin down Lacour's current whereabouts. Amy simply said that no one really knew where he was at the moment.

"He had been staying with his parents, of course, but it seems he may not be there any longer," she whispered.

"Oh, you mean John and Nancy Lacour?" Rucker said, throwing out the first names that came to mind and hoping she'd fill in the blanks.

"No, silly, Mike and Jane," she responded with a laugh.

"Oh yeah, Mike and I go way back," he responded, while laughing at her and not with her.

Having what he needed, he terminated the conversation. Amy seemed disappointed that it had ended. She was seemingly willing to continue babbling all day, but he had had his fill.

When he hung up, he pulled the White Pages back out and looked over the roster of Lacours one last time. There in the middle was the single residence he hadn't been able to contact. Michael and Jane Lacour might just have to receive a visit from their son's good old friend Gerald Rucker.

*   *   *   *

"This is amazing!" Angela exclaimed.

She looked like a kid who had just seen a Santa Claus for the first time.

Nick smiled at her excitement. Being with Angela was like living life through brand-new eyes. The simplest things made such an impression on her. She seemed like a blind person who had just been granted sight.

"I'm glad you approve," Nick said. "It's no Pie Factory, but it will have to do."

"I want the tour reserved for *special* guests," she said, while playfully slapping his arm and wrinkling her nose at his sarcasm.

"Follow me, madam," Nick said, leading her to the great room.

They left their bags in the foyer, and he showed her around his vacation home. He and Pamela had built the house shortly after Justin's birth. They had wanted a quiet place to escape the high pace of their everyday lives. This house on the lake had been a perfect spot. Set in a cove and surrounded by trees, he had paid significantly more for the lot than he had for the home. It wasn't an overly large house, but its setting was spectacular.

The lower level consisted of a large great room, complete with a stone fireplace. The remainder of the floor contained a kitchen, small dining room, master bedroom with a full bath, and a small laundry room. The upstairs loft was made up of two bedrooms adjoined by a larger living room and one and a half bathrooms.

The decorations throughout the house were modern eclectic. Nick couldn't take any of the credit. Pamela was the sole decorator, just as she had been at their home in St. Louis. It was quiet, comfortable, and the perfect place to escape a murderer.

"Here you have the great room," Nick said while making sweeping motion with his arm.

Angela's eyes scanned the room from floor to vaulted ceiling. The hunter green carpeting was plush. A brown, softly cushioned, L-shaped couch occupied the center of the room. There was a forty-three-inch television against the wall to the right. A square, light brown coffee table was in front of the couch.

The room was simple but relaxing. Track lighting above the fireplace had been lowered to a dim setting. Two brass floor lamps provided the balance of the light in the room. Nick and Pamela had often moved the coffee table and assumed positions on the floor in front of the fireplace. He was now looking at the spot, remembering some of the most passionate lovemaking in their marriage. A hollow pain filled his chest. He would never be able to bring Pamela here again. The thought made him feel tiny and alone in the large room. He feebly attempted to remove the memories by guiding the tour to a different room. Adjacent to the main room was a kitchen and eating area, which he referred to as the dining room.

"This is where the gourmet sardines and crackers will be served," he said, pointing to the large country table in the eating portion of the room.

A breakfast counter divided the room, giving the appearance of two individual rooms. The floor in the eating area was parquet. It shifted to tan ceramic tiles in the "kitchen" half. All decorations were completely modern, including an island that contained a grill and downdraft for simulated barbecues. Pamela hadn't gone yellow berserk with this kitchen. The stainless steel refrigerator and black, flat-surface stove made the room look like it belonged in the twenty-first century.

Shiny green ceramic tiles decorated the countertops and backsplash. A black dishwasher was placed just to the lower right of the double sink. It was flanked by solid oak cabinets.

Angela hadn't said much throughout the tour. She followed Nick through the house with wide eyes. This was clearly a standard of living she had never encountered in her own life.

"Show me the bedroom," she smiled nervously.

"I'll show you all three of them, including the separate ones we will each be sleeping in," Nick responded.

She looked somewhat relieved that the unasked question about sleeping arrangements had been resolved before it became an issue.

After spending another few minutes surveying the remainder of the house, he led her to his favorite spot on the property; a large deck that covered the entire back end of the home. They went outside through French doors that stood to the left of the fireplace in the great room. The cedar deck was huge. It was overkill for the size of the home, but Nick said he didn't care. It had been his only request when they had the house built.

Since the house stood on the side of a hill, stilts supported the deck. It was bordered in all directions by heavy undergrowth and large trees. The nearest neighbor was blocked from view by the dense foliage. From the deck, a wooden staircase led to the boat dock below. A thirty-eight-foot scarab occupied a raised slip on the covered dock.

Nick and Pamela had loved to sit on the deck and watch the sun set over the lake. Again, the realization that he would never be able to bring her here again struck him. He stared absently at the still black water. A half-moon cast a silvery glow across the obsidian lake. He was drawn into its dark chasm and hypnotized by the depth of its blackness.

"What are you thinking about, Nick?" she asked, wrapping her arm around his waist.

She was now shivering from the cold.

Surprisingly, he returned the favor and wrapped his arm around her shoulders, momentarily thinking he was holding his wife. He broke his trance with the water and looked at the frightened young girl next to him. He couldn't help but feel for her vulnerability. He didn't know why, but protecting her had become almost as important as catching the killer.

"Why don't we go inside and get something to eat? It's pretty cold out here," he said, releasing his arm from her shoulders.

"Thank you, Nick," was all she could manage. Her eyes welled up like small pools fed by the nearby lake.

She tightened her hold around his waist and brought her other arm across his torso. She was now facing him, arms around his back, looking into his eyes.

"For what?" he asked.

"Well, for saving my life for starters," she responded, wiping her overflowing eyes on his chest.

He didn't say anything. He put both arms around her and returned her hold. He was again overcome by her innocence and near helplessness. She seemed so small and frail in his arms. His need to protect her had intensified.

"It's not just that," she said as she lifted her head from his chest and gazed into his eyes. "It's also because you brought me here and have made me feel safe for the first time in my life."

"You deserve to feel safe, Angela. I'm glad I could help you feel that way," he said, holding her tightly for another moment.

He wanted to say something else, but the words escaped him. He was too confused by his own feelings to risk confusing her as well.

He stood there another moment, fused to this girl by a common fear and something else that went beyond his conscious grasp. The link to her was becoming deeper and perhaps beyond his control. The moment, like their trip to this place, felt like it had been guided by an imaginary compass. The crisp winter air did little to penetrate the heat of their embrace. They felt like one, dependent upon each other for warmth and emotional survival.

"OK, let's get you inside and feed you a decent meal," he said, leading her toward the half-open French doors.

They walked arm in arm back into the house, out of the cold, but still precariously close to harm's way. Together as one, Nick felt they had the strength to fight off whatever remained beyond the doors leading to the deck. Lurking somewhere in the dark shadows of the night, he could feel its presence off in the distance. Something was out there somewhere. The thought made him shudder in a way that the cold winter chill never could.

$$*\qquad*\qquad*\qquad*$$

Rucker got to the Lacour home just before dark. Right away, he could tell that no one was home. He decided to park his car at the end of the street and wait for a while. Once it was dark, he'd consider letting himself in, but he hoped the old folks would return soon. He sat in the car listening to the incessant and noncomical ramblings of a late afternoon deejay.

"Why do these people insist on trying to be funny?" he wondered. "Just play some fucking music and be done with it."

Time dragged on in a painfully slow manner. His legs were starting to cramp, and he had to take a wicked piss. Now fully dark in the neighborhood, he let himself out of the car and took a leak on one of the resident's trees. Feeling much better, he got back into the car and decided to head back to the hotel. It was becoming apparent that the Lacours wouldn't be returning anytime soon. He'd have no choice but to break into their home or the crime scene home, owned by Nick Lacour. He preferred the former, feeling it held much less risk.

Thoroughly unhappy about his failed reconnaissance, he went back to the Motel 6 via a stop at a White Castle drive-through. He ate his Belly Bomber sandwiches in his room and smoked cigarettes while a rerun of *Friends* blared in the background. With his stomach churning from the combination of smokes and greasy, onion-covered burgers, he went back out to get a six-pack and some Tums. So far, his return to Missouri had not been a glorious one. He had to track down Lola and the lawyer soon before he literally lost his mind.

*   *   *   *

"We're going to have to get some groceries tomorrow," Nick said absently.

He had found just enough food to scrounge together a meal for the two of them. It had consisted of pasta with jar sauce and a can of green beans. It was a minor step up from the sardines and crackers he had jokingly threatened.

They ate quietly to the sounds of silverware scraping ceramic. Nick's mind fixated on the strain of their escape and the uncertainty of what lay ahead. He suspected Angela was thinking the same thing. Neither had eaten in more than a day, so despite the tension in their lives and apparent lack of hunger, they managed to polish off the entire meal.

With Angela's assistance, Nick cleared off the dinner clutter and loaded the dishwasher. He had been too emotionally charged to feel the exhaustion that was starting to overcome him. She looked equally as tired. The events of the past couple of months had left an indelible mark on his psyche.

"Let's take the rest of this wine into the living room and build a fire," he offered.

"I'll help. Where's the wood?" she asked.

"It's in the garage," he said, pointing to a door leading from the kitchen to the house's two-car garage.

She left him to gather the firewood while he cleaned up the remainder of the dinner remnants. She returned carrying three fairly large logs. He had finished his duties in the kitchen and was watching her as she lugged the logs the last remaining feet to the fireplace.

"Need any help?" he asked.

"I got it."

"You're pretty strong for a petite waitress," he said as she unloaded the wood onto the hearth.

"You don't want any of this, Nick. I'll mess you up good," she said as she tightened her arms into the exaggerated pose of a bodybuilder.

"Oh yeah? You and how many of your little stripper buddies?" he responded.

"In your dreams, Lacour. Is that why you rescued me, so I'd let you wrestle around with me and my friends?" she mocked.

"You guys do that?" he asked, widening his eyes.

"Not for just anyone," she joked.

"How about for me?" he asked this as he crossed the room to the place where she was crouching by the fireplace. "Can you give me a demonstration?"

"I don't know. You're pretty old. I don't think your heart could take it."

"This heart?" he asked, pointing to his chest.

"Yeah, that heart," she said, while emphasizing her point with a jab to his well-muscled chest. The punch landed harder than she had planned.

"You better run, little girl," he said, while feigning injury.

She started laughing as he reached for her. With that, she took off, leading a chase that began up the stairs toward the second floor. During the chase, his foot caught the last step, and he spilled onto the landing at the top of the staircase.

"Are you OK?" she asked, afraid he might have really hurt himself.

"I think I might have hurt my knee," he grimaced.

"Let me see it," she said, rushing to his fallen side.

Just as she got close enough, he grabbed her ankle and pulled her to the ground with him. They wrestled around on the floor, both laughing. He finally managed to pin the spunky girl to the ground. Sitting on her stomach, he pressed her arms to the floor.

"Say uncle, and I'll let you up."

"Get off of me. You're crushing my petite waitress body," she giggled.

He let up and started to get off of her. She seized the opportunity to wriggle free and pounced on top of him, pinning him to the carpet just as he had done to her.

"Now *you* say uncle, and I won't be forced to hurt you," she said. She then began to tickle him, which was highly successful.

"OK, OK," he laughed. "Uncle."

"Told you I'd whip your butt," she said as she rolled off of him and brushed her hands together like she had just won a big-time wrestling match.

He pulled her down again before she had managed to get out of arm's reach. They lay on the floor next to each other, laughter subsiding. They were inches apart, staring into each other's eyes. He brushed the hair out of her face. Her beauty enthralled him. Only one other woman had ever captivated him like she did. That woman had become his wife.

He lay there, looking at her with his heart pounding from the physical exercise and from the building emotions he had been struggling with. He rolled onto his back, ashamed of what he was thinking. Could he be so shallow as to entertain the thought of sleeping with another woman before his wife's memory was even cold? The question made him sit up and look away from her. He knew all about rebound relationships. The fact that he was starting to make Angela a rebound for the love of his life made the situation even more wrong in his mind.

"Let's finish building that fire," he said, trying to avoid what was sure to happen next.

Angela sat up, too, and put a hand on his face. She drew his head toward hers. Neither of them spoke. She reached up and kissed him softly on the lips. She then put her hand on his shoulder and raised herself off the floor.

"Let's go build that fire," she said.

*   *   *   *

She had been afraid to look at him after the kiss. She sensed that he wanted her, too, but she was all too well aware of his recent loss. She felt guilty for trying to take advantage of him at a time when he was so vulnerable. She was trying to put their desires aside, wondering what it all meant. The attraction was strong. She didn't know if her feelings were caused by the situation, or if they went deeper than that. She had never really been loved by a man. Consequently, she had never been in love, either. Nick came out of nowhere and saved her life, so she was trying not to confuse an allegiance to him for something more substantial. Still, this felt different.

Nick got up and followed her down the stairs to the living room. She watched as he rearranged the logs and added some kindling and newspaper before lighting the fire. She sat entranced as the initial flames blackened the paper and began to lick the underside of the logs. Within ten minutes, the logs were engulfed and began to crackle. Nick slid the screen across the front of the fireplace. Firelight bathed the room and flickered across his face.

She looked at him again without speaking. Words no longer seemed necessary because she felt like she knew what he was thinking. She stretched out on the floor in front of the fireplace. Nick put his arm around her, and she rested her head on his chest. Five minutes later, she was sound asleep, dreaming about what she wished had happened at the top of the stairs.

CHAPTER 19

▼

Rucker was losing it. Lola had vanished, and he was starting to question whether or not he'd ever see her again. Not convinced that she was actually with the lawyer, he had spun by her apartment and The Pie Factory on a couple of occasions. During his last visit to the Factory, he was told that she hadn't been to work in weeks, and no one knew what had happened to her. That was probably enough to indicate that she really was with Lacour, and the realization infuriated him. His anger boiled even hotter because the lawyer was nowhere to be found, either.

He had broken into the senior Lacour home twice but couldn't find anything to clue him in. He had grown so tired of sifting through family snapshots and sappy trinkets that he had half a mind to torch the place. Where the hell were the old folks? Would they ever return to their home?

The search had lasted two weeks and he was no further along now than he had been when he first checked into the motel. In that time, he had smoked more cigarettes and eaten more fast food than most people could in a lifetime. He was tired, bored, and irritated as hell. If it weren't for the still brightly burning obsession he had with Lola, he would have aborted the mission and moved on. It was starting to look like he may not have a choice.

On a whim, he decided to call the Lacour home a final time. If they had been vacationing, certainly they would be returning soon. They had left behind all of their cherished belongings, so they definitely had not abandoned their residence. He took a deep pull from his cigarette and punched in the phone number. After four rings he was about to hang up. Then, a near-miracle occurred.

"Hello," came the tired-sounding, feeble reply on the other end.

"Uhh, h-hello," Rucker stammered, caught off guard by the unexpected voice.

"May I help you?"

"Yes ma'am, this is Special Agent Witter with the FBI," he replied, starting to get it together.

"Oh my! How can I help you?" the old woman screeched.

"Well ma'am, I was hoping you could help me contact your son."

"Oh, I don't know, Agent Witter. Nicholas is out of town."

"Where is he, ma'am?"

"Uh, well, I'm not so sure," she said.

It was obvious that she wasn't a very polished liar, so Rucker seized the opportunity and took a bite out of her wavering confidence.

"Well, ma'am, I think you do know. As a matter of fact, I hope for your sake that you do because I'd hate to think that you'd obstruct justice by lying for your son," Rucker concluded while holding his breath.

He felt that last line was sheer brilliance.

"Agent Witter, may I ask what this is regarding?" she asked after a lengthy pause.

"Yes ma'am, it's regarding your daughter-in-law's murder," he responded, realizing the hook was set and she was on the verge of cracking.

"Oh my, that's what I thought."

"Yes, we believe we may have captured the perp, but we need your son to identify him to be certain," he said, hoping it was a good enough touch to finish her off.

"I see. In that case, I suppose there wouldn't be any harm in giving you his phone number."

"Yes, the number would be nice, but I need to see him right away. Where is your son, Mrs. Lacour?" he asked, punctuating the question with an authoritative voice that was sure to earn a reward.

"Nicholas is at his lake house in the Ozarks," she blurted.

The dam had broken! Rucker felt a ten-ton weight being lifted from his shoulders. The little bit that remained of his questionable sanity had been fully replenished.

"Can you tell me how to find him?" he asked, going for the icing on the cake.

She complied and spilled the remainder of the beans. By the time they hung up, he had an address, phone number, and directions. He was even offered an invitation to the Lacour home for a piece of homemade apple pie after the arrest was final.

Wearing a smile of utter contentment and satisfaction, he snagged his keys from the nightstand and got ready to make the two-and-a-half-hour drive that would eventually reunite him with Lola and her hero. Two for the price of one. He couldn't have hit the jackpot any better than that. He rushed out the door toward his car. It would be all he could do to keep himself from testing every last piston in the four-cylinder Honda on the way toward his final destiny.

*   *   *   *

Daybreak marked the beginning of their third week at the lake. Brilliant sunlight shone through a crack in the curtains in the master bedroom. Angela stirred; the light was cast directly on her face. She rolled over, stretched, and looked at the alarm clock on the nightstand. It was almost noon. She couldn't believe she had slept so long.

She and Nick had fallen asleep on the floor in front of the fire prior to ten the night before. It wasn't the first time in their two weeks alone together that something like that had happened. Angela had wanted the situation to develop, but she still didn't feel right about forcing herself on him. She sensed that he was attracted to her but knew he was still grieving. She didn't want to be *that* person, the one who took advantage of someone during a weak moment.

At some point during the previous night, Nick must have carried her into the largest bedroom. She didn't remember walking there on her own. She couldn't remember waking up during the night. It was the longest, deepest sleep she had had in years. She rolled over and looked at the other side of the bed. It was unruffled. Obviously, he had slept in a different room. She got up and pulled the curtains open. It was the first time the sun had shone in Missouri for what seemed like months. She felt invigorated by the brightness of the sunlight and the fourteen hours of sleep.

She wandered into the living room and peered through the doorway into the kitchen. She saw him standing in the kitchen cooking breakfast. He didn't turn from the stove, but must have heard her coming.

"Good morning," he greeted.

"Morning," she responded groggily, while trying to rub the aftereffects of sleep from her eyes.

"I was starting to think you might sleep all day," he said.

"Yeah, I haven't slept like that since I was a little girl. What was in that wine, anyway?" she joked.

"What, you don't remember when I took you to bed?" he asked.

"Should I remember something?" she replied, raising her eyebrows.

"Yeah, you said, 'Thanks for taking me to the carnival,' and then you went back to sleep."

"I must have been dreaming," she said, now smiling. "I haven't been to a carnival in years."

✳   ✳   ✳   ✳

Nick looked at Angela, who was now standing in the kitchen. The natural light coming through the window shades was illuminating her face. She wasn't wearing a stitch of makeup, but she still looked beautiful. She almost looked like an angel, with the sunlight shining through her nightshirt outlining the curves of her perfect body.

She must have registered the fact that he was checking her out. She seemed to trace the point of his gaze and looked surprised to find that she was wearing the oversized T-shirt she loved to sleep in.

"Mr. Lacour, how in the world did I get into this T-shirt?" she asked, pretending to be horrified by the fact.

"I thought you might sleep better like that, so I helped you."

"Oh you did, did you? See anything you weren't supposed to?"

"No, I wasn't looking. By the way, nice Dalmatians underwear."

"Pervert," she said.

He laughed. She didn't seem overly uncomfortable by the fact that he had dressed her. He found that erotic.

"What are you making?"

"Scrambled eggs, bacon, toast, and hash browns," he responded, while turning over several sizzling strips of bacon.

"Sounds good, I'm starving."

"There's coffee on the table. Help yourself."

✳   ✳   ✳   ✳

She poured a half-cup of steaming coffee into an oversize mug and walked through the living room toward the French doors and took her coffee out onto the deck. The weather had broken for the first time in weeks. It felt like an April morning. You could almost smell the first signs of spring in the air.

She sipped her coffee, holding the large mug in both hands. She looked at the lake below, sunlight reflecting off the surface. Ripples in the water lapped up against the boat dock and the metal joints on the dock creaked from the small swales. The swaying of the shifting dock fixated her. A light breeze rustled the trees around her. For the first time in a very long time, she was happy. She felt she could get used to this kind of life. She had almost forgotten why they were there in the first place. Almost. The door to the deck opening behind her interrupted the pleasant thoughts.

"Breakfast is ready," Nick said.

"Nick?"

"Yeah."

"Come look at this."

He assumed a position next to her on the deck. They stood leaning against the railing looking at the glowing lake water below. It almost looked like bars of gold in the spots where the sun was casting its reflection.

"Isn't it beautiful?" she remarked, stating a fact more than asking a question.

"Yes, it is," he replied truthfully.

He paused to look at the lake for a few minutes before speaking again.

"Come on. Let's go eat."

He led her into the house, and they ate breakfast together. They made small talk about the weather and the lake house. Neither of them wanted to verbalize the deeper feelings that might be stirring within. They were starting to feel comfortable around each other, and it was all they could do to steer the conversation away from their true thoughts and the mounting sexual tension that had been growing between them.

"Where do you think he is right now?" she asked in a nervous voice that burst the bubble and jettisoned them back to reality.

"I don't know," Nick responded, not having to ask who *he* was. "I guess he could be about anywhere."

"He's going to come for me, isn't he?" she inquired in a quivering voice.

He didn't respond at first. Deep down, he felt it was a high probability and he hated himself for appearing to use her as bait. But logically, he couldn't see how the killer would be able to find them.

"I don't see how, Angela. I'm certain he didn't follow us," he said, finishing the sentence, but leaving unfinished thoughts hanging in the air like a cartoon cloud.

"But?" she added, sensing that there was more.

"No buts," he concluded.

They finished the meal.

"Hey, I've got an idea," she said, breaking the brief silence that had followed the discussion about her attacker. Her face had brightened.

"What?" he asked, suddenly swept up by her infectious energy.

"Let's take that boat out," she said, smiling and looking like a schoolgirl who was asking to go on her first date.

"I don't know. I really haven't prepared it for the new season," he frowned, causing her to look disappointed. "But, what the hell? Let's take that thing out, and see what it can do."

"Really?" she asked hesitantly, a smile slowly spreading across her face.

"Yeah, really. You go get some clothes on, and I'll clean up. We leave in fifteen minutes."

"Yeaaah!" Angela shouted. She clapped her hands together and raced from the room.

Her age was sometimes very apparent. This pleased him. Despite the hard years that had forced her to grow up prematurely, she was still full of youthful wonderment and energy. He was starting to feed off of that energy. She made him feel young again, too. What was he getting himself into?

He quickly cleaned up the kitchen and packed a cooler full of Michelob Light, cheese, crackers, and whatever else he could fit into the cooler. On perfect cue, she appeared in the doorway ready to go. She was wearing worn, low-cut jeans that accentuated her exotic figure. She was also sporting one of his sweatshirts.

"I hope you don't mind. It's still a little chilly out," she said, tugging on the sleeves.

"I don't mind at all," he said, thinking that the sweatshirt had never looked better to him. "Let's go boating."

He carried the cooler, and they descended the wooden stairs to the dock. It took him about fifteen minutes to uncover the boat, lower it into the water, and prepare it for their ride. She immediately jumped aboard the minute he took the cover off. She was sitting in the captain's chair awaiting their departure. She looked so excited. He couldn't help but to share in her excitement.

After a few attempts to turn the engine over, it finally roared to life. He slowly backed out of the slip and pointed the boat toward the lake. They crept out of the cove at a snail's pace. A small wake trailed behind the large boat while the guttural rumble of the engines made the only sound on the quiet lake.

When they got into the main channel, he looked in all directions. Satisfied that there were no other boats around, he shut down the engine and turned to his sexy passenger.

"Ever drive a boat before?"

"No," she responded. "I've never even been on one before!" She exclaimed with widening eyes.

"There's nothing to it. Steer it like a car but make small corrections," he said holding the wheel. "Here's the throttle," he added, putting a hand on the silver gearshift to the right of the steering wheel. "Move it forward, and we go forward," he said moving the shift forward. "Bring it back, and we slow down," he said while downshifting and slowing the boat to a virtual stop. "Got it?"

He hadn't even finished the question, and she was climbing past him and assuming the controls. She nudged him out of the way, threw the throttle forward, and they were off. The sudden burst nearly threw him out of the back of the boat. The front end rose up, and the boat raced down the channel, this time leaving much larger waves behind it. The new captain giggled like a child, her hair whipping in the breeze. She looked like she could get used to this kind of life.

∗   ∗   ∗   ∗

They had spent the entire afternoon on the lake. The last remnants of an Indian summer day were fading with the setting sun. A wintry wind poked them with icy fingers, offering a gentle reminder that it hadn't yet succumbed to spring.

Nick steered the boat toward the cove. Angela was wrapped around his waist like a blanket. She held on, using his body to shield herself from the descending coldness of nightfall. He eased off the throttle and guided the boat toward its slip. It floated the last remaining feet until its progress was halted by the submerged lift. With the boat in position, he punched the throttle. The sudden thrust pushed the boat all the way onto the lift. He cut the engine and removed the key. She released her grip from his waist and sat up. She looked slightly dazed from a sudden head rush and the choppy ride. She was forced to steady herself against the passenger's seat.

After a few wavering steps toward the rear of the rocking boat, she hoisted a foot on the edge and jumped to the dock. He followed her and immediately pressed the controls to raise the lift above the water line. When it had finished the cycle, he shut off the lift and began to tie the boat off with lines running from the stern and the bow.

It had been a long day, and they were both worn out. The boat's bouncing course across the surface of the water had taken its toll. Nick felt like he was still bobbing in the water as they ascended the long flight of stairs to the lake house. He had his arm around her and was half-carrying her the final ten steps. They paused at the top, assuming a familiar position along the deck railing. They watched together as the sun slipped seamlessly beyond the glowing treetops and beneath the horizon. Another winter's night had settled upon them. Somehow, things had seemed safe during the bright, sunlit day. He had forgotten who or what they were running from. Darkness restored his memory. She put her arm around his waist and rested her head on his shoulder. It was the gesture of a tired girl, yet she pressed herself against him, suggesting more than just fatigue.

"Thanks, Nick. That was a great day," she said without lifting her head off of his shoulder.

"I had a good time, too," he replied.

*   *   *   *

She was beginning to feel like she had known him for most of her life, and that scared her. She was hesitant to open herself up to these feelings and risk getting hurt or hurting him in the process. She sensed the internal battle of emotions he was fighting. She had been patient and unwilling to put him in a compromising position, but she no longer had the strength to conceal her own growing feelings. What was happening between them was probably wrong and she would most likely regret this moment the rest of her life, but she didn't care anymore.

"Nick?" she asked, releasing her grip around his waist so that she was free to stand before him.

"Yeah?" he responded, looking nervous and uncertain about what words were going to follow.

"I think I could fall for someone like you," she said.

There, she had said it. The words were still echoing in the crisp night air when she began to feel the first pangs of regret.

"I know it's crazy. We barely know each other. Still..." she hesitated, trying to convert her feelings into words.

Everything was tangled inside of her, like a ball of yarn that a cat had been playing with all day. She couldn't seem to grasp the right sentences.

"A lot is going on," Nick said, looking startled while fighting for an adequate response. "I think you're confused and scared right now."

"That may be true," she responded, finally getting control of her jumbled emotions. "I may be confused, and I'm definitely scared, but..."

She had trailed off again, trying to think of a way to explain herself. She was really sorry she had opened her mouth.

"But, what?" he asked, obviously uncomfortable with the discussion.

"But, I know what I feel, and it has nothing to do with our situation," she began. "I've never felt this way around a guy before. Every time I look at you, I feel like all the air has just rushed out of my body. I feel weak when I'm around you," she added, feeling more and more foolish by the second.

She was starting to feel like the little girl he probably thought she was. She wanted to hide from him in shame but couldn't take any of it back now. It was too late.

"I'm sure you are feeling these things because of what we're going through together," Nick tried to assure her, but he didn't sound very convincing in the process. He added, "I'm sure this will all pass."

"Maybe you're right," she said while turning away from him.

She was feeling hurt and even more confused by the second. She was now more embarrassed than ever and felt like it had been foolish to say these things in the first place. He certainly didn't feel the same way about her, judging by the response he was giving. All she wanted to do was race into the house, bury her head in a pillow, and erase the entire conversation from her memory.

He caught her arm before she was able to run to the house and pulled her toward him. She struggled at first, not wanting him to see the tears in her eyes. When she finally looked up, she saw in his expression that he might be feeling some of the same things. He wrapped his arms around her and kissed her. She kissed him back passionately and they held onto each other in a desperate attempt to prolong the moment forever.

CHAPTER 20

▼

The first glimpses of morning were peeking through the slightly drawn wooden blinds. Sunlight was about to usher in another day and sweep away the endless night that had preceded it. Nick reached his arms over his head and tightened his leg muscles, stretching the fatigue from all appendages. He got out of bed and went downstairs to the master bedroom to see if Angela was awake yet. He poked his head through the semi-open door and noticed that she was curled up in the fetal position, sound asleep in the king-size bed.

He left the bedroom and went to the kitchen to make some coffee. He might as well be caffeinated if he wasn't going to be able to sleep anymore. He filled the coffeemaker with water and flipped the switch, which now glowed red. Within seconds, it was beginning to percolate and the smell of freshly brewed coffee started to fill the room.

He took a seat at the kitchen table and rubbed his eyes. What had he done last night? Of course he had been attracted to Angela from day one, but that was no excuse. He was a grieving widower trying to catch the killer of his recently deceased wife. How could he be so weak as to kiss this girl whom he barely knew? Was this the beginning of some kind of relationship or just two people reacting to a period of extreme stress? He had read about post-traumatic stress syndrome and knew that people were often drawn to each other after experiencing a life-altering situation together. Nick and Angela had both brushed up against a serial killer, and it had changed their lives forever. Now they were dependent upon each other to get through the experience. He knew this was more than likely why feelings were being stirred inside, but he was too worn out to fight it.

For whatever reason, Angela was helping him cope, and that seemed good enough for the time being.

Despite knowing what he knew, he still wondered if something was blooming beyond just a reaction to stress. It didn't seem realistic, yet he briefly considered the possibility to make him feel less guilty about bringing a strange girl to his vacation home. He decided to cast the questions aside for the time being. He wasn't going to solve the world's problems this morning. Maybe he would just let things happen naturally without trying to analyze why or how.

After filling a mug full of coffee, he put the pot back on the warmer and took his cup out to the deck. The sky was beginning to brighten, spreading warm shades of pink and orange across its vast canvas. It looked like it was going to be another gorgeous day. It was late winter, and the first tastes of a premature spring were once again filling the air.

He stood on the deck watching the sky brighten into varying shades of blue as he sipped his coffee. He was trying to decide what they should do next. This little trip had been good for both of them, but they couldn't stay there forever. He had a son back home whom he missed desperately. This irresponsible quest for revenge had been completely unfair to Justin. Just picturing the boy's face nearly brought him to tears. Not a moment passed when he didn't feel badly about leaving his little boy behind. He knew Justin was in good hands back home, but it wasn't the same. The child needed his father. He was struggling with the loss of his mother, and now it had been compounded by the disappearance of his father. He was too young to understand why Nick had left.

As dangerous as it might be for Angela, it was time to head back to civilization and face whomever or whatever was waiting for both of them. They couldn't hide forever. He had to get back to his job. His son needed him, and it was definitely time to start repairing his damaged life. Staying away was exacerbating the damage.

The strong dose of reality helped him make a final decision. They would spend the rest of the day cleaning up the lake house. One more night there and then it was back to the city, where hopefully Ramsey and his boys had already been able to put an end to this horrid nightmare. He could picture Justin's face the moment he saw that his dad was home again. His heart warmed at the thought.

The time for chasing ghosts had come to an end. With that realization, he began to feel better. He went back into the house to tell Angela the plan. She wouldn't be happy, but he hoped she would understand. The business of catching the killer had already been left up to the police. He would do everything he could to protect her until the psycho was behind bars or dead. They were in this together now, and there was no way he was going to let anything happen to her. He was suddenly all too aware that his feelings for her had become real and were not just the by-product of a twisted time in his life.

He set the coffee cup on the kitchen counter and made his way back to Angela's bedroom. He was still thinking about the kiss. He wondered if it—or maybe something more—would happen again.

*   *   *   *

Angela's reaction to Nick's plan probably went as he had expected. She nearly demonstrated each of the Kubler-Ross stages of dying in less than a minute. She was shaken by the thought of returning to the place where her life was in deep peril, but she understood his situation. Running away forever wasn't going to solve either one of their problems, although the idea held a lot of appeal.

When she had finally succumbed to the reality of it all, she wrapped her arms around him and held on for dear life. He was her life preserver now, and she wasn't about to let him escape her grasp. She was scared and unsure of the future, but he had come to the conclusion that returning to the city was the proper thing to do. Her thoughts drifted between the past and the future, often intertwining with the present. There was so much going on it was exceedingly difficult to separate all of the emotion and construct a coherent daydream. She had the possibility of a budding relationship to think about as well as the unthinkable—a madman out to destroy her dreams and spray paint terror all over her neatly constructed fantasies.

"Things are going to work out. I really believe that," she said, grabbing his hand and giving it a tight squeeze.

She stood on her tiptoes and kissed him softly on the lips.

"I know," he said, returning the gentle kiss.

She held onto him for a while longer, not wanting to face the daunting task of turning around and heading directly back into a raging storm.

*   *   *   *

Jane Lacour had felt uneasy since she spoke with Agent Witter. He seemed professional and sincere enough, but something about the call hadn't set right with her. She had become rattled that she divulged information that she now wished she had kept to herself. Nick had been explicit when he told her not to let a living soul know where he was going. Witter had caught her off guard, and she didn't have time to think clearly. Before she knew it, she had given away the farm so to speak.

After a sleepless night dwelling on it, she decided to call Detective Ramsey and fill him in. She had attempted to contact Nick all day long, but no one was answering the phone at the lake house. That had her worried, too, and she had the ability to worry with the best of them. Family members had labeled her the world's all-time worry queen, and it was a title she lived up to daily.

She had heard Nick mention Ramsey several times in the past, so he seemed to be the next best option in lieu of not being able to contact her son. If that didn't work, maybe she and Mike would drive to the lake to look in on Nick.

"This is Jack Ramsey, can I help you?" he asked, sounding unpleasant and distant.

"Why yes, Detective Ramsey. This is Jane Lacour, Nick's mom."

"Mrs. Lacour, it's a pleasure. What can I do for you?" he asked. His tone had freshened a bit.

"I'm not sure, Detective. You see, I had a strange call from an FBI agent yesterday, and it just hasn't sat well with me."

"I see. Tell me more about it," Ramsey said, now sounding intrigued.

"An Agent Witter called and was adamant about speaking with Nicholas. When I told him he wasn't available, the agent got mad and threatened me," she paused to swallow hard before continuing. "I guess he caught me off guard, because next thing I knew I had divulged Nick's whereabouts."

Ramsey didn't say anything for a moment. She sensed he was contemplating whether or not to chastise her for being so careless. Surprisingly, he opted for a softer, more subtle approach.

"Mrs. Lacour, I'm sure you did what you thought was best at the time. What did you say the agent's name was again?"

"His name was Agent Witter. I didn't get a first name."

"Uh huh," Ramsey mumbled as he wrote the name in his day planner.

"I certainly hope I didn't do anything wrong, Detective. The last thing in the world I want is to put Nick through more than he's already endured."

"No, I'm sure everything will be fine," Ramsey said while trying to comfort her. "Just the same, I'll get in touch with this Agent Witter and find out what's going on."

"Oh, would you? That would be so kind of you. Will you let me know as soon as possible?" she asked, greatly relieved that she had placed the call.

"Absolutely. Now in the meantime, can you give me the number to the lake house? I'd like to get in touch with Nick myself."

She gave Ramsey the number and directions, not that he had asked. It seemed like a strange recurrence from her conversation with Witter, but this time she felt comfortable releasing the privileged information.

They said good-bye and hung up. She still felt uneasiness in the pit of her stomach, but was satisfied with her decision. If something truly were amiss, Ramsey would know how to handle it.

*   *   *   *

Ramsey set his office phone back in its cradle and cursed the empty air in the room. How could she have been so bone headed? He almost knew without checking that there wasn't an Agent Witter. The fibbies didn't work that way, and they certainly wouldn't have pressed her for the address. They'd already have it!

He plucked the handset back from its perch and punched in Nick's number. After eight rings, it became obvious that no one was going to answer. He tried his cell phone, too, but received the same response. His next call would be to the FBI, where he'd confirm his notion that there wasn't a Witter working the case. He checked his watch. It was after 4:00 PM. If it were the killer who had contacted Jane Lacour, he would have had nearly twenty-four hours to do something with the information.

Ramsey's next call was to the local police in Lake Ozark, Missouri. He explained the situation and asked that they send a cruiser to the house to check on Nick and his guest. He prayed that it wasn't too late. Over the past couple of months, Ramsey had come to think of Nick as the son he'd never had. He couldn't stand the thought that something might have happened to him. On that note, he grabbed his coat from a hook behind his office door and decided to put Jane Lacour's directions to the test.

*   *   *   *

Rucker found the drive to the Lake of the Ozarks nearly as aggravating as the past couple of weeks had been. Getting to the lake wasn't a hassle, but finding the frigging lake house owned by Nick Lacour was an entirely different proposition. What might have taken slightly less than three hours was now going on five, and he still hadn't located the phantom house. The myriad of rural roads and lake coves made the trek maddening. The old broad had laid out uncomplicated directions, but he must have missed something because he simply couldn't find the house. As his irritation was about to reach an all-time high, he spotted the numbers 932 on a nearby mailbox.

"It's about time," he stated, registering the fact that he was now driving by what appeared to be the correct home.

A black Lexus was parked in the circle drive about twenty yards below the street. The driveway was impossibly steep and looked to be inescapable should heavy snowfall hit during the night. It didn't matter to him, because he didn't plan on parking there anyway. He doubted the car would ever need to be extricated from the hilly location again, either.

Now that he had located his target, he continued to wind through the small tributary roads looking for a place to leave his car. He risked not being able to find the house again, but made several mental notes along the way according to various landmarks he passed. He finally located a decent hiding spot just a couple of miles from the Lacour lakefront property.

It was time to sit and wait. He'd make his move after dark and wouldn't be deterred by the presence of Lola's hero this time. He could barely stand the excitement at the thought of the look on their faces when he arrived. This was surely going to be a night to remember.

*   *   *   *

The night of a soon-departing winter fell swiftly upon them. Another premature spring day had given way to a more typical evening for this time of year. There wouldn't be many more nights of biting cold, but Jack Frost ushered in a last gasp with a vengeance. In the scattered moments between the sun's final descent and the moon's triumphant rise, the temperature dropped nearly fifty degrees. A strong southeasterly wind accentuated the cold and took the wind chill factor to a subzero reading. Gone were the remnants of a sixty-degree day. Present was a damp chill that blanketed the lake and encased the gray, barren trees.

Nick pulled the deck door tightly shut and locked the dead bolt. Their forays to the deck had concluded for the trip. He shuddered and clapped his hands together, trying to snap away the iciness that had seeped into his joints.

"Can you believe this shit?" he asked Angela. "I was on the dock without a shirt just a few hours ago, and now it's like the freaking Arctic out there."

"You only had your shirt off to impress the neighbors," she muffled into his sleeve as she fell into the cold wool of his sweater.

"Yeah, you're right. I wanted old lady Parker across the lake to see my pecs," he replied.

They both laughed. The old woman across the cove was probably a by-product of the last two centuries. Nick doubted she could see the hand attached to the end of her arm.

"So what now? I guess fantasy time is over and we have to face the painful reality of life in the city, right?" she asked, speaking the words partly in jest.

They hit home just the same. He didn't respond at first. They had talked about the return to St. Louis. Neither really wanted to leave their hideaway, but both knew it was necessary.

"I want to go back about as much as you do," he said. "But we have no choice. Besides, Ramsey has been staking the guy's place out for weeks. They think he might have skipped town."

The last words didn't come out too convincingly but served the purpose of helping to justify the inevitable return to St. Louis. As his remarks faded into the stillness of the cabin, she removed her head from his chest and pulled from his embrace.

"You're right, but I'm not going to sulk all night. It's our last evening here. We need to make the most of it," she said with a wicked gleam in her eyes.

"What did you have in mind?" Nick asked, with slightly raised eyebrows.

"Well, for starters, we need to change out of these nasty clothes."

Before she had finished the sentence, she was stripping out of her sweatshirt and moving toward the master bedroom.

"I'm going to take a shower while you start dinner," she laughed.

Her half-naked body disappeared into the bedroom before he could respond. She closed the door behind her and vanished into the far reaches of the cabin. Shortly afterward, he could hear the sound of running water as the shower in the master bedroom turned on. He loved this about her. She had a way of imposing her will without making him resent her for it. He actually wanted to make her dinner while she soaked away the remnants of a work-filled day.

He moved about the kitchen on a mission. He pulled what remained of their groceries from the refrigerator and cabinets. There was enough food left to make a pot of soup, two baked potatoes, and some grilled chicken breasts. It was an easy meal to put together, so he was well under way when she reappeared from the bedroom with a towel around her body and another wrapped around her head.

"Smells great. What are you making?" she asked as she dipped a spoon into the simmering pot of broccoli cheese soup.

"Get out of there, and go get dressed. I'll take care of this," Nick remarked with pretend aggravation.

"Oh, you don't like it when I walk around naked?" she asked while threatening to peel the towel from her body and reveal her still wet, sexy body.

He looked her up and down, wanting every square inch of her but somehow was able to show remarkable restraint. He fought back the urge to kiss her and do who knows what else before she skipped away toward the bedroom giggling. Hopefully that opportunity would present itself later on, he fantasized. It was something that had crossed his mind more and more frequently lately, but guilt always made him abandon the thoughts. He was finding it increasingly more difficult to keep his desires in check and he wondered if she felt the same attraction to him.

While she dressed in the bedroom, he put the finishing touches on their final meal at the cabin. They sat in near silence as soft emanations from a Frank Sinatra CD combined with the light clanking of silverware to produce the only sounds in the room. His thoughts danced between an apprehension to return to society, intense longing to be with his son again, and the unmistakable sexual chemistry that had blossomed with Angela. He wondered if tonight would be the night that they shoved aside all inhibitions and gave into a strong desire to share unbridled passion.

The meal was nearly complete when she surprised him with a question that had preyed on his mind for days.

"What's going to happen between us when we get back to the real world?" she asked.

"I don't know. What do you want to happen?" he asked as his spoon slipped silently from his hand into the half-eaten bowl of soup.

He regretted the words even before they escaped his lips.

"Gee, I don't know, Nick. I was thinking I'd become a stripper, and you could become a hot shit lawyer or something," she responded, while not trying to disguise her irritation.

"I was thinking we could do it the other way around," he said, nearly laughing at her sarcasm.

"No, you're too hairy to be a stripper. Besides, lawyers are too boring for me," she finished while gathering up her dinner dishes and moving toward the sink.

He caught her mid-stride and pulled the dishes from her hand, gingerly setting them on the table while corralling Angela around the waist. He pulled her close and enjoyed the way their warm bodies intertwined like pieces of a well-fit puzzle.

"You know what I mean. There's obviously something going on, but it's going to be complicated for a while."

"That's just like a guy. Every one of you views a special connection with a woman as complicated. Why the hell does it have to be so complicated?" she asked, while pushing away from his embrace.

"I guess it doesn't have to be," he said, trying to quell her sudden anger.

"Do you feel something for me, Nick?" she asked very abruptly.

"I probably shouldn't considering what's happened in my life recently, but I think I do," he replied with absolute sincerity, surprising himself that the words had come out.

"Good, I feel something for you, too. Why can't that be enough?"

The question was so simple and made so much sense that Nick, a man with more than twenty years of education, sat speechless for a moment.

"It doesn't have to be, I guess," he said after he finally recovered.

The response wasn't particularly poetic or prophetic, but she seemed to see the honesty in his eyes. Like a shut-off faucet, her anger disappeared and gave way to a brilliant smile.

"Good. I was hoping you'd say that," she said as she caressed his cheek.

She picked up her dishes and moved into the kitchen, leaving him hungering for her. She embodied everything that he admired in a person and everything he missed in Pamela. She was sarcastic, emotional, witty, crass at times, and beautiful. Her spirit enraptured him. It was all he could do to keep from becoming an overzealous schoolboy in her presence. He knew he was powerless to keep his longing in check any more.

He slid in behind her as she rinsed the dishes in the stainless steel sink. He wrapped his arms around her waist and kissed her neck. She set the plate she was holding into the sink and leaned her head back. She held onto his arms and returned his embrace. He could feel the sexual desire raging within himself so powerfully the he felt he could explode at any second.

"I've never felt this way before, Nick. It scares me."

He held her and stared blankly into the distance, somewhat frightened by her words. The gravity of her feelings changed the moment and he once again wondered what he was doing. She seemed to sense his discomfort and turned to face him. She lifted his chin with her hand.

"I think I love you," she said sweetly.

Everything became a blur. They kissed passionately and held each other for a dizzying eternity. The water continued to splash into the sink, blocking out the sound of the howling winter wind. It was beating rambunctiously against the outside of the house, begging to be let in along with the fury it had swept toward their safe haven.

＊　　　＊　　　＊　　　＊

After cleaning up the kitchen mess and the remainder of the cabin, they both retired to their bedrooms and packed their clothes for the morning's trip home. Nick fell asleep among folded clothes in the master bedroom, exhausted by the confusion of emotions he was experiencing. When he awoke an hour later, he saw Angela lying next to him. Her arm was draped across his chest and her head was pressed against his shoulder.

"You know, once this is all over," she said, referring to the stalking of a madman outside their door, "you and I could probably make a pretty decent couple."

He was now fully awake. He hadn't thought of it in those terms, but of course that was what seemed to be happening. A couple, he thought. He turned the phrase over and over in his mind. It had a strange feel to it, and he knew it would be met with scrutinizing eyes back in St. Louis. After Pamela had died, he figured it would be just his son and him for a very long time. He certainly had not counted on this turn of events.

"Do you agree, Nick? You awake over there?" she asked while tapping him on the chest.

"I don't disagree," he responded, not sure exactly how he felt about the question.

She sighed with contentment and tightened her grip on his chest.

He glanced at the clock. It was only five thirty, but it felt like midnight already. He pulled himself upright and began to sift through the clothing scattered across the bed.

"Where do you think you're going?" she asked, still sprawled in the comfort and warmth of the bed.

"I think I'll run up to the gas station. I'm gonna gas up the car and get a few items for the ride home tomorrow."

"Why don't we just do it in the morning?" she asked, with the onset of sleep in her voice.

"Because neither one of us is going to feel like it in the morning. Besides, I want to get some coffee for the ride back."

One of the answers to the question was the fact that he was not a morning person. His career had required mental sharpness at ungodly hours, but he still hated every minute of it. He could stay up all night and maintain a child's level of energy for the duration, but he was a complete slug in the morning. They had that in common, because they both operated under the same mental clock. One of her jobs required late night hours. She was used to sleeping past noon.

The real answer to her question was the attraction between them. He knew if he stayed on that bed one second longer, they'd engage in something they both wanted very badly, but may not be entirely ready for. He needed to temporarily escape into the cold night air to push back his desires, which had become nearly impossible to contain.

"I'll be right back," he said as he kissed her.

She was already drifting off to sleep. They had both become comfortable in the cabin in a variety of ways. It would prove to be their undoing.

✳   ✳   ✳   ✳

Rucker couldn't believe his luck. He almost did a cartwheel when he saw the lights of the black car flip on as it began to drive away from the house. This was a bonus he had not counted on. He continued his vigil until he was certain that Lacour was driving the car. What an amazing stroke of good fortune. He had come to the cabin thinking he would need to expend a great deal of energy disposing of the annoying male presence before giving the girl her rightful passage.

He was sure he could take Lacour, but the man had intensity. It would have been a very good battle indeed, he thought, but would no longer be necessary. Since the nearest signs of life were present on the main road, he figured he had a minimum of twenty minutes to do what he came to do. He wished he had a little more time, but he had been forced to work quickly before. As long as he accomplished his goal, time was irrelevant.

The girl inside would represent his finest conquest. He had stalked her for months now. For a long time, he felt she had slipped from his grasp. He carried anger from that near-fatal night at her apartment, and it burned brighter than ever within his soul. She had been his for the taking until the asshole lawyer intervened. Snuffing her out would avenge that night. He even had to chuckle at the thought that he would be taking a woman from Lacour for the second time.

"Aren't paybacks hell?" he muttered to himself.

He had lurked in the cold outside the vacation home for more than an hour. His bones creaked as he tried to rub life into his arms and legs. He couldn't afford to be slow when he busted into the house. She was a young, strong girl. If he was sluggish, she might elude him yet again. He couldn't bear the thought of that disappointment a second time. He had already managed to cut the phone lines, so a call to the cavalry wasn't going to deter his progress.

When he was convinced he had pulled himself sufficiently together, he began to make his way toward the bedroom window. No need in disguising his entry this time, because there wasn't anyone close enough to hear her cries. No one would be able to help the slut inside.

CHAPTER 21

▼

Angela had drifted off to sleep. Her subconscious mind floated to and from places she didn't want to go. Her sleep was restless and distraught. A storm was coming, and in her dreams she could feel its presence. Over and over the face of a madman tormented her sleep. No matter where she went to escape, he was there, wearing an insane grin and beckoning her "to the promised land" as he once had done while she was awake.

She tossed and turned trying to shake off the images and retreat to a happier place, a place where only Nick could join her. A soft smile spread across her lips as her sleeping mind brought him to the rescue. The scene changed away from the abyss of dark stone tunnels dripping with water to a private beach. Nick stood on the porch of a secluded beach house waving to her.

She waved back and began to run toward him. Emerald waves lapped up against the shore behind her as she streaked across the white sand toward her true love. The sun shone brightly and a gentle breeze rustled the palm leaves above her. She could feel her heart pound as she got closer to him. He stood in the doorway waiting for her, smiling.

With a last effort, she jumped into his arms and hugged him tightly. He had made her fears disappear. He had changed the sky from coal black to the deepest blue she had ever seen. She kissed him deeply and began to beckon him into the house. Wrapped tightly together, they stumbled into the bedroom as one. Steamy passion swept them away. She no longer saw the face of the madman. All she could see was the face of her lover.

*   *   *   *

Nick could see the lights of the gas station less than a mile in the distance. His thoughts had been jumbled since he left the cabin. Part of him was starting to become happy again. He couldn't believe how lucky he was to have met two amazing women in his life. Unfortunately, the second woman brought about intense feelings of guilt. He couldn't help feeling like he was betraying his wife. Her memory wasn't even distant, and he had already kissed another woman and considered doing so much more.

Surely, Pamela would understand. She would want the best for him. He knew that, but it still didn't feel right. His only solace was the fact that he wasn't a womanizer. He had only slept with four women in his life. He had loved three of them. The other had been his first sexual encounter. He never saw the girl again. He wasn't the type to sleep around or use women to satisfy physical urges. He had spent the previous nine years completely faithful to his wife.

Still he couldn't shake the unrest. He figured part of it was brought about by the unusual circumstances he and Angela faced. He had developed feelings for her, though. He couldn't explain why or how it was happening, but she had a strength and energy that drew him to her. With her around, he felt like he was invincible. He was starting to live life through another pair of eyes again. Despite all the guilt, he was powerless to break the spell.

He pulled his car into the BP station. He could see an attendant in the Mini-mart, so he knew the station was still open. Normally, he would just pay at the pump and be on his way, but he needed to go inside to get some items for the next day's journey home.

He fumbled with the gas cap with cold hands. He was finally able to remove it and began pumping petrol. He left the nozzle on and went into the station to pick up some food, coffee, and soda for the three-hour ride home. A brisk wind whipped through his hair as he strode toward the Minimart. A bell signaled his entry as he opened the swinging glass door to the mart.

The door pulled shut hard behind him as he went on his way, gathering up the fuel for their morning ride. To his shock, an uneasy feeling was slowly taking root within, so he hurried his steps and dropped an armload of items on the counter. He had been overcome by this same feeling several times in his life, and its growing intensity was becoming frightfully unsettling.

*   *   *   *

Rucker was now fully ready for the moment of truth. He hunched near the window leading into the bedroom. He had obtained a rudimentary layout of the cabin during his hour-long surveillance from the outside. He had guessed that the girl was still in this room because he had seen no additional activity after Lacour left. This was the last room the two had entered when all of the cabin lights were on. It would serve as the last room the girl would ever enter, he thought to himself.

His defining moment was drawing near. Nothing else in his body of work could compare to this final killing. It would be his twenty-first, a large number, but completely irrelevant to him. He now knew that the twenty before her were only practice for this one final act. She would represent his shining moment. After completing this mission, he would be ready for the next level, a level that did not exist on this earth. With her death, he would be born again.

The time had come. He sucked in a long, cold breath. He pulled his stocking cap over his face, cinched his coat and began to race toward the window. He hit it like a linebacker who had just drilled an unsuspecting wide receiver. With a lowered shoulder, he burst through the glass at full force. It seemed to offer no resistance to his full bore onslaught. He went through with such surprising ease that he catapulted several feet into the room before he landed.

*   *   *   *

Angela's dream raged on. She and Nick rolled in ecstasy on the bed of that deserted island hideaway. They were isolated from the world and surrounded only by palm trees, ocean waves, and tropical breezes. Suddenly, the moment was shattered as something exploded through the bedroom window. Tropical air rushed through, but it wasn't the warm air from the beach. It was icy cold. They were thrown from the bed as the madman crashed onto them, dressed in black.

She shook herself and realized she was now on the floor. What had started as a dream was now reality. It took her a few seconds to shake off the sleep and get her bearings. She tried to quickly assess the situation. She was lying on the bedroom floor of the lake cabin. The monster was rolling around on the bed trying to gain his bearings as well.

Her mind raced. She switched to autopilot and began to function instinctively. She immediately pulled herself from the floor and took two leaden steps toward the door. Her legs were barely moving. She felt immobilized from the waist down. Her heavy steps came in slow motion as she watched the figure on the bed sit upright and jump from his post.

He was coming toward her now, and she seemed too slow and too ravaged with fear to escape. Her mind worked feverishly, trying to send mental impulses to the leg muscles, forcing them to act on their own. Something finally clicked, because she began to move. Weary at first, she gained speed and strength. She could feel the presence behind her.

*   *   *   *

Nick was beginning to hyperventilate. Consciously, he was embarrassed by his growing fear, but his inner self knew it was for good cause. He hurriedly paid the attendant and gathered up his purchases. He didn't even wait for the three dollars and twenty-five cents he was due. He burst through the front door of the convenience mart, leaving a confused eighteen-year-old kid standing at the counter holding his change. When shouting after the customer didn't work, the kid pocketed the change and muttered "dipshit" under his breath.

He nearly dented the driver's side door he hit it so hard. He had built up speed crossing the lot, and a patch of ice prohibited an adequate stop. After fumbling for his keys, dropping them twice, and finally clutching them in his cold wooden fingers, he depressed the button for the automatic lock and ripped the car door open. He wasn't firmly planted in the seat yet, but the car was on and in motion. He squealed out of the lot and fishtailed onto the main road.

"What a *fucking* dipshit," the same attendant once again muttered to himself from inside the Minimart.

Two sharp moves of the steering wheel allowed him to gain control of the vehicle as he continued to roll furiously along the dark pavement. Barren trees lined the sides of the road. They resembled sinister specters with bony claws as he raced past. The world had suddenly turned hostile again.

*   *   *   *

Angela skidded through the bedroom door and sharply disappeared into the blackness of the cabin's main room. Her brain worked overtime trying to remember every nuance of the room's layout. She searched her mental reserves frantically, trying to recall something that might serve as a weapon. Her only thought was of getting to the front door and into the dark disarray of the forest outside.

The madman must have sensed her intent, because she heard him thunder into the foyer. He was in the dark, groping around near the front door. He had turned left toward the front of the house, while her panicked escape had led her to the main room. It was a moonless night, so the only light that penetrated the room came from the dock far below the house. It cast a faint glow through the deck doors and onto the ceramic tiles of the kitchen floor.

She knew where she was. Her eyes were adjusted to the dark, and she moved as swiftly and as silently as she could toward the fireplace. She grabbed a poker from the grouping of tools sitting next to the hearth. She retracted the poker from the stand, but the quick retrieval brought the remaining tools clattering to the ground. She heard her attacker's footsteps stop and retrace. He was now coming toward her again. In her stocking feet, she didn't have the traction that he did. The hardwood floors were difficult to stop and turn abruptly on while wearing no shoes.

She immediately dropped to a crouch behind the love seat in the main room. She could hear his heavy breathing as he entered the cavernous room. He began to search his way around. He was looking for her, while at the same time trying to illuminate the cabin. Suddenly the dark gave way to amber light as a lamp clicked on.

"Come out, come out, wherever you are," he mocked in a shrill, maniacal voice. A deep baritone replaced the shrillness as he growled, "There's no place to hide, bitch. Time to go to the promised land!"

The sound of his voice sent a chill down her spine. He would be on her in a second. Her only chance was the element of surprise. As he came around the corner of the main couch toward the love seat, she gave up her hiding spot with a fierceness and intensity that even the man was startled by. She became the attacker and launched a high-arcing assault with the fireplace poker.

Her weapon found its mark as the curved end came crashing into the attacker's neck. He winced in pain and dropped to one knee. She immediately retracted the weapon and brought it in for another blow. This time, a side-winding, baseball swing found a home squarely in the middle of his back. She could feel the point dig into the muscles between his shoulder blades.

The madman let out a high-pitched scream and dropped face first onto the floor. She wasn't going to make the same mistake that movie victims always make. She wasn't going to try to escape while her attacker lay vulnerable on the floor. It was time to finish him off. With his demise, all of her nightmares would be put to rest once and for all. She felt no fear as she approached her fallen prey.

"It's time for you to go to the promised land, motherfucker!" she yelled.

With those words lingering in the still cabin air, she raised the poker high over her head and brought it down with all the intensity her 110-pound body could muster. It bore a course directly for the back of the monster's head.

Somehow, he managed to roll to his right at precisely the correct moment. The poker hammered into the hardwood floor and bounced out of her grasp. Not to be dissuaded, she lunged after it, but he caught her foot and dumped her to the floor like a sack of flour.

*   *   *   *

Rucker was beyond pain. He was inflamed with anger so intense that it over-rode the pain shooting from his neck and back. Regaining his composure, he dove on top of his victim and pawed wildly at her neck and face. He finally found a hold around her neck and began slamming her head brutally into the floor. He didn't know how many times he did it; he had completely lost count in the heat of the moment.

She now lay motionless on the great room floor. Blood from her nose and a gash under her eye began to pool around her head and mat her hair. Time no longer played a role in the encounter. Seconds felt like hours as they seeped into endless minutes.

He may have knelt over his precious prize for as long as ten minutes without having the strength to finish her off. He was weary from the altercation, and the pain in his back and shoulder had supplanted his rage for the time being. Raw desire became his weapon as he closed in to finish her and get out of the cabin. The whole scene had been all wrong, and an impulse told him to do this one quickly and move on.

In some ways, it was a bit of a disappointment. He had stalked this girl and obsessed over her for months. His fantasies of the final act were always elaborate. Each time he pictured the encounter, it was more glorious than he had imagined it previously. Instead of making one of these fantastical accounts come true, he had instead walked into much more than he had bargained for. No one had ever gotten the better of him, but now he wavered on one knee bleeding profusely while flirting with unconsciousness. Adrenaline had kept him upright to this point, but it was wearing off.

Again the impulse to kill the girl and get the hell out of the cabin broke through the pain and flashed into his mind. With one hand on the back of her neck, he reached above her head and snagged the fireplace poker from the floor. Trying to anchor himself against the couch, he gave up his grip on her neck and rose unsteadily to his feet. From a wobbly stance, he gripped both hands around the end of the poker and lifted it into position to bring home its final destiny.

*   *   *   *

The car marched on toward the cabin at speeds that were highly dangerous for the winding roads around the lake. Nick relied on an internal compass that had been crafted by years of coming to the lake. The road was so dark that at times his headlights shone over the sides of hills as he whipped into sharp turns and slid along the pavement.

What took nearly ten minutes to accomplish on the way to the convenience mart had taken less than five on the way back. His car literally launched over the curb in front of the cabin and crashed to a stop in the middle of the front yard between two large oak trees and just before the front walk. Man, what an ass he'd feel like if his instincts had been wrong, he thought. He nearly chuckled at the thought of explaining to Angela why the car was in the front yard as opposed to its customary spot on the driveway.

The moment of levity passed quickly as he burst from the front seat and sprinted toward the cabin. One look at the dark interior seemed to confirm his fears. He thrust his key into the lock and popped the front door open. What he saw made months and months worth of nightmares come true. The reality of the scene was far worse than his dreams could have ever concocted.

*   *   *   *

Rucker was completely shocked by the opening of the front door. He stood frozen, fireplace poker raised above his head, while his dimming mind tried to reconcile what he was seeing. His puzzled eyes looked Lacour over, and he nearly forgot why he was in the cabin in the first place. Everything seemed so unreal that he remained motionless as the new participant to this macabre play began to race toward him.

*   *   *   *

Nick stood in the opening to the great room and looked directly into the eyes of the beast that had killed his wife and had possibly done the same to Angela, who now lay motionless on the floor at the killer's feet. He had been close to only two women over the past decade, and the inhuman-looking figure standing in the great room had taken both of them away from him.

A myriad of emotions shook his mind. Months of pursuing the beast had led him to this moment. At first, the quest had been about avenging Pamela's death while attempting to bring some measure of closure to the most horrid event of his life. Over the months, the chase turned to an escape as he tried to keep a young, innocent girl safe from the same monster. All of the fears, anger, devastation, and emotional distress brought him to this time and place.

At first, he didn't know quite what to do. His mind was overloaded, and he was no longer thinking coherently. He had dreamed about this opportunity but never quite pictured it to unfold this way. Finally, he had a chance to rid his life of this abomination. Part of him was desperate to race to Angela's side and see if she could still be saved. Logic told him that a move like that would be a death sentence for both of them. He had to take care of some unfinished business before tending to the girl he had vowed to protect.

All at once, he exploded through the room like he had been fired from a cannon. Anger, grief, pain, fear, and desperation had melded together and propelled him into the heart of the great room on a direct line toward the thing that had torn his life asunder.

*   *   *   *

The fierce, maniacal look in Lacour's eyes switched Rucker from a state of confusion to pure animal instinct. He redirected the intended path of the poker and stood facing a new quarry, one that was advancing toward him at an alarming pace. He quickly drew the poker back and started its path forward toward the man charging directly at him. He wasn't fast enough though. Just as he started swinging it forward, Lacour barreled into him and drove him over the couch. Both men ended up pressed against the fireplace stone.

*   *   *   *

Nick pulled the fallen madman from the ground and drove his fist savagely into the jaw of the killer. The force of the blow wrenched the limp body from his grasp. He watched as the thing before him dropped back onto the hardwood. His head bounced a couple of times before coming to a stop. He dragged him back to the fireplace and began slamming his face into the stone base. After five or six violent thrusts into the cold, solid stone, the killer's face no longer resembled that of a living thing.

Nick staggered to his feet and thrust his steel-shank hiking boot into the midsection of his nemesis. The lifeless form folded around his foot in a violent spasm each time he drilled the boot home. Blood foamed from the man's mouth and poured from cuts on his forehead, over his left eye and along the right side of his nose.

After exhausting himself, Nick quickly hobbled toward Angela. He was stunned yet completely overjoyed to discover that she had a pulse and was breathing fairly normally. He cradled her in his arms and jabbed at the cell phone that had been in his jeans pocket. The world spun in slow motion as he exerted much effort to depress three simple numbers. When connected, his voice came out as a hoarse rasp while he attempted to quickly and desperately explain the situation to the emergency operator. She asked him a couple of questions, but he was barely listening.

"Come quick. Someone has been badly injured!" he kept repeating.

When satisfied that his pleas had registered, he dropped the phone on the ground and continued to try to revive Angela. The cuts and abrasions to her face, while ugly, didn't appear to be life threatening. She moved slightly in his arms, and her eyes fluttered.

"Hang in there, baby. Help is on the way," he whispered. "Don't you leave me, you understand? Don't even think about leaving me," he begged.

Her eyes fluttered again, and she weakly grabbed at his forearm. She was coming to.

"That's it, sweetheart, I'm here. Everything's going to be just fine," he said as she made an attempt at a faint smile and tried to speak. "Don't try to speak, I've got you now," he told her.

*   *   *   *

Her eyes began to register full consciousness, like a dimmer switch had been slowly turned brighter. She was now fully awake and looking into his face. For the first time in longer than she could remember, everything seemed to be fine. The pain in her head had dulled and she could feel movement returning to her limbs. She tried to clutch him, but she was still very weak. She didn't know what had happened after she lost consciousness, but assumed that he had arrived at precisely the right moment and saved her from…she couldn't finish the thought.

She tightly closed her eyes, fighting back the tears while tightening her hold on his arm. She loved him like she had never loved another.

*   *   *   *

"Where the hell's the damn ambulance?" Nick cried.

He was relieved that she had regained consciousness, but he was still very anxious to get her medical attention. He was worried that she might have internal injuries and didn't feel that they were completely out of the woods yet.

*   *   *   *

Angela opened her eyes again. What she saw immediately registered in her ashen face and in her eyes, which were now the size of silver dollars. Before Nick could turn to address the source of her terror, the fireplace poker crashed into the back of his head. He slumped forward, teetered to one side and dropped to the floor like a rag doll.

*   *   *   *

The faint sound of distant sirens filtered through the stillness of the dark room. Rucker, barely alive and no longer obsessed by the woman or anything else but staying alive, released the poker and lurched across the room and through the open front door. The overwhelming impulse to escape and remain free had seized him, and he followed his bare instincts out into the cold and toward the safe haven of the woods.

*   *   *   *

Still groggy, Angela hoped what she had just witnessed was a delusion or a bad dream. Her fears were confirmed when she rolled to her side and saw Nick lying next to her. One glance at his marble face made her worst nightmare come true. She didn't need to feel for a pulse to know that he was no longer alive. The blow he had received to the base of his skull was a major head trauma, and he died almost instantly. His eyes still reflected frozen surprise.

She shut her own eyes tightly against the sight, trying to hold back the tears but it was to no avail. Huge sobs racked her body as she shook uncontrollably from the bitter reality of what had happened. In the past twenty minutes, she had narrowly averted death, awakened to find that her attacker was presumably finished off, and finally witnessed the death of the one person she had ever truly loved. The range of emotions had been too much to take. Along with the physical battering she had absorbed in her fight with the killer, she was completely devastated in every way. All she wanted to do was crawl into a deep, dark hole and make the world go away.

She lay on the floor, nearly too worn out to cry, but too crushed not to. Her pain was joined by a new, almost foreign emotion, one that had paid a visit earlier in the evening when she had converted herself from victim to fighter. The anger took hold slowly at first, but began to overcome the emotional wreckage that had been heaped upon her.

She dragged herself across the floor toward the couch and unsteadily pulled herself to her feet. She wavered for several seconds while fighting off the dizziness and nausea that had besieged her. When her darkening vision had cleared, she took several shaky steps toward the front door as the sound of approaching sirens began to grow louder and closer. She stepped on an object near the front door and bent down to pick it up.

CHAPTER 22

▼

Rucker was completely delirious from the pain his battered body wore like a skin-tight scuba suit. Not a square inch was devoid of the hurt. The source of the pain had blended together, making his entire body scream out like one shredded nerve ending. He had hoped the cold night air would sweep away some of the cobwebs, but he still felt shaky and discombobulated as he exited the cabin.

He loped into the woods, looking like a concussed Quasimodo as his slumped frame staggered through the trees. After running for what felt like many hours, the sound of the sirens began to fade into the distance. Pouring sweat had dampened the drying blood on his face and neck. He stopped briefly to catch his breath and began to shudder as the cold air raked across his damp skin. The run had rejuvenated his consciousness, and he began to feel slightly more alert than he had before. He found that he could now recite the alphabet, a menial task he had been unable to accomplish when he fled the house earlier.

He wasn't quite sure where he was, but stopped long enough on a hillside to get his bearings and see the lake far below him. He gauged he was fairly close to his getaway car. He had stashed it on a deserted road about two miles from the cabin. His switchback pattern through the woods had forced him to cover the ground about six times slower than he had early in the evening when he was still fresh and free of the bruises, cuts, and lacerations the man and woman had rained down upon him during their violent altercation.

He was now coherent enough to be pissed off that things had gone so poorly. At least he managed to finish off both of the pricks before they had done so to him. A smile crossed his swollen lips born from the satisfaction of having mostly achieved his ultimate goal and having escaped the crime scene intact. It hadn't been pretty and the encounter was nowhere near what he had fantasized, but the end result was a success.

He had gone to the cabin to own the girl and satisfy the thirst she had inspired in him. He got her boyfriend as a bonus, so all had gone relatively well in his twisted mind. He was still a little pissed that they had nearly gotten the better of him.

"I guess I'm slipping," he thought to himself.

Maybe it was time to call it quits after all. But had he really fulfilled the expectations of the master? He thought this one would be his final test, but a new urge was starting to grow inside him. Retiring after this kind of disaster would not be acceptable. In fact, the sequence of events that unfolded on this particular evening had amounted to several steps backward. He would now need to seek out several new victims to compensate for the near-failure he had just experienced.

Up ahead, the woods began to thin, and he saw a faint flicker of light in the distance. He now knew exactly where he was. The light was a highway patrol speed detector. He had parked his car about a quarter of a mile past the sign just off the road. It had been well concealed below the road's shoulder, and he used the logic that if the police had set up a sign to check speeds, they wouldn't be monitoring the same area in a patrol car. Besides, the road was seldom used from what he could tell. His tire tracks had been the first to pierce the thin layer of frost that glazed the top of the pavement.

He took the last several steps through the woods and reached the road. In just a few minutes, he'd be in his car cruising toward another town, ready to introduce his evil presence to its unsuspecting citizens. He should probably duck back into the woods for the final approach to the car, he thought, but the uneven terrain had begun to hurt his ankles. It was a relief to walk on pavement, and he'd have plenty of warning from headlights if a car was approaching. He decided to stick to the shoulder and dive back into the woods if the need arose.

The dark night had turned as black as coal. He could barely see his feet as they crunched the gravel on the shoulder of the road. The neon yellow zero from the speed detector cast an eerie glow on the pavement. It had become a beacon of hope and guidance as he approached his car and the ultimate freedom it seemed to represent.

Cold had seeped into his bones, numbing his injuries but creating a new kind of discomfort. He jammed his gloved hands deep into the pockets of his heavy wool coat after cinching the collar tight around his neck. He now walked with half his face buried in the coat, exposing only his ears and forehead to the elements.

"Just a few more steps," he told himself as the sign grew closer.

He was now only about a hundred yards from the sign and just a few hundred from his car. He couldn't wait to feel the warmth from the heater as the clunker fired up and aided his escape.

"Why can't any of these bitches live in warm climates?" he mused to himself.

His recent months in the Midwest had become an inspiration to point the ship south and seek an establishment somewhere along the coastal waters of the Gulf or Atlantic. He could almost smell the salt air and feel the ocean's warm breezes blowing in from offshore. Blood probably looks really weird on all that white sand, he thought.

Poking his head out of the coat to get a read on how much farther he had to walk, he was alarmed to see that the zero on the speed unit flashed "25." Then, it became "40," followed by "50"...He was stunned at the change but heard nothing behind him and saw no illumination from headlights. He must be delusional from the altercation back at the cabin he decided.

He turned his body out of the cold and toward the empty pavement behind him just in time to see the faint yellow reflection from the sign cast upon the black shiny hood of a car that was no more than five yards away. The sign behind him blinked "77" and the face in front of him consisted of 100 percent pure, unadulterated hatred. One last thought flickered through his warped mind.

"That fucking bitch!"

He saw or imagined that he saw her icy stare just before the lights went out. A lifetime of evil-laden acts flashed across his mind like a movie projector running a thirty-year horror film in the span of two seconds. His body was propelled high into the air and pitched over the vehicle and into the trunk of a silver maple that was as big around as a 500-pound man. What was left of his lifeless form dropped to the ice-encrusted grass and dirt at the base of the tree. This time, there would be no miraculous recovery or return from near-death. *Near* had been removed from the equation altogether.

*   *   *   *

Angela had crawled into the front seat of the car after picking up the keys from the foyer floor and leaving the cabin. She was driven by something that lay beyond her rational or conscious thought. She gazed blankly ahead as she turned over the ignition and clicked on the headlights. After backing out of the steep driveway and onto the main road, she switched the gearshift into drive and turned the lights off.

Nothing in her mind registered why any of these things had been occurring; she just knew in her gut that it was the way to go. The car crept along the winding road that bordered the edge of the lake. She was traveling away from the approaching sirens and into seeming oblivion.

Every nerve ending stood on edge. Her vision became as sharp as a hawk's and she easily guided the vehicle along the snaking road through a cloak of darkness. Somehow she felt the killer's presence and stalked it like a wounded animal. Rounding a corner just a couple of miles from the cabin, she saw a yellow light off to the side of the road. A form was weaving back and forth, intermittently covering the light and temporarily obstructing her view of its source. She didn't need a closer look to know what constituted that form.

She took a deep breath and pressed her foot slowly into the accelerator. She felt no fear and no remorse. As the accelerator inched closer to the floor, the yellow light, and the dark shadow before it began to come into focus. The light was a speed detector sign used by police departments. The shadow was the most evil living presence she had ever encountered, and there had certainly been many to compete with over the years.

She watched intently as the numbers on the sign counted upward. The digits seemed to expand exponentially; skipping neighboring numbers and growing by fives and tens. She briefly registered a pair of sevens when she saw the penetrating eyes of a madman just before he disappeared over the hood of the car and out of her life forever.

The impact seemed slight, but the car was sent careening off the road and into a dark grove of trees that stood defiantly, braced for the onslaught of the mechanical disruption. After leaping a small dirt rise just past the shoulder of the road, the car sprung through the air before bounding into the brush. The wild ride ended in the embrace of two gnarled trees. Smoke spewed from the demolished front grill and poured over the buckled hood. The horn had become stuck, shrilly marking the crashing car's demise.

Her body had pressed firmly into the airbag upon impact and finally slid to the console as the bag lost its compression. She hung there limply, not thinking, not feeling, and not caring. The nightmare ended just as suddenly as it had begun, all the while smashing her hopes and dreams to bits.

EPILOGUE

▼

Seven Months Later

Angela was released from the University of Missouri Medical Center after two months of intensive treatment. She had been flown there by helicopter after suffering a broken leg, broken arm, several cracked ribs, a punctured lung, a concussion, and internal bleeding. Doctors had told her she was very lucky to be alive. Somehow, she hadn't felt lucky throughout her long road to recovery.

Therapy had been brutal, and her overall will to live now that Nick was gone had hit rock bottom. Why hadn't she died in the crash? Maybe then, they'd be together in another place right now. She couldn't understand why the first really positive thing that had ever happened to her had ended so abruptly.

After passing through a gamut of emotions, she was finally coming to grips with her new lot in life. Seven months had passed since the events at the lake had taken Nick from her. She was walking again and by all rights, sincerely lucky to be alive. Wanting to live was the trick, but that was becoming less and less of a factor. The impulses to take her own life had ended a few months back, and she felt it was her duty to both Nick and herself to pick up the pieces and move on.

She tried to maintain a positive attitude. Nick had brought her a long way before he left, and she did honestly feel like a new person. Her job at The Pie Factory was a distant memory. "Lola" was no more. Sometimes, it was like remembering a faded dream, and she didn't feel like any of it had actually happened. She laughed, thinking that one day she'd be a famous actress or something and be a guest on a popular talk show where she'd bare her soul and tell of her "career" at a topless club in East St. Louis.

One last gift from Nick hadn't hurt her position, either. Just a few days after she was discharged from the hospital, a courier delivered a letter. She had to reread it several times before the content actually sunk in. As it turned out, Nick had established a scholarship fund at St. Louis University in his wife's name. Through some incredible act of God, with additional influence from Nick, she had been awarded the scholarship. She wasn't quite sure when he had done that, but she was shocked just the same.

At first, she didn't think she could accept the opportunity. St. Louis University was a difficult university, and she was sure others deserved it more than she did. It wasn't until another letter, this one from Nick, had been sent to her that she was able to graciously accept the scholarship. Under the heading, Evans, Masters & Lacour, the letter arrived with a brief cover recapping what she already knew; that Nick Lacour had established the Pamela Lacour Scholarship Fund at St. Louis University. The money should be used to provide higher education for a bright individual encompassing all the values and promise associated with a student at St. Louis University. Angela Graves had been chosen as the first recipient.

None of that had been as big a surprise as the attached letter. She didn't know when he wrote it, or how it made its way to her, but enclosed with the cover page was a personal letter from Nick. It read:

Angela—I've been very blessed in my lifetime. As a result, I intend to use some of my blessings to help others. I've done this in my wife's name, knowing that it was just exactly the type of thing she would have approved of. With this gift, I offer you an opportunity to realize your lifelong dream. I understand that at the time of this writing, we've only known each other for a very short time. Not to sound overly cliché, but it feels much longer. When I lost my wife, I never expected to develop feelings for another woman ever again. I had committed myself mentally and physically to repairing my tortured spirit, caring for my son, and re-applying myself to a career in law. Then you came along and touched a void in my soul. I can't explain why or how this happened, but I knew immediately that you were someone very special and that we had somehow become connected in a sort of cosmic way. I hope you'll accept this scholarship and use it to help you become the person you always knew you could be. You deserve it.—Nick

She sat motionless with tears streaming down her face as she contemplated the finality of it all. In a whirlwind this amazing person blew into her life, showed her love and happiness, and was gone nearly as quickly as he appeared.

She folded the letter in her lap and stared off into space for a very long time. She and Nick had discussed her future on numerous occasions, and she was stunned that he was able to make her dream a reality. She hadn't finished high school but had managed to get her GED. Not attending college was one of her many regrets. Through Nick's caring and generosity, she would now be able to right an incredible wrong and do so at a very prestigious university.

Everything had transpired rapidly, and she barely had time to let the fact that she was going to be a college student sink in. After completing all of the enrollment paperwork, meeting with the dean and registering for her fall classes, she drove back to Illinois and packed up her meager belongings. On the way to her new dorm at St. Louis University, she made a stop in west St. Louis County. There was someone she absolutely had to meet.

✳   ✳   ✳   ✳

Angela fought back the tears as the little boy ran out of the house and into her open arms. Nick's parents had assumed guardianship and agreed to let her meet Justin. Nick had told them a lot about Angela. Even though they didn't necessarily approve of their son getting involved with another woman so soon after his wife's death, they knew she had meant a lot to him. Besides, they were probably very curious to meet her as well.

She didn't know why Justin took to her the way he did, but he didn't leave her side throughout the entire two hours of her visit.

"So you knew my dad, right?" he kept asking her.

"Yes," she'd reply. "Your daddy and I were very close friends."

Each time she uttered those words, it brought a big smile to Justin's face.

"Want to see my room?" he asked.

"You bet I do!"

"C'mon, I'll show you the hockey puck my dad got for me."

He led her to his room where she was forced to use considerable effort to stifle tears she saw a picture of Nick and Justin together at some park. They both looked so happy and peaceful. It was terribly unfair and cruel that this cute little boy had been robbed of both parents at such a young age. She wanted to gather him in her arms and squeeze him tightly, telling him that everything would be fine.

In spite of it all, Justin had adjusted to his new surroundings about as well as could be expected. Nick's parents said they had been taking him to a child psychologist for months and that he was making remarkable progress. Even still, whenever Nick's name came up during the visit, he turned his head and tried not to let his new friend know that his eyes had welled up with tears.

At the end of an emotional visit, she bid farewell to Nick's folks and gave Justin a big hug.

"You'll come back to play with me some more, right?" he asked, choked up, but hiding it well.

"Of course I will," she had responded, but she knew that that chapter of her life was about to close.

She had barely pulled away from the house when she broke down. Nick was so present in his son's face that she was almost startled by the resemblance. She couldn't bear the thought that this sweet, innocent child would never see his father again. She couldn't stand the thought that she wouldn't see Nick again, either. He had changed her life in more ways than one, and she would never even be able to thank him for it.

*   *   *   *

A week after the meltdown at the Lacours', Angela was ready to start school. She had probably never been more nervous in her life as she jammed her books in a backpack and walked to her first class. The sun shone brightly on that late August day, and its warmth gave her strength. It had been the worst summer of her existence, but it was now giving way to a new life. She walked through part of the campus on Spring Avenue and watched as a leaf slowly pirouetted its way to the ground. Fall was coming soon; she could almost smell it in the air.

She took her place near the back of a large auditorium. Her first college class was political law, and she was one of the earliest to arrive. She had already decided that she would follow in Nick's footsteps and become a lawyer. In fact, if she had her way, no one like Rucker would be allowed to walk the streets ever again. She was bound and determined to be a relentless prosecutor ensuring that the world was freed from its rampaging lunatics.

Sitting in the back row, she noticed two young boys looking over at her and giggling. They were probably only eighteen years old, but kind of cute. She wasn't a ton older than they were but felt like the events of the past year had aged her well beyond her years. One of the boys got up the courage to approach her seat.

"Is anyone sitting there?" he politely asked while gesturing toward the empty seat next to her.

"Yeah, that one's kind of taken," she said with a smile.

The boy smiled back and returned to his friend, who seemed to mercilessly poke fun at him.

As she looked at the empty chair beside her, she realized that it really was taken in a way. She could almost sense Nick's presence right there next to her. If it hadn't been for him, she wouldn't be here in the first place. He had not only left her with an incredible opportunity to start this new vocation, but also he had instilled her with renewed drive and the vigor to pursue a once-abandoned goal. She could feel his strength and love flowing through her, and the thought of it filled her with an overwhelming sensation of happiness and security.

Still gazing at the empty seat, a big smile spread across her face. She understood at that moment that everything was indeed going to be all right.

ABOUT THE AUTHOR

In *Jagged Fate*, Steve Santel employs a background in psychology to explore the dark recesses of the human mind. Previous publishing credits include a children's book titled *Soccer Dreamin'* (Eakin Press) and a newspaper column for *The Nashville News*.

Santel currently resides in Missouri. He enjoys mountain climbing and golf.

978-0-595-38797-7
0-595-38797-7

29131433R00148

Made in the USA
Lexington, KY
14 January 2014